The
Unleashed
Series
Book 3

THE

WOLF

REVEALED

LEE K. ROGERS

Open Door Publications

The Wolf Revealed
The Unleashed Series Book 3

Copyright © 2025 by Lee K. Rogers

ISBN: 979-8-9871697-5-9

Published by
Open Door Publications
Willow Spring, NC 27592
www.OpenDoorPublications.com

Cover Design: Eric Labacz, www.labaczdesign.com

For my readers. Thanks for following me into my world.

PART ONE
RISEN

PROLOGUE

The red August moon rode high in the sky, casting a hazy reflection on the still waters of the Rivelou River.

Two shadowy figures stood on the northern bank watching intently. One was jittery, impatient, occasionally swiping at a sweat-dampened brow. The other was quieter, seemingly unaffected by the unrelenting summer heat that poured down on them despite the late hour.

"Where is it?" asked the first figure. "What if it doesn't appear? What if it comes up in the wrong place?"

"Patience," retorted the second. "These things take time."

The first figure suppressed a sigh, unwilling to anger the other. A ripple disturbed the moon's reflection. Was this it? Or was it just a lone fish swimming in the moonlight?

More ripples appeared. The first figure glanced furtively at the other, stifling excitement as a few moments later bubbles rose on the water. A giant sucking sound was heard as if something large was breaking free from the muddy bank. The odor of the riverbed, stagnant with decaying matter, floated on the air.

The second figure lifted arms to the heavens, whispering words the other couldn't quite make out. The sound of hundreds of crows was heard, and moonlight shimmered on shiny black metal as the object rose higher. As it came closer they could make out the shape of a car, long and low, it was—or at least had been before being submerged in the river for months—a black sports car. Now, algae hung off the mirrors and draped the roof as it skimmed the surface of the river, moving from south to north, from the Kentucky side of the water to the Indiana bank. It came to rest half-submerged and half out of the water near the edge. The landing site was strategic, just as promised. Magic was all well and good, but the first figure had done the research and knew just where the vehicle should reappear to do the most damage. A flock of crows, disturbed by *the large and ungainly new bird in their midst, rose up suddenly. The clamor of wings and raucous caws disturbed the still night one more time.*

The black Lamborghini, once thought lost forever, did not seem to notice. It hadn't suffered much despite several months in a watery grave. Its sleek shape gleamed in the moonlight. It looked undamaged, its paint as shiny as the first day it came off the factory floor.

"Ah," said the first shadow, in a voice filled with satisfaction. "We have them now."

CHAPTER 1

Dan Bertrand sat back and laughed with his dinner companion. He'd been doing that a lot tonight. In fact, he couldn't remember how long it had been since he'd laughed this much. It felt good to forget about the cares of his business, his family, his pack, even if just for one evening.

"Yes, that's really what Dr. Tormisano sounds like," said his date, Kathleen O'Connor, referring to her new boss at the University of Rivelou.

"I remember him from when I was a student there. I never had a class with him, but he was infamous around campus for his rants on just about everything," said Dan, still laughing. "He'd stand out on the sidewalk and just go on about something at the top of his voice for ten minutes at a time. Then there were his letters to the editor. He wrote one once about why basketball was the downfall of civilization. In western Kentucky! I thought they were going to ride him out of town on a rail."

They both laughed as Dan added, "I don't think the only thing he could have said worse in this town was that werewolves are real."

"Should we be talking about that here?" Kathleen glanced around the room.

"No one is paying attention to us; don't worry," Dan said, as he reached out and touched her hand. "But maybe I should have found a better example of Tormisano's quirks."

"Trust me, I know most of them already. He hasn't gotten better with age," Kathleen said. "You'll have to ask your sister. I know she isn't going to miss *him* when she takes her new job."

Dan had met Kathleen through his sister, Ana, who she was replacing as an admin in the history department. Ana had recently finished her bachelor's degree and was starting a new job as a teacher at a local elementary school. But at the mention of Ana, Dan sobered. "You know, Kathleen," he started to say, looking down at his plate suddenly. "I'm not sure Ana needs to know we went out together."

"Dan Bertrand, are you afraid of your sister?" Kathleen made sure her tone was teasing, but she felt herself tense. She was afraid of her own sibling, and it wasn't a joking matter.

Dan felt his face turning red. "Yes, yes, I am. Not to mention her fiancé."

Kathleen laughed delightedly. Obviously Dan's "fear" was nothing more than the typical joking between siblings. "The big important alpha is afraid of his little sister. That's just too delicious." Kathleen took a bite of her shrimp, rolling it around on her tongue. "This shrimp is yummy, by the way. I haven't eaten here before. I haven't been in town long enough to try out many restaurants. Not to mention, that with just starting my first job out of college I haven't had a lot of money to go to a place like this." She waved her arm to encompass the restaurant's subtly luxurious décor. The walls were paneled in dark wood; the booths were upholstered in leather, deep, comfortable, and private. The river gleamed outside the windows, lit by lanterns along the restaurant's outdoor patio.

Dan's blood heated in an altogether different manner from the way it had at her comment about his sister. "Flannery's may be considered a steakhouse, but I do think their shrimp is the best," he said. His temperature rose even more as she took another bite of her meal. He'd like to take her home this evening and explore those lips. He knew they'd be delicious, too.

That, however, was exactly what his sister had told him not to do. Of course, Ana didn't realize he'd scented Kathleen as his fated mate the first moment he met her. He couldn't heed Ana's warnings even if he tried. He had to be with her. His wolf demanded it.

There was no way he could even try to stay away from this woman. She was his. They hadn't known each other long—this was really only the third time they'd been together, but being with Kathleen was unlike anything he'd experienced before. She was different. Or he was different with her. He felt lighter, as if she lifted the weight of his many responsibilities right off his shoulders.

Whether Kathleen realized it yet or not, she was meant to be his. Had been since the day she was born. That was often how the mate bond worked for shifters, particularly wolf shifters. The male knew at first glance—well first scent, really—that he had found his fated mate, his one true love, the other half of his soul. Then he had to court her and convince her that he was worthy.

"Ana and Chris are just looking out for you," he said now, reminding himself as much as explaining to her why they had cautioned him away from Ana's new friend. They saw him as a player, someone who jumped easily from woman to woman. And he had been, in the past. They didn't know what he knew: that Kathleen was his other half. And he wasn't going to tell them, or anyone else, until he had her wrapped up like the precious jewel she was, protected from anything that might harm her.

"That is so cute. Does she think her brother is the big, bad wolf?" Kathleen teased, biting into another shrimp and drawing his eyes once again to her very kissable lips. Her auburn hair glinted in the soft lighting, making him want to run his hands through it. Her flowered summer sundress bared shoulders sprinkled deliciously with freckles. He wanted to taste each one of them.

Dan groaned and palmed his face in his hand, still unsure whether he was more embarrassed by the talk of his sister or turned on by the woman in front of him. "Big, bad wolf?" he asked, noting the particular way she had phrased the question. "What have they been telling you about me? I'm really not the player Ana thinks I am. I know I have a reputation but…"

"I know how it is with big brothers and little sisters," Kathleen replied. "I'm sure you were just as over-protective of her when she met Chris."

"So you have a big brother, too? What did he think of you moving all the way to Rivelou?"

Kathleen had mentioned she had moved here from some small town down in Tennessee.

"Oh… um… I… he doesn't know yet. I haven't told

him," she stuttered. "But I'm not worried if you are a player."
She changed the subject very deftly, but Dan noted that her
brother was a subject she didn't want to discuss. Right now that
didn't matter, but eventually he wanted to know everything
about her and her family. "I want to have the chance to try out
new things."

The wolf half of Dan growled softly at the thought of
Kathleen trying out new things—new men—other than him. He
tried to calm his wolf down. Kathleen was just out of college.
She was young. Everyone was going to think she was far too
young for him. He was thirty-five and the new CFO of Betrand
Enterprises, his family's company; she was twenty-three. He
had to give her the time she wanted and needed to experience
the world. It wouldn't be fair for him to claim her too soon, to
take her choice away. As long as he was the one to show her
around, that was fine with him.

His wolf disagreed; according to him once he claimed
Kathleen as his mate she'd be happier. He could let her have all
the experiences she wanted as long as she came back to him
each night.

His wolf half was naïve; too emotional. Dan had seen
what happened when the mating bond was forced, when the
woman wasn't ready to settle down. It just led to unhappiness.
He wasn't going to make that mistake.

Kathleen smiled at him as she slowly sucked on another
shrimp. "This sauce is wonderful. I'm planning to save room
for dessert, though."

Did she know what she was doing to him? He subtly
adjusted his suddenly very tight trousers.

He'd first met Kathleen at Ana and Chris' engagement
party, several weeks before. He'd immediately realized she was
his mate and had planned to escort her home that night and get
to know her better. But she seemed shy and had left the party
early.

That had probably been a good thing, he thought now.
Kathleen seemed very innocent, an introvert. What happened
after she left might have sent her running back to that small
Tennessee town she talked of coming from. The celebration had

turned—complicated—a short time later when his younger sister Channing brought an unexpected guest.

Damn Channing, anyway, for bringing Dolan McTier to a family party, he thought now. Dolan was the son of the head of the McTier pack from Lexington. The McTiers had made it clear they thought that his grandfather, and Alpha of the Bertrand pack, was old and weak and didn't take his responsibilities seriously. Michael McTier thought the Bertrands were ripe for takeover.

The ensuing scuffle that evening between Dolan and Dan, complete with both combatants changing to their wolf form, might have resulted in Kathleen listening too closely to Ana's warning about him. She might have been so concerned by his lack of control that she would have never wanted to see him again, much less go on a date.

Control had been one of his problems when he was younger. He'd come a long way since then. He had duties now, and he couldn't afford to let his emotions run away with him.

You'd be happier if you didn't keep me on such a tight leash, his wolf responded, giving him a mental picture of how good it had felt to leap on Dolan McTier and rip a strip of fur and flesh off of him. He shoved that thought down as fast as he could.

Though a shifter, Kathleen hadn't had time to officially join the local pack, the Bertrand pack which his grandfather led. From what Ana said, Kathleen had been so busy learning the ins and outs of her new job as one of two admins to Dr. Tormisano and moving into her new apartment that she'd had little chance to hear the local paranormal gossip.

And that, Dan thought, was good for him. She hadn't heard about the fight at the party. Tonight he would keep his cool and not move so fast he scared her off. *Calm down,* he told his wolf half that panted to take her home and possess her. *We need to take it slow.*

"So, what type of dessert are you interested in?" he asked, trying to keep it light.

"Maybe something we can share?" Kathleen tossed her red wavy hair over her shoulder again, making Dan want to run his hands through it.

"Or maybe we should just order dessert to go and take it back to my place." He gave in to temptation and reached over to gently run a lock of her hair through his fingers. Yes. It was just as soft as it looked.

Kathleen smiled. "That sounds like a plan. What should we get? Maybe something gooey?"

Dan mentally rolled his eyes. Was she really this naïve, or was she toying with him? Did it matter whether she had any idea what she was doing to him? Yes, he had been a player, and he could usually tell the difference between true innocence and the usual banter of another player. But this girl. She bounced from innocence to seduction faster than he could turn from human to wolf. Just what did her wolf look like, he wondered. Was her coat as soft and red as her hair? She'd be magnificent. He signaled the waiter. "Box up a couple of your chocolate lava cakes to go, please, and bring me the check."

"Of course, sir."

"Now, what were we talking about?" He turned back to Kathleen, ready to give her his full attention again. Before she could answer him, they heard a commotion at the front of the restaurant and turned to listen.

"Sir, you can't just barge in here," the maître d' said.

"This gives me the right."

Through the tables of people, all turning their heads to watch what was happening, Dan could just make out a man wearing a police uniform hand something to the maître d'.

"Of course, sir."

"Uh oh, someone's in trouble," Kathleen singsonged, her eyes wide.

"Maybe he knows about the trouble I plan to give you as soon as we get back to your place," Dan teased.

Kathleen blushed, and Dan had to shift in his chair again. This time his pants seemed to have shrunk a full size smaller than they had been a few seconds ago. Ana was wrong. Dan wasn't trouble. This young, inexperienced girl spelled trouble with a capital T for him. He couldn't wait to get her home.

Their attention was drawn away from the front of the restaurant when their waiter reappeared with their desserts in a box along with the check. Dan got his credit card from his wallet and handed it to the waiter, who quickly walked away to take care of it.

As he turned back to Kathleen, he was startled when a voice spoke to him from behind.

"Well, look who's come up in the world. Fancy meeting you, Bertrand, in a place like this." This must be the cop he had glimpsed at the front desk a few minutes ago.

He tensed and his wolf growled audibly. He clamped down on it quickly. He couldn't make a scene here in a public place. And in front of Kathleen, too. "Assistant Chief Walker, what a surprise to see you here," he said, his voice cool as he turned to face the man. Despite his effort to seem unaffected, his voice sounded harsh, even to his own ears. His words were rude, but he couldn't stop himself. "I didn't think Flannery's let in people like you."

Kathleen looked startled. This was not a side of himself he had meant to show her tonight. He'd been taught by his family to always be polite. He was a Bertrand. He had a reputation to uphold in the community—both communities in fact, the paranormal and non-para. But this was different. This was personal. And there was no way he could control his reactions to this man.

"Not assistant chief anymore. I'm sheriff now, in Herndon County."

"Congratulations, I suppose," Dan said, dismissively. "Then what are you doing harassing people on this side of the river? Herndon is in Indiana, not Kentucky, you know."

"We're here to arrest someone."

"Ah, so that's why you brought your favorite playmates with you," he replied, nodding to two large and beefy Kentucky State Police who stood behind him."

"Yeah, needed them with me to be legal. And you know me, I always like to be strictly legal."

The waiter returned with Dan's card, and he made a show of signing it and returning it to his wallet, ignoring Walker and the sheriffs. "It's been nice, Walker, but my friend and I are ready to go," he said.

He made as if to rise even as he knew instinctively that he wasn't going to be walking out of this restaurant so easily tonight. Despite the antagonism he'd always had for Dan, Walker was a straight arrow. He wouldn't have stopped to harass and insult Dan if he were here to arrest someone else. But Dan had to put up a good front. It was his nature. And he was here with his mate, the woman he planned to spend the rest of his life with even if she didn't know it yet. He would not back down in front of her.

Walker reached out and put a hand on his shoulder, pushing him back into his seat. "You seem to think that now that you're a fancy corporate executive in your family's business, you don't have to follow the law. But enough small talk," Walker said. "Daniel Henry Bertrand, you are wanted for questioning as a material witness in the disappearance of Alexander Fontaine."

CHAPTER 2

Ana Dugan and Chris Spier snuggled on the couch watching "Van Helsing" in their home near downtown Rivelou. Ana's fourteen-year-old daughter Sophie was upstairs on her computer, chatting with friends.

"I can't believe you like this movie. It has no socially redeeming qualities whatsoever," said Ana, grabbing a handful of popcorn from the bag sitting on her lap.

"Hey, it's a great movie. And what about Kate Beckinsale? I think she adds a lot of socially redeeming value to the plot," Chris protested as he, too, ate some of the snack. "Not to mention Hugh Jackman has to turn into a werewolf to kill Dracula. You should like that part. The werewolf is the hero."

"Hah! The werewolf is the anti-hero. Jackman has to be cured of being a werewolf at the end. But at least the werewolves are slightly—very slightly—more realistic than the vampires."

"Yeah, I've never seen a vampire who looked quite like those girls," Chris chuckled, grabbing another handful of popcorn.

"Thank goodness for that—I'd be jealous all the time. And thank goodness your job is nothing like Van Helsing's."

"Fortunately for me, the movie is nonsense. Three quarters of what I do is collect evidence and research while I sit at a computer and work on PackNet," Chris said, referring to the dark web internet site that only paranormals had the ability to access. "And now that I've got the support of your pack and the Rivelou cops, I don't often have to go in alone to take down a troublemaker."

"Good. I don't want you hurt. Couldn't live without you," Ana replied, kissing him soundly.

At that moment her phone rang. "Pause that. Hugh Jackman is just about to take his shirt off." She laughed as she dug her phone out of her pocket. "Hey, Kathleen. How are you? What's up?... What? Just a minute, I'm going to put you on speaker so Chris can hear you."

"Ana, they arrested Dan." Kathleen spoke breathlessly, and Ana could hear the panic in her voice. "They said he was being arrested for the disappearance of someone called Alexander Fontaine. Dan said to call you. That's all he had time to do before they took him away. Ana, it doesn't make any sense."

Chris took the phone. "Kathleen, where are you? Are you safe?

"I'm at Flannery's." She mentioned the well-known riverside steakhouse where she and Dan had been eating. "I don't have my car, and I don't have Dan's keys. They wouldn't let him give them to me." She was so upset she began to stutter. "Th-They said they were c-confiscating his c-car to look for evidence." Chris and Ana exchanged worried looks as Kathleen began to cry.

"I don't know what to do. Chris, it was such a mess. It was unreal. Everyone was shouting, and all the people in the restaurant were watching us like we were Bonnie and Clyde. And then outside all the reporters…"

"But you're inside the restaurant now? You're okay?" Chris asked again, trying to break through her hysteria and get some concrete information.

"Yes, the nice manager is letting me sit in his office here at the restaurant."

"Good, I'll be there to get you as soon as possible."

"I want Ana," she said, tears in her voice.

"I know, Honey, but I'm going to leave her here with Sophie. I'll bring you back to our house and get you to her as soon as I can. Now you just sit tight, and I'll be there in about fifteen minutes."

"Okay, Chris. Thanks. I don't know what I'd do without friends like you and Ana."

He hung up the phone and gave Ana a quick kiss as he went to get his car keys and wallet.

"What was Kathleen doing with Dan? I told him not to

date her. And now look what's happened," Ana fumed.

"You know, it doesn't make any sense to worry about that right now. Dan and Kathleen having dinner together is certainly not what got your brother arrested."

"I know, I know. Anyway, I should go with you. Sophie's old enough to stay by herself for the time it will take to get to the restaurant and back, and Kathleen doesn't know you as well as she knows me. She sounded so scared." Ana got up to look for her purse.

"No, I don't want you anywhere near that place," he said protectively. "You heard Kathleen. There are reporters, and this has something to do with Fontaine." He spit out the name as if it were a curse. "Stay here and call your grandfather; then, get hold of Connor Morrigan and get him over to the police department as soon as possible." Connor, a friend of Dan's since high school, was now the family lawyer.

"All right. But Chris, why are they arresting Danny now? What evidence could they have? And if it's about Alexander, shouldn't they be arresting me? Not my brother? I'm the one who…"

Chris kissed her hard. "I don't even want to think about them arresting you. As soon as I get home I'll check some of my contacts on PackNet for any additional information. Maybe there's something new on Fontaine we haven't heard about. And an even better question is where is Chief Anderson, and how did he let this happen? He knows all about what went on that night. That's another reason you need to get hold of your grandfather ASAP."

As Chris headed out the door, Ana started making phone calls, beginning with Connor. This was going to be so awkward. She'd also been friends with Connor since high school, but in the middle of the mess with Fontaine last year, he'd suddenly told her he had been in love with her for years. She'd never felt anything but friendship for him, and now things were strained between them. He'd always been someone she could talk with, confide in. And then she'd found out that he had never been honest with her. She thought back to the night he'd professed his love—when she'd finally admitted to herself it was Chris that she was in love with. What timing!

She pictured the tall, lanky shifter. His blue eyes always looked serious, his blonde hair constantly falling across his forehead. Sure, she'd had a crush on Connor back in high school. What might have happened if one of them had been courageous enough to act on their feelings back then? But now, well, she knew she would never feel anything for Connor like she felt for Chris—like apparently Connor felt for her.

Why hadn't he just kept his mouth shut? It made it so damn awkward to call him. But Danny needed his friend's help, and she'd just have to suck up any feelings of discomfort and call.

***

"What's wrong, Ana?" the man said immediately when she got him on the line. "Do you need help?"

Ana gave a tearful smile even though her friend couldn't see her. That was Connor. He'd do anything for her. And for Danny, too of course.

"Connor, it's Danny. He's in trouble."

"What kind of trouble?"

"He's been arrested."

"What? You've got to be kidding me. We aren't seventeen anymore. I can't see him out drag racing by the dunes. He was just going out to dinner with…" Connor stopped.

"With Kathleen. Yes, I know. She's the one who called me. And yes, I told him to stay away from her. I'm really not worried about your keeping that secret at the moment. We have too many other issues," Ana replied. "All I know is Kathleen just called me. She said while she and Dan were eating dinner at Flannery's, he was arrested for something to do with Alexander Fontaine."

"Why would they arrest Dan for Alexander Fontaine's disappearance? What could he have to do with that? And why now? The man's been gone for months."

"It's because…"

"No! Sorry. It's not professional of me to ask that. Don't tell me anymore, Ana. I'm the lawyer for your entire family, but right now I'm going into the police department as Dan's attorney. I don't want to know anything you know. Only what he tells me."

"Okay. You'll get over to the police station right away?"

"As quick as I can. I'm really surprised Chief Anderson did this so publicly. He must be getting pressure from somewhere..." He broke off that thought. "Ana, don't worry. Whatever this is we will fix it. It can't be anything as bad as we got up to as teenagers," Connor said, trying to lighten the mood.

Ana took a deep breath. Connor had no idea of the real story of Alexander Fontaine's disappearance. Or how she was involved. She started to speak, then remembered his warning and closed her mouth.

"By the way," the attorney continued, "where's Kathleen right now? From what I've seen of her she seems pretty shy and inexperienced to handle something like this."

"She's still at the restaurant. Chris went to pick her up."

"Good. We don't want her on her own. We don't know much about her. She's only been in town a short time. She could be a loose cannon in all this. Or something worse."

"Dammit Connor, just because she wasn't born and raised in Rivelou doesn't mean she's involved with Danny getting arrested. She's a very nice girl."

"What do you know about her, Ana? She comes to town and makes a play for Dan, and suddenly he's arrested for something that happened months ago. Do you even know what pack she was born into?"

"No, the subject hasn't come up. I was planning to bring her to the next pack meeting. And she didn't make a play..." Ana took a deep breath. Now was not the time to get into a discussion with Connor about Kathleen or who had made a play for whom, her brother or her friend. "Just fix this, Connor. Please."

"I will, Ana; you have my promise. Dan can't have gotten into anything too terrible."

Ana shook her head as she hung up the phone. Connor didn't know the full story. She flashed back to Fontaine's apartment, last Halloween night. Chris tied and helpless, his sister Shannon unconscious on the floor. Ana had had no choice.

She'd shifted and taken Fontaine out. She'd had no choice. He was threatening to kill them all. She could still feel the blood in her mouth as she sank her fangs into his throat.

But Connor knew nothing about it. The only people who did besides Chris and Kathleen were her grandparents, Dan, and Chief Anderson. So why would Anderson arrest Dan now? The only way to find out was to do exactly as both Chris and Connor had said and call her grandfather. Hank Bertrand was head of their shifter pack and needed to be the next one informed. After that she called her parents on their home line. Neither one was good about checking their phones or leaving them on when they were home. She prayed that her father would pick up, not her mother. She wasn't so lucky.

"Mom, this is Ana. Can I talk to Dad?"

"Oh, Ana, how are you dear? It's rather late to be calling us, don't you think? I always worry something is wrong when the phone rings after 10 p.m.," her mother, Donna, said.

Ana rolled her eyes. "Mom, I really need to talk to Dad."

Her mother barreled right over her. "But I'm really glad you did call. I was going to talk to you tomorrow. I've got color samples for the bridesmaids' dresses. Can you come over in the morning? We need to get them chosen right away."

Mom, I'll be happy to look at the samples in the morning. Right now, I really need to talk to Dad."

Something in her daughter's voice finally got through to Donna. "He's right here. I'll put him on," she said meekly.

Ana explained the situation. "Grandpa said we'd all meet here at my place. Connor will bring Danny here as soon as he gets him released."

"I don't understand this, Ana. Where is Chief Anderson? And why would he let this happen?"

"I know, I know. Everyone's been saying that. I guess we just need to wait until Connor gets Dan released to find out the answers."

"We'll be right over. And don't worry; I'll handle your mother."

Ana nodded thankfully at her dad's words. If anyone could keep her mother "under control" during an emergency, it was her dad. They were a classic case of opposites attracting she thought as she headed to the kitchen to make coffee and see what she could offer people to eat. Her dad was always the picture of calm while her mom tended to turn every molehill she found into a mountain.

By the time Chris and Kathleen got to the house, other cars were pulling up. Her grandparents, parents, her younger brother Tyler and his girlfriend Winnie all converged on the home at once, and Sophie, of course, came downstairs to see what all the commotion was about.

"Oh Kathleen, I'm so sorry this happened. I can't imagine what is going on," she said, hugging the younger woman as she came through the door.

Kathleen was trembling, her eyes wide. "I'm the one who's sorry, Ana; I broke your trust and went on a date with your brother. I don't know what you must think of me." Kathleen wrung her hands nervously.

"Kathleen! That's absolutely not important now. And it's good you were with him. If he'd been alone, we might not have learned about his arrest so quickly."

"I know, Ana. The sheriff seemed to really not like your brother and…"

"Sheriff?" questioned Hank, stepping into the conversation. "Where was Chief Anderson?"

"W-Who is that?" asked Kathleen." The man wasn't just the head of the Bertrand pack; he was a large and imposing figure. Ana understood why Kathleen might feel nervous around him. She had noticed the girl often seemed tense when men she didn't know well were around. She put her arm around her friend.

"He's the head of the Rivelou police department," Hank explained.

"But he's not the…"

Before Kathleen could say anything more, the doorbell rang again.

"That must be Channing," Ana said, turning from Kathleen and hurrying to the door. Channing was her younger sister.

"I hope she's had the sense not to bring McTier with her," Hank muttered as he, too, turned from Kathleen and followed Ana.

Left alone in the living room, Kathleen realized that Dan's family thought he'd been taken to the Rivelou city police department. Hadn't she mentioned to Chris that the sheriff had been from the Indiana side of the river? No, she realized. She'd been too intimidated by him to do more than wring her hands and stutter thanks for him rescuing her from the restaurant; then, she sat silently as they drove to his home. She needed to clear up the mistake right away. She was looking around to find someone to tell when the commotion at the door grew louder.

"Channing, why would you bring him here?" she heard Donna say loudly. Kathleen raised her eyebrows. That seemed rather rude. She turned to see who Dan's mother had objected to coming. And stopped short and blanched when she recognized the man entering the door.

Oh no! What was he doing here? He couldn't see her. He didn't know she was in Rivelou. She'd taken great pains to make sure no one knew she was here. If he found out he'd drag her away. She'd be locked up…

She quickly found Ana's fiancé, the need to clear up the mistake about exactly where Dan was being held forgotten in her panic. Dolan couldn't see her here.

"Chris, I really feel like I should get out of here. I'm not family; I'm just in the way."

Chris took one look at her pale face and kindly put a hand on her arm, ushering her toward the back door where his car was parked. "You must be exhausted. I'll take you home."

CHAPTER 3

Dan sat on a hard chair in the lone interrogation room of the Herndon County, Indiana, jail. He had no idea how long he had been there. There was no clock on the wall, and they'd taken his phone and watch. It may have only been an hour, but it felt like all night. He would pace back and forth if he could, but they'd handcuffed one of his hands to the desk. He flexed his hands; his claws lengthened. He suppressed a growl of frustration and forced his hands to relax and his claws to retract. Who knew if someone were watching him through the one-way glass in the wall?

He could get out if he tried—not just the handcuffs. He could leave the entire building if he really wanted. That would mean he'd have to shift to his wolf. And that was taboo under these circumstances.

He took a few minutes to imagine it. The crack as his bones reshaped themselves. The hot, fierce pain that was almost pleasure as he changed from human to wolf. His nose lengthening to a snout that could scent exactly where his enemies were throughout the small building. His ears growing longer until he could hear the fear-filled beats of their hearts. His fangs sharpening, ready to bite into anyone who stood in his way. The snap of the metal handcuff as his teeth tore into it. Then he'd break down the door, find Sheriff Walker, tear him from bloody limb to bloody limb, and run off into the night, howling at the moon as he went.

It would be so satisfying.

And it would betray his pack, every shifter, and every other paranormal he had vowed to protect.

No. No matter how personally gratifying it would be, getting angry enough to lose control was not the answer this time. He'd been out of control as a teen, and that's how he'd first met Sheriff Chip Walker, at the time Assistant Police Chief Walker of the Rivelou Police Department. He'd been the wild child of the family—determined to break every rule his parents, his school, or his pack set for him.

He and his friends, Connor and Gabe, had torn up the town. They had drag raced at night at the track down by the river when no one was supposed to be there. They'd driven drunk and high. It was a miracle they'd never hurt anyone. Their grades had been terrible. All three had been in danger of being kicked out of school. They'd dated every girl whose parents would allow it—and several whose parents never knew what was going on, too. That's how his reputation as a player had started. Funny, he thought now; he still had that reputation even though his date tonight with Kathleen had been the first he'd had in over a year—and look how that had turned out.

Finally, Chief Anderson and Dan's grandfather, Hank, had taken the trio in hand. Chores—yes. They'd spent lots of time at his grandparents' farm doing everything from mucking out stalls, to driving the tractor, to planting and harvesting corn.

The chief had taken them on some ride-alongs, where they had a chance to see just what happened to the criminals, and the victims, the chief dealt with every day. It had been eye-opening for Dan. He'd had a privileged life; he had known it even as a teen. But his two mentors had shown him that being a shapeshifter was about more than power and privilege. It was about responsibility.

His grandfather had begun taking Dan with him when he went to meet with various pack members to find out their needs.

That's where he learned that being the pack leader meant more than dominating other shifters—certainly a lot more than being able to fight well. It meant taking care of everyone in the pack. If a pack member lost a job, the rest of the shifters were there with food, supplies, money, and, if possible, new employment. If someone were ill, everyone in the pack pitched in. Dan had found his calling.

And that's when his grandfather had helped him learn to channel his anger and manage his need as an alpha wolf to dominate others. The lessons he'd learned at that time were why Dan was able to sit in the jailhouse now and just visualize what he'd like to do to Walker but know he would never act on it. He didn't feel patient, but he could at least act that way.

Those lessons had worked for his friends, Connor Morrigan and Gabe Legato, too. Now, at 35, most people in town had forgotten their days as the wild boys of Rivelou and saw three young, respectable businessmen. Gabe ran his own IT business. What people outside the paranormal community didn't know was that Gabe was the brains behind PackNet, the secret, internet-based paranormal communication system. Connor was a respected lawyer and handled most of the legal business for the Bertrand family as well as the pack. And Dan was the new CFO of Bertrand Enterprises.

While some people thought he'd only been appointed to the position because he was part of the Bertrand family, Dan knew better. His father and grandfather would have found someone else to head up the company's financial department if they hadn't trusted Dan. Bertrand Enterprises was too important to the welfare of the entire pack to have someone in charge of the money who wasn't more than just competent.

Everyone seemed to know that he had turned his life around except for Sheriff Chip Walker, he thought bitterly. He hadn't seen the man in years, of course, hadn't even paid enough attention to realize he'd moved across the river and become a sheriff here in Indiana.

The door finally opened, and Walker came in, followed by one of his deputies.

"Well, Bertrand, older but no wiser, I see," the man said. About 50 years old, with thinning grey hair cut military short, Walker had never been a physical match for Dan and his friends, even when they were still in their teens. Now that he and his wolf had come into their own, Dan knew he could easily intimidate him physically. It wasn't a smart play to make, though, and he held back the need to straighten and flex his muscular arms. He could just as easily get under the sheriff's skin with words.

"Oh, I don't know about that. I haven't been caught after hours on any drag strips lately. That's got to say something for my maturity."

Maybe it wasn't the smartest way to start a conversation with the sheriff when he wasn't even sure why he was sitting here handcuffed to a table, but the man just brought out the 17-year-old bad boy that still lurked inside him.

"You may think you're some big shot now that your daddy and granddaddy got you fixed up with a fancy job at their fancy company. I look at you, and I see the same snot-nosed rich kid who thinks he's above the law, just like you were back in high school. Well, you're going to find out differently. Now that you're in my territory, no one's going to be able to protect you."

"That's great, but what do I need protection from? I have no idea why I'm here."

"What do you know about Alexander Fontaine?"

"He was a professor at the university—disappeared a while ago." Dan made sure his face gave nothing away as he answered the question. There was a lot more he could tell Walker about Fontaine—things no one in the non-para world knew. But that was never going to happen. Fontaine's secrets had died with him. At least so Dan hoped.

"I notice you said 'was' not 'is,'" put in the deputy. "Do you know something we don't know?"

"I assume he isn't a professor there anymore since he hasn't been seen for several months. That's pretty much common knowledge—his disappearance was all over the local news last year. Is there something else I should know?"

"This is Deputy Rossi, by the way," said Walker. "You'll treat him with the same respect you treat me."

"That won't be hard since I have no respect for you." Dan inwardly cringed as the words came out of his mouth. This was not going well, but he couldn't seem to just shut his mouth and say, "Yes sir," and "No sir," like he knew he should. He swallowed another growl of frustration. The way he was feeling it would come out much too wolf-like to be acceptable in his present company. Sitting here handcuffed in front of Walker and his deputy made him feel like a smart-assed teenage truant again. All the lessons his grandfather had painstakingly taught him had flown out the window.

"So, where were you the night Professor Fontaine disappeared?" Rossi asked.

"He disappeared over in Rivelou. That isn't even in your jurisdiction."

"Just answer the question," said Walker.

"You know, I don't think I want to answer any more questions until I talk to my lawyer. Can I have my phone call now?"

"We can hold you for a 'reasonable time' before allowing you to make that phone call," said Rossi. "And we have forty-eight hours to arraign you. I guess we've got quite a few hours to go and still be considered reasonable."

The answer did nothing to reassure Dan. Whatever was going on, Walker and his little deputy friend were going to go out of their way to follow the law to the letter. It had been a long time since he'd had to worry about this type of thing. Yes, his family and his pack sometimes skirted the laws of the non-para world, but only to keep the paranormals in their care safe. Well, he had one ace up his sleeve. Kathleen would surely have gotten in touch with his sister by now and told her where he was.

"I think someone is going to notice I'm gone a long time before then."

"Yes, I'm sure they will," answered Walker. "The press is already outside waiting to find out just exactly why the chief financial officer of the mighty Bertrand Enterprises has been arrested."

Dan groaned inwardly even as he tried to keep his face blank. Staying low-key and not causing any waves was a motto not just of his pack, but of every paranormal in Rivelou. No one wanted the non-paras to ever get the idea that anything strange happened in the town. The mess with Fontaine's disappearance had finally started to die down. And now this. His grandfather, his parents, and the pack council were all going to kill him.

CHAPTER 4

Dan must have sat in the tiny room for at least three or four more hours, still handcuffed, still chafing to leave. He shifted restlessly, trying to get comfortable. Were they going to keep him here all night? No window, no clock, no clue as to how long he had been there. Maybe it was morning already. Where was his family? Someone should have been here by now. He'd seen the reporters when he was taken away. It would have been on the news by now. And if that wasn't enough, Kathleen must have called them. Or had she been too worried about Ana's reaction to finding out they'd had a date to let her know?

No, he was sure that wasn't it. Kathleen might be shy, but he'd watched her stand up for herself. And while his sister had warned him off Kathleen, it had only been because she was afraid he would hurt the younger, more inexperienced woman, not that Kathleen would hurt him. His thoughts circled around and around. Why had Walker arrested him? Had Fontaine's body been found? Where was Connor or someone to spring him out of this place? What did Kathleen think of him after seeing him dragged away in handcuffs? Had he lost all chance with her? Finally, he heard a commotion in the hallway outside and recognized Connor's voice.

"I have a right to see my client now," he was shouting. "I don't care what Walker says. I want to see Dan Bertrand immediately."

The voices faded; then, a few minutes later he heard more noise outside as the lock clicked. "Hey, Connor," he said. "You're a sight for sore eyes."

"And you look like shit," his friend replied entering the tiny interrogation room.

"Thanks for that. What the hell took you so long?"

"A little mix-up about which side of the river you were on. Took a couple of extra hours to figure it out."

"Kathleen didn't tell you who'd arrested me?"

Connor had the grace to look embarrassed. "She was trying, but apparently no one was listening to her."

Dan's anger rose even higher. "Not even Ana? I'm sick and tired of everyone acting like Kathleen…"

"Worry about that later, man. We've got bigger problems right now," Connor told him as Sheriff Walker entered the room. "Sheriff, I demand you take the handcuffs off my client. He's done nothing to warrant this type of treatment."

"Well, being held in the suspicion of connection with the disappearance of a well-known professor could be thought of as a reason," the man drawled. He did, however, take a key out of his pocket and unlock the cuffs.

Dan rubbed his wrist. "Can I get out of here now?" he asked, looking at Connor.

"Not so fast, boy," Walker said. "You said you'd answer questions once your lawyer got here. Seems he took his good, sweet time, but he's here now, so I think you can answer those questions."

"Before my client answers any questions, I have a couple for you, Sheriff," Connor said.

"Well, look who thinks he's a big-shot lawyer now. I remember when you were just a little punk like your friend here."

Dan watched Connor take a deep breath. He'd always been the calmest of the three friends, but apparently his patience was tried by the sheriff just as much as Dan's.

"First, what is my client charged with? Second, why did you not allow him a phone call? I'd have been here sooner if I'd known exactly where he was, and finally, have you read him his rights?"

"He hasn't been charged with anything—so far."

"But I understand you used the term 'arrested' when you publicly handcuffed him at a restaurant earlier this evening."

"What I said was he was 'wanted for questioning.' Someone wasn't listening. Get your facts straight, boy."

"Then I'm guessing my client has not been read his rights?"

"That would be correct," interjected Dan.

"He hasn't been charged, so no need to read him his rights."

"Fine, that's on you if down the road we get all charges thrown out of court because you can't be bothered with procedure. Dan, you ready to answer questions?"

"If it will get me out of here faster, yes, I'll answer the ass... er, Sheriff Walker's questions."

"Wait a minute while I get someone in here to record your answers," Walker said.

"You'd better make it quick, Walker, or my client is out of here," Connor said.

Dan sighed and got up to stretch as Connor turned to him and hissed, "Keep it under control, Dan. He's just looking to find something to charge you with."

Dan rolled his eyes. He sat back down and flexed his claws as Connor shook his head. "I said keep it under control!"

"Rossi, come on in here with a tape recorder so we can get a statement from our guest," they heard Walker call. The man must have been standing just outside since he appeared almost immediately, his phone set to record, and a notepad in hand.

"Alright, let's get this party started," said Walker, sitting down on the only other chair in the room, forcing Connor to stand. "How well did you know Professor Alexander Fontaine?"

"Not well. I met him a few times at social events at my grandparents' farm."

"That would be Hank and Ida Bertrand?"

"Yes, as you well know, those are my grandparents."

"And what was he doing there?"

Dan's voice was tight. "Like I said, he was invited to some social events."

"Seems like a stretch to me. A couple of elderly farmers and a fancy professor who's nationally known for his books on paranormal claptrap."

"Sounds like you don't think much of the professor's books," Dan replied.

"Just answer the question, boy. Or maybe I need to bring

your grandparents in and talk to them."

Connor put his hand on Dan's shoulder as he started to rise. "Don't let him bait you. Frankly, I'd enjoy watching him try to get one over on Hank Bertrand."

Dan snorted at that idea. Yeah, he wanted to take Walker apart piece by piece, but Connor was right. That was what the man wanted—for Dan to do something to provoke an arrest.

"What was the question again? I'm not sure I heard one," he said. Maybe he couldn't hit Walker, but that didn't mean he had to be polite.

Walker's mouth tightened. "How did your grandparents know Fontaine?"

"You'd have to ask them."

"Keep it up, boy, and I'll be over there at that fancy farm asking them all sorts of things."

Dan's fist clenched again as Walker noted, "You don't like the idea of my talking to your grandparents? Why is that?"

"I don't want you bothering them."

Well then, what about your sister, Ana Dugan? I hear she was dating Fontaine. Funny how she got engaged to someone else right after the good professor disappeared."

"Do not bring my sister into this," Dan said, his voice tight. "She has nothing to do with Fontaine."

"I thought they were an item. I heard he took her out to dinner at some fancy restaurants, took her to a party at the country club. Maybe you didn't like Fontaine sniffing around your sister. Decided to take care of the matter?"

Connor stepped in. "You certainly seem to have been listening to a lot of gossip about the Bertrands, Walker. Particularly when they don't even live in your jurisdiction. What's your problem with the family? Jealous you don't have as much money as they do? This could start to look like harassment. What does the Bertrand family knowing Fontaine have to do with anything? And why are you apparently looking into his disappearance all these months later? If you don't have a reason for questioning my client, we're going to leave right now."

"Oh, we've got a reason. And we've got jurisdiction.

Fontaine's car was found this morning. It came up from the river over in Harmony Park, right here in Herndon County."

"That's still no reason to question my client. It sounds like you're making a lot out of some gossip and vague rumors. Come on, Dan." Connor stood up. "We're leaving."

"Oh, not so fast, Morrigan. We've got a lot more than circumstantial evidence. Your client's prints were found all over Fontaine's car."

CHAPTER 5

Kathleen lay on the couch in her apartment, refreshing the page for the local news station on her computer every few minutes. It was Saturday afternoon, and she had heard nothing new about what had happened to Dan since she had left his sister's home the night before.

Why was there nothing? There had been several television news cameras at the front of the restaurant when they had taken Dan away in handcuffs. The photos had been all over the 11 o'clock news and were splashed on social media and various local information websites this morning. She would have been filmed in those videos, too, if the nice maître d' hadn't hustled her into the back office.

That would have been a disaster. She was sure her family had heard this news. They might not live close to Rivelou, but she'd always heard about the Bertrands. About how they thought they were better than everyone else, how they didn't follow shifter tradition. They even thought women were equals! That was what the men of her pack railed about the most. How could shifters who gave women equal say in pack business be as successful as the Bertrands? Her father, for one, was sure it was only a temporary situation. The Betrand pack would be taken down soon. Maybe that was why…?

She shook off thoughts of her old pack. She never planned to go back there again. Thank goodness Chris, her friend Ana's fiancé, had hustled her out the back door of the restaurant and into the safety of his car. He'd even brought a hoodie to help her cover her face so no one would recognize her. Kathleen understood that the Bertrand family was important in Rivelou, but she hadn't realized just how influential they were until last night. It had helped her understand some of her old pack's jealousy. They strutted their importance every chance they got, but they had nowhere near the influence of the Bertrand pack. She'd heard the questions being shouted at Dan and that sheriff before she'd managed to get away.

"Why is he being arrested, Sheriff?"

"What happened to Fontaine?"

"Did you kill him?"

"What evidence do you have against him, Sheriff Walker?"

"Hey Dan, will your family still keep you as CFO of Bertrand Enterprises after this?"

Dan had made no response to any of the shouts from the reporters. He'd kept his eyes straight ahead, his face expressionless. She admired his control as she watched the video one more time. She admired more than that, too, if she were being honest. Her gaze was drawn to his bulky shoulders, his thick biceps, evident even on her small laptop screen.

She refreshed her computer again. Nothing new about why Dan had been arrested or whether he had been released. Just a lot of speculation about Alexander Fontaine, the professor who had gone missing last October at the university where she now worked.

She thought about calling Ana to see what the family knew, but it had been obvious last night when Chris brought her to his and Ana's house that the Bertrand family was circling the wagons to protect one of their own. And Kathleen was not one of theirs and was not welcome. Although she'd like to be. But would they accept her into the pack? Would Dan want to see her again… once they knew just who she was? Just who her father was?

Ana, of course, had been very apologetic. And then her sister, Channing, had shown up with Dolan. She'd escaped the house as fast as she could. She'd pleaded the stress of the evening and asked Chris to take her home. It was obvious that no one in the family liked Dolan McTier. Kathleen snorted at that thought. She wasn't that fond of him either. Because the two packs had never gotten along, she'd been surprised to see the man there.

One of the reasons she'd chosen to come to Rivelou was because she was sure she'd never run into anyone from the

McTier pack. And now here he was and obviously connected to a member of the Bertrand pack. And not just the pack, one of the family. How had he managed that? If he had seen her, she'd have had to run. Find someplace new to start all over again. She didn't want that; she wanted to stick around and make a home here, maybe explore this attraction she felt to Dan.

Dolan and Channing arrived just as Kathleen had been about to explain everything to the family—that Dan had apparently had history with the Indiana sheriff who had taken him away in handcuffs. She'd quickly feigned feeling ill—not too hard under the circumstances—and had managed to get out of the door before Dolan noticed her.

Ana and Dan's grandparents had stopped her in the entryway to thank her profusely for letting them know about the arrest. Dan's mother had been rather useless, Kathleen noticed, wringing her hands and crying about "her baby." But it had been plain that Kathleen was in the way. Being in the way was an easy excuse to leave, and no one had to know she was making sure Dolan didn't see her.

Chris had taken her back to her apartment. He'd been apologetic, thinking the family had made her feel unwelcome. "It's just their way," he'd told her kindly as they pulled up at her apartment building. "They've just barely begun to accept me." He and Ana had been engaged for almost a year and would be getting married in two more months.

At that moment her doorbell rang; Kathleen wondered for a moment if she should bother to answer it. Her hair was barely brushed, and she wore an old T-shirt and pajama bottoms. She hadn't even put on makeup this morning. She never let people—even her best friends—see her this way. It wasn't just vanity. It was self-preservation. Growing up in her pack, where females were considered important only for their ability to reproduce and make more strong, alpha wolves, appearance was everything. One of the earliest lessons a female learned was to never look sloppy. To always act as if you were ready to host the pack alpha, and that as a female, you were subservient to even the lowest male in the pack. Never miss a chance to capture the attention of the most important alphas.

Falling head over heels for a lower wolf only meant a life of more subservience.

The bell rang again. The person obviously wasn't going to leave. With a sigh, she told herself she was in her own home, and she didn't have to impress anyone these days. It was probably some salesman who was not going to care what she looked like. She headed to the door and opened it, prepared to quickly get rid of whoever was there.

"We never had time to eat dessert last night," Dan said as soon as the door opened. He was leaning against the door jamb, holding a bakery box. "I thought I'd make it up to you."

He looked as yummy as whatever was in that box as he stood in front of her, staring at her intently. He wore black jeans and a black t-shirt shirt that showed off those lovely muscles she'd been admiring on video. They were even more impressive in person. But that was just the icing on the cake that was Dan Bertrand. His dark hair was worn just a little too long for the responsible CFO position he held, and in his T-shirt and jeans he looked like a rebellious teenager. That bad boy image was emphasized by the edge of a tattoo she could see peeking out of his left sleeve. He'd always worn a long-sleeved shirt the few times she'd been with him before. She'd never noticed the tattoo, and right now she couldn't see enough to tell exactly what it was.

She stared in surprise at the man in her doorway for so long that he grinned impudently at her. "Aren't you going to let me in?"

"Oh! Uh, yes, come in." Kathleen blushed as she held the door wider for him. "Just give me a minute. I'll go get cleaned up."

"Don't bother. I like you this way."

He put the box on the island that separated the living room from a tiny kitchen and strode toward her. He grabbed her tightly, possessively running his hands up and down her back as if trying to memorize the feel of her in his arms. She gazed up at him spellbound as he slowly, slowly, bent his head toward her. Their lips met, and everything else faded to the background. It was as if Kathleen couldn't see, or hear, or feel anything but

Dan in her arms. He tasted like coffee and smelled like fresh air and cedar. The kiss might have lasted a moment or a day, she wasn't sure.

Finally, he lifted his lips from hers and gave a sigh of pleasure or relief, she wasn't sure which. "Now that's how I planned to end last night before we were so rudely interrupted."

"Oh," she said again. She stepped back quickly, almost falling. Dan reached out and grabbed her waist, supporting her. She laughed in confusion.

"I didn't mean to scare you," he said remorsefully.

"No. No. You didn't scare me. I, um, I just lost my balance."

"I was afraid I was maybe a little too intense there; I mean especially since you don't..."

"Since I don't what?"

He shook his head. "Nothing. It doesn't matter."

He grinned again, that naughty-boy look back in his eyes. "Besides, I think I like you off balance. But for now, let's see about the dessert I brought." He walked around the island to her cabinets. "Where do you keep the forks?"

CHAPTER 6

"What happened last night?" Kathleen asked as Dan cut a couple of slices of the chocolate lava cake he had brought with him. Then she grimaced. "That sounded stupid, didn't it?" she asked, turning the shade of a boiled lobster. "Obviously I was there at the beginning. I meant, what happened after they arres... er... took you away?"

"You meant arrested me? Don't worry; you won't offend me by saying the word. That's what happened." Dan scowled as he handed her a plate and pulled a couple of paper towels off the roll hanging under her cabinet. "Despite Walker trying to characterize it differently so he didn't have to read me my rights."

Kathleen gasped. "He didn't..."

"Don't worry about that right now. Here we are," he added, handing her a plate with a slice of cake. "Let's dig into this before I tell you about last night and lose my appetite."

"I hope it didn't take Connor too long to find you. I tried to tell your family that you weren't at the Rivelou Police Department, but over in Indiana, but there was so much going on that no one was really listening to me."

"Yeah, that's my family for you. Never listen to the one person who has the answers," he said a little bitterly.

Kathleen felt blindsided by the whirlwind shifts in Dan's mood. She'd never seen him this way before. One minute he was kissing her as if he needed her to breathe. The next he was making jokes, then he was sounding off about his family. Of course, she thought, she barely knew him. She'd met him a few times when she'd been with his sister, then had a couple of dances with him at Ana's engagement party. But last night had been their first date. And after all, wouldn't she have felt a little "unsettled" after being arrested? "But I thought your family..."

"Was the perfect example of wholesome shifters? *Father Knows Best* with fur and claws?" he asked sardonically.

"Trust me, we have our moments just like everyone else."

Kathleen looked down at her plate, worried that she couldn't seem to strike the right note with the man today. She took a bite of the cake. "Delicious. Did you get it at Flannery's?" Changing the subject seemed like a good idea.

"No, I stopped at a bakery down the street from my place. It was easier, and I wanted a shower after spending all night sitting in an interrogation room."

She breathed a sigh of relief. Dan seemed to have gotten back on a more even keel, so she took a chance. "What exactly did happen? No one's told me anything, not even Ana."

"Yeah, well Ana's busy being a good little girl now that she's back in the family's good graces. I guess she doesn't want to upset that apple cart," Dan said.

"What do you mean?"

"I just meant that now that she's engaged to a man the family approves of rather than being married to her ex, Jonathan, she's getting a lot more support from the family— particularly our mom." He paused, and she could tell he heard just how he sounded.

"Hey, I'm sorry; Ana's your friend. She's had a hard time of it and didn't always get the support from the family she should have had—not even from me," he admitted. "I know you haven't lived here long enough to know all the gossip. And some of the nuances of her situation only the paranormals would understand."

"I know she has a 14-year-old daughter and a fiancé, so I kind of assumed there was an ex in the picture somewhere," Kathleen said lightly. "And yeah, I get most of my gossip from Monica." Kathleen mentioned the other admin in the history department. She was a good friend of Ana's, but she was a non-para.

Dan chuckled when she mentioned Monica. "Yeah, she's totally unaware that her best friend howls at the moon at night. Can you imagine how fast the gossip would spread if she knew all the paranormals living in Rivelou?"

Kathleen chuckled also. Monica was well-known as a gossip.

"Anyway, please excuse my mood and any disparaging remarks I might make about my family or anyone else."

"You've had a shitty twenty-four hours, so I think you get a pass on some things."

"Nah, only a shitty twelve or so hours. The first part, where I was having dinner with you, was great right up until the end."

"You, Mr. Betrand, are full of bull."

"No, it's the absolute truth." Dan reached over and ran a hand lightly down her cheek. He couldn't help himself. He knew he should take it slow—not that the kiss a few minutes ago had been "taking it slow." He took a deep breath and moved his hand away.

"The part of yesterday with you was great. And the fact that you let me in the door today after I pretty much dumped you at a restaurant last night being hounded by reporters makes it even better. Like I said, that certainly wasn't the way I had planned to end the evening."

"Well, I'm sure you hadn't planned on getting arrested. And at least you paid before they took you away. If you hadn't, I'd have thought you had gone to really great lengths to get out of paying the check," Kathleen teased.

Dan laughed. "Well, a lot of women wouldn't be quite so forgiving. And hey, according to the sheriff, I wasn't arrested, just 'taken in for questioning as a material witness.' That's what I meant about him not having to read me my rights."

"Sounds pretty typical when non-paras run the police department and arrest paras. At least where I come from."

"We never did get to that part of the evening," said Dan.

"What part?"

"The part where I find out all about you. Like exactly where are you from?"

"Oh, no place you've ever heard of. A little town a couple of hours from here. I was in college in Tennessee." She quickly changed the subject. "This cake is delicious, by the way. It really makes up for the whole leaving me at the restaurant thing."

Dan grinned and lifted his fork as if to toast her with it. Kathleen laughingly returned the gesture. "But seriously, what did happen last night?"

She was avoiding his questions. *Does it matter?* His wolf asked. *She is ours. Where she was before we found her is of no significance.* Maybe his wolf was right, he thought, letting her get away with evading his questions—for now.

He finished his cake and wiped his mouth on the paper towel. "Are you going to finish your piece?"

"Um, I'm not so hungry right now. I really want to know how you are after everything that happened."

Dan picked up her plate and took a bite.

"You must be starving after spending such a long, long time in jail," Kathleen teased.

"Hey, I couldn't get cake like this while doing hard time for twelve hours."

So how did you get sprung?" she said, continuing with the teasing tone, but still insisting on finding out what she wanted to know. "I mean, I have heard of bail, but apparently you're a hardened criminal. Maybe you dug a tunnel and escaped?"

"You don't know how close I came to considering it. If Connor hadn't shown up when he did... Come on, let's sit down. It may have only been only one night, but it's a long story."

He took her hand and walked her back to the couch, sitting down and putting his arm around her possessively. She snuggled in. She rather liked it. She felt safe with this man, she realized. It was a new sensation. Something she'd never experienced with the males in her pack.

"Well, I don't know how much of the conversation between me and good ole' Sheriff Walker you caught."

"Enough to realize you two have some history."

"Yeah, you could say that," he laughed shortly. "Well, it may surprise you to learn I haven't always been the paragon of virtue you see before you—the suave and charming CFO of Betrand Enterprises. Member of half a dozen Chamber of Commerce committees. Advisor to the mayor, and everything else the press has mentioned about me in the last twenty-four hours while trying to simultaneously smear my name."

"Well, now that you mentioned it, that tattoo I saw under your sleeve rather surprised me."

"That's the least of it," he gave a short laugh, then ran his hand over his hair and around the back of his neck. "Okay, I guess you need the short, ugly history of Daniel Bertrand to understand everything."

Kathleen looked up at him and waited as he took a breath. She could see he was trying to decide where to start.

"In high school I was bored. My friends Connor and Gabe were, too. We didn't have enough to challenge us, I guess. Oh, I'm not using that as an excuse..." He put up a hand as if she had started to say something. "...just an explanation. I liked fast cars—still do. We kind of got in with the wrong crowd. We had been the good kids all through elementary and middle school, and then suddenly we found ourselves popular with the bad kids. They knew we came from money. They were using us."

Kathleen looked away. She knew a little about being used because of who your family was or where you came from. Now wasn't the time to talk about that, however. She wasn't sure there was ever going to be a right time to tell Dan Bertrand exactly who she was.

"Well, to make a long story short, we had a few runs-ins with the law. Sheriff Walker was the assistant police chief here in Rivelou at the time, and he didn't take kindly to 'rich kids getting off the hook so easily.'"

"I take he's a non-para? And he's not aware of us, right?"

"Right. But just coming from well-known, influential families was enough for him. He thought we were entitled." He looked ruefully down at her again. "He was probably right. We had been let off the hook because of our family connections. Well, finally my grandfather and Chief Anderson took us in hand, gave us our own personal "scared straight" program, and kept the three of us from becoming criminals—which, frankly, is where we were heading. The way we were going we would have ended up outing the whole paranormal community." He shook his head.

"It's very important to you to take care of your pack, isn't it?"

"Of course. I learned that from my grandfather, and Chief Anderson, too. With their help, Connor, Gabe, and I turned our lives around. But there are still people around the area—and obviously Sheriff Walker is one of them—who don't want to accept that we've changed."

"Okay, so I understand the animosity, but why was he arresting you last night over this Professor Fontaine? I've heard his name around campus a few times. Isn't he the teacher who disappeared last year?"

"Apparently they found Fontaine's car after all this time. It's been in the Rivelou River, and for whatever reason, yesterday it floated up onto the bank on the Indiana side. I'm astonished that fact hasn't been all over the news. Walker must be keeping a really tight lid on that part of the story. He's just so happy he can tell everyone that he's arrested me, he's not worrying about getting credit for finding out something about Fontaine."

"But what did their finding the car have to do with arresting you? And have they learned anything about what happened to this Dr. Fontaine?"

"The car had my prints on it." Dan looked away again.

"Your prints? Really? Why? I mean how?"

"Well, Fontaine let me drive it a couple of times when he was dating Ana. Did you know that? He took Ana out for a while before he disappeared. It wasn't anything serious, of course. But Fontaine was planning on joining the pack and..."

"Wait. Fontaine was a shifter?"

"Yeah, didn't I mention that?"

"No, I haven't heard it mentioned by anyone else when they've talked about him. Of course, I'm not really sure who I heard the story from, if they were paranormals or non-paras."

"Well, he was a shifter although of course no one over in Indiana realized that—at least not the people who questioned me at the sheriff's department. Unlike here in Rivelou, it's pretty much run by the NP's.

"Anyway, when Walker finally got around to telling me why he was questioning me, I told him that Fontaine had let me drive his car. Several other people know that, too. If Walker had just asked politely, it could all have been taken care of without the drama."

"Somehow I doubt that," Kathleen said skeptically. "From what I saw the chances of you and that sheriff having a polite discussion were pretty slim."

"Okay, you've got my number. Anyway, no polite questions were asked or answered until Connor arrived."

"You've mentioned him a few times. You said he was one of your friends in high school?"

"Yeah, and now he's the family lawyer. Ana sent him over to sort things out and get me sprung from jail. I'm still listed as 'a person of interest,' but there is nothing they can charge me with—at least that's what Connor says. A lot of people will testify that they saw me drive his car—several days before he disappeared, too, by the way. And since they still haven't found the…" he paused just long enough for Kathleen to look at him questioningly, "…where Fontaine has gotten to," he continued, "they can't take it any further than that."

"Where do you think he is?" Kathleen asked. "Why would he have left so mysteriously? You don't think he's dead, do you?"

"Well, finding his car in the river certainly can't be a good sign," Dan said. He stood up abruptly, again running his hands through his hair. One more change of mood for Kathleen to wonder at. She got up and followed him. Was he angry that she'd asked so many questions? She started to apologize, but he turned around again, smiling.

"Enough about Fontaine, Walker, and all the rest of it. Let's get back to our date."

He took her hand and walked her back to the couch, turning so he could watch her as they continued to talk. Nothing heavy, nothing serious, and certainly nothing about how he'd spent the last twenty-four hours. As they chatted, he thought how much he needed this. The normalcy of an afternoon spent with a pretty woman. He reached over and brushed his fingers along her cheek. She smiled and turned her head to catch his fingers with her lips.

He drew her closer and kissed her—lightly. That's how he planned it. Just a light kiss on the lips. His wolf took over, turning the kiss into something deep, intense, dark.

No, it was too soon. She was too young. He pulled away, panting. "I'm sorry, I…"

"I'm not." She grabbed his shirt and pulled him back to her, taking his lips, his mouth, just as passionately as he had hers. She pushed his shirt up to run her hands over his bare skin. He loved the feel of her hands on him. He reached up and pulled the shirt over his head, so she could run her hands more freely over his chest, his back. She pulled away from their kiss, still running her hands lightly over his chest. "You have a beautiful body," she said.

He laughed. "You aren't supposed to call me beautiful. You'll hurt my manly pride."

"Oh, I think you have enough pride. You're not in any danger." Her hand headed up his arms again, and he shivered. "Oo, you like when I touch you, don't you?" she teased. "Here, let me see your tattoo. I've been wondering about it all afternoon. It's been peeking out at me from under your sleeve.

He turned so she could better see his shoulder and upper arm and rolled up his sleeve. The black image showed a stylized wolf with the words *"Veritas Vencit,"* underneath.

"It means truth prevails," he said.

"Truth is important to you," she said softly, her face turning sad.

He turned away again for a moment, and when he looked back to her, his gaze was serious. "Of course. Maybe because as paranormals we are always keeping secrets. But in the end, the truth is what is most important between two people who love each other. I'm learning, though, that there are times we need to hide the truth."

His words gave Kathleen a glimmer of hope. Maybe, when Dan did learn the truth, he would be able to accept why she had hidden it from him.

CHAPTER 7

Moonlight shimmered on the path through the trees as two wolves chased each other in a playful game of cat and mouse. One finally flopped down, panting, while the other prowled the area for a few moments, searching to make sure they were alone and that they were safe. Then he crossed over to her and nuzzled her cheek.

Are we okay to change here? Channing asked through the mental connection all werewolves shared whenever they shifted into wolf form. They could communicate with other shifters within a few miles of each other.

Yes, no one around, Dolan replied.

As they began the transformation from wolf to human, the crack of their bones interrupted the silence of the empty forest. Small creatures would scatter when two apex predators were out for a midnight run.

As Dolan completed the change to human he stood up, giving Channing a chance to admire the sleek, taut muscles of his chest and abdomen. It was a hot, muggy night, and sweat immediately coated his skin, making his body glisten in the soft glow of the moonlight.

She gave a little shiver of delight. How had she gotten so lucky as to attract the attention of this man? He wasn't part of their pack. It was complete coincidence that they had run into each other when she had been at a meeting in Lexington for her job doing public relations for the Rivelou Chamber of Commerce.

Dolan's father, alpha of the McTier pack which was located near the Kentucky capital, had always had a problem with the way her grandfather ran the Bertrand pack. Their territory bordered each other. Michael McTier thought the Bertrands were too welcoming of other paranormals. He didn't allow mixing of the paranormal races in his pack. No intermarriage between werewolves and other paranormals was allowed, not even with different shifter species; even friendships were discouraged.

He would most certainly disapprove of her sister marrying a Hunter. Although Chris Spier preferred the title "hunter", he was a witch. His special skills enabled him to track rogue paranormals and bring them to justice. That was fine with McTier as long as the rogues were not werewolves. But Chris treated everyone equally. If a werewolf violated the laws of the paranormal world, they were brought to justice, just like a member of any other species.

Dolan had assured her he didn't agree with his father's policies. When he was in charge of the pack, things would be different. And he wanted Channing to help him with that goal. He'd told her that often since they had met in the spring. And he treated her as an equal most of the time, so she was sure he meant it—even if sometimes he said some things that were... well... maybe a little chauvinistic. She'd called him on it at first, but he'd looked so uncomfortable, she no longer mentioned it. He'd been raised to think that women were merely breeders. It was difficult not to slip up sometimes and say things that grated on her. She'd excused his words because he always treated her well.

Channing was beginning to fantasize about becoming the next Luna of the McTier pack. Dolan hadn't promised anything yet. He hadn't said he loved her. He hadn't suggested they were fated mates. But that was how he made her feel. Now if she could only convince her father, her brother Dan, and her grandfather that Dolan was a good guy...

"Wait here a minute; I'll get our stuff," Dolan said, bringing her out of her thoughts and back to admiring the beautiful body of the man in front of her. Shifters were comfortable with their bodies. They had to be, since everyone in their pack saw them naked each time they changed, beginning with their first change at about age fourteen. Dolan seemed particularly unselfconscious as he walked away from her with a quick grin, fully aware that she was admiring him.

He left the path and headed into the trees a short way to where they had left their clothes to change into after their run. He brought them back and handed hers to Channing, taking a minute to admire her body in return before handing them to her. He leaned down and kissed her lips gently, then moved down her neck to take one taut nipple into his mouth. She giggled. "Not here, Dolan. We need to get back to my house before we start that."

"Okay. For now," he said. "That was just a preview of what I plan to do to you when we get back to your place. I want you constantly, Channing; you know that don't you? I find you the sexiest thing I've ever seen."

Channing smiled and blushed. "I don't often feel that way. Have you seen my big sister? She's so beautiful."

"I've never noticed. I only see you. But speaking of your family," he continued, pulling his shirt over his spectacular abs. Channing wished he didn't have to cover them up. She liked looking at him.

"What happened with your brother last night? There hasn't been a lot on the news about it. The Bertrand family influence at work keeping it quiet?"

Channing tensed at the sarcasm in his voice when he mentioned her family's influence. "Well, I don't know how quiet we've kept it. Maybe the results aren't out in the public, but Danny being taken in for questioning surely was. I think the sheriff needs to release a statement saying that Danny was cleared of suspicion."

"He was? That's good. But why was he arrested in the first place? I thought no one knew where Fontaine had gone. He might have just taken off on his own. He's a grown man, after all." They headed down the trail toward the state-forest car park, Dolan taking her hand as they walked.

"Why do you think it had anything to do with Alexaner Fontaine? Nothing on the news said anything about him."

"Come on, Channing, everyone heard on the news that your brother was taken in for arrest over something to do with Fontaine. And I've heard some fancy car was found in the river the other day. Fontaine drove a black Lamborghini. It's obvious the cops think your brother had something to do with putting it there."

"How do you know Alexander drove a black

Lamborghini?"

"Um, well, it was all over the news back when he disappeared. You know, to be on the lookout for it."

"I wouldn't have thought you were keeping up with the news in Rivelou before you met me." Channing tried to make the comment sound teasing. Maybe she wasn't successful, though.

"Well, he was a nationally known author. His disappearance made it farther than the smalltown Rivelou newspaper," Dolan replied defensively. "And now that he's been gone this long, I assume he's dead."

"You just said he was a grown man and could have left on his own."

Channing, don't double-talk me. I can put two and two together. Yeah, when he first disappeared, he might have just left. Now they've found his car in the river. Sounds like either suicide or foul play to me."

Channing let out a sigh, then grabbed Dolan's hand. "You're right. It sounds like one or the other. But I don't like it when you assume my brother had something to do with it. Dan wouldn't have had any reason to be involved with what happened to the man. Dan had driven his car a few times, so his prints were on it. That's why they took him in for questioning.

"And it wasn't an arrest, by the way. Please make sure you don't call it that. Connor has said he wants everyone in the family who is asked about it to make that clear. He was only brought in as a witness to see if he knew anything. He wasn't arrested."

"So don't get mad at me if I think there's something fishy about it when obviously his lawyer is worried."

"I'm not mad at you. I just think you should support my family if you want to bring our packs closer together, like you say you do."

"Hey, I'm sorry. I didn't mean..."

Channing stopped walking and swung around to face him. "I'm sorry. I know you didn't mean anything by it. I know you want to get along with Dan and the rest of my family."

Dolan pulled her in and kissed her. She started to draw back, but he held her harder, turning the kiss from something light and playful to dark and drugging. "I want you, Channing," he said when he finally released her.

"I know. I want you too, but I'm part of my family, just like you are part of yours."

"When a man takes a woman, she gives up her birth pack and takes his."

Channing pulled back. "We've had a few dates. I'm not ready to…"

"I can't help thinking ahead, baby."

These were the words Channing had wanted to hear. He was thinking of her as more than just a casual relationship. So why did it make her uncomfortable?

"That is very old school of you, you know." She turned and began walking to the car. When Dolan tried to take her hand, she pulled away.

"I need you to believe in my pack and what they stand for," she told him. I know you and Dan don't get along, but you can't think he would be involved in anything related to Fontaine's disappearance."

"Don't always get along? He attacked me on sight at your sister's party, Channing. I'd say 'don't always get along' was an understatement. Fontaine was dating your sister, and then poof, he's gone. If Dan's welcome of me as a potential beau was any example, he could very well have offed Fontaine."

"Dolan! That's ridiculous. And you know why Dan had a problem with you. I shouldn't have surprised the family by bringing you to Ana's party unannounced. They thought you were there to disrupt things. I should have warned them ahead of time, but I was just too cowardly." Channing turned away, embarrassed, and bent down to make a show of retying her shoe.

"Just because my last name is McTier doesn't mean I hate every Bertrand; I think that is obvious," Dolan said. He helped her up, giving her another of those drugging kisses that made it hard for her to think.

"Yes, it's obvious," Channing said when he released her. She stood on her tiptoes to give him a quick kiss on the cheek as they continued to walk. "And if you and I can become friends, I'm sure we can help the two packs get along." She deliberately understated the feelings she was beginning to have for him. She didn't want to be embarrassed if she were wrong about the way he felt about her.

"I thought we were more than friends." Dolan put his arm around her and pulled her in close. "Your grandfather is as set in his ways as my father. Maybe it's time for some of the old guard to step down."

"I'm not sure my grandfather is ready to step down. What about your dad?"

"He plans on being leader until he dies. That just leaves me sitting around with nothing to do but wait on his orders. And his ideas are so damned old-fashioned. And every one of his alphas is, too. I want to bring the pack into the 21st century," Dolan grumbled. "At this rate, I'll have to wait until the next century to do that."

Channing patted his shoulder sympathetically. "I know how you feel. But maybe I can help you with that. Maybe us being together can help change people's minds—particularly our pack leaders. When are you going to take me to meet your family? You've met mine."

"And that went so well," Dolan said sarcastically. "I think we need to take this slowly. I'm not sure they should see us together for a while."

That hurt. She was already madly in love with Dolan although she would never tell him that. He said it wasn't the right time for her to meet his family. She shook her head at herself as she realized she was doing the same thing Dolan was. He was afraid to let his family know they were seeing each other, and she was afraid to tell him she loved him.

When they got back to the apartment, Dolan distracted her with kisses. Well, to be honest, they were distracting each other, she thought.

"Let's not talk about our families anymore. In fact, let's not talk about anything," Dolan said, leading her into the bedroom. "I have to leave in the morning. I'll be over in Lexington all week, and you'll be here. We have much better things to do right now than talk."

CHAPTER 8

Dan had often sat in on pack council meetings but never when he was the main topic of discussion. It wasn't a comfortable place to be.

The council included his grandfather, Hank, and father, Remy, as well as Marianne Legato, the owner of the Strawberry Moon Restaurant and grandmother to his friend, Gabe. Tim Means and Maddie LaBlanc rounded out the group that made all the major decisions for the pack. While Hank had the final say, he took the advice of his councilors seriously. Tim and Marianne were close to his grandfather in age while Maddie was a new member of the council, a female shifter only slightly older than Dan. And Remy, Dan's dad, was in between them all. Unlike other packs Dan knew about, Hank tried to make sure that he had not only males and females, but people of several generations on the council.

"What if something happens?" Hank explained when Dan questioned why his policy was so different from other packs. "We need to have young blood that knows what's what to carry on. And besides, old people get hidebound. Who would keep us on our toes if the younger generation weren't around?"

Tonight, several of that younger generation were present, but Dan knew "keeping the council on its toes" wasn't the reason they were all here. His sister, Ana, and soon-to-be brother-in-law, Chris, were there although neither was a member of the council. Since Chris wasn't even a shifter, his presence raised several eyebrows as everyone walked into the basement of his grandfather's farmhouse. The large and inviting room was the setting for many pack events, from parties to more formal meetings such as tonight.

When everyone had greeted each other and settled in the comfortable couches and chairs grouped in a circle, Hank cleared his throat. "I know you all have questions and would like to learn the full story from my grandson, Daniel, about what happened this weekend. But before we hear from him, there is a backstory that very few in this room are aware of. You know that I welcomed Alexander Fontaine into our fold last fall. That was my mistake, and I take full responsibility for bringing him in. As you also know, just a few weeks after joining our pack, he disappeared.

"While there was some suspicion about his disappearance at the time, he was known for never staying too long in one place. After the police looked into it, they concluded that there was no evidence of foul play, so it was assumed he had decided to move on. I'm here to tell you that the official police report was not accurate."

The council members stirred and mumbled to each other, and Chris reached over to grip Ana's hand as Hank continued. "It's time you heard the entire tale. But I must ask you to keep whatever you hear in this room to yourselves. Up until this time only seven people have known the whole truth about what happened to Fontaine that night. Hunter Chris Spier is one of them. I'm going to ask him to tell you the portion of the story that you do not yet know."

Chris stood up and began to talk. He seemed perfectly at ease, and Dan admired his cool. It wasn't too long ago that most of the people in this room, himself included, had been out for Chris' blood.

"I know you all remember the rogue shifter attacks that occurred last year. I came to Rivelou specifically because of those incidents. My sister had realized that they followed the same pattern as certain attacks that occurred in Chicago the year before. In one of those assaults her husband, Jason, was killed." Maddie made a small noise of sympathy. While not everyone here knew the whole story, she and Tim were the only people in the room who were completely unfamiliar with it. Chris nodded his thanks at her and continued.

"As Shannon and I investigated, we became convinced that Alexander Fontaine was the perpetrator of the attacks. Unfortunately, I had the problem that he had already gone a long way toward convincing Hank, here, that I was the one responsible. Luckily, Ana wasn't convinced of my guilt."

He paused to smile at her, and Dan felt a stab of jealousy. He wanted someone he could look at like that—as if just being close made everything better. Now that he'd scented his mate, Kathleen, he wanted to court her and marry her as soon as possible. She was so much younger than he was though—ten years. He'd need to give her time...

He quickly shook off his daydream and tuned back into what Chris was saying.

"But we needed evidence to prove Fontaine's guilt. Ana, Shannon, and I developed a plan where my sister and I would break into Fontaine's apartment while he was giving a speech at the university. Ana, as his assistant, would be at the university to warn us if the shifter left for any reason.

"I'm sorry to say that I was not as versed in Fontaine's alarm system as I thought I was," Chris continued, grimacing at the need to make this embarrassing admission. As a Hunter, he was supposed to be an expert not in just non-magical alarms, but the magical ones, too. That's what had tripped him up at Fontaine's place.

Ana reached up from her seat and took his hand as if she knew how badly he felt about this one mistake. It could have cost Chris and his sister their lives.

"I triggered one of the alarms in his building. It was connected to his telephone, and Fontaine left the university to find out what had happened. He knocked my sister unconscious and was holding me at gunpoint when Ana arrived to rescue us. She shifted to her wolf and killed Fontaine."

At that revelation the room erupted.

"Where was Chief Anderson? And why isn't he here now?"

"What else are you hiding from us, Bertrand?"

"But how does this involve Dan?"

"What did Fontaine want from the pack, anyway?"

Dan's and Ana's father's voice rose above the others. "Why wasn't I told about this? Ana's my daughter. You should have informed me. I'm tired of being kept out in the cold in this family."

"Dad, no one is trying to keep you out of the loop with

your family," Ana said.

"We would never do that, Dad," added Dan. He rose from his seat to try to calm his father down.

"No, don't try to placate me," Remy continued, raising his arm as if to ward off Dan's approach. "It's been this way since your grandfather here decided I wasn't worthy of being the pack leader and made you his heir."

"Remy you know you never wanted the responsibility. Why…"

Dan cut his grandfather off before the discussion could get farther afield. "Dad, Grandpa, we need to get back on topic."

"And that's why he'll make the best alpha," Hank mumbled under his breath.

"You're right, son," said Remy, turning back to Chris. "Spier, you've explained how you and your sister involved my daughter in this mess, but how did you get my father and son tangled up in it, too?"

There went all the hard-won goodwill Chris had developed with his soon-to-be father-in-law, Dan thought. He didn't want to be seen as the potential heir to the pack right now, but it was obvious he needed to step in to help smooth things over. "Dad, obviously Ana called Granddad when she realized Fontaine was dead. He's her pack leader. Who else would she call?"

"I think you are forgetting yourself, Remy," Hank said sternly as he stood up. His calm strength was all that was needed to silence everyone in the room, reminding Dan why he had been the pack Alpha for over fifty years. It wasn't only his physical prowess as an alpha wolf, his leadership ability was a large part of it, also.

"I am the leader of this pack. I told Ana to keep what she knew a secret for her own good. No one needed to know that she had killed Fontaine. No, not even her father," he added sternly, looking toward his son as Remy started to object once again. "Chris, please continue."

"Fontaine's apartment was on the tenth floor of a downtown condominium, and his body had obviously been torn apart by a wolf. There was no way we could explain away everything to the non-para's, and if it had been officially reported, there would have been far too many of them involved for our witch friends to suppress their memories."

"I agree with that," said Tim. "We get along well with the coven. That doesn't mean we need to go running to them for favors every time someone in our pack has an indiscretion we need to cover."

Hank nodded his thanks to his friend. "I absolutely agree. And to answer another question that was asked earlier, I did call in Chief Anderson. He was there at the time and knew what had happened. He agreed with my assessment on how to handle things. As to where he is now, he is on a much-deserved vacation. He's spending a few weeks at his childhood home on Jamaica. I'll only call him back early if it becomes absolutely necessary."

"Well, that explains in part why Danny was arrested last night," Remy said, using his son's childhood nickname. Dan grimaced. While his family often called him 'Danny,' this was not the moment when he wanted to be seen as a child. It was time for him to step into the conversation.

"Hank asked me to get rid of Fontaine's Lamborghini. I drove it into the river, made sure it sank, and assumed it would never be found. We all know that things often disappear in the Rivelou River and are never seen again. It was just bad luck that the car floated up."

The conversation rose again, this time with various members of the council questioning how Dan could have been so careless in getting rid of such an incriminating piece of evidence.

"I did everything I knew to keep the car from coming up again," he said, standing up so he could face all of the council. "I rolled the windows down so it would flood quickly. Then I drove it into the river from the parking lot at the Indian Mounds Park. There's enough space in the lot, and enough elevation— it's at least twenty feet above the bank at that point. I sped up to 200, then ran off the lot into the river."

Remy gave a gasp of alarm when he heard the way in which his son had disposed of the car. Chris, however, gave a low whistle. "Two hundred miles per hour? That shoulda done it," he said admiringly.

"Yeah, it should have. I shifted to my wolf as soon as it hit the water and swam out. The river's deep at that spot. It should never have come up again."

Questions sprang up from everyone in the room. Dan appreciated his father's exclamations of worry over the dangerous way he had disposed of the car, but it was not the most important thing at the moment. That danger was past.

"Where is Fontaine's body?" Marianne asked.

"I left it in the woods. There should be nothing to be found by now except maybe a few bones. And yes, the body was well-wrapped when I put it in the trunk of the car to take it out to the park. There was no blood in the car. I think we can be sure of that because Walker would have loved to arrest me for murder.

"It was autumn. There are a lot of hungry predators who could have made good use of some extra meat over the winter. Fontaine's body shouldn't be a problem by now," Dan said callously. They were, after all, wolves. Every one of them had hunted, killed, and eaten fresh meat. They were predators at heart, and that was their way.

Hank allowed everyone to talk for a few minutes, then held up his hands to quiet them. "What's done is done. I made the decision to handle things this way. Now, we need to make sure that there is no fallout on the pack, or on Ana, Dan, Chris, or Chris' sister, Shannon."

"And I won't let Danny take any of the fallout for what I did. I'm the one who killed Fontaine. I don't regret it, but if there are repercussions, I'll be the one who steps up and confesses what I did. I just don't want Sophie to suffer from her mother being accused of murder," said Ana.

Chris put a supportive arm around Ana as she stood up next to him.

"And I'm not letting anyone arrest my sister for murder," Dan told her.

"Alright, alright, settle down the two of you. No one is going to be arrested for murder. They can't declare it a murder unless they find a body, and from what Dan says, that won't happen. Right, Dan?" his grandfather asked him pointedly.

"I haven't been back to that spot, but I could go look tomorrow," he suggested.

"No!" objected Remy. "Leave it alone. The last thing we want is for someone to notice you going to that area and get suspicious."

"He's right. We should leave well enough alone," said Chris. "If anyone goes to check, it should be someone with no connection to the family."

"And how are we going to find someone like that? We're going to say to a perfect stranger, 'Why don't you head out into the woods and make sure you don't find a body at this location?' That's not suspicious or anything," Tim said sarcastically.

"I was thinking about someone like Gabe."

"Oh, yes, let's get my grandson involved. That may solve something for the Bertrand clan, but not for my family," Marianne said. "That's how it's always been with you, Hank."

Tim and Maddie nodded in agreement.

Suddenly, Dan was seeing cracks in the tight pack council that he had never noticed before. Had they always been there, and he had just not noticed? Or was this something new? He'd always seen his grandfather as totally in control, totally in charge. What if the pack decided it was time for a change? Panic gripped him. He wasn't ready to step up as alpha. He needed more time.

He took a deep breath; he'd just let his imagination run away with him. Maybe the rest of the pack agreed with the three council members, but maybe they didn't. He looked across the room at his sister and Chris. They'd noticed the tension, also. He'd have to discuss this with them later.

"Someone going to look for the remains of a body that has been in the woods for a year is not a top priority right now," Chris said, cutting through the tension. "We have a bigger problem. The real questions are how did the car float upstream from where Dan put it? And isn't it convenient that it came up in the jurisdiction of a man who seems to have a grudge against Dan?"

CHAPTER 9

Chris' words caused a new outbreak of conversation among the council members.

"That's certainly something to think about," said Hank. "Chris, can you quietly look into it for us?"

"Of course."

"Yeah, your pet hunter will look into it," muttered Tim. Dan noticed Maddie nodding her head in agreement, one more sign of the cracks he'd never noticed before.

"He's the best suited to the task," Hank retorted. "Because of the way in which the car reappeared, we must consider the possibility that it was not a natural occurrence." Ana turned to Chris, who shook his head slightly. What was that all about?

"Hmph, you just don't want to admit your boy, here, made a mistake. We know you've been grooming him to take over from you. Maybe it's time someone other than a Bertrand led this pack," Tim replied.

It was no coincidence that Means had a son who was the right age to be considered for pack alpha if his grandfather stepped down, Dan thought. How had he never noticed these conflicts and tensions before? Had Hank known and just not told him? Or was this a surprise to his grandfather, too? He watched the man speculatively as he began to wind down the meeting.

"Now that everyone on the council has heard the entire story, I'd like to remind you that council business is private. Nothing said in this room should leave it."

They all murmured in agreement as they headed up the stairs, stopping in the kitchen to say their farewells to Dan's grandmother and mother, Ida and Donna, neither of whom were on the council.

When everyone except the family had left, Hank went over to the pantry and pulled out a bottle of Kentucky bourbon. "I think we could all use a little something after that cluster of a meeting."

The seven family members chuckled as he got out glasses, filled them, and handed them out, then headed into the home's living room across the hall. The setting here was more formal than downstairs, with antique walnut end tables placed on either side of a camel back sofa. The chairs were covered in a floral fabric but were still large and comfortable. "I'm too big to sit in a tiny chair that I have to worry about breaking," his grandfather always said. Ida had compromised by adding one leather recliner so Hank could always be comfortable.

"So, tell us everything that happened," Donna demanded as soon as everyone was settled.

"Honey, you know we can't discuss council business," her husband, Remy, said in a gentle voice.

"What happens in council stays in council," she replied, sarcasm dripping from her voice. "Oh, please! You know the rest of them are going home and telling their mates everything that was said. If you don't tell me now, I'll just get it out of Jan Means tomorrow."

"If I hear one word of what was said tonight being whispered around the pack, there will be hell to pay—and that includes members of my own family," Hank said sternly.

"You won't hear a word, dear," his wife Ida said, patting him on the knee. "Trust me; there are things that happen in the pack outside of council that you never know about. That's why you kept me off, remember? So the other shifters would feel comfortable talking to me about things they didn't want to become official business."

Hank smiled at his wife and put his hand over hers. "I do remember, and I'm grateful you handle all the things that you do so discreetly. But this is different. We need to keep everything about this business quiet. For the sake of our pack and of our family."

Donna pouted, obviously put out that apparently Ida already knew about what had been discussed in the council meeting. She was seemingly the only one in the room who did not know anything about what was happening.

"And Donna," Hank continued, "that means that we need

to tell you everything, too, because this is about our own family just as much as it is about the safety of the pack."

Donna gave a gratified smile as he went on to fill his daughter-in-law in on all the details that had been talked about at the meeting. As he spoke, Dan watched his mother become more and more upset. Obviously, his father noticed, also. He put a comforting arm around her, but Donna shook it off and stood up.

"I can't believe you never told me any of this," she said to the room at large, then turned to her husband. "Remy, did you know about this? How could you not tell me that our daughter was involved in something that could get her arrested by the non-paras."

Ana winced. She obviously didn't want to think about being arrested. Their mother had never had any tact.

Remy put his hands up. "Honey, I didn't hear a word about any of this until tonight." He looked around at the rest of the group. "And I said much the same thing as you just did when I found out. Ana, I still can't believe you didn't trust your parents enough to let us know what was going on. This was taking pack secrecy way too far."

"You should have told us when you first suspected that awful man, Professor Fontaine." Donna said the name as if it were a dirty word.

Ana laughed. "Mom, if you remember, you were all for Alexander Fontaine. You thought he was just the type of person I should be looking to marry. And that's all he wanted—to marry into the Bertrand family so he could start taking over the pack. Chris loved me, yet you wanted to throw him into the middle of the pack and let them tear him apart." She reached over to Chris, who sat in the chair next to her, and he took her hand.

Dan felt that small surge of jealousy again. Everyone in the room, all of his family members, had someone to support them, someone to turn to. Even his youngest brother, Tyler, was dating a nice witch, Winnie. And Channing had Dolan. He gave an inward grimace. He really didn't like that shifter, but he did seem to be supportive of Channing. Dan wanted to claim Kathleen as his own. He wanted her now. Would she accept him as her mate, the one person he could always turn to for understanding and acceptance? *Yes, just ask her!* shouted his wolf.

At her daughter's words about Chris, Dan noticed that his mother had the grace to look sheepish. "Chris, you know I've changed my mind. You are an excellent choice for Ana to marry, and you'll encourage Sophie's shifter side—unlike her father."

That was a little unfair, Dan's thoughts continued. Seeing as Ana's ex-husband and Sophie's dad was a non-para and wasn't even aware that shapeshifters existed. But his mother was on a roll, and she wasn't going to let little things like fairness or reality stop her. He tried not to roll his eyes when his mother's gaze fell on him. Now he was in for it.

"And what about my son? You got him into this, Hank. It's your fault. If you hadn't asked him to hide that car, he wouldn't have been arrested in a public restaurant. And have it plastered all over the news, too!"

"Alright, alright, we are getting off track here." Hank clapped his hands to get everyone's attention and get the conversation back to what was important. "The point is there are some things that are pack business and some things that are family business. I don't want us to take privacy and secrecy too far. Is there anything else any of you know about this? Now is the time to speak up."

Dan looked around and caught Ana and Chris exchanging a look again. What was that all about? Chris noticed him watching them, quickly schooled his expression, and cleared his throat. "There is something I'm worried about."

Hank nodded for Chris to go ahead.

"It's PackNet. I'm starting to wonder if it's been hacked."

Everyone in the room responded with surprise. PackNet was supposed to be totally secure. Gabe had designed it with the most up-to-date non-para security as well as spells and protections provided by every paranormal expert he knew. It was not hackable. At least that's what they'd always been told.

"Why would you think that?"

"It's something Dave Thorne told me," he answered, mentioning the cop who was also a witch and was dating his sister Shannon. "When they were investigating Harrison, the guy who was responsible for the Artificial Witch murders, the man said something about it being possible to find out all sorts of interesting things on the internet 'if you had enough juice to get there.'"

Dan watched his sister's face as Chris told his story. There was more to this than they were saying, but he wasn't going to call them on it now in front of the rest of the family. He would have to talk to them another time. So much for the truth prevailing. Everyone kept secrets, apparently. It was not the time to worry about that, however, because Chris' remark had set off a new storm of comments.

"It's impossible."

"I've never felt comfortable with PackNet."

"What would happen if PackNet were hacked by the non-para's?" His grandmother's final comment brought silence to the room. PackNet hacked? It would spell disaster, not just for the Bertrand pack, but for all paranormals everywhere. So much information was stored on PackNet. The paranormal dark web held everything from the bloodlines of the Vampire sires to websites for shops which catered to paranormal needs. The emails between heads of packs or covens held enough damaging information to take down the worldwide paranormal community from the inside—let alone what would happen if non-paras got hold of them.

"Dan, can you ask Gabe to double check everything about PackNet security tomorrow?" Hank said.

"Of course. I'll check with him first thing in the morning."

Dan's family seemed ready to continue discussing the same things over and over again all night. He gave them fifteen minutes, then decided he'd had enough. He was done for the night and kissed his grandmother, his sister, and finally his mother on the cheek. "I need to go, he said. "I have a late date with Kathleen."

CHAPTER 10

It wasn't true. He didn't have any plans for the evening. But it wasn't that late, only 10 p.m. Not late for a shifter who ran almost nightly in the moonlight. Wolves were nocturnal, after all. But maybe it was too late for Kathleen. Shifter or not, she worked daily as an administrative assistant for a cranky professor. He wavered even as he started his SUV. Maybe he shouldn't. Maybe she was already asleep. Finally, he decided he could at least stop by her apartment and see if she were available.

He remembered his time with her the day before. They'd had a great time. He'd felt more relaxed yesterday afternoon than he could remember feeling around a woman in years. Kathleen didn't seem to have expectations of him, like so many of the shifters or other paranormals or even the non-paras he had dated. They thought of him as the heir of the pack Alpha, the responsible businessman, or "a great catch." He found that one rather amusing, particularly from the non-paras. What would they think if they knew what he really were? He let his fangs slip out just a little as he imagined the horror of the particularly pushy mother of one girl he'd taken out on a date. Kathleen didn't act as if she considered him any of those things; she just accepted him for who he was.

He couldn't think of an excuse for stopping by so late. There certainly weren't any bakeries open at this time of night. He could be making a fool of himself. But somehow his car seemed to be driving in the direction of her apartment even as he was still debating whether or not he should stop.

When he got to the parking area, he turned off the motor and just sat for a few minutes. At least the light was still on in the front room of the apartment. That was a good sign. As if pulled by a magnet, he got out of the car, staring at that lighted window like a moth attracted to a flame. That was his mating bond, pushing him to be near Kathleen. She was his. She might not know it yet, but she belonged to him. His wolf clamored for the connection, for her voice, her touch. He slammed the car door shut and headed toward her. He could hear a movie playing softly inside as he knocked on the door.

"Who's there?" Kathleen asked cautiously, not opening the door.

"It's just me."

"Danny? What are you doing here so late? Is something wrong?" He grinned when she called him Danny. When his family did it, he was irritated, but from this woman it felt intimate.

She opened the door, pulling her hair off her neck as the heat of the late summer evening invaded her air-conditioned apartment. She was dressed in a pair of short shorts and a tiny T-shirt that slid up over her stomach as she lifted her arms, emphasizing her curves. She pulled it down self-consciously and crossed her arms in front of her. Dan immediately missed the view.

"I've just come from meeting with my family and the pack council. They all want an explanation of what happened. Of why I was arrested."

"And, of course, you don't have one since you didn't have anything to do with it," she said. "I can imagine it felt like you'd been called to the principal's office. Come on in."

Dan felt like a fake. Kathleen only knew what he'd told her—and even without his grandfather's warning, he couldn't reveal all the information he had about Fontaine's disappearance without incriminating his sister, Chris, and Chris' sister Shannon, as well. Not to mention his grandfather and the chief of police, who were the ones who had ordered him to get rid of the body and the car in the first place.

He sat down on her sofa, head in hands. When had his life gotten so complicated? Kathleen sat down at the other end, watching him, concern in her eyes. "Can I get you anything? Coffee? Are you hungry? I could make you a sandwich."

"You," he thought. *"I just want you."* He wanted to take her in his arms and kiss her like he had the day before. It had felt like coming home. He wanted that feeling again.

Who was he kidding? He wanted that feeling every night. With Kathleen. Not with any of the suitable shifter girls his mother kept throwing at him. Why did he have to be attracted to the one girl he shouldn't have? She was too young. He would be bad for her. She hadn't had an opportunity to experience life. He should give her time. But his wolf wanted to claim her now. Right now. And on top of everything else, here he was linked to the disappearance of Fontaine. If the press learned of his relationship with Kathleen, she'd be hounded.

He was being framed. He felt it in his bones. It was no accident that the car had come out of the river in Sheriff Chip Walker's jurisdiction. But who knew about his background with the Indiana sheriff and had the power to move the car upstream and land it right in the sheriff's front yard?

His face still in his hands, he groaned softly.

"Dan?" Kathleen reached over and stroked his hair.

Damn it. He should not be doing this! Still, as she softly stroked his head, his arms went around her. He pushed back her curls so he could fondle the soft spot at the base of her neck, leaning down to take little nips of her sweet-smelling skin. "I don't need coffee. I don't need a sandwich. All I need is you," he whispered, capturing her lips with his.

The kiss was soft, gentle, healing.

"You can have me," she told him. "Anything you need, I'm here for you."

The kiss turned darker, bolder, as he plundered her mouth. "Kathleen. I shouldn't... we shouldn't. You're too young."

"We're both adults. I'm tired of every male I know telling me what I should and shouldn't do. I think we should." She sat up, pushing away from him. "Unless you don't want me?" Her vulnerability in that moment was clear. He couldn't let her think that.

"Of course I want you. You're beautiful. You're sexy. I can't seem to stop wanting you."

A fleeting shadow crossed Kathleen's face, but it was gone so quickly Dan wasn't sure he had really seen it. Maybe it had just been a trick of the soft light flickering from the television set that was still turned on across the room.

"If you're sure," Kathleen said. Taking his hand, she pulled him from the couch as he followed her down the tiny hallway to her bedroom.

In her room she turned on a lamp, illuminating it with a soft glow. The bedroom was stark, bare. She had only lived here a few months. She'd had no time to decorate. The walls were painted a basic white. Her nightstand and dresser were empty of photographs or other personal items, except for a necklace and earrings lying on her bedside table, probably discarded when she took them off earlier.

"I haven't had much time to spruce things up since I moved in," she said, looking a little embarrassed at the plainness of the room.

He placed a kiss on her forehead. "You have the most important thing—a big bed."

She laughed. "I guess I do. I planned to get my living room and kitchen the way I want them before I started in here. It seemed more important at the time."

"I'm glad. That means you didn't plan to have anyone over who would see this room. I've got no problem with that." He pulled her to him and placed a soft kiss on her lips.

"Do you want to be the first one to help me christen it?"

"I would be honored." He bent toward her for another long, fiery kiss.

CHAPTER 11

The soft glow of the bedside lamp made the room feel less stark, less unfinished, Kathleen thought, still nervous despite the pleasant ache that was growing deep inside her. The bed was covered with just a blanket, and the pillows had mismatched cases, not the lovely, flowered duvet and pillow covers she hoped to have some day. Now, though, the soft light painted the room in warm, golden hues and cast long shadows across the walls. Outside, the night pressed against the sheer curtains at the windows. It was tranquil and quiet, save for the sound of the television still playing softly in the living room. Dan withdrew from the kiss and took a step away. She crossed her arms over her chest in an unconscious gesture of defense.

What was it about this man that made her feel like a child again? A lonely little girl with no one to care for her. She'd banished that girl a long time ago. She'd left her hometown near Lexington. Left her family. Left her pack. No one in Rivelou knew who she was. She'd even changed her last name. She was reinventing herself here, where no one knew her, where she could join a pack that promised a different type of life, different values. Now, as she stood near the bed, hugging herself as if to hold herself together, it all came back to her.

"Girls are useless," her brother taunted her.

She stood in the middle of the circle, surrounded by his friends.

"Go away. We don't want you following us. Girls don't need to learn to fight and hunt. Go play with your dolls like the other females."

The other boys echoed his taunts as they all turned away, her brother leading the pack of boys toward the woods. One of them, Ric, turned back, grabbed a stone, and threw it in her direction.

"You heard him. He said go home. He's going to be your alpha someday. You have to do what he says," Ric told her. He

turned and followed the other boys.

She stood for a moment staring after them. She'd show them. She'd learn to do everything they could do, but better.

Slowly she turned away, but not to go find the other girls and play with dolls. She'd find someone who was willing to teach her to fight.

Dan's tall frame seemed as if it could barely be contained in the small room. Maybe, she told herself, if she had done as her brother said and just played with her dolls, she'd be intimidated by him now. But she wasn't. She wouldn't allow it. Dan's eyes caught hers, the dark amber swirled with something raw and feral, and for a minute seemed almost to glow, as if he tried to tame a wild beast hidden inside him.

Despite her just-made promise to herself, she took a step away from him, his large presence mixing with the old memory. No, she told herself again, she would not allow herself to be overwhelmed, no matter how large and powerful this man was. He wasn't like her brother; he wasn't like her father. He wasn't like all of the men in her old pack. He wasn't like anyone she'd ever met before.

Dan noticed. "Did I scare you? I didn't mean to; what made you draw away?" he asked.

She shook her head, bringing herself back to the present and automatically giving him a bright smile. It was an old habit. Despite her new resolve, those lessons from her youth reared their head. Her instincts told her to make sure that she pleased the man. *Don't bother him; live up to his expectations. Never even imagine that he might try to live up to yours.* "I'm not sad. I'm just... not sure what you want. In my old pack..."

He reached out his hand brushing her arm. The heat of his touch sent a shiver up her spine. "It doesn't matter what your old pack told you. It sounds as if they were old-fashioned and didn't value their women." He stopped for a moment, something in what he had just said triggering a memory. He shook it off quickly. Now was not the time. "It's not just about what I want," he continued. "It's about what we want. We'll figure it out together."

The words settled something deep inside her; a knot of

uncertainty unraveled. Slowly, she uncrossed her arms and allowed him to draw her closer. One hand rested gently on her waist. His other cupped her face, rough but gentle, his thumb brushed over her cheek. She sighed and let go of more of her tension.

"You feel it too, don't you?" he asked, his voice dropping to a whisper. "The connection?" Again, he wanted to add the words "the bond," but those were sacred words to a shifter. A fated mate—bonded wolves shared everything. They could even read each other's thoughts. Was he ready for that? Was she?

Kathleen nodded, her breath catching as his forehead came to rest against hers. The air between them was charged. They breathed in each other's scent, their breaths mingling, and for a long moment, neither of them moved. He smelled deliciously of cedar and woodsmoke and musk. It was a scent she'd never forget. She breathed deeply again, and he smiled at her, as if he knew exactly what she were feeling.

Then his lips brushed against hers, tentative, testing. Silently asking her what she wanted. He knew she was inexperienced. Oh, it wasn't as if she were a virgin. She'd been with males before—at college she had dated. But those were boys. Dan was a man. He understood she was nervous. Her hands found his chest, and the warmth beneath his shirt made her fingers curl instinctively, holding on. The kiss deepened, slow and unhurried, as though they had all the time in the world.

When they finally broke apart, his hand stayed on her face, his thumb tracing the curve of her jaw. "We don't have to rush this," he murmured. "I'll give you all the time you need."

"I know," she whispered, her voice trembling but certain. "But I don't want to stop. I seem to keep saying that to you, but it's true."

He smiled then. "The truth will prevail?" he said lightly, referring to the words of his tattoo. She knew he hadn't had much to smile about in the last few days. She wondered if he ever did. It felt like a rare and fleeting occurrence, softening the sharp edges of his face. Carefully, he guided her to sit on the edge of the bed, kneeling on the floor in front of her, his hands resting lightly on her thighs.

"This is about you," he said, his gaze never leaving hers. "Whatever you need, however far you want to go. However fast or slow. Just tell me."

Her fingers threaded into his hair, tugging him closer. "I need you to stay."

Through the sheer window curtain, she could see the moon hanging heavy in the sky. Its pale light comforted her. Like all of her kind, she had a special connection to the faraway orb. She reached over and turned off the bedside lamp, so that only the moonlight cast its silver streaks across them. Everything else faded away. They were cocooned in a place of safety, away from the cares and problems of the daytime world. The only thing that mattered was the deep, steady cadence of his breathing and the wild pounding of her own heart.

He knelt before her, his presence commanding but not overbearing, the heat of his body rolling off in waves that made her skin prickle. She could feel his gaze on her, intense and unwavering, as if he were taking in every detail, committing her to memory. Her wolf stirred inside her, restless and eager, the instinct to bare her throat in submission warring with the desire to show her teeth and challenge him.

"You're trembling," he murmured, his voice a low rumble that made her heart skip a beat. He reached out, his fingers brushing her cheek with surprising tenderness for someone so rugged and powerful. "Are you afraid?"

She met his golden eyes, their depths glowing faintly with the otherworldly light of his wolf. She could see his face clearly, even in the darkened room. "No," she said, her voice steadier than she felt. "I'm not afraid of you."

His lips curved into a slow, almost predatory smile at odds with his words as he said, "Good. You shouldn't be."

He closed the slight distance between them until their bodies were nearly touching. The scent of him—earthy, rich, and unmistakably male—wrapped around her, filling her senses and awakening something primal inside her. Her wolf growled its approval, the sound reverberating in her chest.

"Tell me if you want me to stop," he said, his voice

softer now, almost a whisper. His hand slid down her arm, leaving a trail of fire in its wake, until his fingers intertwined with hers. "If this isn't what you want, tell me now."

She shook her head, her breath hitching as his free hand traced the curve of her jaw. "Don't stop," she whispered. "Please."

That was all he needed. With a growl that was more wolf than man, he pulled her against him, his mouth claiming hers in a kiss that was fierce and consuming. She gasped against his lips, her hands finding their way to his broad shoulders as he lifted her effortlessly from the bed and turned to press her back against the wall. The contrast of the cool boards against her bare, heated skin only heightened her awareness of him—the strength in his arms, the controlled urgency in the way he touched her.

Her legs wrapped around his waist, anchoring herself to him as his lips trailed down her neck, his teeth grazing the sensitive spot where her shoulder met her throat. This is where he'd make her his own; he'd bite just there, where he could see her pulse beating in her neck. He'd claim her and she'd be his. Forever. They'd share everything. The thought made her tense. They'd share everything. He'd know where she came from, who she was. He'd hate her then. They'd be bonded and he'd hate her.

He must have felt her tense because he pulled back.

"I told you we don't have to do anything more. If you don't want this… if you're not ready."

"You called me 'mate' before. Did you mean it?"

"I hadn't planned to tell you—I wanted to show you. I wanted to wait. To give you a chance to…"

"Shh," she whispered. "It's alright. I'm not ready to bond with you, but I am ready for more." With that her wolf surged forward, a growl escaping her lips as she arched against him, her fingers tangling in his hair. She could feel his restraint slipping, the carefully controlled edge that was his nature giving way to something raw and unrestrained, and much more dominant. If she'd ever doubted his alpha status, she wouldn't any longer.

"You drive me mad," he muttered against her skin, his breath hot and ragged. "Do you have any idea what you do to me?"

She answered him not with words but with action. She tugged at his shirt, pulling it over his head so she could revel in the feel of the hard muscles of his chest. Her nails dragged down his back, leaving marks as she claimed his mouth again, this time with equal fervor. Their movements became a dance of give and take, dominance and submission, each of them pushing and pulling, neither willing to yield completely but both utterly lost in the moment.

The world around them faded. The only sounds were the mingling of their gasps and growls, the rhythm of their connection building to a crescendo that left her trembling in his arms. Her wolf howled in triumph; her human side surrendered to the overwhelming rush of sensation as they came undone together.

When the storm finally passed, they remained tangled together, their breaths mingling as they slowly came back to themselves. He pressed his forehead against hers, his golden eyes softening as he cupped her face in his hands.

"You're mine now. You're my mate—my fated mate," he said, his voice rough but filled with a surprising tenderness. "I haven't claimed you yet, but I will." He pulled back so he could look at her. Was she upset? Intimidated? Scared by his admission?

She smiled, her fingers tracing the lines of his jaw. "And you're mine. But there are things…"

No 'buts' tonight. We'll deal with the real world tomorrow. Tonight, you're just mine. And I'm yours." He kissed her one more time. In that moment, with the light of the moon shining in the window, they were not just two people but two wolves, bound by something deeper and more primal than words could ever capture.

CHAPTER 12

It had been two weeks since Dan's arrest by Sheriff Walker, and the reporters had moved on to new stories. The excessive heat and lack of rain that were threatening crops and creating a danger of forest fires had moved to the top of the local news. The word had gotten out that Fontaine's car had been found with Dan's fingerprints on it, creating a news sensation for a day or two. But after a threat of legal action from Connor, Walker had made a statement that Dan was not a suspect in the disappearance of Alexander Fontaine. Now the story no longer even rated a mention in the local news. He'd been replaced by advice on how to identify heatstroke, keeping pets out of the heat, and the locations of "Cooling Centers" where residents could go if they had no air conditioning. He couldn't be happier.

Dan breathed a sigh of relief as he left his office and found no waiting reporters or photographers ready to snap a photo or annoy him enough to make him say something controversial. Life was returning to normal, he thought. At least he hoped it was. That little nagging worry that something else would drop when Dan least expected it had sent him out to meet his friends.

Connor and Gabe were already at the local bar, The Night Crawler, when he arrived. Near the river on the outskirts of town, the non-paras thought of it as a fishing bar. A bait and tackle shop was attached to one side. He, however, knew that the back room of the bar, which was hidden from anyone without power, was a secure hangout for paranormals of all kinds.

Witch, shifter, vampire, or any other paranormal could safely meet for a game of shifter pool, in which the balls magically moved between each play, or a magically enhanced drink. Often rowdy, the bar had a "no magic on the premises" policy that kept the fights clean. Calls to the police were rare.

The large bear shifters who acted as bouncers made sure of that.

"Hey, how ya doin'" he greeted his friends as he sat down at a table in the back of the bar. The pair were opposites in almost every way. Connor, long and lanky, had blue eyes and blonde hair. As a lawyer, he usually wore a suit. Tonight, he'd obviously come straight from work. He'd discarded his jacket and tie, and the sleeves of his white dress shirt were rolled up. Gabe had dark brown eyes and hair, along with the physique of a body builder, a hobby of his. He wore jeans, boots, and a t-shirt that said, "Run Code. Raise hell." It amazed people that the pair were such good friends since their personalities were as different as their appearance. Connor was quiet and serious while Gabe was constantly joking and laughing.

"More important, how are you doing? Things calming down for you?" asked Gabe. "And how are things going with Kathleen? You mated yet?"

"Don't even joke about it," Dan growled at his friend. Gabe was known for his sometimes inappropriate sense of humor, which was as often turned on himself as it was on his friends. But Dan's relationship with Kathleen was too new and precious to make jokes about. Kathleen was his fated mate. He'd known it from the first moment he sensed her. But as usual with werewolves, the male sensed the connection, then had to convince the female of the fact.

Yes, he'd told her the other night, and she'd said she wasn't ready. It was up to him to court and persuade her to accept him. It kept the balance of power between males and females equal in a culture where strength and fighting ability were often valued over everything else. While her reaction had been encouraging, Dan knew he had a long way to go to get her to accept him as her mate. She was hiding something; he didn't know what yet. He needed to get her to trust him. And once again a pang of guilt shot through him at all the things he was keeping from her.

Gabe held up his hands. "Okay, okay. Forget I mentioned her. I won't even say her name."

"Better not." Dan was testy; he hadn't been able to see Kathleen for much of the week. They'd both been busy, and

Kathleen said she wanted to take it slow. She'd put him off when he'd suggested coming over or going out. Well, he couldn't blame her for worrying about being seen with him in public. Until the last day or so he'd been click bait for every social media influencer located in the area, and for a few who had traveled from as far away as Nashville and St. Louis to attempt to get pictures or quotes from him.

"Isn't she a little young for you?" Connor questioned.

"She's my mate," Dan said in a tone that made it clear that that was the end of the story. Then he drew a breath and started over. "Sorry, my wolf's ready to claim her right now. But I want to let her take it at her own pace. And she's hesitating, too." His annoyance was clear. His friends ignored it. They continued to joke and talk about his love life. Finally, he put a stop to it.

"Look, that's not why I got you both here tonight."

"I know you've been worried about the security of PackNet. I've gone over everything at least three times since your grandfather mentioned it and..."

"Hey, that's not why I'm worried. I trust you. If you say it's secure, it is. I've got a favor to ask the two of you."

"Anything, man, you know that," said Connor.

"I do. And I appreciate it. I'm thankful that things have calmed down. Walker has backed off. The media isn't interested in the story anymore."

"For now," said Gabe.

"For now," Dan agreed.

"Look, I don't think you have to worry about this anymore," said Connor. "From a legal standpoint, there's no evidence that you had anything to do with Fontaine's disappearance. Walker knows I'll hit him with a harassment suit so fast his head'll spin if he comes at you again without anything more than we've seen so far."

"Again, I appreciate it. But Walker finding more evidence is exactly what I'm afraid of."

The conversation stopped as the waitress came over to take their orders.

"I'll have a burger and fries to go with that," Gabe

added, and Dan and Connor ordered the same thing. They kept their conversation light for the next few minutes, knowing the waitress would return quickly with their drinks. Finally, she left them to see about other customers.

"Look, I need to get you both up to speed on everything about Fontaine's disappearance." Dan continued the earlier conversation.

"You don't have to," said Gabe. "Grandma already clued me in. And I told Connor. Damn, you could have called us, you know. We would have helped—even Mister Straight Arrow Lawyer over here."

"Yeah, I'd be happy to help you bury a body anytime; you know that. I'd just charge it to your attorney's fees." Connor tried unsuccessfully to hide a grin as he said it.

Dan slapped the man on the back. Connor really was a straight arrow, especially for a shifter. As a group, shifters tended to have a fairly loose interpretation of non-para laws, but Connor took his oath as an attorney seriously. Coming from him, the promise to bury a body in secret really meant something.

"Thanks guys, really. But number one, I didn't want to get you in any trouble. And two, my grandfather ordered me not to tell anyone."

"You know we'd do anything to protect Ana," said Connor.

"Of course. But before the car reappeared the only people to know about it were family—and not all of them at that. In fact, Channing and Tyler are still in the dark about it. And my mom is pissed that she only found out when I was arrested." He rolled his eyes. "She thinks I should have told her immediately."

"Hey, bro, what am I in the dark about?" a familiar voice asked.

The trio had been so involved in their discussion, they hadn't noticed Dan's youngest sibling, Tyler enter the bar. He was accompanied by his girlfriend, Winnie.

"Hey, what are you doing here, kid?" asked Dan. "Aren't you a little young for this place?"

"We're both 21 now," said Tyler. "We're celebrating Winnie's birthday."

"Happy birthday, Winnie," Gabe said.

They all knew the girl. She and Tyler had been hanging around together since grade school. They'd just been friends then, but it was evident by the way Tyler kept his hand protectively at her back that they were more than that now. Tyler had helped save Winnie's life when she was abducted by a non-para couple pretending to be witches earlier in the summer.

"So, what's up with you three? No dates tonight? Or is this what old farts do? They hang out at the bar with their friends instead of finding hot chicks?" Tyler asked. He dragged a couple of chairs up to the table, and he and Winnie sat down.

"What would you like, Winnie?" he asked her when the waitress hurried over to them.

She asked for a Tequila Moonrise. Similar to its non-magical version, the drink swirled in shades of purple and midnight blue. It was garnished with candy stars and was known to give the drinker a boost of confidence. "I've heard so much about this drink, and I'm finally old enough to try it," she said. It was the signature drink in the back room of The Night Crawler.

"Just a beer for me," said Tyler to the waitress who had appeared at their table.

"Winnie, I know it's your birthday, but go easy with those things," Dan said when the drinks arrived. "They taste harmless but can really pack a wallop."

"Bro, I won't let anyone take advantage of her," Tyler growled protectively and pulled her chair closer.

"It's not 'anyone' I'm worried about, Bro, it's you," Dan replied.

"Oh stop, you two. Tyler won't take any more advantage of me than I want." Winnie giggled as she spoke. The drink was obviously taking effect already. "Tyler, can't you tell that your brother and his friends were talking about something important and don't want us here?" asked Winnie.

"Of course they want us here," he replied.

"Little brother, you are so obnoxious, I don't see how

Winnie can stand you. Winnie, you are a saint for being with my brother."

"I know," she replied. Then she put her arm around her boyfriend to make sure he knew she was joking. "But he knows how good I am to him."

The three older men looked at each other and rolled their eyes.

"Well, since you three are no fun—it's like partying with Grandma and Grandpa, by the way—we're going to find some people our own age," Tyler said as he helped Winnie up. They took their drinks and wandered over to the pool tables.

CHAPTER 13

"Were we ever that bad?" Connor asked, taking another sip of his beer and shaking his head in amazement at Tyler.

"We were worse," Dan admitted.

"Yeah, I guess we were."

When the couple was out of earshot, Gabe returned to their previous conversation.

"So, about Fontaine, what is it that you need from us?"

"The way the car came up out of the river smacks of magic," explained Dan.

"Yes, it does," agreed Connor. "It shouldn't have reappeared upstream, that's for sure. Nature doesn't work that way without a little help from the supernatural."

"I disposed of the body in the woods—wanted to let nature take its course; that was my theory. Now I'm worried."

"You think that if someone used power to find the car, they could also use power to find the body?"

Dan nodded, then looked up as he heard a familiar voice coming from the other end of the room. He hid his face in his palm and shook his head. "Why did I think this was a good place to have a private conversation? Particularly on a Friday night. My entire family seems to be here. Next Grandpa and Grandma will be coming through the door."

Gabe and Connor looked around to see who he was talking about. Channing and her boyfriend Dolan were standing at the bar.

"Oh shit," Gabe said. "Dan, you've got to keep it together this time. She's of age and has a right to date anyone she wants."

Dan gritted his teeth. "Easy for you to say. It's not your sister dating the heir to a rival pack."

"And I'm not the heir to the Bertrand pack. I know. That just means that getting in a public fight won't help things. It will only make them worse.

"And look at the way she's dressed."

"She's not dressed any differently than any other female here," pointed out Connor. Channing wore short shorts, Doc Martins, and a plaid shirt tied at the waist. And Connor was right. In the August heat most of the women were wearing shorts or tight miniskirts with tank tops or crop tops.

"It looks different on her," Dan growled.

"No different than on Winnie." Gabe laughed. Winnie, too, had been wearing a miniskirt and crop top.

"And Winnie has my brother to watch her back. I don't trust Dolan as far as I can throw him. Certainly not to take care of my sister."

Gabe and Connor exchanged grins. They knew better than to call Dan out on that prejudice right now. Winnie had obviously dressed for Tyler. Maybe he was the one who needed looking after tonight.

As the trio kept their eyes on the front of the bar, Dolan put his arm around Channing's waist, his hand sliding down to cup her backside barely covered in the tiny shorts. Dan ground his teeth, growled, and started to get up. Connor and Gabe each grabbed hold of one of his shoulders and held him back.

"Dan, calm down. Do not create a scene. You've just gotten yourself out of the news. We don't want you arrested again," said Connor.

"Then one of you go over there and talk sense to her. Get her away from Dolan."

Connor and Gabe exchanged glances.

"Alright, I'll go. But you owe me big time for this, Dan," said Gabe. "A hell of a lot more than you'll owe me for searching the woods for a dead body."

He stood up, but before he could go very far, Dolan turned, and Dan watched him notice their table. He said something to Channing, and she slowly twisted to look, seemingly reluctantly, toward Dan. She waved sheepishly, then allowed Dolan to walk her toward their table as Gabe sat back down.

"Hi Dan; I didn't expect to see you here," she said. She gave him a quick hug.

"Dan, I've been wanting to talk to you for weeks, but I'm not in town that often, and I try to spend as much time as I can with your sister. Can we sit down?" Dolan was pulling out a chair for Channing even as he asked.

Dan was about to open his mouth. He wasn't sure exactly what he was going to say, but Connor seemed to know it wouldn't be a polite "Yes, you can." His friend jumped in. "Of course." He motioned to the two extra chairs. "You know your brother and Winnie are here tonight, too."

Dolan ignored the conversational gambit. "Look, Dan, we got off to a really bad start at the party. I shouldn't have let Channing talk me into just dropping by that way. I should have done what my instincts said and stayed away. I caused a scene, and I'm sorry."

Dan was taken aback. Dolan trying to ingratiate himself? The party wasn't the first time they had met. Dolan had gone to school at the University of Rivelou at the same time Dan had. He'd always been arrogant and contemptuous of Dan and all the Bertrands.

But what could Dan say right now? Or do, when the other man was holding out his hand, and his sister was looking at him so hopefully. Despite the fact that the man was blaming her for "talking him into" coming to the party unannounced. He ground his teeth, thought Dolan should have enough spine to own up to his own mistakes, an then shook his hand. "Hey, no harm, no foul. We were both out of hand that day."

"I'm glad you see it that way. I'm going to be around a lot more."

"Oh?"

"Yes, I want to spend as much time as possible with your sister, so I've convinced my father to allow me to open up a branch of our business across the river in Herndon County."

The McTiers ran Moonlight Security, a private agency which used the wolf shifters' strength and agility to have a security agency with one of the best reputations in the area.

"Really," Dan said in a stern voice. What was Dolan up to? Herndon County was rural. Why would he be opening a branch of his security company there?

"What, the cows and corn need bodyguards?" Gabe apparently thought the same thing as he stepped in with a very bad joke. He'd known Dolan while at the university also. If anything, their relationship had been worse than Dolan's and Dan's.

"It's central to a lot of larger, more urban areas, and the land's still cheap there. My dad thought it would be a good investment when I brought it up. Besides, it will give me a base that's a lot closer to your sister."

Dolan put his arm around Channing and pulled her close. She responded by giving him a lingering kiss. Dan clenched his fists under the table to keep them from seeing his claws extending. He couldn't help it. He didn't trust Dolan, and he certainly didn't think this sudden romantic interest in his sister was anything but a ploy to worm his way into the Bertrand pack.

That, after all, was what Fontaine had tried with Ana. Luckily, he mused, Ana had seen through Bertrand's ploy. He hoped like hell his younger sister would wake up just as fast and figure out what he was sure was going on with McTier. He couldn't object. Herndon County was not his pack's territory. In fact, it was unclaimed—neutral territory, between the McTiers, the Bertrands, and the Westfield pack centered in the Indianapolis area. For decades it had been a buffer designed to give the packs a safe space. There was nothing that said the McTier's couldn't open a branch of their business there, but it was a subtle insult, nonetheless. Why couldn't Channing see that, Dan wondered.

After a few more minutes of small talk, Channing and Dolan got up from the table to say hello to Tyler and Winnie.

"What do you think is with him wanting to open a branch of Moonlight Security in Herndon County?" asked Connor.

"Well, I'm pretty sure it's not just his sudden great love for Channing—no offense, Dan."

"None taken. I had the same thought. In fact, I'm wondering if he wants to make a run at our territory. Being closer would make it easier—he could poach any disgruntled pack members, start to expand that way…"

"Disgruntled pack members?" Connor questioned. "How many of those can there be?"

Dan and Gabe exchanged a look, and Dan realized his friend Gabe had heard a lot more about the last council meeting than he had realized. Yeah, "what happens in council stays in council" was a rule apparently only Hank Bertrand ascribed to.

"You'd be surprised," Dan replied to Connor's question.

"Yeah, you'd really be surprised," Gabe added.

Dan took a deep breath. "Let's take this elsewhere. I'd like to finish the conversation somewhere else before the rest of my family walks in."

"Good idea," said Connor. "I think we definitely need more privacy."

They paid their bills, then headed to their cars, stopping to greet several more people they knew along the way. They agreed to meet back at Dan's condo.

CHAPTER 14

Dan's condo was downtown, ironically, next to the building where Alexander Fontaine had lived. It had a fabulous view of the Rivelou River. Sunsets were beautiful, and moonrise over the water was a spectacular sight. But Dan had begun to think this wasn't the space he wanted anymore. It wasn't the right place to raise a family. He wanted little red-haired cubs running around, looking like miniature Kathleens. They'd need space to run. All cubs did. Maybe he'd start looking for a house in the country. Something near his grandparents' farm would be nice.

"Okay, let's go over it again," said Connor with his logical, legal mind. "What exactly are you worried about?"

"When things went down with Fontaine, my grandfather called Dr. Lazard in, also. He thought as coroner he could easily take care of the body. But Lazard couldn't help that week. The hospital where the coroner's office is located was having an inspection. Lazard couldn't afford to have an extra body just lying around. So we agreed that I'd drop it in the woods when I took care of the car.

"We all wanted to make sure no evidence could ever be found. Fontaine was too well-known in the non-para world. If a body were found, there would have been calls to find the murderer, have a trial—you know, exactly what happened to me in the last couple of weeks."

Gabe and Connor nodded. Gabe reached for another beer and took a long drink. "So, you decided the best place for the car was the river. But you didn't leave the body with it?"

"No, I thought the body was better off just left in the woods. I couldn't burn it without taking a chance of someone seeing it, but if the car ever were found, I didn't want the body to be with it. I decided it was best to leave it to return to nature. I thought the animals would find it and dispose of the problem. But now I'm not so sure."

"Why? What makes you think that's not exactly what happened?"

"It's something Ana told me the other day. I thought she was keeping something from me when my family talked about the whole Fontaine problem a few weeks ago. I finally got it out of her. You remember last spring when everything was going down with the Artificial Witch murders?"

The two men nodded.

"Well, Chris and Ana were out to dinner with his sister Shannon and her boyfriend, Dave Thorne."

"He's a good guy. A witch, right? I've met him several times," said Connor. "He's on the police force. I've seen him in court; he makes a good witness."

That, from a lawyer, was high praise, Dan thought, hiding his smile.

"I hear from my grandmother that Cassandra is training him to be the next high priest of their coven," added Gabe.

"Yeah? I didn't know that. How serious are he and Shannon?" said Connor.

"Pretty serious, from what Grandma says. She already has a reservation down at the Strawberry Moon for November for an engagement party for them. After Ana and Chris' wedding, you know."

"Okay, back on track, guys. You two gossip like girls.

Gabe gave him a cheeky salute. "Yes sir, Alpha sir."

"Okay, you know who Shannon and Chris' mother is, right? Beatrix Spier. She was rather notorious as a dark witch until about ten years ago. Then suddenly, nothing. Poof. She's hasn't been heard from since. Well, Shannon and Chris thought they saw her here, one night while the four of them were out to dinner at the Strawberry Moon. They couldn't be sure but…"

"Damn it, Dan, you're dragging it out like it's some horror movie. You're giving me the creeps here," said Connor.

Dan rolled his eyes. "We're werewolves, Connor. We *are* a non-para's horror movie."

"Yeah, but we don't do magic. Not like witches." He gave an exaggerated shiver.

"Okay, okay, you two, knock off the bickering and finish

the story," Gabe said.

"So, the night they caught the guy responsible for the Artificial Witch murders, Shannon thought she saw her mother, Beatrix, in the woods. She didn't have time to go after her. And Harrison, the one they arrested, was babbling about someone telling him how to get power.

"Unfortunately, the guy's been loony ever since. Can't get a straight sentence out of him, according to Chris and Shannon. They've heard that from Captain Anderson, by the way. So, the two of them got worried about where their mom was. It turns out Shannon had used her magic to restrain Beatrix. They went back to where Shannon buried her mom behind a wall in the basement of their old home, but there was no one there. Nothing."

"Damn, that's freaky. She'd buried her mother alive behind a wall? Shades of *The Cask of Amontillado*. I hated Edgar Allen Poe in high school. He was way too scary—and he wasn't even a paranormal."

The other two men turned and laughed at Connor as he said this.

"You've got to be kidding, Connor!" said Dan. "You grew up with witches. Winnie's a witch. How scary is she?"

"Yeah, but she's just a baby witch and your brother's friend. She was shy. I always felt like we had to protect her."

"I forget sometimes that Chris is a witch. I just think of him as a Hunter, but of course, that's what a Hunter is," added Gabe.

"So, if his mother, Beatrix, wanted to get revenge on him and Shannon, a good way would be to frame Chris for Fontaine's death—and make it public," Dan continued. "You know there's probably no one in the paranormal world except Fontaine who was that well-known in the non-para world. His disappearance made news. Maybe bringing up the car was just the first step. She couldn't know it would have my fingerprints on it. But it worked in her favor just the same. Hurt me, hurt Ana. Hurt Ana, hurt Chris."

"Sounds pretty convoluted to me," said Connor.

"Maybe she thought the prints would either be Chris' or

Ana's."

"Yeah, it's as good a theory as any, I guess," said Connor. "But don't you think you are being a little paranoid here? I mean the river's been very low this summer. No other evidence about Fontaine has been found. And no one's actually seen Beatrix Spier, not even her children, right? They just had a 'feeling,'" said Connor using air quotes around the word.

Dan nodded. "I hope you're right, Connor, and I'm just paranoid. If so, this will all blow over. They can't investigate Fontaine's death unless they have a body, and if we're lucky there will be nothing but a couple of bones left for evidence by now. Not enough to do any more than tell who it was. Not how the person died. But if I'm not right…"

"Better safe than sorry," finished Gabe.

Dan nodded.

"So how do we go about setting your mind at ease?" asked Connor. He leaned back, spreading his arms along the sofa as if looking relaxed could make them be relaxed. He was still not willing to admit there might be a problem, Dan realized.

"Gabe and Chris go out to where I left the body and see what they can find. Gabe because, as a werewolf, his sense of smell and his ability to track things will be an asset. Chris, because he's a Hunter, and if his mother is involved, he's probably the best person to spot that evidence."

"What about his sister, Shannon?"

"She's a cop, just like her boyfriend Dave. I don't want to put anyone into a compromising position if I don't have to."

"Alright then, the first step is to check on the body. If it is still there, or more than a couple of bones, that's one problem. It's summer, and there are hikers. Anyone could find it by chance. If that's the case, we just make sure the evidence is totally erased."

"There should be some trace evidence that you or Chris can find. But if there is nothing there, no evidence at all, that's when we suspect magic. And someone who does not have the best interests of Ana or the Bertrand pack at heart," Dan said. "I'll protect Ana the best I can, and so will Chris. But I'm afraid if she thinks I'm in danger of being arrested, she'll come out and confess to the killing."

"She would. That sounds just like her; always taking care of others," said Connor.

There was something in the man's voice that made Dan turn and look at him closely. Connor turned his head away. He wouldn't look Dan in the face. Well, that was interesting. But damn, it was bad, too. Ana was never going to be interested in Connor that way. Particularly now that she had Chris.

"Hey man, I'm sorry. I didn't realize," Dan said.

"Realize what?" asked Gabe, clueless to the undertones around him.

"Nothing," said Connor quickly.

"Okay, back to business," Dan said, to distract Gabe from probing any further into Connor's business, "I don't know if I should be more worried if the place where I left the remains has been disturbed—or if looks completely undisturbed."

"And you want us to go check on it. Have you talked to Chris about this?" Gabe asked.

Dan nodded. "He's free tomorrow night."

"Alright then, I'll put my nose to the problem, and you'll have what you need."

CHAPTER 15

Gabe sat at the desk in his home office, fingers flying as he logged onto PackNet's developer console, the nerve center of the massive site that connected paranormals throughout the world. Before PackNet, paranormals had been dependent on either non-para methods of communication—old-fashioned snail mail and telephones, or arcane methods, such as witches or other paranormals who could send mind-to-mind controlled communications throughout the paranormal world. Most shifter species could only speak mind-to-mind over a distance of a few miles, and only in their animal form. This left them at a distinct disadvantage. And often at the mercy of sometimes unscrupulous witches or telepaths. Of course, there had also been the World Wide Web, but paranormals had always considered it much too insecure to trust their secrets to a non-para invention that seemed to leak like a sieve.

Gabe had changed all that.

Now, he picked up the ever-present can of Diet Pepsi that sat on the desk and took a long drink as he watched the interface unfold before him. Rows of scrolling logs, system metrics, and real-time user activity cascaded across the screen. At the top, a sleek navigation bar gave him access to server health reports, security alerts, and database performance stats. It also had another feature not seen on the desktops of most computer programmers: a second bar for tracking the wards that protected the site from magical tampering. This was what made PackNet secure; this was why the paranormals depended on him.

He clicked into the Network Operations Panel where a map of global traffic glowed in pulsing arcs of light, showing the flow of data through the vast infrastructure. He smiled. He was proud of his invention. It was as world-changing to paranormals as the invention of electricity to the non-paras. The System Log Feed flickered with timestamps and status codes, highlighting server requests and login attempts. It occasionally flagged an anomaly.

Gabe leaned back in his chair, rolling his shoulders. It had been a long day. He wasn't sure if Dan was paranoid or if a witch really was out to wreak havoc with the Bertrands, but he'd do his best to protect his pack. Tomorrow night he would go with Chris and search for any evidence of Fontaine's body. But right now, it was important to give his baby one last good-night check to make sure everything was fine, then hit the rack. And for once, enjoy eight solid hours of sleep.

The system logs scrolled by in orderly lines of green and white, nothing out of the ordinary. No security flags, no major traffic spikes, no magical probing of his security. Just another night on the massive network. He glanced away, stretched his arms, and took another drink from his Pepsi can. It was warm, but he often drank it that way—couldn't be bothered to get a glass of ice.

"What the fuck!" He spewed his Pepsi as a single query request buried in the log kept repeating. It wasn't often—every few minutes at most—and it wouldn't trigger any alarms for someone who hadn't built this entire system line by line. But it was there. Recurring. Subtle. Wrong. Like the slowly beating heart of a vampire's victim just before taking a last breath.

It looked like a standard API call. But the origin ID was blank. Impossible. Every call left a trace. Unless someone was masking their footprint... or altering the logs after the fact.

He clicked into the process. The subroutine wasn't behaving like anything PackNet was designed to run. It nested like a Russian doll inside a diagnostic module. He clicked deeper.

A three-second pause.

Then the magical security bar flashed—a red flicker. Not a breach. Not quite. More like the wards had hiccupped, then smoothed themselves over with practiced ease. Too smooth. Like a glamour covering a wound.

He froze. Someone had altered the protections. Not broken them—rewritten them. It was like finding a security camera in your house that looked like yours but reported to someone else. Who could have done this? He was the best in the business at combining high tech and paranormal magic. He wasn't being vain when he thought this. It was the truth. No one could out-program him. And what he didn't know his staff of shifters and witches did. At least that's what he'd always believed.

The screen flickered again, then resumed, calm and clear. The logs rolled forward like obedient soldiers, one after the other. But he noticed the timestamps—off by four seconds. A few lines had been edited. One signature was there. It belonged to Ramona, his lead network engineer. And then it was gone. Replaced by an ID he didn't recognize: Hytheris.null.

He watched for fifteen more minutes. No more anomalies. No more glitches. Just a faint sensation crawling along his spine.

As he reached to shut down, a faint sound leaked from the speakers. A sigh. A whisper. And then a line of binary scrolled across the screen, too fast to catch—except the final phrase hung on the edge: DO NOT FOLLOW.

CHAPTER 16

There was nothing Dan could do about the Fontaine problem until Chris and Gabe had the chance to check things out. It was a good thing he had a date set up with Kathleen for Saturday afternoon and evening, or he would have gone crazy wondering and worrying about what was going on with the search.

As it was, the day dragged until it was time for him to pick her up for an afternoon matinee at the art cinema on Washington Avenue, near the university campus. They were going to see *Rocky Horror Picture Show*. Kathleen had never seen it, and Dan had a good time gathering all the supplies they would need to really enjoy the movie as it should be experienced—toast, rice, noisemakers, water guns, and newspapers were in a small backpack to take with them although he had warned Kathleen to bring a jacket with a hood as well in case the "rain" was particularly heavy in the theater that afternoon.

He enjoyed seeing Kathleen watch the movie. She knew some of the more popular songs and quickly learned to duck whenever he warned her that things were about to be thrown.

They came out into the late afternoon sunshine, laughing and shaking rice kernels from their clothing. Dan had already made reservations at The Strawberry Moon, the restaurant owned by Gabe's grandmother. They should arrive just in time to watch the sunset on the Rivelou River. He knew Marianne would make sure they had a table near the window.

***

"Dan, it's so good to see you," Marianne greeted him with a kiss when they arrived. He felt a little uncomfortable after her outburst at the pack meeting a couple of weeks before. After all, her grandson was heading out to the woods tonight, just as she had predicted, to help him and his family by looking for the body of Alexander Fontaine.

He didn't believe there was any danger. And besides, Gabe had offered, both as a member of the pack and as a friend. Still, a chill of unease spread through him. He was sending his friend along with his future brother-in-law on a mission whose sole purpose was to keep Dan out of a jam. How was that for putting the pack's needs before his own? How would he look Marianne in the eye if something happened to her grandson tonight? Gabe was the only family she had left.

He shook off his uneasiness. It wasn't a prediction, he assured himself. Just feelings of guilt for not being the one out looking for Fontaine's body. He tuned back into the conversation just as Marianne was greeting Kathleen.

"You look so familiar. What's your last name again? Do I know your family?"

"N-no, I'm sure you don't," Kathleen stammered. "I moved here from Tennessee, where I was in college. I'm sure you wouldn't know any of my family."

Kathleen was shy, Dan told himself and put his arm around her. "She hasn't had much chance to get out and meet people since she's gotten here," he said to Marianne.

"Well now that she has you, I'm sure it won't be long before she's involved with the pack." Marianne gave a knowing smile at the way his arm had tightened possessively around the girl.

"Kathleen, I'm sure I'll see you at the next pack meeting; it's terrible of me to keep you standing in the doorway when you came here to eat." Marianne gestured to one of the hostesses to take them to their seats. "I'll check in on you later to see that everything is fine with your meal."

As soon as they were seated at their table, the waiter approached with a plate of appetizers sent over by Marianne. Dan could feel Kathleen settle down and relax, obviously hoping that Dan would forget her earlier nervousness at Marianne's questions. "What do you recommend?" she asked, closely perusing the menu.

"Everything here is excellent, but I'm particularly fond of the lamb curry," he said.

"That sounds different, I'll try it."

They began the meal with a pear and pecan salad, perfect for a warm summer evening. The lamb curry was served in a spicy

Chu-Chee sauce with fresh carrots and baby peas on the side.

"Mm, this is delicious," said Kathleen, taking a bite of the curry.

Dan smiled; he really did enjoy watching Kathleen. Just like the other night at Flannery's, seeing her savor her meal turned him on. Of course, everything she did seemed to turn him on. His wolf agreed. He could feel his inner beast's longing to hurry up with the courting and just make her his mate. It was the part of him that didn't care about pack politics, the age difference between him and Kathleen, or any of Dan's other concerns. It just wanted his mate claimed and by his side. Always. He told the restless animal inside him to chill. He was feeding her, taking care of her. What more did it want? And didn't he need to find out what secrets she was hiding before he claimed her?

His wolf dismissed that thought. Once claimed, they'd know everything about each other. They'd be able to read each other's thoughts and emotions. It wasn't a reassuring thought. Wasn't he hiding as much from Kathleen as she was from him? *She's our mate. You don't need to hide from her,* said his wolf. Dan mentally rolled his eyes. It just wasn't that simple. She might never forgive him for lying to her.

They were finishing their dessert, a Victorian rose geranium cake with rosewater-infused icing when Marianne approached the table.

"Mrs. Legato, this cake is delicious. I've never had anything quite like it before. The flavor is so delicate," Kathleen said.

"I'm so glad you like it. It's been on the menu here since my mother opened the restaurant fifty years ago.

"Everything is wonderful as usual, Miz Marianne," said Dan.

"I'm so glad you are enjoying it. Kathleen, I finally realized why I thought I'd seen you before. You said your last name is O'Connor? You remind me so much of an old friend of mine. Her maiden name was O'Connor before she married into the McTier clan—Alice O'Connor."

"N-no. That's doesn't sound familiar," Kathleen said. Dan noticed her looking down at her lap as she said the words.

"Marianne is an expert at genealogy. She probably knows your ancestors better than you do. You'll have to have her look into it for you."

Kathleen forced a smile, but her fingers tensed around her fork.

"I doubt she'd find out much about me; I'm nobody important," she said lightly. Dan caught the slight hitch in her breath. Her scent had changed, become a little sharper. Not quite fear, but something close.

Dan wondered if his grandmother had put Miz Marianne up to learning more about his new girlfriend. The two of them had been best friends for years.

"Well, Alice and O'Connor are both common names," Marianne said. "I'm sure you'd know if you were related to her. She married Michael McTier, the head of the McTier pack over near Lexington."

Kathleen blushed, her fair skin turning beet red under the older woman's scrutiny. "You're right, I'm sure I'd know if I were related to someone that important," she said again as she looked down and fumbled with her napkin.

"Yes, I'm sure you would," Marianne said, looking back and forth between Dan and Kathleen.

"Miz Marianne, this has been lovely, but we need to get back to town," Dan said, to break up the air of discomfort between the two women. What was this all about?

"Of course, Dan. I'll have the waiter bring you the check."

"You know," Dan said, "as he handed the waiter his card a moment later. "I've been to your place several times, but you haven't seen mine. The view of the river at night is even more spectacular than it is here."

Kathleen blushed again. "I'd like that very much," she said.

Dan's wolf rolled over, almost purring like a cat at the thought of his mate finally tucked away in his own den. This was going to be a much better end to the evening than the last time he had taken Kathleen out to dinner.

CHAPTER 17

"You were right; the view is spectacular," Kathleen said as they stepped onto the balcony of the eighth-floor condo. Rivelou was a small city. There weren't too many tall buildings, even in the downtown area, so the top level penthouse was one of the highest locations in town, other than the Bertrand Enterprise offices, and that didn't have the spectacular river view that this condo had.

"It's great. My family loves it. They come here all the time to watch boat races, fireworks, anything going down on the river," Dan replied, coming up behind her to circle her waist with his hands and leaning in close. He sniffed her hair. "You smell wonderful, you know."

She could feel herself blushing again. It seemed she'd spent the night turning twenty shades of red. She tried to tell herself that she was strong, competent. But her body never seemed to get the message. It betrayed her with a blush any time she felt the least bit unsure or embarrassed.

And Marianne Legato's comments had certainly made her uncomfortable. The woman was too close to the truth. She'd have to stay away from her in the future. She knew Dan had noticed even though he hadn't mentioned anything. At some point she would have to tell him everything. Would he hate her then?

She battled with her wolf, which just wanted her to tell Dan everything. *He'll understand. He wants you as his mate. And I like him.* She could feel her wolf's thoughts. Unfortunately, that part of her didn't understand the nuances of human relationships. She sighed. Yes, she would have to tell Dan—just not tonight. She was enjoying the evening too much to spoil it.

She focused again on the soft glow of the city lights shimmering against the dark water. The waning sliver of the moon still had enough light to cast a silvery ribbon across its surface. Kathleen curled her fingers more tightly around the wrought-iron railing, watching the water move in slow, lazy currents. They could hear the noise of traffic faintly on the streets below. A jazz band played in the bandshell by the river; she could see the small crowd that had gathered for the concert. She could feel the cool, air conditioned breeze floating out from inside the condo, contrasting sharply with the humid warmth of the late summer air that wafted up from the banks.

"There won't be too many more nights like this," Dan said. His steadying presence was a comfort behind her, solid and unyielding, just like the man himself.

She felt him move closer before he touched her, his heated body pressing against her back, his hands moving from the railing to settle lightly at her waist.

"You're thinking too much," he murmured when she didn't respond. She felt his breath against her hair, his voice rough and low.

She huffed a quiet laugh, leaning into him. "I usually do."

Dan's arms tightened, drawing her against his chest. "Then stop," he said simply. "Just be here. Whatever it is can wait."

"If I tell him, he'll hate me. If I don't, he'll eventually find out. And then he'll hate me even more. There's no good option," she thought. She turned, ready to explain everything… or leave, runaway… she wasn't sure which. But then he moved his hand to her cheek, lightly running his fingers up and down, and all her worries dissolved. For now.

She sighed, half relieved, and pressed her cheek against his hand. He was giving her permission to keep her secrets tonight.

See? What did I tell you? Her wolf thought smugly.

She looked up into Dan's storm-dark eyes, and for once, she let herself drown in the moment. This tension between them had been simmering for weeks. Yes, he'd taken her to bed— several times. They'd even run together as wolves late one evening. But their schedules, their responsibilities, had made it difficult to see him as much as she would have liked; as much as he would have liked, too, she thought. Those lingering touches, the little glances that he'd given her all evening while they ate at the restaurant must mean that he wanted more.

Kathleen had always been shy. She'd never had much self-confidence. She didn't trust that this powerful alpha male could really want her for more than just a casual relationship, despite what he had said about fated mates. There was no way she could be the fated mate of a powerful alpha. Her family had spent years telling her she had no value. How could so many of them be wrong and this one male be right?

He turned her toward him, as if sensing her insecurities, and bent low to steal a kiss. How could she doubt he wanted her when everything he did showed her how much he cared? But she did doubt it. And if he wanted her now, he would hate her all the more when he found out the truth.

"Let's go inside. You haven't seen the whole condo yet," he said, drawing her back into the living room.

She looked around at the open plan room, the kitchen, large enough to fit two of hers inside, was fitted with the latest appliances, including a fancy coffee machine. "What have I missed?" she asked lightly.

"My bedroom," he said. He leaned down to kiss her again, then swept her up in his arms and walked down the short hallway, turning in at the first door.

He laid her gently on the bed. The world narrowed to the faint glow of moonlight through the curtained window, the hushed sound of jazz music floating up from below, and the quiet rhythm of their breathing. She would do nothing to stop this moment. She might regret later that she hadn't told him everything. She knew she certainly would if he turned away from her, but for now, nothing could stop the inevitable.

Kathleen reached up, brushing her fingers over the rough line of his jaw. "This is dangerous," she whispered.

His lips quirked. "I know."

She didn't care. Not tonight.

Their mouths met, slow and unhurried at first, the taste of the wine they'd shared at dinner and something uniquely Dan lingering on her tongue. His hands slid up her back, threading into her hair, and she melted into him, heat unfurling in the pit of her stomach.

His kiss deepened as his hand moved slowly, teasingly, under her blouse. She moaned; she could hardly wait for him to reach her breasts. Her nipples tingled at the thought.

A sharp, jarring noise cut through the haze like a knife.

Dan cursed under his breath, his forehead resting against hers for a beat before he pulled away. He pulled his phone from his pocket. I'm sorry. I've got to check in case…"

The number flashing on the screen made him frown.

"This better be good," he growled as he swiped to answer. "What?"

Kathleen reached out to touch him, and he brushed her hand away; his body tensed, his jaw tightened. The heat between them evaporated in an instant.

"Slow down," Dan said, his voice edged with something colder than she'd ever heard from him before. "What the hell went wrong? Is it bad? I'll make the calls. Someone will come get you… as soon as possible."

Kathleen's stomach dropped.

The night had just taken a very different turn.

CHAPTER 18

It was early evening when Chris met Gabe in the parking lot of the Indian Mounds State Park. They wanted to begin their search while there was still daylight, and the sun wouldn't set until about 8 o'clock. They could switch to other senses, or powers, if they hadn't found anything by the time it was dark.

"Did you let Ana know what you were doing this afternoon?"

"If I told her she would only worry. I figure if we find out anything, one way or another, I'll let her know. If not, well, what she doesn't know won't hurt her."

"Hurt you, you mean," Gabe laughed, and gave him a slap on the shoulder. "I've known the Bertands my whole life. Ana might be the quietest of them, but that doesn't mean she can't bite when she wants to."

"Yeah, you got that right," Chris laughed. "Hey, you need me to carry anything?" He pointed to Gabe's backpack.

"Nah, right now it's just some extra water, a couple of trail bars, and some tools in case we find anything we need to dispose of. If we decide I need to shift, you can keep my clothes handy for when I change back."

"Sounds good," Chris replied as they headed down the trail into the woods.

"I figure we head straight for the coordinates Dan gave us, and if we're lucky, we'll find some evidence of bones or other remains. Then we can head right back out and go for a beer."

"That would be nice," Chris answered, the skepticism clear in his voice. "But in my business, I've learned the easy way almost never happens."

The coordinates Dan had given them were about a mile down the trail away from the water, then another few miles into the woods. As a wolf, Gabe could have covered that distance in half the time it would take him on two legs, but it was too early to shift. Wolf shifters were never at full power in the daylight, and besides, Chris couldn't keep up with him in wolf form. For now, they'd rely on Chris' magic to detect anything unnatural.

They hiked steadily on, the shade from the trees relieving the heat. It took over an hour to get to the spot Dan had indicated, but there was still plenty of light. They searched the area thoroughly. There was no indication a body had ever been there: no bones, no scraps of cloth. Nothing.

"I don't know," Gabe said, "this could be either very good or very bad."

"It doesn't feel right, you know?" responded Chris, wiping sweat from his face. "There should be some trace evidence. It's as if there haven't been any animals at all in this particular area for months, not even a bird or squirrel. Think you can sniff out more if you shift?

"I'll give a go." Gabe stripped his clothes and shoes off, stuffing them in the backpack, then shifted to his wolf. The change took only a few seconds. First there was quick sharp pain as his bones reshaped themselves. He hunched onto all fours as his face began to change. His nose elongated; his ears moved from the side of his head to the top. They twitched as he listened for any new noises he'd missed in human form. There was nothing.

As Chris stuffed his shorts, shoes, and t-shirt into the backpack, Gabe began to sniff around the site. It was just as Chris had said, notable not by what he could smell but by the absence of odor. Gabe began to walk in an ever-widening circle. His fur was a mottled grey with white markings around his eyes. He would blend perfectly into the forest as the night grew darker, which made him an excellent choice for what they needed to do. The only problem, while he could communicate telepathically with other shifters, and even some witches when he was in his wolf form, Chris's magic didn't include telepathic communication. They weren't going to be able to "talk" while he was a wolf. He sniffed the area systematically, then gave a short, sharp bark telling Chris to follow and headed deeper into the woods.

They walked slowly for another hour, Gabe moving deliberately back and forth over the area, taking his time to track any possible lead. As they moved farther from the spot where Fontaine's body should have been, he began to pick up the scents of a variety of animals. He had to rein in his wolf, who would have enjoyed a few side trips to track down something small for a quick snack. Finally, he shifted back to his human form.

"There is nothing here—absolutely nothing. A few squirrels and rabbits who have moved in recently, but as for older scents, it's as if the place had been swept clean," he said as Chris handed him the backpack. He pulled out his clothes and boots and put them on.

"What do you think we should do? Tell Dan there's nothing and he can relax?"

"No, I'm not getting that kind of vibe. It's not a natural absence. It's magical. There's an area where there is nothing at all, then around that, a larger circle where the only scents are more recent. And none of the scents are from a predator. Not a fox, not a hawk, not even a damn vulture. Something has swept this place clean."

"All right, but what else can we do?"

"I've got an idea—it may be a waste of time, but I'll feel better once we check it out."

"Not a problem. I'm even more anxious to put this to bed than you. I want to make sure nothing can blow back on Ana about Fontaine's disappearance."

"I say we head over to the other side of the river, near where Fontaine's car was found, and check there. It wasn't a coincidence that the car came up on the Indiana side of the river right in Sheriff Walker's territory. Whoever is orchestrating this has looked into us—you, Dan, Ana, maybe even me. They know there's bad blood between Walker and Dan."

"Sounds reasonable. Let's go waste some more of our Friday night hiking through another patch of woods," Chris said.

***

By the time they got back to their car, then drove across

the bridge to the state park in Indiana, it was nearing midnight. They followed the same procedure as before. Gabe walked with Chris until they were far enough away from the parking lot not to be seen. Then he shifted and began to check the area thoroughly for any signs of magic, of Fontaine's body, or anything else that seemed out of place.

The farther they went the more they felt it: a subtle wrongness. Gabe, now in wolf form, whined.

"Yeah, I feel it, too," Chris said. "I think we're getting near the right place." They trudged on for several more minutes, going deeper into the forested portion of the park and away from the designated hiking trail. The farther they went, the more silent the woods became. Even at night they should have heard the sound of animals hunting for dinner, the croak of frogs, a rustle of leaves. Something.

Just as he was about to give up, Gabe's sensitive nose caught a new smell. The faint odor of decay had it twitching. But this was more than just the scent of a dead animal. Someone had used power here—magical power. He shivered, barked once to alert Chris, and took off at a faster pace. Chris hurried to keep up.

They headed through the trees, not really noticing at first how far they had come. They had hiked far enough through the shallow strip of woods that made up the park that they were now close to its northern edge. Gabe could make out the lights of houses from a suburb not too far away.

Chris stopped abruptly. "This doesn't feel right," he said.

Gabe barked once more in agreement, but he also knew they needed to continue. They were close to finding something. He nosed through the soft dirt near the edge of the trees. The odor of decay and magic became suddenly stronger as he uncovered a bone—obviously human from the ragged plaid flannel shirt that still clung to it. He looked up, cocking his head questioningly at Chris.

"Yeah, I see it. We're too damn close to those houses over there." Chris moved closer, studying the body. "And there's more, Gabe. Look at this." He held out his hand, something in it. A small, withered bone was wrapped in tarnished silver wire that bound it to a crow's feather. He stood up slowly, searching the area, but saw nothing. "I've seen this type of thing before. This is really not good…"

Gabe stepped back to give Chris room to investigate. At that moment, a shadowy figure appeared next to the bones. Gabe tensed to strike but the figure gave him no time. He saw its fingers twitch. Before he could do anything, Chris had collapsed on the ground, and the figure had disappeared with only a trace of smoke to show where it had been.

Gabe turned to his friend. Chris clutched his chest, gasping in pain as if his heart were about to explode. Heat radiated from within him. Gabe could smell his skin and saw it turning red and blistering as if he were burning from the inside out. His veins glowed like molten lava, spreading from his chest to his arms and neck. The pain was obviously unbearable—he clawed his throat trying to scream, but it was as if the fire had already scorched his voice away.

Gabe quickly shifted back from wolf to human as quickly as possible, the crack of his bones sounding loud to his ears. He looked toward the houses, hoping no one was out walking in the suburb now that it was night and a breeze had sprung up to cool the air. "Chris, what can I do?" he said, frantically pulling the backpack off the man and scrambling into his clothing."

"Nothing. I don't know." Chris panted. "It feels… like I'm burning from the inside out."

"Damn it, even if you could walk, it's too far back through the woods to the car. I'm going to call Dan to come and get us."

Chris nodded as he continued to clutch his chest. "I need… I need Dave Thorne. He'll know how to heal this," gasped Chris.

Gabe pulled out his phone, dialed Dan, explaining the situation, and where they were.

"Someone will be there to get you as soon as possible," Dan told him. Gabe hung up the phone.

"Chris, we've got to get to the street—as quietly as

possible. Dan's going to have someone pick us up, but we need to make sure no one sees us near these bones before they get here."

He helped Chris to his feet, slung the man's arm over his shoulder, and stealthily helped him away from the woods. The skeletal remains still lay half-covered by dirt, more exposed than before they had come, but there was nothing Gabe could do about that now.

CHAPTER 19

Saturday morning, and Kathleen once again was sprawled on her sofa, idly scrolling through social media. At least she wasn't wondering if Dan was in jail this morning, she thought, even though she did have a bad feeling about whatever had happened last night. The way he had left, almost pushing her out his door in his haste, had told her that whatever it was, it wasn't good. It had sounded as if someone had been hurt.

As a shifter, she was used to seeing others in her pack injured. She understood pack emergencies. Her father and brother dealt with them all the time. It was an inherently dangerous way of life but there were compensations. Shifters generally healed quickly; they had a much longer lifespan than non-paras, too. Still, accidents and injuries happened.

Kathleen left Dan a text, hoping everyone was okay. Curious, but also realistic, she knew that since she wasn't yet a part of the Bertrand pack, she had no need to know what had happened. She hit the link for the local news app, wondering if anything important had happened in the world lately.

And suddenly she sat up straight, turning the volume on her computer to its highest setting.

"...CFO of Betrand Enterprises, was arrested for the second time in a matter of weeks by Sheriff Chip Walker of the Herndon County, Indiana Sheriff's Department. Sheriff Walker declined to comment on the charges, saying only that he will hold a press conference later today."

The picture showed Dan once again in handcuffs. His hair was a mess, there was a bruise on his cheek, and even though he was wearing the same dark jeans and casual shirt she had seen him in last, they were now torn and dirty.

What had happened? Panic grabbed her by the throat, and she carelessly pushed her computer off her lap onto the floor and grabbed her phone. She tried Dan's phone first even though she had called him this morning and had no real expectation that it would be answered. When it went straight to voicemail she tried Ana.

Again, no answer. She threw the phone on top of the computer, squeezing the bridge of her nose between her fingers in thought. Who else's number could she call? She grabbed the phone off the floor and searched through her contacts. Monica? She wasn't a paranormal, but she was a good friend of Ana's.

She hit her number and waited. This time, someone answered.

"Hey girl," came Monica's cheery voice. "What's up? You looking for something to do on this fine Saturday? We could go shopping."

"Monica, I'm so glad I got hold of you."

Her friend obviously heard the strain in Kathleen's voice. "What's wrong? Can I help you with anything?"

"Have you heard from Ana?"

"Ana? No, I didn't really expect to; you know we've got that farewell lunch for her on Monday, but I haven't heard anything since we left work yesterday afternoon. What's up?"

"I take it you haven't seen any news today?"

"No, you know I never listen to the news. It just starts your day off wrong to hear all that bad stuff. Particularly on a Saturday. I've been listening to music all morning. I've been running my faves channel on Spotify and…"

Kathleen waited for her friend to slow down enough that she would hear her trying to interrupt.

"Monica… Monica… stop. Have you heard from Ana at all?"

"I just told you, I think she and Chris had plans to go away for the weekend…"

Kathleen gritted her teeth. Monica had said a lot, but she had not managed to give her that one crucial piece of information. "I need to get hold of her, Monica. Her phone's turned off."

"Well, yeah, if I were planning a romantic weekend, I'd turn my phone off, too."

"Monica, listen to me. Her brother has been arrested again. I need to know what happened."

"Arrested? Again? You mean Dan, right. Well, of course you do. It wouldn't be Tyler. He's such a sweetie."

Kathleen rolled her eyes. "Monica, I'm trying to find out what happened. He and I were together last night, we went to dinner…"

"Ooh, you go, girl. Dan is so hot. I didn't know you were seeing him. But isn't he a little old for you? And does Ana know? She's always warned me away from him."

"Yes, Ana knows. Monica, I've got to go. If you do hear from Ana, tell her I'm trying to get in touch with her."

"Okay, of course but…"

Kathleen didn't wait for Monica to finish her sentence; she just hung up the phone. Now what was she going to do? She'd only met a few of Dan's friends. Her shyness took over. Could she really call someone she hardly knew and ask why their friend had been arrested?

She took a deep breath and put her shyness on hold. Dan had mentioned his two friends, Connor and Gabe, quite often. Now if she could only remember their last names. She picked up the computer again and googled "Connor… attorney… Rivelou, Ky." The town wasn't that large. How many attorneys with the name "Connor" could there be?

More than she thought, she found when the return information came back a few seconds later. There were several attorneys with the last name of Connor, and a couple of O'Connors as well. And of course, the search engine gave her several ads to look through for attorneys who had nothing to do with her search.

She continued scrolling and finally found "Connor Morrigan, Rivelou Ky. Family Law" listed. His photo was next to the listing. Yes, this was the right man. She dialed the number.

"This is Connor Morrigan; leave a message, and I'll get back to you as soon as possible."

"Connor, I met you once or twice with Dan Betrand. I just saw on social media that he's been arrested. Again. Connor, what happened? He was with me most of the evening. I just need to know that he's okay. Please call me as soon as you get this message."

She got up to make some coffee, then went back to google Dan's friend Gabe. That was harder. She couldn't remember exactly what his job was, or his last name.

She searched for another half hour when her doorbell rang. She jumped up to answer.

Dan stood at her door, just as he had two weekends before. His hair was still a mess, just as she'd seen on the internet. The bruise stood out on his cheek; there was dirt on his clothes and a tear in the shoulder of his shirt. He obviously hadn't stopped home for a shower this time. But he was dangling a bakery bag from one hand.

"Oh, thank God, I've been so worried."

And just like the last time, Dan bent down and gave her a scorching kiss.

CHAPTER 20

"Aren't you going to let me in?" he said when he finally released her.

She felt a bit unbalanced after the kiss, and he reached out and took her arm to steady her.

"Yes, of course, come in." She held the door wider for him. "And I remember. You don't care if I get dressed up."

"Not at all, in fact, I hope to have you a lot less dressed before too long."

He stalked over to the kitchen island and put the bag down. "You liked the lava cake the last time, so I brought more." Then he pulled her to him and gave her another kiss. "Why don't we ever seem to be able to finish our dates?"

"Maybe something about you getting arrested all the time?"

"You heard," he growled.

"It's all over the local news and social media."

"Of course it is."

"Can you tell me what happened?"

"Most of it. Some of it I'm not sure I even understand myself."

"Coffee?" she asked.

He nodded, and she got him a cup. "Let's take these over to the sofa and get comfortable, and you can tell me whatever you can."

"Some of it's pack business. Some of it's all over the news. And some of it, well, it just doesn't make sense," Dan said.

Kathleen nodded. She took his hand and pulled him over to the sofa. She folded her legs under her and got comfortable, facing him as he dug into the dessert.

"When I left you, I went to get Ana. Gabe had been helping Chris look into something, and they got into trouble. Chris was hurt."

"Is he alright? Ana must be so upset. I've tried calling her... and you... and everyone else I could think of, but no one picked up but Monica."

Dan put his head in his hands. "Oh Lord, what rumors is Monica spreading?"

"Nothing bad. She thought Ana and Chris were away for the weekend."

"Unfortunately, Monica was wrong. I wish she hadn't been," he said. She could see the guilt in his eyes.

"Well, she's not spreading rumors. She didn't know anything. But keep going with your story."

"I had already called Connor to go find Gabe and Chris..."

"You're not making a lot of sense here. Why did Gabe and Chris call you? And why couldn't they get the help they needed by themselves? What were they doing?"

The more Dan explained, the more confused Kathleen became.

"They were out in the woods, too far away from their car, and Chris couldn't walk. Anyway, Connor got them over to Dave Thorne's. Do you know him? He's a witch, and he's dating Shannon, Chris' sister."

"I've heard of him, but I don't think I've met him yet."

"He's skilled at healing, particularly magical curses. That's why Chris wanted to be taken there. Like I said, after I dropped you off, I went over to Ana's and told her what was going on and took her to Chris."

"But what was going on? And poor Ana, she must have been so frightened."

"Yes, she was." He closed his eyes, trying not to remember how scared and angry Ana had been when she found what Chris had been doing, and that Dan had asked him.

"What exactly happened to him?" Kathleen reached over and ran her hand softly over his bruised cheek. "I can tell you're upset. It must have been bad. Just tell me what you can."

He took a deep breath, pushing away thoughts of Ana and worry for Chris. Yes, the man was fine now—at least his body was no longer burning inside. But there was a brand on his chest that hadn't been there before. A crow. It was his mother Beatrix's mark. Dave didn't know what kind of side effects Chris might still be suffering from...

He couldn't worry about all of that now though. He needed to think about Kathleen. He had to tread carefully. He didn't want to lie to her, but how much should he tell her? It seemed every time he opened his mouth around Kathleen another lie came out. Well, he'd tell her as much of the truth as he could.

"They'd come across a body, and once we knew Chris was going to be okay, Gabe and I went back to check it out. By the time we got there, though, there were cops all around. They arrested me on the spot. That's how I got this." He motioned to his cheek. "They weren't inclined to play nice. And I wasn't inclined to go with them. But you should see the cop who gave it to me." His grin turned feral, and he cracked his knuckles.

Kathleen knew she shouldn't find it sexy, under the circumstances, but she did.

"They assumed the body was Alexander Fontaine's. Chip Walker was practically pissing himself with joy," Dan continued. "And then I showed up and they thought it was confirmation that I was the killer. They took me in for questioning... detained Gabe, too. It was a mess. Luckily, this time they let Gabe make a phone call—must have been a mistake by one of the deputies. I heard Walker reaming him out. Anyway, Connor got to us much quicker than last time. And guess what?"

"What?" Kathleen asked breathlessly.

"The body wasn't even Fontaine's. It was a woman."

"A woman?"

"Yeah, Chris and Gabe had only seen an arm before Chris'... um... accident. They didn't know who it was. That's why we went back and..." he trailed off

"And what?"

Dan looked away, ran his hand through his hair, if he said more he could give away more than he meant to. "How much more do you need? Wasn't all that enough for one night?"

He sounded upset and frustrated, she realized. Was it at her for asking? The old Kathleen would not have pushed. She could hear her mother's voice. "Never question a male. They will think you are challenging them, and that's no way to find a mate... or keep one happy."

She was not her mother, she reminded herself. That's why she'd left home, so she would be free of those hidebound traditions and rules.

"Obviously there's more," she said slowly. "The body wasn't Fontaine, so it shouldn't have anything to do with you, right? And maybe the sheriff thought he had caught you at something, but there wasn't anything—at least nothing you were involved in. You shouldn't have to worry anymore."

Dan stood and began to pace back and forth in the small room, looking like a caged animal with not enough space to run. "Chris and Gabe were looking for Fontaine's body. That's why we assumed it was him and went back to move it. The cops... well, Walker was just hoping it was. He wants to score a big case."

"But before you said you didn't think Fontaine was dead."

Damn it, the woman was too smart. He ran his hand through his hair again. How much should he tell her? He didn't want to lie. He laughed silently. So much for *"Veritas Vencit"* as his motto. He'd told so many lies lately he couldn't keep them straight.

"You're a shifter, an alpha, and so is Gabe. I can understand your concern when you thought it might be Fontaine, but it wasn't. But I can tell you're still worried. What's going on, Dan? You can tell me. And what about Chris? What happened to him?"

Chris' injury. Another topic he couldn't discuss with his mate. Damn it! How could he claim her when he couldn't tell her the truth about so many things? What could he say that wasn't a lie but didn't compromise anyone else? He took a breath. "Yeah, I guess we really can't hide the fact that Chris and Gabe were looking for Fontaine's body."

"Well, I can see why they might think he'd be in that

area; I take it that it was close to where the car was found?"

"Yeah. I sent them. I wanted to get ahead of things if Fontaine had died up there. You know, find the body. Help the police out."

"Help the police out? Dan, you've got to be kidding me. I know you wouldn't lift the tip of a single claw to help Walker."

She knew what he was saying was a lie, he realized, knew it didn't make sense. How was he ever going to get out of this complicated network of half-truths, evasions, and outright deception? Everything he said just dug the hole deeper. And, while he had told Kathleen she was his fated mate, he hadn't really had a chance to tell her just how he felt about her. That he couldn't live without her. That he loved her. If he claimed her, there'd be a connection. They'd know everything about each other—their thoughts, their feelings, their memories. God, would she even want him once she knew everything about him? She'd probably run as fast as she could back to that little town in Tennessee if she knew the whole story.

And then he'd just have to chase her. She was his mate. He wouldn't ever give up on her. His wolf stirred at the thought, painting a picture in his head of the two of them, in wolf form, chasing each other across a wide expanse of grass. He'd catch her, roll her on her back and…

He closed down the wayward thoughts. This was not the time. Just explaining the whole story was beyond him. He paced some more, trying to figure out how much he should say.

"Do you think the body might have something to do with the murders earlier this summer?" Kathleen interrupted his thoughts.

He stopped pacing and looked at her. Was this something he could tell her? There was something connecting the murders and this body, just not what she thought.

"The Artificial Witch murders? I suppose so. I haven't even had time to process everything that went on in the last twelve hours, let alone wonder about the body, other than that it looked as if it had been around awhile." He sat down again, head in his hands, frustrated and confused by his thoughts, his feelings, his worry about what to share.

Kathleen moved closer, putting a comforting arm around him. "I'm sorry," she said. "You've had a rotten time, and here I am badgering you with questions. How can I make you feel better?"

She slipped around to sit on his lap, facing him. Taking his face in her hands, she leaned in for a long, slow kiss. This. Just this. His mate. It was all he needed. He shoved his worries aside and thought only about her.

CHAPTER 21

It was late afternoon when Kathleen and Dan left her bedroom and wandered out to the kitchen to find something to eat. Kathleen turned on the television.

"Do we really need that?" Dan questioned.

"I like the background noise."

He shrugged and headed over to the refrigerator to see what was available.

"You've got a lot of vegetables here. Not much red meat," he said.

"This wolf is trying to keep her figure."

"Your figure looks perfect to me," he replied, turning from the fridge and grabbing her by the waist. "I like your curves. Every one of them."

"I do have a couple of steaks in the freezer," she said. "If you're willing to wait, we can thaw that. I've got a little grill on my patio."

"Sounds like a plan. While we're waiting, I can find something else to snack on." He pulled her to him and nibbled her neck.

"You're incorrigible; you know that don't you?" she giggled as she allowed him to move her toward the couch. She sat on his lap again. Facing him, she could enjoy the feel of his hard, muscled arms around her, run her hands over his chest and abs, feel the gentle kisses, so much in contrast to the moody, fierce wolf he showed to the rest of the world.

The TV continued to play softly. The words of the anchor on the cable news channel were just a blur of noise. Suddenly Dan stopped and looked up.

"What's wrong?"

"Did you hear that? Turn up the volume."

She scrambled for the remote, which had fallen beneath the couch pillows, and hit the volume button.

"...the body was said to have unusual markings, as if

the victim had been attacked by a wild animal, possibly a wolf," the anchorwoman was saying. "Sheriff Chip Walker, of the Herndon County, Indiana Sheriff's Department, will be giving a press conference shortly to update us on the discovery of the body and how it is linked to other mysterious deaths in the Indiana/Kentucky border area near the Rivelou River. We'll bring you that press conference as soon as it happens. And now, we'll take a break for a few minutes. Stay tuned for the news you can use."

"It's made the national news? I can't believe it," Kathleen said as Dan's phone began to ring.

"Grandpa... Yes. I heard.... I've got no idea. We need to wait for this press conference... Here's Connor, trying to call me... I'll call you back."

This time Kathleen could hear Connor's voice coming tinnily from the phone. "We're gonna sue him for everything he's got if the name Bertrand is so much as whispered," were the first words out of his mouth, his anger obvious.

"Hey, let's just hear what he says first. Maybe it's all more of the Walker bullshit campaign," Dan said as the news anchor returned to the screen, a video feed of the front of the Herndon County Sheriff's Office in a box at the side. "I'll call you back when it's over."

He hung up, and Dan and Kathleen stood in front of the TV as the newswoman introduced the topic of the missing body again. Then the screen switched to the Herndon County sheriff's office—Dan recognized it all too well at this point. Walker came out of the door with Deputy Rossi a step behind him. A small podium had been set up on the sidewalk. A group of officials stood behind Walker and Rossi, some in suits, some in uniform. Dan recognized the mayor of the small town of Gibson City among them. They looked very important standing in a solemn row, the officers with their hands behind their backs at parade rest.

"Thank you all for coming today," the sheriff began. "We have evidence of a new crime which links to other unsolved crimes in our area in the past year. While many of these events have taken place across the river in Rivelou,

Kentucky, we now have evidence that the perpetrator or perpetrators are working on this side of the river, in Indiana, also.

"The body of a woman was found late last night in the woods near Harmony State Park. We have yet to identify the victim, but she was in her late 20s or early 30s and died from an attack that looks like it was carried out by a very large animal, possibly a wolf. We have to wait for forensics teams to do their work to pinpoint exactly what killed this woman. We are asking that any persons that might have any information about this woman to please contact us at...."

Dan and Kathleen turned to look at each other in horror.

"Who would do this?" Kathleen asked. "Shifters are taught never to take someone like this... and even a feral shifter knows better than to leave a body where it can be found..."

Dan put his arm around her. "These must be the bones Chris and Gabe found. But what's Walker up to saying so much on tv? I can't imagine... I don't believe it's anyone from our pack."

He quieted to continue listening to Walker, who was now discussing the still-missing Alexander Fontaine and the reappearance of his Lamborghini. Then he took questions from the group of reporters surrounding him.

"Do you have any idea how long the body has been there?"

"At least several months," was the response.

"Do you know who the person was?"

"As I've already said, we have not yet identified the body." Walker was already showing his impatience at dealing with the repetitious questions reporters always asked. Dan, who'd had a lot of experience with this kind of thing lately, suspected the tactic was just aimed at riling a person up so they'd say something foolish. He didn't really expect Walker to fall for it no matter how irritated he seemed.

"What about the reports that the victim was killed by a werewolf?" another questioner asked. Dan recognized her as an influencer for a popular blog that purported to look into all things supernatural, the Paranormal Heartbeat.

"Really Ms. Dark, do you expect me to answer a ridiculous question like that?"

"So do I take your answer as no comment?" responded Delaney Dark, who Dan knew was named Vivian Greenblatt in real life.

"Why has nothing been done in Rivelou about this problem? They have more resources there than you have, as a county sheriff," Bob Baker, an older reporter from the local Rivelou newspaper asked. Baker was known for uncovering inefficiency and scandal in local politics.

This was a question Chief Walker was obviously anxious to answer although he might not appreciate the way it had been phrased. "I have no idea why Chief Luther Anderson of the Rivelou Police Department has been unwilling to pursue some of the obvious suspects in these cases," he said. "You should ask him if he is protecting wealthy and influential people in his town. Maybe even some business and government leaders."

That caused an uproar from the small group of reporters.

Dan growled, his claws unsheathing without him even realizing it. Kathleen put a hand on his arm to soothe him, and he smiled gratefully at her, retracting his claws and pulling her to him.

"Who is he protecting?" and "What else do you know?" rang out from the group.

"You are going to have to discuss that with Chief Anderson and the rest of that pack over in Kentucky," Walker said, with scorn in his voice.

Dan stiffened and his eyebrows raised again. Did Walker know something about the shifter pack? Or was this just a derogatory phrase he happened to use?

Officer Ricci stepped up to the podium at that point, hands raised in the air. "That's all the time the chief has right now for questions. We'll have another press conference…"

He was cut off by one more voice.

"Chief Walker, what do you know about PackNet? The secret website for the paranormals in your community?"

CHAPTER 22

Channing got up her courage. She'd never been to Dolan's place before; they'd always gone to her apartment. Granted, when he'd stayed in Rivelou in the past, he'd either just stayed with her or gotten a room in a motel. But now that he was planning to move here, he'd rented an apartment close to the Twin States Bridge, which linked Indiana and Kentucky in this part of the world.

While his business was located on the Indiana side of the line, he wanted a place closer to her, he told her. As a member of the McTier pack, he really wasn't supposed to stay in Rivelou without permission from the pack alpha. Her grandfather. Channing didn't think he'd bothered with that.

Dolan, she'd learned, wasn't big on rules. Or pack protocol—unless it were his own pack. He didn't really seem to respect the Bertrand traditions she thought now as she drove toward his new place. It bothered her although she'd never admit it out loud. Certainly not to her family. Or even her girlfriends. Though she hadn't seen them much lately. There never seemed to be time. All of her free time was taken up by Dolan. If he were in town, she'd be with him, and when he wasn't, she hurried home from work to Facetime or talk to him on the phone.

She put on her playlist and sang with Billie Eilish to "Birds of a Feather." Yeah, she wanted to be with Dolan until the day she died. She sighed. It was going to be hard to convince her family that she'd found her mate. But she wouldn't feel like this about a shifter who wasn't her true mate, would she?

She'd always been independent. But Dolan wanted to know where she was all the time. It made her feel so safe and protected when he called to check in on her.

She'd mentioned getting together for dinner with her friends, Nova and Brittany, so he could meet them, but Dolan always came up with an excuse. He said when he only got to see her a short time each week, he wanted to keep her to himself. She sighed contentedly, thinking about how romantic that was.

Dolan made her feel wanted. Sexy. Particularly since all he seemed to want to do was to keep her in bed. Not that she minded. She'd never had anyone treat her as if she were beautiful and sexy before. They always seemed to want her just for her family connections. Like her last boyfriend, James. That had been a disaster. And look at what had happened with Ana and Alexander Fontaine. Everyone thought he was so wonderful—even her grandfather. And it turned out the man had only wanted her for her position in the pack. He believed if he married into the Bertrand family, he could take over and become pack leader. Hah! He'd certainly underestimated her sister. Thank goodness Dolan wasn't like that. He was already in line to become the alpha of the McTier pack. That's how she knew he had no interest in her as a Bertrand.

The music change to Jada Thirwall's "It Girl." Yeah— just like Jada, she had claws and fangs, she thought with a laugh. And it turned out her sister did, too.

Channing had been totally surprised when she learned that Ana had killed Fontaine. She would never have guessed her quiet sister had that much gumption. Guess a woman would do anything when the man she loved was threatened. That's how she felt about Dolan. Her family might not approve, but she'd do anything to help him. Anything...

She pulled into the parking lot of his apartment complex and took a deep breath, gathering her courage. She got out of the car and carefully took the planter she'd put together for him out of the back seat. She'd planted lavender for serenity and healing, sage for wisdom, thyme for courage, and sweet basil as a symbol of her good wishes for Dolan. Would he like it? She hoped so. She got up her courage and knocked on his door. He didn't answer, but she thought she heard voices inside. She put her ear closer to the door to try to decide if Dolan had heard her. Yes, someone was definitely there. She waited another minute and knocked again.

She was just about to leave when she heard Dolan say,

"Who's there?"

"It's me, Channing."

He opened the door just a crack and peaked out. "Channing? What are you doing here? I was going to see you later tonight. At your place."

"I know. But I thought... well I thought..."

"You didn't want to wait for me until tonight, huh Baby?" he asked with a smirk. He ran his hand down her back, stopping on her butt. "And what's this?" he asked, looking at the planter in her hands.

"It's some herbs. I thought you could use them. For cooking or..."

His frown appeared and disappeared so quickly she wasn't sure she'd actually seen it. "Yeah, hey, that's nice." He took the heavy pot from her. "Look, I'd ask you in, but the place isn't ready at all. I've still got boxes everywhere. Don't even have my bed set up yet." He smirked again. "Why don't I just come over to your place tonight like we agreed?"

Before she could say anything else, he'd given her a kiss, said, "That's to keep you thinking about me until later," and closed the door.

Channing stood for a moment, a little shocked. She thought she heard voices again. He must be listening to something on the television, she told herself.

As she turned to leave, she was surprised to see Dan come out of an apartment a few doors down. A redheaded girl she thought looked familiar was with him. They didn't notice her as she watched Dan put an arm around her waist, and they looked soulfully into each other's eyes.

Dan had a girlfriend? It was news to her. Of course, she hadn't spent much time around her brother lately. Not since he and Dolan had that fight at Ana's engagement party, she thought sourly. Of course, he had been polite when they'd seen him at The Night Crawler a few days ago.

"Dan, hey!" she called now. She ought to try to be friendlier with him.

The couple turned to her. "Hey Channing," he said, as she walked over to them. "You remember Kathleen, don't you?"

"Hi, you're the friend who let the family know when Dan was arrested. The first time," she added to tease her brother.

He rolled his eyes.

"Nice to meet you," Kathleen said, shyly holding out her hand. "I haven't had a chance to meet many of Dan's family yet. I don't count that night. Everyone was too upset."

Dan leaned in and gave her a light kiss on her neck.

Channing raised her eyebrows. Not so much at her brother's display of affection, but at Kathleen using the word "yet," as if she just expected Dan to bring her to the next pack meeting. Well, she hoped it went better for him than it had for her. "When is my brother bringing you to a pack meeting?"

"Yeah, we need to make you official, Kathleen. You're settled here now. I'm going to have to make sure you get to the next one. The full moon is in a week. You can get introduced then. Although I think we're going to have more than the usual business to discuss."

"What do you mean?" Channing asked.

"You haven't heard the news?"

"What news? I haven't listened to anything today. I had my Spotify list on." She continued to talk, paying little attention to what her brother was trying to tell her. She was more interested in Dan's new girlfriend than any local or national news. "Where are you from, Kathleen?"

"Oh, um, Tennessee. But what are you doing here? I haven't seen you in this complex before. Do you live here?" Kathleen asked.

Now it was Channing's turn to hesitate. "I was just visiting a friend who's moving in here."

"A friend?" questioned Dan, a sudden suspicious note to his voice.

"If you must know, Dolan is getting an apartment so he can spend more time in this area."

Kathleen suddenly turned pale and looked ill.

"Are you all right?" Channing asked her, concerned.

"Baby, what's wrong?" Dan said at the same time.

"It...It's nothing." Kathleen put her hand to her forehead to wipe away the cold sweat that had just broken out.

"It must be the heat. I.. um…" She swayed a little.

"I'm so sorry, Baby. Let's get you over to the car. I'll turn on the AC for you. Hey, Channing, let's talk later," Dan said as he quickly helped his girlfriend to the car.

Channing stared after them. That had been odd. Kathleen had gotten ill so suddenly. Right when Channing mentioned Dolan.

Or could it be something else? Had her big brother knocked up his girlfriend?

Channing chuckled at the thought. Dan was always the sibling the family thought could do no wrong. That looked like it was changing. First he gets arrested, now he gets his girlfriend pregnant. She was going to enjoy this.

CHAPTER 23

As Dan, Gabe, and Connor entered The Night Crawler a few evenings later, the crowd grew suddenly silent.

"Looks like they've heard about the breach," Gabe said. He gave a laugh that couldn't quite mask the strain in his voice. His friends knew the guilt he was feeling about the internet breach. PackNet was his baby. And it had been violated. He hadn't slept since he'd gotten an alarm in the early hours of the morning after Chris had been injured. He'd still been at Dave Thorne's home, waiting to make sure his friend was okay, but when the alert sounded, he'd taken off immediately for his office. He, Ramona, and the rest of his team had spent hours ensuring that everything was patched and secure. They'd spent every moment since working to understand just how the breach had been accomplished.

"I know how it was done now," he told his friends as Connor ordered three beers and they headed to their usual table. "It was a combination of magic and technology. It took someone who is very good at both. More than very good actually. A wizard—a tech wizard and a paranormal. I've stopped them from getting in that way again, but who knows?" Gabe sat down heavily and put his head in his hands. "Maybe they're better than me; maybe no matter what I do, they'll find a new way in," he said despondently.

"Gabe, cut yourself a break. From what you're saying, whoever did this was apparently both a magical and technical genius. I've never even heard of a witch with those kinds of abilities," Dan told him. "Beatrix Spier might have had the magic, but not the technical know-how." Dan lowered his voice to just above a whisper as he said the name.

Gabe had just put his head in his hands. "If they got in once, they can get in again. It's like they always say. I have to be secure all the time. The hackers only need to break in one time. My team can see what was done, just not how they did it.

I don't know that I can ever guarantee that PackNet is safe again."

Dan looked up as the hush that had fallen over the bar at their entrance changed to whispers and accusing looks. He exchanged a look with Connor. Gabe had needed a night away from his computers, but right now he wasn't sure The Night Crawler had been the best idea. As the muttering grew louder, he could tell that not all of it was directed at Gabe. The Bertrands had vouched for PackNet—had pushed for PackNet. And whether they were witches, vampires, shifters, or other paranormals, the name "Bertrand" was being muttered in the bar tonight just as often as "Legato."

"Hey, I seem to be the only one someone doesn't want to throw a dart at," Connor tried to joke. He'd apparently noticed the same thing as Dan.

"Maybe you'd be better off not being seen with us," Gabe told him morosely. This was so unlike Gabe, who usually found the humor in every situation, that Dan and Connor exchanged another worried glance.

"Man, it happened. You're fixing it. That's all anyone can ask of you," Dan told him. "And if you don't get your head out of your ass, you're not going to be much good to anyone."

"But what about the people who've already been hurt? Abby's shop was vandalized last night. Someone threw a rock through the window with a note saying, 'Get on your broom and leave Rivelou alone.'

"What if it had happened earlier in the day? What if she or Winnie had been there and been hurt? I couldn't forgive myself." Their friend Abby owned a boutique, The Wolf's Den, where Winnie worked part-time. It was popular with both paranormals and non-paras. Or at least it had been. Who knew if she'd be able to reopen now that the world knew she was a witch.

"Look, I feel just as bad as you do. The pack is doing everything we can to minimize the damage. We're relocating anyone who feels threatened. We're…"

"And why should they feel threatened?" Connor broke in angrily. "We are the paranormals. We're the ones with power.

We should fight back." His voice grew louder as he spoke.

Dan and Gabe looked at him in surprise. This wasn't the Connor they were used to. He was gentle; he believed in the law. Out of the three of them, he was the one who always looked for the least violent way."

"We're shifters. We have power. And the witches and vamps—they've got even more. If we wanted to, we could take over from the non-paras."

One of the waitresses passing by with a tray for another table, heard him. "Yeah! That's right. Why are we the ones living in fear? We could take over this town and run it our way if we wanted," she said loudly.

Some of the paranormals at nearby tables heard her and nodded in agreement.

"Yeah, why are we the ones who are worried? They should be afraid of us," a bear shifter sitting at the next table said loudly.

"Please, be careful," Dan told him. "Everyone in this bar is on edge tonight. You don't want to stir up anything you can't keep under control."

"I've been keeping control for too damn long, and what has it gotten me? I sit at home alone," Connor said.

Dan grimaced, realizing that Connor was talking about more than the breach, or even his career. He was talking about Ana and his reluctance to tell her how he felt about her until she was already involved with someone—first her husband Jonathan and now Chris Spier. Dan started to say something, although he didn't know exactly what he could say that would make the other man feel better, when the door of the bar was slammed open and three figures walked in.

They were tall and dressed in leather like many of the other patrons, but there was a subtle difference, not just in their dress but in their manner and bearing, that made everyone at the bar notice them. For the second time that night the bar went quiet.

CHAPTER 24

The three strangers stood in the doorway looking everything over, an unmistakable hint of superiority in their gazes. The tallest man was dressed in fitted black jeans, combat boots polished to a mirror shine, and a charcoal button-up shirt with a subtle embroidered pattern of sigils that shimmered as he moved. Despite the warm summer night, he wore a long, black leather coat that fitted him like a suit of armor. A silver cuff in an intricate design could be glimpsed at his wrist beneath the coat sleeve. His hair, dark, long, and tied back from his face, shone with a metallic undertone that reminded Dan of Nero Helene, the glittering metallic black paint used on Alexander Fontaine's Lamborghini.

His companions, a male and female, were both fair, with pale golden hair and silver-blue eyes. The woman's long tresses were highlighted with gleaming blue streaks that matched her eyes. Dan wondered if the male were her brother because of the resemblance between them. His eyes were also blue, and he wore his golden hair short and tousled, curling around his ears. Both also wore leather, but unlike their companion's hard biker look, these two held themselves with an aristocratic bearing as if they were runway models in a world of tourists.

Without acknowledging anyone else in the bar, they walked straight toward the table where Dan, Gabe, and Connor sat, coming to a stop a short distance away.

"You are Daniel Henry Betrand," the fair-haired male said. It was a statement, not a question.

"Yes, and who may you be?" Dan put on his best dominant alpha male veneer, difficult with these three looking at him as if he were a specimen in a bottle.

"I am Serelith Virelyn. Although I go by Sierra Vale when in the human world." The woman stepped forward, making it clear she was in charge, and managing to infuse the words "human world," with a universe of scorn. "This is my brother Kailin, and our paladin Theolin Duskbane."

"Theo Knight," the dark-haired man said, then snapped his mouth shut as if acknowledging a second name were more than he should have said.

"Please, have a seat." Dan stood and pulled a chair out for Serelith. "It's been many years since we've had a visit from the Fae. To what do we owe the pleasure?"

As Dan said the word "Fae," Gabe and Connor gawked at him, their mouths falling open comically. Out of the corner of his eye he saw them turn to each other as Gabe mouthed the word "Fae," again, his eyes almost bugging out of his head.

"My Lady, Sirs," said Connor, standing and bowing his head. "It is a great honor to have you here."

"Ah," said Serelith. "Connor Morrigan. I see that some in the New World still have manners."

"The rumors of your beauty and your courage have long been told in my family," said Connor.

Gabe continued to stare open-mouthed, his glance moving from Connor to Dan, to the elves and back.

Dan noticed that the silence in the room had continued, with everyone straining to hear what was being said at their table.

"And the favors owed by our family to yours have not been forgotten," Kailin said.

"You are much too kind."

"But enough of pleasantries. Brother, we are wasting time. We are here to discuss the events of the past week. Word of your catastrophic breach has disturbed us, even as far away as Otherworld. We have been sent to make sure that you shifters have things under control,"

"Your queen has never allowed any of your kind on PackNet," said Dan. "You should not be affected, so what business is it of yours?"

"The paranormal world is intrinsically connected in all ways. You have put us all in danger," Theolin said. "Our queen made clear the hazards and her disapproval to your grandfather when he first proposed this scheme." Though ostensively speaking to Dan, he stared at Gabe as he said this, condemnation clear in every word and glance.

Serelith placed a restraining hand on his arm. "Theo, please, we are here to help them, not threaten them."

"And how can you help us? Do you know code?" Gabe finally found his voice.

"You would be surprised what we know, Gabriel Legato. We have seen more things both here and in the Otherworld than even a shifter can guess, despite his knowledge of 'code.'" Kailin said, a subtle offense clear in his tone if not in his words.

"Kai, just as I said before, we are here to offer help, not trade insults," Serelith said. "Gentlemen, please forgive my brother and cousin." She turned toward Gabe, putting out a hand to lightly touch his arm. "Gabriel, while my brother may not want to admit it to you right now, he and I have both been fascinated with the technical world for many decades, and our knowledge of the dark magic that was involved in breaching your system is greater than any of your current experts. Our queen has sent us to help you repair your system in such a way that it cannot be breached again."

Gabe seemed unable to speak. He stared in amazement, his mouth hanging open for so long that Connor finally kicked him under the table. "I… um… thank you?" he said.

As one, the three elves stood from the table. "We will be at your door tomorrow morning prepared to work on the problem." Serelith addressed her statement to Gabe, then turned and led the way through the bar and out the door.

As it closed behind them, the noise in the room picked up again as the patrons turned to each other to discuss what they had just seen. Gabe stared after the trio for a long minute, then finally turned to his two friends. "Their ears," he said.

"What about them?" asked Dan.

"They're not pointy. I always thought the Fae had pointy ears."

CHAPTER 25

The basement of Hank's home was filled with many more shifters than just the council. Every sofa and chair held angry males and females. Several guests were in attendance also: Cassandra, the head of the local coven; Chief Luther Anderson; vampire Dr. Nathan Lazard, who was the county coroner; hunter Chris Spier as well as the heads of the other shifter clans in the area, the bears, the bobcats, the deer, and the eagles. The walls were lined with members of the pack. Alphas, Betas, Omegas, they were all shouting.

"Is PackNet safe?"

"Are *we* safe?"

"What about our children? They're afraid to go outside."

"I can't send my kids to school. They're being bullied."

My name was released. I was doxed."

"I might lose my job. No non-para woman wants a wolf giving them a haircut."

"Can't the witches help? Conjure everyone to forget they've heard anything?"

"Why did we ever let *him* talk us into this?" The male shifter stood at the front of the room, his feet spread, body rigid. He pointed an accusing finger toward Hank, making it obvious who he blamed for the breach in security.

Dan took a step forward, but his grandfather quickly motioned him back. Dan understood. Tempers were hot, and it was better to allow everyone to unleash their anger in words. The last thing the Betrand pack needed was a challenge fight by another alpha right now. Or even just a brawl here in the basement. Dan took a breath, clenching and unclenching his fists in attempt to stay calm—not his natural inclination when he felt his family was challenged. He stepped back next to his grandfather and Gabe; the other council members were arranged behind them at the front of the room.

Gabe could barely meet anyone's eye, his usual cocky

demeanor nowhere in evidence. He was still taking the breach in PackNet to heart even though he and his team had made great progress in securing the system in the last few days. The assistance from the two elves, Serelith and Kailin, had been invaluable. Theolin mostly just stood and glowered at everyone, making it clear that he took his job as bodyguard seriously. Gabe wasn't sure, but he had the distinct impression that the two Virelyn siblings were some kind of royalty.

He knew he should be grateful for their help. And he was. Really. But PackNet was his baby. He'd planned it, executed it, and had been largely responsible for promoting its use, not just to the Bertrand pack, but to paranormals worldwide. Even though he'd closed the breach almost as soon as it appeared, he had failed, and millions of paranormals' data and personal information were now at risk.

"Alright, alright, settle down," Hank shouted, raising his voice to be heard in the crowded room. "The sooner you stop shouting, the sooner we can all get some answers."

Slowly, the shifters settled until finally you could hear a pin drop on the basement's floor.

"Gabe, tell us what you know," Hank said without any additional preamble.

"Um, yeah, okay," the younger man stumbled as he began his explanation. Dan reached over and grabbed his shoulder in support. Gabe looked at him gratefully, then took a breath and began.

"As we all know, information from PackNet was leaked to a social media influencer, Delaney Dark of the Paranormal Heartbeat podcast, and discussed during a televised press conference given by Chief Walker over in Herndon County last Sunday afternoon. We all know Dark. She's been sniffing around every rumor of the paranormal for years, from Chupacabras to the Loch Ness Monster."

This brought a few laughs, and the tension lowered slightly throughout the room. "Yeah, she's an idiot. She was here all last spring about those murders. Kept coming into my bar to try and interview people," called out George Merlin, owner of The Night Crawler. "Of course she never even knew about the back room, where she'd have found out all the goods. That's because I keep my place secure for paranormals." Merlin got his barb in as he referred to the back half of the bar, the magically concealed section where Dan, Gabe, and Connor had gone for drinks a few nights before.

"No one's gonna believe her. She's a nutcase, chasing all these silly rumors," said someone else in the crowd

The irony of that statement made Dan want to smile. So many of the so-called rumors were very true facts about shifters.

"Unfortunately, it's not just Dark this time," Gabe continued. "Information was released to some of the more mainstream sites, like cable news and the big national newspapers. Apparently most of those sites paid no attention at first, but the same information was put out in so many places at one time that they started to take notice.

"Luckily, we closed the breach before most of these people had a chance to check on the sites. When they tried to go to the links, they found nothing. But Dark and a few other paranormal researchers and mainstream journalists had already been inside PackNet. We don't know exactly how much, or which particular sites were visited although we do know about some of them because of the doxing or other harassment that has occurred. We also don't know exactly what information may have been copied, so that even if the breach is closed, the data can be shared through other sites."

"That's why we need the covens to get together and cast an obliteration spell—make everyone forget what they saw," called out a woman from the back of the room.

At that, Cassandra stood gracefully from her seat near the front of the room. "I'd like to answer that, if I may," she said politely to Gabe.

He nodded and she stepped next to him, turning to the crowd. "An obliteration spell can wipe out memories for a small group of people. For example, I could cast a spell that would wipe out the memories everyone in this room has of what was said in the last hour." Cassandra, who usually dressed in elegantly casual jeans and blouses, tonight wore all the trappings of her position as the High Priestess of the local coven. Her long, black gown was decorated with the Wiccan symbol of the tree of life embroidered in silver. Silver pentagram earrings hung from her ears, and a tiger's eye cabochon pendant denoting her power and rank hung from a thick silver chain around her neck.

She smiled graciously when several of the shifters made exclamations of shock. "Of course, neither I nor any of my coven would consider such a thing," she said reassuringly. "I am just giving you examples of what is possible and what is not in the hope that it will dispel rumors. We must all stand together right now and not allow speculation based on misinformation to tear us apart.

"That said, I could also create false memories in a group of people, making them believe in something that had not really happened. But what neither I, nor all the witches in the world working together can do, is to eradicate the memory of a specific event from everyone on earth. That is what we would need to do to hide this breach, and it is just not possible."

"What about the elves? We heard the Fae were at The Night Crawler over the weekend. Aren't they more powerful than you witches?" called another voice in the crowd. At that, the murmurs rose again. Some of the younger men who stood at the back of the room grumbled even louder. Dan caught a few phrases. "Then what good…" and "the McTier pack…" He noted who they were. He'd have to keep an eye on them.

At that moment, his grandfather stepped back up. "This meeting is not about what we can't do, nor is it about laying blame at anyone's feet."

Dan heard more mumbling, including Gabe's name from the same group of men, as well as the phrase "old man," obviously aimed at his grandfather.

Gabe took the floor again. "Yes, we have had assistance from three Fae experts in the last few days. They've been invaluable in helping us secure PackNet once again. I understand many people may be leery of using it now, but I assure you, it is as safe as we can make it. That said, we have to assess the damage that has been done and wonder why it happened. With help from the Fae, we've developed a few theories." He began to count off points on his fingers.

"Whoever breached the system made sure certain information was released to several influential people— reporters, government officials, scientists. Other information was only given out once or to the less credible sources.

"Information released included details about certain packs and individuals, everything from services and shops that cater to paranormals to specific well-known individuals who happen to be paras. One interesting fact is that much of the information that was leaked centered here, on the Rivelou area— not exactly the largest or most well-known town in the world. You would think that whoever was responsible for the leaks would have focused on a more important city or area—New Orleans, Paris, Bahla in Oman, or Haiti or Jamaica. Any of these areas already has a reputation as a paranormal center and would have been a more likely choice than Rivelou. That leads us to believe that whoever is behind the leak had a particular grudge against one or more of the paranormals in this area."

Again, there were mutterings in the back of the room, but they quickly quieted when other shifters turned to hush them. That, Dan thought, was a good sign. More shifters were here tonight who wanted to listen than those who just wanted to air grievances and make trouble.

"It is also obvious that the information could only come from PackNet," Gabe continued to make his points, holding up another finger. "The information that Alexander Fontaine was a shapeshifter could only have come from there. Fontaine was very careful. No other source had that fact. In fact, until he joined the Bertrand pack last fall, he was not registered anywhere as a paranormal. And no other source could have known that Dan Bertrand and Ana Dugan are werewolves or that Chris Spier is a hunter—or what, exactly, being a hunter means."

"Okay, whoever did this wanted to get back at us here in Rivelou. Or at least the Bertrands. You don't have to convince us anymore. Now tell us what you're doing about it," shouted one of the young males in the back of the room.

"Why didn't you know about the breach before you heard about it on the news?" called out another. "Aren't you supposed to be the all-knowing tech guru who would keep us safe?"

Gabe rolled his shoulders and continued. "PackNet is set up so that I, or one of my techs—who are all paranormals by the way, I don't have any non-paras on my team—should have immediately gotten an alert if someone were even starting to try to breach the site. That didn't happen."

"So you failed." The man at the back heckled Gabe again. He ignored it and continued.

"We immediately set about fixing the breach as soon as we knew about it. It was closed within minutes of our learning about it. That said, you can't put the genie back in the bottle."

"I can… just watch me squash one of those little fuckers so they fit in an olive jar." This comment was met with laughter and some good-natured ribbing of the large shifter who was known for his prowess in fights. He'd beaten everyone in the pack except Dan. Of course, he'd never challenged Hank. No one in the pack, so far, had been foolish enough to challenge Hank, Dan thought. He was glad the mood had lightened.

When the noise died down, the atmosphere was finally a bit more relaxed. Gabe looked a little more at ease, too, and he ventured a joke. "Good to know, Adam. I'll call on you the next time I'm having trouble with a genie. That said, my people and I have closed the breach, and we've set up new safeguards to make sure the same thing doesn't happen again. We are in the process of notifying anyone whose personal information has been compromised. That includes not just our pack, or just shifters and paranormals in this area. As I've mentioned, data was stolen worldwide, and we are working with other para tech groups throughout the world to ensure everyone's safety.

"Other than the emphasis on Rivelou, we haven't detected any pattern to what was released and what wasn't. Chief Anderson is looking into that part of it, and he'll talk to you in a minute. But I want to mention one more thing that is of concern. This breach could only have been done by a paranormal, or a group of paranormals, with extremely powerful magic and excellent tech skills. Think about it; there can't be too many paras out there like that. And whoever it is wanted to out us all."

CHAPTER 26

At Gabe's words, the crowd erupted noisily again until Hank raised his hands for quiet. This time, the shifters were quicker to calm down. "I've invited Chief Anderson here today to talk to us about his search for the culprits. Let's settle down and listen to him."

Gabe, with obvious relief, changed places with the chief. He sat down between Chris and Cassandra. Chris, he noticed, still looked pale. There were dark circles under his eyes. Gabe hoped the aftereffects of the magical attack wouldn't affect him permanently. It was obvious to anyone who knew him that he wasn't okay.

Chief Anderson, a large, dark-skinned man with a commanding presence, stood up and moved to the front of the room. Anderson's mother had been a siren and his father a witch. Luther Anderson had inherited only his mother's abilities to control people with his voice. He used it now to gain the attention of everyone in the room. He held up his hand over the crowd, and as he began to speak, Dan could feel a calmness steal over him. He knew Anderson did not use his powers lightly. He would be a very dangerous paranormal if he did.

In this case, Dan wholeheartedly approved of anything that helped to calm his pack down—even if only for a short time. But what if…? Right now he knew Anderson was on the side of the shifters, in particular the Bertrand pack. Watching him work his particular brand of magic at this moment made Dan suddenly understand just how dangerous the chief of police could be if he weren't on their side. Not only could he calm an unruly crowd, but he could also persuade both paranormals and non-paras to believe almost anything. Yes, Chief Luther Anderson was a double-edged sword. Dan wanted to make sure he continued to be a friend of the Bertrand pack.

Now, the chief quietly looked over the room and began to speak.

"First, I want to assure everyone that the Rivelou Police Department, as well as our associates in paranormal law enforcement around the world, are working with us to solve this problem. We are looking at both the technological and the magical components of the breach."

The chief continued to update the crowd on the work that was being done, and this time, instead of the antagonism they had shown as Gabe was speaking, Anderson's voice calmed and reassured them. Dan noticed that even the young hecklers in the back of the room were quiet. When he was done speaking, Hank said a few more words, and the pack began to file out of the basement, chatting easily with each other. The tension and anger that had been present at the beginning of the meeting seemed to have dispersed. While Dan knew at least part of that was because of Anderson's powers, he hoped the siren's influence had allowed the shifters to listen to reason and that their reassurance that all would be well would last until everything was straightened out.

As he walked onto the porch he noticed Dolan waiting for Channing. He and Kathleen were the only two wolf shifters in the area that Dan knew had not been at the pack meeting. Dolan, because as a member of the McTier pack, was not invited. And Kathleen because she had asked not to come even though this was the meeting where Dan had planned to officially introduce her to the pack.

"I'm not yet a pack member, and I am your girlfriend." She'd said the last word hesitantly, looking up at him as if she expected him to correct her.

"Yes, you are my girlfriend. That's why I'd like you to be there. That's why you need to formally join the pack."

"I think it would be better to wait to introduce me to the rest of the shifters some other time. You'll have enough questions to answer, and having me there might just make people uneasy or suspicious."

"Okay," he said reluctantly. "You make a good point. I don't want to jeopardize anyone's reaction to you when I introduce you officially."

"That's not what I meant. I'm thinking of me, not you,"

she'd protested.

"And that's just one of the things I love about you."

She blushed and turned away, but he'd taken her chin in his hand, forcing her to look in his eyes. "I meant what I just said. I'm in love with you. I was from the moment I met you. I don't expect you to feel that same way about me. I plan to court you, to cherish you until you realize for yourself that I am your mate, and then I will claim you."

He pushed away the memory and focused on the shifters on his grandparents' porch and yard. He needed to be alert; he wanted to test the waters to see just what some of the young alphas were thinking.

***

As soon as Channing got outside, she walked over to Dolan, who was standing under a large oak tree in the front yard. Several shifters hailed Dan, but he only waved at them and moved on into the night. As he rounded the corner of the house, he quietly shifted into his wolf form, then moved stealthily through the bushes to position himself close enough to hear his sister's boyfriend.

"So, what did the great tech wizard have to say about the PackNet breach?" Dolan asked Channing.

"You don't have to be so sarcastic about it, Dolan," Channing replied defensively.

"Sorry, Baby, I didn't mean to be." Dolan leaned down and kissed her lightly. Dan had to suppress the urge to growl. "There's a rumor he's got some kind of techie Fae guru working with him. Is the guy any good? Did you get a look at him?"

"The guy is a female," Channing said with asperity.

"Yeah, really? Have you seen her? It's hard to believe the Fae would let some chick learn about computers."

Channing huffed. "Dolan, I can't believe you just said that. I thought you were more enlightened. You keep telling me you're not like your father, but…"

"Hey, I didn't say I thought like that, but I do know something about the Fae. They are some of the ones who aren't known for their enlightened views—particularly not when it comes to technology." Dolan leaned over and kissed her lightly on the cheek. "I promise, I'm not like my father."

"I know, and that's just one of the things I love about you." Channing returned the kiss. Dan had to hold his wolf under tight control—always harder when he was in wolf form. He really wanted to force Dolan's hands—and mouth—off his sister.

"Let's go back to your place, and I'll show you just how I feel about you." Dolan put his arm around Channing's waist and began to turn her toward her car when he was stopped by someone calling his name.

Dan crouched down, hoping he wouldn't be noticed. The last thing he needed was for his sister to find out he was spying on her boyfriend.

"Hey boys," Dolan said now as three of the young men who had done the most heckling during the meeting came up to him. "What did you think of the meeting? Get all your questions answered? You all know Channing, don't you? She's Hank Bertrand's granddaughter."

The three younger men acknowledged Channing respectfully, then turned back to Dolan.

"I'll wait for you at the car," Channing said, and headed off.

"You shoulda been in there, man," one of shifters said to Dolan as Channing walked away. Dan recognized the voice as Anthony, one of the young men who'd been doing a lot of the jeering from the back of the room. "We gave it to those old dudes real good. Legato thinks he's got real big brain energy. But if so, then why did PackNet get hacked so easy?"

"Boys, boys, go easy on the guy," Dolan said.

Hmm. Maybe Dolan was on their—well, Channing's side, Dan thought. He'd been decent at the bar a few weeks ago. He didn't want to alienate Channing, but he couldn't help being suspicious of the heir to a pack that had always considered themselves superior to his own. He continued to listen, hoping to hear something that would definitely put Dolan in the "good enough to date my sister" category.

"So... do you think Gabe practices his speeches in the mirror, or does he just wing it with that much cringe?" Dan recognized Jax, one of Tim Means' younger boys, and brother to Isaac, the oldest son who Tim was not-so-subtly pushing as the next Alpha of Bertrand pack.

"There's a Notes app monologue in his phone. You know there has to be," said Anthony.

"With bullet points and dramatic line breaks." Dan didn't recognize this voice.

"Mica, you seem... unconvinced by the leadership." Dolan identified the third speaker for Dan. He'd seen him running around with the other two at various pack events. He wasn't a bad kid, but he definitely had an Omega personality: a follower, not a leader.

"Look, I respect the hustle," Anthony shrugged. "But if Legato's our first line of cyber defense, we're one bad meme away from total collapse."

"Hank called this fancy elf tech guru a 'computer whisperer,' like that's even a thing." Jax' joke had all the boys laughing.

"Show some respect boys, that's Alpha Bertrand to you," said Dolan. Dan would have applauded the sentiment, except for the subtle undertone of snark behind the words. Just what was Dolan up to?

"Yeah, yeah, that's what my dad always says," said Mica.

"Maybe these elf dudes know more than Gabe," added Anthony.

"You mean like they're actual experts?"

"Or at least someone who doesn't think 'reboot' means kicking the server."

"I always value initiative; thanks for keeping me informed. It's good to have sharp minds watching from the shadows." Dolan slapped the boys' backs. "Let me know if you hear anything else interesting. I need to get back to my lady."

Dan stayed in the bushes, thinking, until long after everyone had cleared out of the yard. Dolan had definitely been egging on the younger members of the pack. But he couldn't have been so successful if the seeds of discontent weren't already there.

Had his family become too complacent? Had they started to take for granted that they would always lead the pack, just because their several-times great-grandfather had founded it? He needed to check in with his brother Tyler. He was closer in age to Anthony, Jax and Mica.

And what about Channing? Dolan was obviously using her. Wasn't he?

Part Two
Revealed

CHAPTER 27

The moon was waning when the two figures met again on the bank of the Rivelou River. There was a hint of autumn in the air this time, the dank odor of the river overlaid with the crisp scent of autumn leaves and the hint of wood smoke from a firepit some non-paras had set earlier in the evening to roast marshmallows.

That wasn't the only difference between this meeting and the last. A third figure approached them slowly, a flashlight wavering in the late-night dark as he stepped deliberately on the uneven ground.

"Why in hell did we have to meet out here, McTier?" the person groused as he came up to them. "Couldn't you have found someplace where we would be less likely to break our necks?"

"Hush, you idiot. Don't you know there are ears listening everywhere?" the first figure spoke in a hissing, evil voice.

"What do you mean? I own this side of the river. And before long, I'll be in charge on the Rivelou side, too."

"You didn't tell me he was a fool," the first figure said to Dolan McTier.

This time, unlike that night in August, it was McTier who was calm, his companions both nervous and jittery. "He may be a fool, but he's done what we needed."

"Hmph!" snorted the other. "He's framed the wrong Bertrand. I want my son to suffer. I don't care about the other one—or all your machinations."

"Patience, these things take time. Isn't that what you told me when we were here before?"

"I don't know what the hell you two are talking about, and I don't care," said Sheriff Walker. "I want Alexander Fontaine's body, and you told me you knew where it was."

The sheriff jerked his chin toward McTier, who

suppressed a sigh. Working with these two was becoming very boring. But he was unwilling to anger either one right now. He still needed them if he wanted to pull off his plans. Both were so eager to claim their own victories they could not see past the ends of their noses.

"If we all work together, we will get what we want," he said soothingly.

"I don't know what she wants, and I don't care," Walker said belligerently, pointing at the older woman who stood next to McTier. She was gaunt, her clothing disheveled, and she looked as if she had been ill. The cane she carried suggested to Walker that she was crippled in some way. He discounted her immediately and wondered why McTier was bothering with her. "I want to find Fontaine's body and prove Dan Bertrand murdered him. Then I can destroy that damn arrogant Luther Anderson and get myself appointed chief in Rivelou."

"What either of you want is only important if it helps me get my revenge on my children—the ones who did this to me." She gestured to herself.

Walker didn't know exactly what she meant and didn't care. He dismissed her and turned to McTier. "And what is all this crap about witches and wizards? Why'd you have to blindside me with that stupid influencer? He said the word "influencer" as if he'd uttered the vilest of curses. "I've had nothing but ridiculous calls ever since. First from more reporters, now from people who think their neighbors are witches and vampires. What the hell is wrong with these people? And don't deny it. I know it was you, McTier, who started all this nonsense. And why the damn fake body? It would have worked just as well if it had been Fontaine—and I could have kept Bertrand under arrest."

The woman threw back her head and laughed. "An unbeliever! Dolan, you didn't tell me. How delicious."

"I figured you could show him some things, Beatrix. Make his day."

Still chuckling, the woman lifted her arms to the heavens, whispering words neither Dolan nor Walker could make out.

There was a disturbance in the air. The two men heard a fluttering sound as if hundreds of birds were flying over their heads. Walker put his hands up and ducked. "What the hell! It's crows." He batted his hands in the air. "Keep them off me!"

Beatrix only laughed. The night grew even blacker as the birds blocked out what dim light the dying moon had given them. Then as quickly as they had come, the birds were gone.

"There!" Beatrix pointed to a spot several yards away. The earth was disturbed as if some animal had been pawing at it. "Send someone to 'discover' this tomorrow, and you will have the body you need."

"Ah, yes," said Dolan in a voice filled with satisfaction. "We have them now."

CHAPTER 28

Channing pulled up at Ana's front door the following Saturday morning. All of her sister's bridesmaids, along with her and Ana's mother, were getting together to try on the bridesmaids' dresses that had just arrived. As she got out of the car, she saw her sister's ex-husband, Jonathan, storming down the porch steps. Ana hurried after him. "Jonathan you can't do this to Sophie. It's not fair to her."

Wondering what the irritating man was up to now, Channing got out of the car and walked over. Was she being nosy? Yeah. But if the pair were going to bring their business out to the sidewalk, Channing figured it was fair game.

"You're a werewolf! Damn it, I was married to a... a... monster."

"We call ourselves shifters, not werewolves." Channing couldn't resist. She'd never liked the man. He was pompous, he'd treated Ana abominably, and he used Sophie as a photo prop for his political ambitions. He only wanted her around when it was convenient.

Both Ana and Jonathan turned to glare at her. She held up her hands and backed off a few feet, still close enough to hear and intervene should her sister need help.

"You cannot keep Sophie from seeing her baby brother. It'll just kill her. She loves Baby J." That was what Jonathan and his second wife, Melanie, called their three-month old baby, Jonathan Jr.

"I can, and I will. She's dangerous. She can't be around a baby. You saw what she did in there!"

"She's not dangerous. Your daughter just shifted to show you the truth of what she is. She's always wanted you to know. She's proud of her abilities."

"Proud! Proud! She's a monster. You're a monster. The whole damn lot of you. And if you come near me or my family again..."

"Sophie is your family."

Channing noticed that Leslie and Joe, Ana's neighbors and good friends, had come out on the porch. Pretty soon other neighbors would be popping their heads out to see what all the commotion was about.

"Guys, guys," she stepped forward cautiously. "I think you need to wrap this up or take it inside. You don't want to air the dirty laundry—or wolf skins—in public do you?"

They both looked up, and Channing nodded toward the neighbors.

"Ana, you'll be hearing from my lawyer. We'll be taking a look at the child support payments. I won't support a monster." He jerked open the door to his BMW, slid in and slammed it, then gunned the motor and raced down the street.

"Come on, Honey, let's get inside," Channing said to Ana, putting an arm around her shoulders.

"I don't know what Joe and Leslie are going to think. Will they still let Sophie be friends with Emily?"

"I hope so," Channing said as she ushered Ana into the house. They'd been such good friends to Ana and Sophie, but who knew now that all their secrets were out in the open. "Tell me what happened before Mom gets here."

Inside they found Sophie crying on the sofa; Ana's fiancé, Chris, was comforting her. "You know he'll relent, Sophie, he was saying as he patted the girl on the back. "He loves you. He's just in shock."

"I shouldn't have... shouldn't have..." the girl hiccupped.

"Well, you probably did shock him a bit." Chris couldn't keep the amusement out of his voice. To know Jonathan was to disdain him, and Channing was sure that Chris had suffered quite a few digs by Jonathan in an effort to keep the peace for Sophie's sake.

"So Sophie, I understand you came out of the closet to your father, full claws and fangs," Channing said, trying to keep the atmosphere light and bring a smile to the girl's face.

"And he wasn't happy about it," said Ana. "I'm going to get us some coffee and let Sophie tell you all about it."

At that moment, the doorbell rang and Shannon, Chris' sister and also a bridesmaid, opened the door and came in.

"Hi, I saw Jonathan driving like a bat out of hell down the street," she said. "If I weren't off-duty and walking, I'd have taken great pleasure in giving him a ticket." Shannon and her boyfriend, Dave Thorne, were both officers in the Rivelou Police Department.

Sophie gave a strained laugh. "I wish you had Aunt Shannon."

"He deserved it," said Channing.

"Wow, apparently I missed a lot this morning."

"I only got here in time for the end; I was about to hear the rest of the story."

"Ana, why don't I make the coffee, and you tell the girls about your morning," Chris said. As he stood up, Channing caught her breath. He looked ill. He was thinner, his face pale and gaunt. She knew he had been injured a few weeks ago, but she'd never heard exactly what happened. She'd assumed he'd recovered. Had he looked this bad at the pack meeting, and she had just not noticed? She had been at the back of the room, more interested in leaving quickly after the meeting to see Dolan than in sticking around to talk to family.

Chris headed to the kitchen to make the coffee. "Is he alright, Ana?" she asked quietly.

"He's going to be fine," Ana said in a voice that made it clear there was no discussion on the matter. "Shannon, did Dave come up with any new ideas to try?"

"Not yet, Honey. He's spending every free minute researching the curse, and so have I. I'm trying to remember anything my mo…" She stopped herself and looked over at Channing. "Well, let's just say we're trying everything we can think of."

At that moment the front door opened again. "Yoohoo, anybody home?" their mother's voice rang out. "I've got Monica with me, and we're ready for some pre-wedding fun." Channing and Ana rolled their eyes at each other.

As they noisily greeted each other, Chris came in with a tray of coffee cups. "This is my cue to leave you ladies by yourselves." He kissed Ana. "Honey, I'm meeting your brothers for a tuxedo fitting. Let me know when it's safe to come home."

Chris left, letting the final member of the bridal party in as he went out the door.

"Oh Ana, I'm so sorry I haven't called you all week." Monica rushed to hug Ana. "I can't believe everything they're saying about your family. It's just horrible for people to make up stuff like this. And the ones who believe it! I can't imagine how ridiculous they are. You know everyone who knows you has your back, don't you?"

The other women stared at Monica in disbelief. The breach of PackNet and the outing of paranormals had been the only thing on the local, national, and world news for days. There had been interviews with prominent celebrities—both paranormal and non-paras—on their opinions on the subject. Videos were all over the internet of witches performing magic, shifters demonstrating how they changed into wolves or bears or eagles. Even vampires were coming out of the closet and showing off their fangs.

The hotels were booked solid in New Orleans and other cities with reputations as paranormal hotspots. And of course, given that this was where the news had broken, Rivelou was packed with journalists, both from the mainstream media and influencers and podcasters. Delaney Dark's following had grown to 100,000, and she had been hired as a special contributor on one of the cable news channels. There were rumors that Dan Ackroyd would film an episode of his paranormal television show from the Rivelou Courthouse, where a ghost of a murdered Civil-War-era bride had been sighted often throughout the decades.

And Monica, the queen of local gossip, friends with everyone in the most prominent shifter family, didn't believe a word of the juiciest scandal the town had ever seen.

Donna recovered first. "Oh, Monica, I always knew I liked you," she said, prying her off Ana. "You have such a good head on your shoulders. I knew we could count on you not to believe some silly rumors."

Channing's mouth hung open. This day couldn't get any

stranger, and it wasn't even 10 a.m. yet. Her mother, for once in her life, was saying all the right things. She'd settled Monica on the sofa with coffee and cookies. "Now, let's forget all of this nonsense and just focus on the wedding. It's only six weeks away, and we have to make sure everything is perfect."

They spent the next hour trying on their dresses, a deep, coppery velvet, perfect for an autumn wedding. The ceremony would be outdoors under the full moon, so the sleeveless gowns were complemented with faux fur shawls in a silvery grey that closed with a glittering silver moon pendant at the throat.

"The way the material shimmers in the light—it looks absolutely magical. And the fur shawls look so real," exclaimed Monica. "Are you sure…"

"Of course," Ana said. "I'd never condone killing an animal for its fur."

Sophie, who would be a junior bridesmaid, had thoroughly enjoyed trying on her dress and had recovered from her encounter with her father. She hid her face in the sofa cushions trying not to giggle. Of course, shifters were taught to respect all animals, that didn't mean in their wolf form they didn't have the occasional… snack. Channing gave her a light smack on her thigh. "Sophie, behave!" she whispered.

"Mom, Emily texted. She wants to know if I can come over."

"You're sure it's okay with Joe and Leslie?" Ana asked.

"Yes, Emily says her mom said to tell you specifically that I was invited."

"See, your friends will stick by you. And when all this supernatural nonsense dies down, things will just go back to normal," Monica said as she got up to leave. "Sophie, I'll walk out with you."

CHAPTER 29

As Monica closed the front door, Ana collapsed into one of the armchairs. "I'm exhausted. I felt like I couldn't talk about anything in front of Monica. It was so much more difficult than before the breach. Then, no one noticed if a shifter joke was made. Now, everything anyone says seems like it's a double entendre."

"Here, Dear, let's get you something to drink. I think we all deserve cocktails with our lunch," said Donna. She gave her daughter a concerned pat on the shoulder, then went to the kitchen to make Old Fashioneds for all of them as Shannon and Channing brought out the salad that Ana had ready for lunch.

"You know this whole PackNet breach reminds me of stories my grandmother used to tell of the Shifter War," Donna said, as they sat down in the living room with their salads and cocktails.

Channing stiffened. "Oh, Honey, don't worry." Donna nodded to her younger daughter. "I know the McTiers and Betrands were on opposite sides, but it's ancient history now, and it's got nothing to do with you and Dolan dating."

"I'm pretty sure Grandpa doesn't see it that way—not to mention Dan."

"Your father would tell me not to say this, but sometimes I think Hank, and Ida too, spend too much time worrying about the old days. This happened before they were even born—if you can believe that. And they are still holding a grudge."

"So what happened?" asked Shannon.

"You've never heard this story?" Donna asked, taking another large gulp of her Old Fashioned. "I'd have thought sure your mother would have taught you paranormal history—especially since your family was involved, too."

"What do you mean my family was involved? I've never heard anything about werewolf wars."

"Well the Callich Coven was definitely a part of it," Donna said. Callich was Shannon's mother's maiden name. "Now don't roll your eyes at me, girls," she added, looking at each of her daughters. "It's history, not gossip. And if Shannon's mother didn't tell her how her own flesh and blood was involved in some very important events in paranormal history, then someone should. And you should know, too, Ana, since it's part of Chris' ancestry. And if you two have children it will be part of theirs. You are planning to give me more grandchildren, aren't you?"

"Mom! Let me get through the wedding first," Ana protested.

"Well, that would be better than the last time, I suppose."

Ana and her first husband Jonathan had eloped when Ana realized she was pregnant with Sophie.

Donna, as usual, was getting way off the track. "You know, Ana and I aren't the only ones who can give you grandchildren, Mom," Channing said, thinking of her suspicions about Dan's girlfriend.

"Well, I'm sure Tyler and Winnie are much too young for that," Donna said. "And Winnie's such a good girl."

"Mom! I was Winnie's age when I had Sophie."

So back to the story, Mom." Channing wanted to push her back on that track. She wasn't sure about Kathleen, anyway, and it was more likely Ana would get angry, or their mother would start questioning Channing's plans on supplying her with grandchildren. Plus, she did want to hear more. She vaguely remembered learning about the Shifter War from her days as a young Were Scout, but she didn't really recall much about it.

Donna settled herself more comfortably on the sofa. "So the Shifter War happened in the 1920s. Rivelou was just a small town back then. The Bertrand pack already had a firm grasp on the shifters in the town although the other paranormals were not as friendly to us as they are today. That is something Hank has accomplished." Donna nodded her head in gracious acknowledgement that her father-in-law had done at least one thing she approved of.

"At the same time, the McTiers were consolidating several smaller packs over in the Lexington area. It's only a few hours away from Rivelou, and it was becoming obvious that if the McTiers wanted more territory, they were going to have to make a move on Rivelou." Channing must have made some gesture or expression because her mother stopped and turned to her. "Now, Channing honey, I'm not trying to make out that your boyfriend's family was to blame. But everyone knows they made the first move.

"They began moving their pack closer and closer to the Bertrand territory. They were merging—well some said taking over by force—smaller packs in the area, expanding their reach. They even started to move in right across the river in Herndon County.

Channing swallowed wrong and began to cough when her mother mentioned the McTiers had moved into Herndon County a hundred years or so ago. Ana quickly got up and brought her a glass of water, which she accepted gratefully as their mother continued.

"There were a lot of smaller packs over there at the time; they were either wiped out, moved away, or joined our pack at the end of the war. There are no shifters there now—in fact very few paranormals of any kind. As the McTiers expanded, they were making it more and more difficult for our pack. And then, to top everything off, the Callich Coven got involved. They were notorious dark witches even then, Shannon."

Donna nodded at Shannon as she said this, and Channing had a fleeting moment of being glad that Shannon was coming in for the same matter-of-fact treatment of her past as Channing was about her boyfriend's family. Sometimes her mother was clueless about people's feelings, but in this case maybe that, "Nothing personal, I just tell it the way I see it," attitude actually made things a bit better.

"When you call it a war, Donna, just exactly what do you mean?" asked Shannon.

"Oh, I mean a war. Bloody battles. Good wolves killed and maimed. Women captured and taken. It was the 1920's after all, and there were a lot more uninhabited areas between here and Lexington. There was plenty of room for pitched battles between shifters that the non-paras never even knew about. At any rate, with the dark coven on the McTier side, the Bertrands were losing—badly. That's when the Fae came to our aid."

"The Fae!" Mom, I never heard that," said Ana.

"Yes, the Fae helped us out."

"I never knew there was a whole coven of witches related to me. I thought it was only my mother," said Shannon.

"Yes, and that's because of the Shifter War. By the end of it, most of the witches who sided with the McTiers were dead. They specialized in blood magic, necromancy, and forbidden rituals. And the Fae just couldn't stand that. You do remember something from Were Scouts, don't you?" Donna asked disapprovingly of her daughters. "I was your leader. I taught you all of this when I made sure you both got your Paranormal History badges."

"It was a long time ago, Mom," said Ana.

"Yes, and Sophie doesn't attend regularly. I'm going to have to make sure she learns this."

Ana took a deep breath, ready to argue again, but Channing gestured for her to be quiet. "I want to hear this, Ana."

"Thank you, Dear," said her mother, settling in her chair as if for a long lecture. "Now, as I was saying, you should remember from your lessons that the elves—or the Fae—are the guardians of the Old Magics. They balance the realms. While we live here in the human realm, they prefer to live in Otherworld. They guard the boundaries between the mortal world and the supernatural Veil.

"Dark magic, by its very nature, pulls energy from the suffering of others. When the McTiers invited dark magic practitioners into the shifter war, the Fae saw it as a red flag— not just a political alliance but a supernatural threat. 'One does not plant a rotted vine and expect the garden to thrive.'"

"Mom, that's so corny."

"I didn't make it up. It comes straight from *Claw, Elm, and Charm.* The compendium of the wisdom of elves, witches and shifters was Donna's bible. She quoted from it often. "There's a lot you can learn from it." She looked around at all three younger women. "The McTiers obviously haven't. If they'd read that book, they wouldn't have taken up with dark allies. You think I'm being silly, but until the McTiers joined with the Callich coven, the Fae just watched. They didn't want to get involved. They're very clannish, you know, and never want to get involved with any of the other races—unless it is something that benefits them."

"Well, this time they had to step in. The dark magic the McTiers and the Callich coven unleashed was causing the veil between the realms to thin. It had happened before, and they knew the consequences if they didn't do something.

"We Bertrands had not used dark magic. Now, I'm not going to tell you our pack are saints; you all know by now we aren't, but there is something we have never abided, and that is dark magic. We keep to the older shifter traditions."

"Older shifter traditions? Dolan is always saying we're the ones who don't hold to the old ways," said Channing.

"Don't let Dolan tell you that," said Donna. "Old is relative. And whose old are we talking about, anyway? We are an old race, but the elves are even older. They wouldn't officially 'join' our side in the Shifter War. They consider themselves above all that kind of thing. But they did supply support. They gave us enchanted weapons and wards to protect us from breaches. But after it was over, they withdrew; they wanted nothing more to do with such warlike creatures as shifters."

"But we aren't..." Ana started to say.

"Oh yes we are, Dear," her mother stepped in. "I know we don't like to think of ourselves that way—and your grandfather has gone a long way to finding more civilized ways to deal with conflicts and challenges. But at heart we are wolves. We are fighters. The elves understand this. They respect the Bertrand pack, and they've kept the alliance with us. But we aren't friends. I don't think anyone has seen an elf in Rivelou for almost a hundred years."

"But that's not what I heard," Shannon interrupted.

"There were elves at The Night Crawler just the other weekend. They talked to Dan and Gabe. Jake Waseaux told me about it. He and Abby were there getting dinner, and they saw it all. Jake said they offered to help Gabe fix the PackNet breach."

"They must really be worried that the PackNet problem will allow humans to enter their realm because from what you say Mom, they wouldn't be here for anything less," said Ana.

"You're right, dear. They have to be worried there is still an alliance between the McTiers and a dark witch. The Callich coven was destroyed except for one or two people. Your mother, Shannon, was one of the last."

Channing had gotten very quiet.

"Elves understand that when dark magic is unchecked it can fracture the veil that protects the seven realms, allowing the horrors of the Underworld to enter both our domain and Otherworld. We've seen it before. You do remember your lessons on The Sundering?"

"Wasn't that when the worlds were torn apart, separated into the seven realms?" asked Shannon.

Donna gave her a big smile, as if she were a particularly dense pupil who had finally gotten an answer correct. "That's right, Dear. The Sundering is what shaped our worlds as they are today. Some of us, the witches, shifters, and others who could pass as human, stayed with the non-paras here in the human realm to protect them—although you would never think it from the way they act. Of course, most of them forgot us over the centuries, or began to think of us only as myths and legends.

"But *our* history tells us the war was started when a group of witches realized the additional power they could attain by using dark magic. And who better to steal from than the most powerful of us all—the elves. That's when a Callich ancestor entered the Fae realm and attempted to entrap a High Fae Lord. His name was Lirael Thorne. And though the attempt failed, the witch carved a rune of binding into his soul, leaving him scarred and broken."

"Thorne? You mean like Dave?" asked Shannon.

"Well, yes, I believe David does have some Fae blood."

"And my ancestors... They... some witch... carved a

rune into his… soul?"

"Well, Dear, it was a long time ago. You can't be held responsible for something your ancestors did."

"I know, but this…" She glanced over at Ana who was also perking up. "Maybe this is how we cure Chris."

"I'm not sure what you mean, Dear," Donna said. "What's wrong with Chris? I know he didn't look well today, but is it more than just a little early flu?"

"You didn't know about the attack, Mom?" asked Ana.

"I haven't heard anything either, except that someone said Chris was attacked. What exactly happened?" Channing jumped in.

"It was when Chris and Gabe went out to make sure there was no evidence of Alexander's body left. They were attacked by something—or someone. A spell was cast on Chris. You didn't hear this? It's what happened the night Dan was arrested—the second time that is." The irony was clear in Ana's voice.

"And you say in this legend there was a rune carved on his soul? Do you know any more?" Shannon asked anxiously.

"Not legend—history," Donna said sternly.

"Was there a physical manifestation?" Shannon's voice sounded hesitantly hopeful.

"Why yes, there was a brand on his chest. A bird of some kind."

"I have to go talk to Dave right now," Shannon got up and left.

"Before you go, Shannon, remember, you can't talk to anyone about this except Dave. No one else can know. Channing, Mom, I mean it; you can't tell anyone." Ana reminded them.

"Of course I wouldn't tell anyone," said Channing.

CHAPTER 30

Kathleen woke up relaxed and turned into the warm strength of Dan next to her in bed. It wasn't often that he spent the night even though they'd now been seeing each other exclusively for a month.

Morning light filtered through the window, golden and soft. His arm draped across her, heavy and possessive, as his hand tightened his grip around her waist, then moved slowly up to caress her breast. She sighed and stretched like a cat—or wolf—pushing back on his delicious hardness.

"You're awake," he murmured, voice thick with sleep and something darker. Deeper. He growled low, nuzzling into the crook of her neck, inhaling deeply. "You smell like mine."

"That's because I am."

"My mate. Are you ready for that?"

"I…I think so…"

He shifted, rolling her onto her back, bracing his weight on his elbows as he hovered over her. "That didn't sound very sure."

She lowered her eyes. "I'm just afraid."

"Of what? Of me? I'd never hurt you. You don't believe all the stuff they're saying about me on the internet, do you?"

She heard the hurt in his voice and tried to reassure him. "Of course not. The rumors really have gotten ridiculous. I could never believe three quarters of the stuff they're saying— remember, I'm a wolf, too. I know you don't eat babies for lunch every day."

"Yeah, only on Sundays, right?" he joked, then made sure to get the conversation back on track. "So if it's not the rumors, then what are you afraid of?"

Kathleen turned her head. "It's not you; it's me."

"Oh no. Please don't give me that excuse. It sounds like you're breaking up with me."

"Never. I just worry you'll want to break up with me."

She turned her head away and put her arm up over her face, shielding his gaze from hers.

"Kathleen, there is nothing you could tell me that could make me break up with you." He gently pulled her arm down. "You are my mate, remember. My fated mate. I knew it the moment I saw you—smelled you. Your scent intoxicated me."

"Promise me?"

"I'll do better than that; I'll show you." His dark eyes had a golden glint, the wolf close to the surface. He bent down and kissed her like he was starving, like every cell in him needed her. His mouth was rough but still reverent. Their bond pulsed, a tether of heat and hunger Kathleen felt even as she wanted to deny. Her wolf hummed, happily chiming in with *Let him claim you. Now. Then you'll be bonded and nothing else will matter.* Kathleen ignored the thought, arching into him, her nails dragging down his back. He groaned like it physically hurt to hold back.

"Dan," she breathed, wrapping her legs around his hips, "I need…"

"I know," he said, kissing down her throat, nipping gently where her pulse fluttered. "I know exactly what you need."

He moved with the confidence of a man who understood her body—and the desperation of a wolf who'd been dreaming about her all night. Each thrust was deep, deliberate, in sync with the rhythm of their bond. His hand slid beneath her thigh, lifting her to meet him harder.

The air was thick with heat, musk, and the unspoken words only mates understand. Their heartbeats pounded together. Her moans turned feral. His growls became words again—barely.

"You're mine," he said, biting gently where her neck met her shoulder. Not enough to break skin, not enough to call up the bond—but enough to remind her who she belonged to. "Only mine. Never forget it."

When they came, it was together, shaking and tangled, the connection between them thrumming like a live wire. Dan collapsed against her with a satisfied grunt, still buried inside her, breath coming in pants.

"You've ruined mornings for me now. If you're not here, I miss this," Kathleen said, brushing sweat-damp hair from his forehead.

"You're telling me I'm better than coffee?"

"So much better. And so much more addictive."

"Good," he murmured. "I want every morning to start with you under me."

They lay there silently for a few minutes, each engrossed in their own thoughts.

Finally Kathleen stretched. "We can't spend the entire day in bed even if it is the weekend."

"We could try," Dan said, turning to her and running his hands over her breasts. "Let's see if I can convince you.'

"Dan," she giggled. "No, you're tickling me. You can't be ready again this soon."

"That wasn't quite the reaction I was going for. But how about we compromise. Breakfast first, then a run, and then back to bed."

"That sounds like a plan. "I love seeing your wolf. You are so sexy." She ran her hand down to feel his hardness again. "So yes, let's go for a run. I could use some exercise."

***

An hour later they had hiked through the woods to an out-of-the-way spot Dan knew where they could strip and shift.

Dan was a black wolf, his fur as dark as his own hair with almost no color variation in his coat. Kathleen was a classic red wolf, with auburn hair that matched her natural coloring, fading to pale blonde behind her ears, down her legs and on her belly. Dan thought she was the sexiest thing he'd ever seen, and his wolf agreed, taking a few moments to nuzzle her fur behind her ear before they took off running. They took turns chasing each other and following the scents of the smaller animals who made their homes in the area. Kathleen surprised a family of deer sleeping in the afternoon sun, then took off running again in another direction, Dan following.

Suddenly she stopped.

What is it? Dan's voice in her head grounded her,

reminding her she was not alone. But what had she just heard?

I don't know. Someone is out here, too. I don't think they've seen us, but they are here.

You're sure? Dan held so still she almost couldn't see him breathe. He heard it then, too, and took a slow, silent step in front of her, protecting her from whatever danger was out there.

Kathleen growled softly. *I can take care of myself.*

She thought of her Uncle Brendan, the man who had taken her under his wing, despite his older brother's orders, and taught her how to fight, to hunt, and to survive without the help of anyone else. She always wanted to make him proud. He was the one who had encouraged her to go to college and had fought with his brother, her father, to make sure it happened. In fact, he was the only one in her pack who knew where she was right now. That was why this scent was so disturbing. It was definitely McTier. And it was *not* her brother. How many other shifters from her pack were here in Rivelou?

She moved cautiously forward, turning to make sure Dan was following her. He was as close as he could be without actually stepping on her tail. She slunk down. She could hear sounds now, the murmur of voices. They weren't that close. In wolf form she could see and hear much farther than as a human.

Nose to the ground she followed the scent. She didn't want to get close enough that they would scent her, also. They would recognize her as quickly as she had them. Luckily, she was upwind. She continued to silently close in until she could make out the voices more clearly even though with the trees in the way she could not yet see them.

"As soon as Fontaine's body is found, we'll have what we want."

That was Ric's voice. She knew it well. He'd been her brother's best friend for as long as she could remember.

"And when will that be?" Another voice she recognized, Sean. He was a little younger than she was, not to mention her brother, but he'd always hung around trying to ingratiate himself with the son of the pack leader.

"I'll give it a week to let some hiker stumble on it by

chance. If it doesn't happen then, I'll set something up."

"Wait! Did you hear that?" Sean hissed.

Kathleen stopped moving, stopped breathing. She could feel Dan behind her pause, too.

"Someone's out there. We'd better make sure they can't tell anyone what they heard."

CHAPTER 31

At that, Kathleen turned and fled as fast as she could. Uncle Brendan always said the wise wolf knew when to stand and fight and when to run. Now was the time to run. Dan followed her, running just as quickly. He could easily have overtaken her, she knew, but he kept to her flank, a rearguard protection.

Finally, they stopped near a small stream that led to the river. Kathleen stepped in, rolling in the water, enjoying its cool wetness. Dan did the same. They walked on in the stream, using it to cover their scents, and followed it to as near as they could get to where they had left their clothes. They quickly changed, neither of them speaking until they were back at Dan's car.

"Did you hear what they were saying?" she finally asked when they were back on the road to town.

"Yes. They know where Fontaine's body is, and they are going to make sure it is found," Dan said harshly. "Do you have any idea who it was?" he asked her. "I thought for a moment you recognized them."

"No. No," she said quickly, and looked out the side window, away from Dan. "I was just startled."

"Right."

There was a world of doubt in his voice, she thought. He had no proof she knew the pair. She'd only lived here a few months. Who would she know? That's what she'd say, anyway.

"Do you want to get something to eat?" he asked as they pulled out of the parking lot. His tone was conciliatory, and he put one hand on her knee.

"Sure, where would you like to go?"

"We aren't that far from Strawberry Moon,"

"Oh, I don't think so," she replied.

He looked over at her again. Her eyes were glued to the side window.

"You didn't like the food?"

"No… no… it's not that."

"Umm. I'd suggest Flannery's, but I might get arrested again—after what we just heard." He tried to sound snarky, but it just came out strained.

"I don't want that; you know I don't."

In the end, they headed out to the highway to one of the many chain restaurants, silently thinking their own thoughts. When they were finally seated in a booth and had ordered their meals, Dan brought it up again.

"You knew who they were, didn't you, Kathleen."

She looked away from him without speaking.

"Why won't you tell me? I thought you had my back."

"Can't someone have loyalty to more than one person?" she asked.

"Not to more than one pack. You know that."

"I'm not part of your pack. You haven't even taken me to a pack meeting yet."

"You know I've wanted to; it's just been an... unusual time."

"It doesn't have to be the perfect time; you keep saying I'm your mate—your fated mate. But you've never introduced me to anyone in your family. The only one I really know is Ana. What am I supposed to think?"

"Well, you did meet them all when I was arrested, didn't you?"

"Barely. They were a little too busy worrying about you being in jail to notice some shifter who'd just had one date with their son and grandson."

"Is that what this is about? You don't think they treated you well enough? I didn't think you were that kind of person."

"Dan Bertrand, you know full well that's not what this is about. It's about you... you say you want me as a mate but you're hiding me."

Kathleen couldn't meet his eyes, and Dan noticed it. "That may be part of what this is about, but there's more. You're keeping secrets from me, Kathleen."

She was about to respond when the waitress returned with water and iced tea for both of them. Kathleen thanked the waitress and made a show of fixing her tea.

"What aren't you telling me, Kathleen?" Dan asked gently, reaching a hand out to hers.

"What aren't *you* telling me, Dan? There's more to this Fontaine story than you're letting on. Why do you get angry at me for having secrets when you have your own?" She decided it was time to change the subject. "Do you think Fontaine's body was somewhere near where we were?"

"It could be. But they didn't exactly say that. If you know something…"

"Know something! Dan Bertrand, I'd never even heard of the man until I moved here."

"I meant about the men we heard."

Luckily, their meals arrived, and they were both saved from saying anything else, anything they would regret, for a few minutes. The silence lasted until they were almost done eating.

"Kathleen, I know this has been difficult," Dan started, reaching out toward her again. "I haven't wanted it to be. You probably won't believe this, but until a few weeks ago my life was simple. Then I met you and…"

"You know, considering what's been going on, trying to explain that meeting me has turned your life upside down doesn't seem very convincing."

Dan laughed. "How about you're the only good thing that's happened to me? Is that better? I hope so because it is the truth."

Kathleen smiled and reached for his hand.

"Well, well, well. If it isn't my little sister. And here you've been telling everyone that you're in Tennessee for the summer finishing up some classes."

Both Dan and Kathleen jumped at the familiar voice. They had been so absorbed in each other they hadn't noticed Dolan come in the restaurant with Ric and Sean.

CHAPTER 32

"Dolan! What are you doing here?" Kathleen tried to look surprised, Dan noticed, but she couldn't look anyone in the eye. Not himself, not her... brother... not the two McTier pack members who were now leering at her in a way that made Dan want to shift into his wolf and challenge them. He shook himself, trying to catch up with what was going on. Dolan and Kathleen had continued to talk in tones that got louder and louder the longer they went on.

"Kathleen, why don't you calm down," Dolan said in a patronizing voice. "We don't want the entire restaurant to know our business." He slid into the booth next to his sister, motioning for his friends to slide in next to Dan, effectively trapping him in his seat.

Dan seethed.

"So, *your* sister didn't tell me you were seeing *my* sister; I'm going to have to have words with her," Dolan said.

"Leave my sister out of this. In fact, just leave her alone altogether. Nothing could make me happier."

"And leave you to date—or is it mate—my sister? I've heard rumors the great Dan Bertrand, most sought-after bachelor in Rivelou, had been lassoed by a pretty face. I just never thought my sister qualified. But she's my sister, Bertrand. And you're not going to like what she's hiding."

Dan didn't know if he was angrier at Dolan right now for the insults he was throwing at Kathleen, or at Kathleen for managing to never mention that she was Dolan McTier's sister. That almost certainly meant her father was Michael, the head of the McTier pack.
Unless they had different fathers? Dan wanted to think the best of her that he could. Maybe she hadn't been raised as a McTier, after all. It happened.

"Why don't you introduce me to your friends, Dolan?" he asked now, motioning to the two shifters next to him.

"Oh, I think Kathleen knows them as well as I do, don't you, Kathleen?"

His comment made it clear that he'd read Dan's thoughts and was making certain Dan knew that Kathleen was very much a part of his pack.

"Dan, I'd like to go now," Kathleen said in a voice so low it was almost a whisper. She was wringing her hands and looking down at her lap.

"What? You don't want to stay and have a happy family reunion with your packmates?" he asked bitingly, still unsure of whether he was angrier at Kathleen or Dolan.

"N...no. Please. I understand you're upset with me, but this isn't the place to explain."

"Well, if not here, then where better, Kathleen?" asked Dolan. "Maybe I should just pick you up and take you home to Lexington and let our father deal with you."

It was very much a threat. And Dan didn't like it.

He threw some money on the table. "Excuse me, gentlemen, it's time for us to leave now," he said in an overly polite voice to the two shifters next to him.

Neither one moved, and Dan growled low enough that only the five people in the booth could hear him. He bared his teeth just slightly.

The pair looked to Dolan, who nodded. "Let him up, Ric... Sean," he said.

Dan stood, but Dolan made no move to allow Kathleen from her side of the booth. She pushed at him, but he wouldn't let her leave.

"I've got nothing left to lose, McTier. Everyone in town already knows I'm a feral wolf at best—maybe even a mad killer at worst. But what do you have to lose? What will your daddy say if you have a fight with me in a public restaurant? I notice your family haven't been mentioned at all in any of the PackNet leaks. You're still in the closet. Want to come out right now in a big way?"

He was baiting Dolan, but right now he was so angry he didn't care. What would Dan do if Dolan did shift right now, right here? *Don't worry. I can take him,* said his wolf.

That's not the point!

Dolan took a deep breath, and Dan could see that he was

fighting the urge to cast it all to hell and just turn wolf on Dan. Finally, he got himself under control.

"Kathleen, I'll be seeing you later, and we'll have a long chat about why you've lied to your pack leader and just what you're doing in Bertrand territory."

Kathleen scooted out of the booth and hurried past Dan toward the door.

"She doesn't have to see you if she doesn't want to, you know that, don't you, Dolan?"

"She's not a member of your pack yet, Bertrand. If she's called back to Lexington, she'll have to go."

There was nothing he could say to that. Dolan was right. Dan turned and hurried after Kathleen, who had already left the restaurant.

"I'll get an Uber," she said when he reached her. "I understand you don't want to see me anymore."

"You're right. At the moment, I don't even want to look at you, but I'm also not leaving you where your brother can get his claws on you. I can tell you're afraid of him. Besides, you owe me an explanation. Get in the car."

She bowed her head submissively and obeyed. Dan gritted his teeth. The gesture was so unlike the Kathleen he knew. It was as if seeing her brother had knocked all of the confidence out of her. It tore at him, but he tamped down the sympathetic thought. She'd lied to him. Could he ever trust her again?

He got in the car, slammed the door forcefully, and pulled out of the parking lot. Once they were on their way, he said, "All right, now tell me why you never bothered to mentioned your real name is McTier. Did your father send you here to seduce me?"

"No. Dan, no! It's just like Dolan said. My entire family thinks I'm still in Tennessee for the summer."

"And why should I believe you? How do I know that wasn't a big set-up just now, to gain my sympathy."

"You must really believe I'm a terrible person if that's what you think. Why would I do that? I've been trying to get away from my father and brother—not to mention his friend Ric—for most of my life."

"And you thought hooking up with the heir to the Bertrand pack was a good way to do it?"

"Who chased whom, I want you to remember? I went out of my way to avoid you. Particularly after Ana warned me you were a player."

"And that's another thing. You come to Rivelou and just happen to get hired for the job my sister was leaving. That's way too much coincidence."

"Well, you don't have to worry about me anymore. I'll be leaving town just as soon as I can pack."

Why did Dan suddenly feel as if he couldn't breathe? Kathleen couldn't leave. His wolf howled in his head. "Wait. What? Why are you leaving?"

"Because I don't want my father to find me. He'll drag me back home and force me to marry one of his lieutenants. It's done all the time."

"Not in my pack."

"And that's why I wanted to come to Rivelou. I'd planned for years to join the Bertrands as soon as I could. How did I know you all were going to have this crazy summer, and there would never be the right time for me to introduce myself to the pack?"

"I'm not letting you run away, Kathleen."

"But you don't want me anymore, Dan. Admit it. I disgust you now that you know I'm a McTier."

"I'm hurt, yes. I don't know if I'll get over it. But that doesn't mean I want you in the hands of Dolan McTier. My God, I don't want my sister associating with him, let alone my…"

"Your mate, Dan? You can't even say the word right now. I think it would be better for me to just go."

"No, if you run, they'll be looking for you. Maybe we can find a place to hide you."

"And have my brother challenging your pack for keeping me from him? That's a terrible idea."

"Then we'll hide you somewhere else. I'll take you to Shannon's. She's not a wolf; she's a witch."

"Okay, but can I at least get some of my clothes first?"

"You have fifteen minutes to get what you need. Then you are going into my Wolf Protection Program."

CHAPTER 33

Kathleen had giggled at the idea of a "Wolf Protection Program," but it wasn't too far from the truth. Or maybe it was actually a "Witch Protection Program," since the person who was guarding her was a witch.

When they got to her apartment, he was true to his word and gave her exactly fifteen minutes to gather some belongings. While he'd waited for her, he'd called Shannon to give her a heads up, then stood in Kathleen's doorway, tapping his foot impatiently until she brought out a small rolling suitcase. She stopped to grab her laptop and shove it inside. Dan watched silently, then took her suitcase and rolled it out to his car—ever the gentleman even when he was so mad she was surprised his claws and fangs weren't showing.

He put her suitcase in the back of his car, then walked around and held open the passenger door for her.

"I'll follow in my own car," Kathleen said.

"No. It's too dangerous. And you won't need it. You won't be going anywhere. Now get in."

"But…"

"Get in, or I'll tie you up and throw you in."

Looking up into his eyes, Kathleen knew he meant it. She shivered. His threat shouldn't make her belly tighten with anticipation. She should feel threatened, not excited. That's exactly how she would have felt if Dolan, or Ric, or Sean had said those words. But no matter how angry Dan was right now, he'd never hurt her. She got in the car.

He slammed her door shut, rounded his vehicle, and got in.

"Dan," she said in a quiet voice. "I need my car. I have to go to work. I can't lose my job."

"You can call in sick for a couple of days until we figure some things out."

"Okay," she said and waited a few moments, hoping

Dan would say something that would show her his anger was dissipating.

He stayed silent.

"Won't Shannon find it odd, your dumping me on her?" she ventured

"No."

She couldn't think of anything else to say to ease the tension between them, so they rode in silence until they arrived at Shannon's home, a rambling Victorian that was obviously being restored. Scaffolding was in place on the side of the house, where a couple of painters were working hard at scraping the old white paint off. The front of the house had been recently completed. It was painted a dark grey with its trim highlighted in reds and creams. A round turret on one side had a peaked roof that reminded Kathleen of a classic witch's hat. A pink climbing rose covered the porch railing, its blooms still vibrant in the autumn afternoon.

"It's beautiful," she said, getting out of the car and staring at the home.

"Shannon's spent a lot of time and energy on it. She's done as much of the work herself as she could," he told her as he got her suitcase out of the car and gestured for her to proceed him up the walk. "I wish those painters weren't here, though," he said. "I'd rather no one saw you come in."

As soon as he rang the bell, Shannon came to the door dressed in paint-spotted jeans and t-shirt and holding a brush in her hand. "Hey, come on in. Kathleen, I met you once at my brother's and Ana's engagement party, but I'm not sure you remember."

"Not really, no. I've met so many people since I moved here," Kathleen admitted. "Thanks so much for taking me in. I think Dan is worrying about this more than necessary but..."

"Hey, no problem. Better safe than sorry. Dan, do you want to stay for dinner?" Shannon asked.

"No, I need to go. Thanks, Shannon."

He turned and headed out the door.

"Wow. Dan can be intense, but that was a little awkward," Shannon said. "Let's go in the kitchen, and I'll clean up my paint for the day. Then you can fill me in on everything."

Kathleen followed her through the hallway, which had been recently wallpapered with a Victorian style motif of red roses on navy blue with a subtle pentagram pattern in the background. It was dark, formal, and just a little spooky—very suitable for a witch's home. The kitchen, however, was bright and modern, with white cabinets and granite countertops. The late afternoon sun shone in through big windows over the sink.

"This is so lovely, Shannon. And thank you so much for taking me in on such short notice."

"It's not a problem," Shannon said as she began washing her paint brush in the sink. "Dave's on duty tonight, and I'm off, so you can keep me company. He's still got his place out in the country, but he spends so much time here, he's thinking of offering it to his cousin Winnie. It was their grandparents' home, originally."

Shannon put her brush on the counter to dry. "Let's have some sweet tea and tell me all about it," she said, going to the refrigerator and pulling out a pitcher. "I'm from Chicago originally, but since moving here, I've adopted sweet tea as my official drink. It's good anytime of the day; and since it's getting close to five o'clock, we can add a little bourbon."

"That sounds wonderful. My mother..." Kathleen took a deep breath. "My mother always says sweet tea can fix anything." Tears came to her eyes as she thought about her mom.

"Dan didn't tell me much about what's going on. Just that you needed protection and to keep you out of sight. I take it whatever is happening has to do with your family?"

Kathleen nodded. "Yes, you see my last name isn't O'Connor. That was my mother's maiden name. My real last name is McTier."

"What! And so Dolan is your..."

"Brother. Yes."

"And Dan..."

"Didn't know this until this afternoon."

Shannon stood and gaped at her, the tea pitcher forgotten in her hand. She was silent for so long that Kathleen stood up and said, "If you want me to leave, I'll understand. I'll just get my things."

No! No, I'm so sorry. I just don't think I've been this surprised in years. That at least explains why Dan was acting so dark and growly."

Kathleen grinned at the description. "Yeah, I kept meaning to tell him, but somehow…"

"You just couldn't find the right words? I feel you, girl. Been there myself." Shannon poured the tea. "You're lucky Dan trusts me," she said handing a glass to Kathleen. "He doesn't hand people off lightly. Especially not people he…" She stopped, then sipped her own tea.

Kathleen arched a brow. "Not people he what?"

"Never mind." A flicker of something unreadable passed behind Shannon's eyes. "You've rattled him. That's rare."

Kathleen felt her stomach twist. "He barely spoke on the way over."

"He's scared." Shannon looked straight at her. "Not of you. For you."

Dolan's voice echoed in her ears, "She's my sister, Bertrand. And you're not going to like what she's hiding."

Kathleen sipped her tea and swallowed hard. "Am I safe here?"

Shannon's smile faded. She walked to the doorway and pressed her hand against a carved sigil in the wood. A shimmer of blue light ran through the grain, not just in the doorway, but Kathleen saw it travel across the wood in the hallway, and presumably the other rooms of the house.

"You're not just safe. You're now invisible to anyone I don't invite in. That includes wolves, witches, and anything in between."

Kathleen raised an eyebrow. "Even Dolan?"

Shannon's eyes glittered. "Especially Dolan. He reeks of dirty magic. I've met him once or twice. Someone's been teaching him tricks."

Kathleen opened her mouth to ask more, but the wards shimmered again, pulsing faintly against the quiet.

Shannon turned her head slightly. "Someone's trying to scry for you."

Kathleen's blood went cold. "What does that mean?"

"It means," Shannon said calmly, reaching for a small jar filled with powder the color of crushed sapphires, "we're not the only ones asking questions tonight."

CHAPTER 34

Dan called Connor as soon as he left Shannon's. He knew Gabe was working every minute on hacking issues, so he didn't even try him. They opted to meet at Flannery's, and when Dan arrived, he found Connor had already gotten a corner booth half-shielded by an old whiskey barrel turned planter. Dan was grateful for the shadows. He didn't want to be recognized. Not by other shifters, not by paranormals, not by non-paras, and definitely not by anyone asking questions about Alexander Fontaine.

Connor slid into the booth across from him and signaled the waitress with two fingers. "Whiskey. Two."

The waitress brought their drinks a moment later, and Connor raised his glass. "To poor decisions and the wolves who make them."

Dan didn't toast. He drank.

"You look like hell. Again," Connor said, leaning back. "Which means either the Fontaine mess just got worse, and you called me here for legal advice, or you finally had to admit your girl's got secrets."

"She's not..." Dan stopped. Swallowed. "It's complicated."

Connor snorted. "When is it not? Of course it's complicated. You're complicated. She's complicated. I'm the only one around here with a normal relationship, and I'm dating a woman who thinks it's fun to set things on fire with her mind."

"You're dating? Who? Since when? I thought you were still crushing on..." Dan stopped suddenly. He didn't want to let on that he'd figured out Connor's infatuation with his sister Ana.

"It's only been a week or so. We met online. After the breach."

"I take it she's a witch?"

"Yeah. She's not local. She lives in New Orleans."

"That's complicated."

"Nah, I think it makes it easier. We've only seen each other in person twice. But she can astral project, so we've had several dates."

"You call it a date when her actual body is in New Orleans, and you're here? How do you have sex?"

"Haha. I told you we've been together in person twice."

"And she sets things on fire with her mind?"

"Yeah, she's pretty good at it, too. Very controlled. I watched her light a campfire from twenty feet."

"And does this witch have a name?"

"Vivi."

Dan gave a short laugh despite himself. "You're kidding. Sounds more like an exotic dancer than a witch."

"Hey, watch it."

"Sorry man, I don't want to make fun of your girl."

"She's not my girl. We're just having some fun. It's not like we're fated mates or anything."

Connor suddenly looked bleak, and Dan felt bad that he'd teased him. He was a good guy. But happiness with women always seemed to elude him.

"We didn't come to talk about me," Connor said, signaling the waitress for another round. "Tell me what's going on with you and Kathleen. What's got you drinking here with me, rather than sitting cozily at home with her? If it's just that you've figured out she lied to you, don't forget you've been lying to her, too."

"I didn't lie," Dan said flatly. "I just didn't tell her everything. That's different."

Connor raised a brow. "Is it? Because the way I see it, you're sitting on a secret that involves a missing man, a river, and a hell of a lot of legal gray area."

Dan's jaw clenched. "She knows a lot more about that now than she did a couple of days ago. And besides, I didn't kill Fontaine."

"I didn't say you did."

Dan looked away, fingers drumming the edge of the glass. "Her secret was worse than mine."

Connor raised his eyebrows. "So *she* killed someone?"

"No, you ass. She's Dolan McTier's sister."

Connor stared at his friend for a moment, then slowly put his drink down on the table. "You've got to be kidding me. She told you this?"

"No We were sitting in a restaurant, and Dolan and two of his underlings came in. Dolan saw us and came over to taunt her."

"Taunt her?"

"Yeah." Dan sighed. "I don't know what else you could call it. Apparently, she's been hiding out from her pack.

"Wow. I really don't know what to say. And you believe her? That she was hiding from Dolan?"

"Yeah, I do. I think. I don't know. But she seemed damned scared of him, not to mention his two minions—Ric and Sean their names were."

"So, you just left her with her brother?" Connor's disapproval was clear.

"No, I did not leave her with her brother. I wouldn't leave my parrot with that ass. I took her back to her apartment, had her pack a few things, and brought her over to Shannon to protect her."

"That should be pretty safe. What Shannon doesn't know about magic, Dave does. But back to your secrets. What have you told Kathleen about Fontaine? If—and I don't really believe it—but if she is spying for the McTiers, she could have spilled everything to him before today."

"She knows he's dead. She doesn't know how he died."

"So, you told her half the story."

"Actually, no. McTier's wolves handled that for me. Kathleen and I went out for a run today, and we heard something in the woods. Turned out it was McTier's two minions, and they were talking about making sure that Fontaine's body is discovered. Said if it weren't found in a couple of days, they'd call it in themselves."

Connor slammed his glass on the table. "Damn it, man, as your lawyer, I've got to say, you sure really did bury the lead here. So McTier's pups know where Fontaine's body is stashed and plan to go public with it this week? Is there some way we can find it first?"

"You're planning some kind of *Weekend at Bernie's* reenactment?" It was the first time since Connor had gotten to the restaurant that he saw his friend grin. Connor didn't find it funny.

"No! I'm hoping to keep you and your sister out of jail!"

"Hey, keep your voice down. You talk any louder, and we won't have to wait for someone to find the body."

Connor ran his hand down his face in frustration. "Okay, so let me sum this up. Kathleen is either running in fear of her brother and the McTier pack, or she's a spy for them, and she's been reporting to Dolan everything she knows about you. Channing thinks she's in love with Dolan." Sarcasm dripped from his voice as he said the words "in love" while rolling his eyes. "Anything Kathleen hasn't told Dolan about our pack, Channing probably has. The McTiers have discovered Fontaine's body and plan to make sure Sheriff Walker gets hold of it soon. And half the shifters in Rivelou want to string up you, Gabe, and your grandfather because they blame you for the PackNet breach. Is that all we have to deal with?"

"Yep, that it," said Dan, holding up his glass and toasting his friend with it. "Cheers."

CHAPTER 35

Gabe blindly reached for the Pepsi can on the desk next to him, ran his hand across his face tiredly, and continued to plug in numbers. He shook his head as the screen blurred in front of him. He'd been working day and night for the past two weeks to repair the PackNet breach

Make that breaches. Every time they thought they had the damned thing secured another leak sprang up somewhere else. It was as if PackNet were suddenly made of Swiss cheese—holes and more holes wherever he looked. How had it been so secure, absolutely hack-proof for over fifteen years, and now had a breach at least every other day.

He ran his hands one more time through his already messy hair. He'd barely stopped to shower or shave in the last few weeks, let alone take time for a haircut. His dark locks, which he usually kept short, were now a mess of unruly curls, and his usually clean-shaven face sported the beginnings of a beard.

Ramona knocked on the doorframe of his office, walking on in even as she did so. She stopped to admire his rumpled good looks. He seemed so tired. She wished she could do something to help him. Rub the tension from his neck and shoulders or maybe take him to bed for a few hours to help him forget everything.

Of course, Gabe had never given her any indication that he thought of her as anything except a great software engineer. He'd never treated her any differently than any of the "other guys" on the team. As an employee, she appreciated that she got the same respect from her boss as Landon and Jace. He never discriminated, never treated her differently. As a woman, however, well... Gabe hadn't seemed to notice that she was a woman.

And now that elf girl was here. How was Ramona, merely a werewolf and a geeky one at that, supposed to compete with a damned Faery. Serelith "Call Me Sierra, It's So Much Less Formal" Virelyn was exactly what any red-blooded shifter computer nerd would go for. She should know; Jace and Landon had spent hours in the last few weeks telling Ramona everything they found sexy about the elf.

Sierra's long blonde hair was streaked with silvery blue that exactly matched her eyes—and turned Ramona's pale brown ones a deep shade of green every time she thought about her. Ramona was sure that it wouldn't matter how hard she searched the internet for that exact hair color, she'd never find it on the Garnier, Revlon, or Paul Mitchell sites. And not on any other human beauty site, either. That color was pure magic, and it had her coworkers panting. Not that they were allowed to get very close to her, with her "bodyguard" Theo Knight glued to her side every minute.

Ramona sighed. She had to admit Serelith—or Sierra—and her brother Kai knew their stuff. Not just the techno end of it either. They excelled in magical technology as well. They knew more than even Gabe's other staff member, Jessa Vance, about techno magic. And Jessa was one tech-savvy witch.

Sierra and Kai had been happy to share their knowledge with everyone. The problem was even the two elves couldn't figure out why the system was constantly breaching.

"Hey, I brought you a sandwich," Ramona said, stopping beside Gabe's desk. She wished she could lean down and kiss away the frown lines or just nibble on his neck for a moment. But she was just an employee.

"Thanks." He looked up and smiled at her. "What would I do without you to look after me?" He opened the paper wrapping and took a bite out of the sub. "Oh Lord, that's good. How did you know this was just what I needed?"

"Maybe because you eat a Wolfie Burger from 'Wich Witch almost every day?"

"What's not to like? Beef, lamb, and bacon—a growing wolf needs his protein." He stuffed another giant bite into his mouth and spoke around it. "Damn, this is good;

I guess I am predictable. I just wish we could predict whatever is going on with this software. I've never seen anything like it. I've got to fix it."

He put his sandwich down and took a deep breath. "This is all my fault, Ramona. Paranormals are being outed—they're being put in danger and all because of me."

"You didn't create this problem. Someone else did." She tentatively put a hand on his shoulder.

"But I'm the one who made the software. Convinced the entire paranormal world to use the damn thing. Now, Congress wants to start some investigative committee to 'explore whether paranormals are real.' Did you hear that yet?"

"I heard. Who are they going to call?"

"Well Hank, for one. So far, thank God, no one seems to know that Chief Anderson is a siren. And they're calling Sable Benoit."

"Wow! She's really famous. Winnie Thorne was telling me all about her the other day. She's Winnie's hero."

"Yeah, and she's been working the tourist trade in New Orleans for years. It wasn't any surprise she came out as soon as the breach occurred—and her site wasn't even hacked."

Ramona chuckled. "Well, at least someone is getting something good out of this. If it brings her business, more power to her."

"They're calling paranormals from throughout the United States—shifters, witches. Even a couple of vamps are being subpoenaed to testify."

"Well, that should be interesting."

"And they're calling Delaney Dark—our local 'expert' so she can get everything else about us wrong."

"Well, then what are we worrying about? Delaney Dark will give them so much misinformation, they'll be wearing garlic around their necks and waving crosses at us," Ramona laughed.

"Gabe! Gabe!" Sierra's voice rang out in the office. Her urgency had them up on their feet and out into the main office at once.

In the outer room everyone was crowded around the elf. Despite the note of fear in her voice, Ramona noticed how sexy she still managed to look in tight black leather pants and a white lace camisole. *Now is not the time, Ramona!*

Serelith's fingers danced across the projected interface on the screen, blue code scrolling faster than any human eye could follow.

"This isn't just corrupted data," she said as she narrowed her eyes at the string of obfuscated code. "This is a ghost."

CHAPTER 36

Sierra's brother Kailin leaned in, frowning. "Define ghost."

"Access logs that don't exist. Like someone's been inside PackNet and cleaned up after themselves—but not clean enough. I think they're getting sloppy. They've been running circles around us for so long they weren't as careful this time."

She isolated a pattern, an unregistered packet sequence embedded deep in the system's root. A vulnerability. One she hadn't seen before. One no one had.

"It's a Zero Day," Gabe whispered, watching her screen.

Kai straightened, the tension in his shoulders immediately evident. "That's impossible. Gabe, I know you would've accounted for…"

"He didn't. No offense, Gabe. No one could have predicted this," Sierra said. "No one. This flaw isn't in the source code. It's underneath it."

"You're saying someone found it before we even knew it was there?" Ramona asked.

"Not just found it. They used it." The elf's voice was low and grim now. "Someone's been siphoning PackNet from the inside. For weeks. Maybe longer."

"It can't be. No one could have gotten in. I used my Lock Hex Protocol charm," Jessa said defiantly. "No one can break that."

"But they did," said Sierra. "How else do you explain what happened?"

"I told you, no one…" Jessa began to argue when Gabe cut her off.

"We know you did your best, Jessa, and no one's blaming you. The only thing we need to do now is fix it." Gabe's exhaustion was evident as he sat down heavily in a nearby chair.

"How do we know they aren't the ones who 'broke' it in the first place," Jessa said defiantly, pointing her finger, long nails polished a glittering black studded with tiny silver stars, at

Sierra and Kai.

Theolin stepped smoothly in front of the other two elves. He didn't say a word. He didn't need to; his message was clear, "Make another move and feel my wrath."

Jessa put her hand down slowly, reminding Ramona of a TV suspect lowering her gun for the police.

"Chill, everyone." Gabe stood back up, his arms out to separate the two factions. "Just chill. Jessa, if they were the ones responsible for the breach, they didn't have to come here and point it out to us. They could have just kept on hacking us from Otherworld—or wherever the Fae keep their mainframes."

There was the tiniest hint of humor in Gabe's response. The first Ramona had seen from him in days. She didn't know whether to be grateful or angry that Sierra was the one responsible for the quick glint of humor in his eyes.

Kai reached out and placed his hand on Theolin's shoulder. "It's fine, Cousin. No one here is going to hurt us."

The dark-haired elf slowly relaxed his posture but kept his eyes on Jessa. "They could try—but they will not succeed," he said in a low voice.

"Humph." Jessa made a dismissive gesture and turned her back on the trio. "They don't know the half of what I can do," she muttered as she walked off.

"All right, if the drama is over, we need to shut this down—now. And make sure that no one can use it again," Gabe said, sitting back in the desk chair and rolling over next to Sierra at the computer.

"No. Not yet. Before we shut it down, we need to trace it," said Kailin. "If we don't, we'll never be sure who did it in the first place."

"Can you do that? Trace it before it does more damage?" asked Ramona.

Serelith nodded; she sat back down and turned to her keyboard, fingers flying again even as she spoke. "If this is what I think it is… it's not just code. There's magic layered in here."

Jessa reluctantly walked back over to watch as Landon put a comforting arm over her shoulders.

Sierra ran a quick scan, activating a code none of the

others had seen before. "What's that?" Landon pointed at her screen.

"It's an elven code designed to detect arcane residues. I developed it myself." Landon and Jace exchanged glances, obviously impressed.

As they all watched in silent anticipation, faint wisps of dark violet, almost like smoke, flickered across the screen.

"Shit! May their very marrow mold," Sierra cursed.

Ramona and Jessa exchanged surprised glances. This was a new side of the very elegant elf girl. They'd never heard her swear before.

"Is that…?" asked Kailin.

"Aetheric residue. Not elven—and definitely not natural."

"What the hell is aetheric residue?" Gabe ground out.

"It is magic from the ether—from the air," she explained, looking at the group gathered around her and choosing her words carefully. "And while that may sound like white magic, it is not. It is a particularly vile dark magic that uses nature—the very air around us—and turns it into dark energy. Someone has used an aetheric spell to detect the vulnerability in PackNet. And then exploit it."

"Beatrix Spier." Gabe spat the name out as if it tasted foul. "It can't be anyone else."

"I know she's a legendary witch, but I thought she had disappeared years ago," said Jessa. "Why would you think of her?"

"There's a lot more going on than I've told everyone," admitted Gabe. The four staff members muttered to each other at this statement.

"Look, there have been reasons I haven't filled you all in. Hank said it was need-to-know, and until now you didn't need to know."

"Hank's too damn tight with the information these days," said Landon.

Gabe looked at him sternly. "Hank is our alpha. We do what he says."

"He's not my alpha," said Jessa defiantly. "I'm not a

werewolf, and I don't follow him. Cassandra is the leader of my coven."

"Look, things have gotten to the point where all of you…" his glance took in the elves as well as the others in the room "…need to know everything that's been going on. And remember, I only found out some of this a few weeks ago. Until then, I was just as much in the dark as the rest of you."

CHAPTER 37

"I think you all know that Beatrix Spier is Chris and Shannon Spier's mother," Gabe said when he had everyone's attention. They were all now seated in office chairs, surrounded by their computers, coffee, or cans of pop in their hands.

"Say what!" said Jace.

"Where have you been, Jace. The name 'Spier.' Could be a clue they're related," don't you think?" Landon asked sarcastically.

"Well, I've got to say I never really thought too much about legendary dark witches until a few minutes ago."

Ramona gave him a light smack on the head. "Well, now you have, so listen up."

Gabe smiled at her. "Thanks, Ramona."

"This all starts about a year ago with Alexander Fontaine." Gabe quickly explained Fontaine's death and how Dan had been called in to help hide the shifter's car and body.

"Meek little Ana Dugan. I can't believe she had the gumption to kill Fontaine," said Jace, earning him another smack from Ramona.

Gabe ignored the interruption and continued. "Let's fast- forward a few months to the Artificial Witch murders. That's when Chris' sister Shannon and her boyfriend, Dave Thorne, got involved."

"Dave's a very well-respected witch." This time it was Jessa who interrupted.

"He's very knowledgeable for one so young," added Sierra.

"How do you know Dave?" Jessa asked.

"Even in the Otherworld we keep track of what is happening in this realm," she replied.

"Okay, guys, let's get back to the story," said Landon. "Gabe, please continue."

Gabe grinned and nodded his thanks. "As you know…"

Gabe looked over at the elves. "Shannon and Dave are with the Rivelou Police Department. They were part of the team investigating the murders. Chris, as a hunter, was also called in. On the night they captured the murderer, Shannon thought she saw her mom, Beatrix."

Jessa gasped and put her hand to her throat. "I thought she was dead."

"Well, so did Shannon, apparently. Because Shannon had used some type of magic on her—and no, I don't know exactly what—and walled her up in a basement, then left her for dead ten years before."

Theolin stood with his arms folded across his chest. "She should have known one so evil, and so steeped in dark magic, could not be killed that easily."

"She was very young at the time, Theo," Sierra said. "She would not have been at her full powers yet."

Gabe nodded. "And she was desperate to keep her mother from killing her brother, Chris. But what is important now is that last spring Shannon and Chris went back to Chicago to check on their mother's body. And it wasn't there."

Ramona gasped. "But what happened? How did she…?"

"We don't know all the details of how Beatrix escaped—probably never will. But at any rate, it became clear that not only had the witch escaped, she also had a hand in the murders here in Rivelou last spring. Fast forward to a few weeks ago when Fontaine's car suddenly appeared in the Rivelou River, and Dan Bertrand was arrested."

"But Dan didn't kill Fontaine, you said," Ramona asked, confused.

"You're right. But he did help hide the car—and his fingerprints were all over it. Luckily, there were a lot of witnesses who saw Dan driving the car before Fontaine disappeared, so the Herndon County sheriff couldn't hold him."

"Why do you bother with these human laws?" Theo asked. "If it had happened to one of us, we would just have disappeared the human sheriff and been done with it."

"Because we've chosen to live among humans, we have

to respect human laws," Gabe explained. "Without that, there would be chaos."

"Or at least we follow them when we can't get around them," Jace added with a grin. "I got a story or two…"

"Another time, Jace. Let me finish this. We don't know exactly what Beatrix' plan was, or is, but we think she wanted to target Chris and Shannon, and Dan got caught in the fallout. That means her plan isn't finished."

"Or," said Sierra, "she is working with someone who would like to see harm come to Dan and the Bertrand pack."

"That's another possibility. At any rate, Dan was worried that Fontaine's body would somehow turn up. He thought he'd hidden it in such a way that nature would finish it off, but after the car fiasco, he wasn't so sure. He asked me and Chris to see if the body—or what was left of it—was still safely hidden. We went out to look, and that's when another set of bones was found, and Chris was hurt."

There was muttering again. "I didn't know Chris was injured. What happened? Is he alright?" Ramona always worried about everyone.

"He's better, but there are still some side effects—and we're worried that… But the important thing right now is that he was struck by a magical curse. And it's obvious that the curse came from his mother, Beatrix."

The three elves exchanged glances. "We have not been told about this," said Sierra. "You should have mentioned it."

"When you approached us, we were discussing the internet breach, not dark magic. I had no idea Beatrix Spier was involved in the hack, or that Chris' injury was related."

"Humans think so linearly. They miss the trees for the forest." Sierra said. The others hid their grins at her reversal of the cliché.

"Do you think you can help him?" Gabe asked anxiously. "He looks bad; he hasn't been well since he was cursed three weeks ago."

"We will look into it," Sierra promised. "But first, we need to find this breach and shut it down for good."

"And that's another thing I don't understand. Beatrix

may be involved in this, but as far as I know, she's no techno expert. Obviously, someone else is also involved—another witch or..." said Jessa.

"A werewolf?" Gabe asked. "Like maybe Dolan McTier?"

"McTier!" Landon said in astonishment. "I know there's always been bad blood between our packs, but why would you think he's involved?"

"Especially when he's now dating Dan's sister, Channing," added Ramona.

"Say what?" asked Jessa.

"Honey, you just haven't been keeping up with your shifter gossip," said Ramona.

"Excuse me, I've been a little busy over here trying to keep PackNet from spilling the secrets of the entire paranormal world," Jessa said huffily. "You were supposed to keep me up to date with something juicy like that."

"Well, you're updated now," Ramona grinned back at her.

"Ladies, please," said Sierra. "While I enjoy spilling the coffee, now is not the time. We need to get this breach fixed as fast as possible before more information leaks out."

Ramona and Jessa giggled as Sierra once again mangled a cliché, and Kailin stood and headed back to his console, jaw clenched. "Beatrix Spier may be good, but we're better. All of us, together, are going to beat her."

As Kai began to type, the others crowded around to watch. Suddenly a black crow appeared on the screen.

"They know we've caught them," said Gabe. "And that is definitely Beatrix Spier's signature. We just triggered a Zero Day Event, Kai."

"Then let's pray we're not already too late to fix it."

CHAPTER 38

For the last two weeks Shannon had spent every spare moment working on finding a cure for Chris. Since the night he and Gabe had gone looking for Fontaine's body, her brother had been getting weaker. He was now having occasional blackouts, too. The crow brand, their mother's signature mark, looked more livid on his chest every day. Although there were no other visible magical chains, Shannon feared the mark might be a link meant to somehow control Chris, to be used to spy on the Bertrands, or even—at its worst—make Chris do something that would harm Ana, Sophie, or someone else. He'd confessed to Shannon that he was beginning to have thoughts that were not his own, thoughts about hurting loved ones, as if someone else were trying to control him. So far, he'd been able to resist, but as he grew weaker physically, Shannon feared he'd be unable to fight their mother's attempts to control him. Could Beatrix truly have tethered his will to hers?

As soon as she'd learned of her boyfriend Dave's ancestral link to elves, she'd gone to him. He'd been surprised—dumbfounded was a closer description.

"You're telling me I'm related to elves, and I never even knew it? You've got to be kidding me, Shannon," Dave had said when she'd told him, disbelief clear in his voice.

"No, that's what Donna Bertrand said."

"Donna Betrand. She's a bigger gossip than Monica Garros, and that's not meant as a compliment, either."

"Look, you're trying everything you can to help my brother, I know that. But what if there's something else? If the elves know something that could help? I don't think they'd do it for me. I'm Beatrix Spier's daughter, and they have a long-standing hatred for anyone from her original coven. I think they're more likely to get involved if you talk to them."

Dave had given in, and they'd found the elves at Gabe's office, hard at work on the PackNet breach.

Dave hesitated outside the office door. "They're busy, Shannon."

"It's lunchtime. Even elves have to eat."

Dave rolled his eyes. "Okay, look, I feel silly barging into Gabe's office and going, 'Hey, guys, I hear you've got some elves in here who might be my distant cousins. I know they're busy helping y'all out with the PackNet problem, but can I ask them a favor?'"

"So, you're embarrassed to do this in front of Gabe, Jace, and Landon. That's what you're saying."

"No, of course not, but… well…"

"Oh," Shannon said knowingly. "I forgot you used to date Jessa."

Dave grimaced, and his face turned a bright red. Before he'd met Shannon, he'd been a player. He'd never denied it. That didn't make it any easier when he came across an old girlfriend while his new, and much more serious girlfriend, was with him.

"And if the elves can help Chris? Nothing else we've tried has worked, and he's getting weaker every day."

"I know. I'm sorry. I'm being an idiot. Your brother's health—maybe his soul—is at stake, and I'm embarrassed to ask a favor of someone in front of an old girlfriend."

Shannon stayed quiet. She knew when she'd won. Dave pushed open the door, and they walked in.

"Hey guys. What are you doing here in the middle of the day" asked Jace, the first to look up when they walked in. "We haven't broken the law or anything yet today. I promise."

"Uh, we'd, uh, like to speak to your guests," Dave said.

"Our guests? Oh, you mean Sierra, Kai, and Theo. Which one?"

"Whichever one has a few minutes to spare," said Shannon.

"Okay, well let me get Theo for you first. He's kind of their bodyguard, I guess you could say. If it turns out you need Sierra or Kai, you probably should go through him."

As Jace headed into the office's back room, Dave muttered, "I can't believe we're doing this. Asking an elf for a favor. Everyone knows they don't do favors for anyone."

Shannon looked up as a tall male with dark hair worn long and tied back from his face came out. It was clear to anyone with the least bit of knowledge of paranormals that he was an elf. It was evident in the extraordinary beauty of his features, that made it difficult to look away from his dove grey eyes, and in the metallic glimmer of his coal black hair. Shannon caught her breath. It was just plain difficult to look away from him.

"I'm Theo Knight," the elf said. "I understand you would like to speak with us." He stood with his arms folded across a broad chest that practically rippled with muscles that Shannon noticed even underneath his rather mundane black, button-up shirt. He gazed at them now with a cool but wary gaze.

"My name's David Thorne, and this is Shannon Kelly." Dave held out his hand in greeting, but the elf continued to stand unmoving, arms still folded across his chest. After a moment Dave put his hand down. Shannon knew he did not like the rebuff. She also knew he stayed and continued the conversation only for her sake. "We've come to ask for some information."

At that moment several other people came out of the back room. Shannon and Dave knew most of them—Landon, Ramona, Jessa, and of course Gabe. But the two strangers who accompanied them were also obviously elves.

"David Thorne, you said?" asked the female. "My name is Serelith, but you can call me Sierra. You are very well met, Cousin."

Every one of Gabe's staff stopped what they were doing and stared at Dave, still standing near the front door. Shannon particularly noticed that Jessa, looking as sexy as always in a tight black mini-skirt and low-cut tank top, her nails painted blood red, was near the doorway of the back room, unabashedly listening. Shannon pushed down a wave of jealousy. She would never have the figure to pull off that outfit. But then, Dave always said he liked her curves. She pulled her attention away from Dave's ex and back to the conversation.

"Cousin. It's true then… I guess," David said. Shannon

told me, but I wasn't sure… I mean… no one in my family…"

"Our link to your line goes back many hundreds of years; it is unlikely you would know. Even witches do not have the memory we elves do." Sierra said it kindly, but Shannon noticed the hint of superiority that came through even as she tried to politely hide it.

"That's what we've come to ask you about. Well, it's more than just curiosity about my ancestors. I know you're not Ancestry.com, or anything." Dave, who was always calm and had a good dose of his own sense of superiority, was obviously intimidated by the three elves. Shannon had never seen him like this before. Gabe and his gang of computer nerds weren't helping the situation, either. They'd been working with the trio for over a week now and had obviously gotten used to the effect they had on mere witches and shifters.

She took pity on him and stepped in. "My brother, Chris, Chris, has been injured—cursed we believe."

"And what does this have to do with us? He's a Spier. A member of the Callich clan. We are old enemies," said Theo.

"Theo, please, don't be so hasty. You know full well that Shannon Spier Kelly has worked tirelessly to stop her mother's evil. Long before she was of age or had come into her full power, she slowed Beatrix Spier down. I'm Kai, by the way." The third elf came forward, and unlike Theo, held out his hand for both Dave and Shannon to shake. He held Shannon's hand a few moments longer than necessary, his smile widening as he glanced between her and Dave, as if he knew exactly what emotions his attention stirred up in both of them. Shannon pulled herself away from the elf's gaze. "How do you know this? No one knows this. I told no one at all about what I did until a few months ago."

"Elves are tasked to act as the guardians of the Old Magics. We keep an eye on everything that could affect the balance between the realms," said Serelith. "As such, we have always kept our eyes on Beatrix. As two of the last of the Callich line, we have also kept our eyes on you and your brother, of course."

Theo stared at Shannon in a way that made her think he

knew every bad thought she had ever had. She felt like a disobedient child sitting on Santa's lap, certain he has a list of all of her naughty behavior. Sierra put her hand on Shannon's arm and turned to glare at Theo. "Don't let him intimidate you; he enjoys it way too much," she said. "We know you and your brother are nothing like your mother or her coven."

"Elves do not learn; they remember. That's what my mother always says," Jessa stepped into the conversation.

"Seriously?" Shannon said, giving her a scornful look. "You couldn't wait to drop that old saying in, could you?"

"The elves also say, 'Envy is the mark of one who cannot see their own magic,'" said Sierra. "But we do not have time to stand here trading elvish aphorisms."

"Then can you help my brother? He was struck by a curse from our mother. He hasn't been the same since. I'm worried about him. His fiancée is worried about him. He is supposed to be married in a few weeks. He's fought evil his entire life; he deserves this chance at happiness."

"Gabe, can you do without us for the afternoon?" Kai asked politely.

"Please, if you think you can do anything to help Chris, please try. I feel as if I let him down by not getting to Beatrix fast enough."

"You would have been no match for her that night, friend," Kai said. "I do not mean that as an insult to you. Only that Beatrix' power has always been substantial, and it has been growing over these past months. She is a threat to all of us unless she is stopped. That is as much a part of our mission here as is closing the PackNet breach."

CHAPTER 39

"Let us adjourn to Otherworld," Kai suggested as they discussed where to begin their research into a cure for Chris.

"No!" said Theo. "If Spier is connected to his mother in even the slightest way, it could spell disaster. We haven't spent centuries protecting ourselves from the Callich coven to bring one of her lackeys into our midst."

"My brother is not a lackey—of anyone, let alone of my mother. He's been fighting against her his entire life."

"I don't mean that he is intentionally doing her bidding." Theo softened his tone as he turned to Shannon. "But if he is tied to her, she may be able to weaken our defenses. We can't risk it."

"Otherworld may not accept you either, Shannon," said Sierra apologetically. "It would recognize your blood and reject you. Just as it will recognize David's Thorne bloodline and accept him."

"See, I'm special," Dave wisecracked, grinning at Shannon.

"Especially annoying," Shannon retorted.

Finally, they decided that Dave's home was the best headquarters for their magical research. It was in the country and more secluded than Shannon's house.

***

They had been researching a cure for the curse for over a week when Kathleen arrived at Shannon's, and she was scheduled to meet with the elves and Dave the next morning. She arranged for her friends, Abby Mohr and Jake Waseaux, to stay with Kathleen while she was gone. Not only were they both witches, Jake was also on the force with Shannon and Dave.

"It's not that I don't trust you," Shannon assured Kathleen when she questioned why she needed, "babysitters," while Shannon was gone. "But Dan asked me to keep you safe. And that means someone with magic needs to be here to protect you."

"You said your protections make me invisible to the outside world."

"Yes, they should. But one thing I've learned in both witchcraft and policing—always have a backup plan."

At that moment the doorbell rang, and Kathleen let in Abby and Jake. The couple were in their 30s. He was tall with blond hair and blue eyes. Abby wore her long, dark hair pulled back in a braid; her wide-legged jeans and a lightweight sweater were perfect for the early autumn morning. After the introductions were made, Shannon left the trio in the kitchen sampling some muffins she had made the night before and headed off to Dave's home.

***

Shannon arrived at Dave's house to find the others already gathered in the sun-drenched living room, books and scrolls spread like relics of some forgotten war across the old oak table. The scent of strong coffee mingled with the sharp, metallic tang of magic in the air.

Chris sat in the armchair by the fireplace, which had been lit for his comfort, despite the growing warmth of the day. His skin was drawn and pale; a cold sweat darkened the collar of his T-shirt.

Shannon gave him a kiss on the cheek. "How're Ana and Sophie?" she asked.

"They're worried, particularly Sophie. We tried to hide this from her as long as we could but..."

Dave handed her a mug. "Are you sure you're up for this?" he asked Chris.

"I think I have to be," he replied.

Theo stood rigid near the window, arms folded, expression unreadable. He didn't acknowledge either Shannon's or Chris's presence. Sierra and Kai sat at the table. While they seemed to be studying the scroll unrolled on it, Shannon noticed them surreptitiously glancing between Theo and Dave. Had something happened before she arrived, Shannon wondered. The elf and the witch had clashed constantly since they'd begun working on finding a cure for Chris.

Dave glanced at Theo, and set his mug down with a soft clink. "We've traced the rune on your chest, Chris, to an ancestor of mine—Lirael Thorne. He was marked, too. Same sigil. Same curse. It nearly destroyed him. There are some differences in the story. Lirael was an elf. And the witch who cursed him was one of your ancestors—a Callich."

"So, who cured him?" Chris asked.

"Another of my ancestors. A witch named Coraly Knightbridge. After curing him, she married him. And that, apparently is how I come to have elven ancestry—something I didn't know until I met our friends here." Dave gestured to the three elves. Theo walked over to stand by the table, not quite part of the group, but not quite separate, either.

"Let us show you," said Kai. He raised his hands, and a magical light flickered in his palm as a vision took shape between them.

"Wow, magical Netflix," Dave said irreverently to Chris. "I'm going to have to have them teach me this trick once we get you fixed up."

Chris grinned back, but Theo gave Dave a scornful look. They turned their attention back to Kai as a translucent figure appeared between his hands. It was Lirael, Shannon deduced. The crow brand blazed red-hot on his chest, and from it sprang tarnished silver chains, wrapping his body. A new figure entered the picture, a woman dressed in a flowing red robe embroidered with stars. Her face reminded Shannon of Dave's cousin, Winnie. As they all watched, she performed a ritual, and slowly, the chains fell away, and the brand ceased to glow and faded from Lirael's chest.

"It was a gamble," Sierra said softly. "But it worked. He lived."

Chris let out a shaky breath. "So, what—some great-granddad of Dave's got magically rebooted, and that's your plan?"

"It's a lead," Dave said. "And better than none— which is more than we had before."

Theo moved forward, his eyes narrowed. "Let me see for myself," he said, kneeling beside Chris, placing a palm over the rune on his chest. His lips moved almost silently. Shannon could just barely make out the Elvish words he sang. Slowly, they sensed a change in the room—the fire blazed in the hearth. A mist curled out of the walls and surrounded Theo and Chris, whose eyes fluttered shut.

Dave's voice cut through the quiet that had descended on the room. "You're just skimming the surface."

Theo's head snapped up. Chris' eyes flew open, whatever spell he had been under, broken.

Dave stepped forward, lifting his own hands, fingers splayed. His voice was steadier than Theo's had been, a chant, not a song, the rhythm sharper. Dave's magic—witch's magic—surged in. It was brighter, louder, as if the power itself pulsed to a more modern beat than that of the elves' ancient rituals. A shimmering spiral suddenly showed itself, a second band, this one golden, wrapped just as tightly around Chris's chest as the first that Theo's incantation had forced to appear.

"There, look," Dave murmured. "There's a second tether. Subtle. Your elvish magic didn't see it. But it's there."

The spell snapped shut like a clasp and with it, they could see the bands on Chris's body tighten. He gasped, clutching his chest. Theo rose slowly, a flicker of surprise, maybe even respect, crossing his face.

Sierra grinned at Shannon, clearly enjoying herself. "Told you not all witches are wild wands and bad ideas. This one's ducks aren't running around."

Shannon tried to hide her grin as Sierra once more mangled a common saying.

Theo's voice was cool. "He has skill. But skill is not wisdom."

"We don't have time for either to be optional," Shannon said. "So what's next?"

"The soul-weaving ritual," Theo replied. "We map the damage. Reconstruct Chris's essence from within."

"Too unstable," Dave countered. "It could re-entangle

the rune in one or both of the tethers. We need to isolate the rune from the bindings. Reverse the intent behind it with a spiral unbinding. Or something stronger."

Chris looked around at each of the five who stood over him. "I, if anyone, can appreciate the differences between elven and witch's magic, but while you all are having an academic debate on which is better, our mother"—he nodded at Shannon—"is using me as a conduit to learn all of your secrets."

The room fell quiet. Dave and Theo glanced at each other. Theo nodded his head at Chris. "I understand your concern, and I agree. But Elvish magic weaves slowly. This witchcraft forces forgetting."

"That's why we need both," Shannon interjected. "You bring memory. Our spells bring motion."

"And we need to move quickly—more quickly than your magic," added Dave. "Chris doesn't have a hundred years. I'm not sure he even has a hundred hours."

Suddenly, Chris convulsed. His eyes rolled back. A low, foreign voice curled out of his throat—silky, mocking. Shannon reached out toward her brother, then drew her hand back as she recognized the voice.

"You were always the weaker sibling, Shannon. I was fooled when you were younger. Your magic is showy and impressive. It blinded even me to Chris' power. I regret that now."

"That's her. Our mother, Beatrix," Shannon whispered.

Theo stepped forward instinctively, magic flaring in his hands. But Shannon held out an arm. "You might hurt him!"

"She's watching us through the mark," Theolin said grimly. "The tether is a doorway. If she completes the binding, he won't just be cursed. He'll be hers."

The crow rune shimmered, darkened, then flared again, and Chris groaned, though his eyes did not open.

Sierra's voice was hushed. "We'll need something of hers to unbind this spell. Shannon, do you have anything?"

"I do. I kept a box. It's locked away. I burned almost everything, but I was afraid I might need…"

"Thank goodness you did keep it," said Dave.

Theo turned to her, his voice stern. "If you go digging into your mother's lair, be prepared to find pieces of yourself you thought long buried."

Shannon didn't flinch. "I have to. Chris won't survive without it. As soon as I find something of our mother's that you think will work, and you and Dave figure out the spell, we'll finish this."

CHAPTER 40

Kathleen had been holed up at Shannon's for a week, and she was beginning to go crazy. No, she decided as she thought about it some more; she wasn't just beginning to go crazy. She was already there. She was camping in the middle of crazy. She had her tent set up and a campfire roaring right in the middle of Crazyland.

Shannon got to leave the house every day. Either she went to work, or she went off on some mysterious mission that Kathleen wasn't supposed to know about. She heard whispers when her "babysitters" came over to stay with her. But they all made it obvious that she wasn't supposed to know what was going on.

It didn't matter who her "caretakers" were; they all kept her in the dark. When Shannon was on a different shift from Dave, he stayed with Kathleen. Abby and Jake came several times, and once Tyler and Winnie were her chosen minders. Shannon kept telling her that she had it wrong. They were bodyguards, not jailers. But it certainly didn't feel that way.

They didn't trust her. She was sure of that. They thought if she were left alone for a moment, she'd go running back to her brother and father. Never mind that they were the ones she had run away from in the first place. She had explained it all to Shannon, who seemed sympathetic. She'd even told Kathleen her own story—that her mother had been the infamous witch Beatrix Callich Spier.

Shannon had questioned her on how she had gotten the paranormals of Rivelou to trust her, but Shannon had just shrugged and said, "There was more to the story," and that her brother's relationship with Ana had helped. That wasn't very useful. Dolan's relationship with Ana's sister, Channing, certainly wasn't bringing the Bertrands and McTiers closer together as one big happy pack. And the one person who hadn't come—had not even stopped by for a few minutes to say hello or see how she was doing—was Dan.

That hurt worse than anything. Finally, late Sunday afternoon as Shannon was getting ready to work and Kathleen was wandering aimlessly around the house, the doorbell rang. Can you get that, Kathleen?" she called from her bedroom.

Kathleen was surprised. She hadn't been allowed to answer the door since she arrived. "I guess she just assumes whoever she has lined up to babysit me today is too strong for me to overpower and then run off screaming into the night," she mumbled to herself as she headed downstairs to the front door. She flung it open rather ungraciously, then stopped in shock, holding the door with one hand, blocking the entrance with her body.

"Are you going to let me in?" Dan asked after they stood like that for a moment. There was a scowl on his face as he stalked passed her into the foyer.

He seemed to loom over her as she closed the door. The days were getting shorter; it was already dusk outside. The soft glow of the lamp on the entryway table had seemed cozy and welcoming to Kathleen when she'd turned it on earlier. Now it just cast large, gloomy shadows on the midnight-blue wallpaper with its silver pentagrams, making Dan's figure all the more imposing.

"What, no kiss this time?" Kathleen straightened her shoulders, pretending an indifference she didn't feel.

"I'm not here to fight with you, Kathleen," he said resignedly. He ran his hand through his hair and across his beard in a tired gesture that was so familiar she just wanted to take him in her arms and take care of him. Her hand reached out toward him almost of its own accord. She quickly pulled it back. No. Dan didn't want her anymore. He had already made that obvious. She was not going to show him how much that hurt.

"So, you're my babysitter tonight?" She turned toward the kitchen just as Shannon came down the stairs. She was dressed in jeans and a sweater rather than her uniform. Obviously, this was not a night she was on duty, as Kathleen had thought. She must be headed out on whatever mysterious project she and Dave had been working on for the past week.

"Hey Dan, I've got a stew on the stove ready for us. Come on in and eat."

Kathleen grimaced. She was hungry. She was going to have to sit down and eat with the man. There was no way around it. She followed the others into the room and watched from the doorway as Shannon dished up three bowls of stew. The aroma of beef, garlic, and vegetables made her stomach growl. She sat down reluctantly as Dan politely pulled out chairs for both of the women.

"How's the project going?" Dan asked cryptically.

"Much better." Shannon brightened. "Si... uh Dave... thinks we have that spell figured out."

Dan glanced toward Kathleen, who made a show of not paying attention to what they were saying. "That's great!" he said. "I really hope this works."

After that the conversation died. It was obvious Dan and Shannon wanted to talk about the mysterious project and couldn't in front of her. Shannon finished her meal quickly, set her bowl in the sink, and said, "Thanks Dan. I'll be back in a few hours."

"Yeah, I hope everything goes well. Tell... well you know..."

"I do. And thanks." She headed out the door and Kathleen began to clear the table. Dan just sat and watched her for a few minutes.

"You could have told me, you know," he finally said in a low voice. He didn't sound angry; it was worse. He sounded hurt. When Kathleen turned, she saw that his fists were clenched on the table like he was holding himself together with sheer willpower.

Kathleen took a deep breath. She'd wanted a chance to talk to him. To explain. Then why, now that she had the opportunity, did she just want to run away and cry?

"I wanted to," she finally said. "A dozen times I started to tell you. But you..." Her voice broke. "You hate him, and I get it. I do. But I'm not him."

Dan turned away, jaw working. The wolf in him was howling—not in rage, but confusion. *She's your mate,* it growled.

She lied!

She was afraid.

She's a McTier.

Claim her, and she's a Betrand.

Dan gave up. His wolf would never understand. It was all so simple for the animal inside him. Kathleen was his mate. Claim her, and she became his. If only the real world were so simple.

"You let me fall for you. And all that time, you knew. You are his sister. You know what that means. And you said nothing."

"*I* let *you* fall for me! You've got to be kidding me. You chased me. You pursued me. You told me I was your fated mate. That you loved me. I didn't tell you about Dolan because I was afraid. I was afraid of exactly this happening. That you wouldn't be able to see past my last name."

"It's not your name. It's that you kept secrets from me."

"And what about you?"

Kathleen had been filling the dishwasher with the dirty bowls; now, she slammed the door shut and turned to face him. "You are just like all the men in my pack. You say you want to love us—to cherish us—but all you really want is someone to control while we warm your bed and do your bidding."

"Kathleen! That's not true." Dan stood up and walked toward her. She moved away from him, scooting along the counter until she was near the door. He held up his hands in a gesture of surrender. "Please, you're killing me here. You know I'd never hurt you."

"Do I? How do I know that? You're keeping secrets from me, too. You've hidden me here surrounded by your witch guards. Don't think I haven't noticed that everyone who has been here to watch me has been a witch. Even when one of them was a werewolf, they always had a witch with them—someone with power. Someone who can make sure I don't leave or even attempt to contact my brother. As if I would want to!"

"That's not it at all. It's not that I think you want to contact your brother. I saw your fear. I believe you don't want to go back. Your 'guards' as you call them are to protect you. Not just from your brother, but from Beatrix Spier."

"What! What are you talking about? Shannon told me about her mother. I thought she was long gone."

"No, she's not. Kathleen, you're right. I haven't been honest with you. I haven't even been honest with myself. I've been so damned high and mighty. Thinking I knew everything. *Veritas Vencit.* Truth prevails! Well, turns out despite everything I've done to keep the truth hidden, it has prevailed. The truth is, no matter who you are or what you've done, I love you. I've never felt... never let myself feel... like this before. And then you..."

He turned away, unwilling to let her see the hurt on his face. "It's not just me. It's my whole pack. It's falling apart. We're at each other's throats. I've never seen it like this before, and I don't know what to do. I can't walk away from you, and I can't bring you to the pack. Not right now."

She took a step toward him, reaching out tentatively. "I am Dolan's sister, but I was never his ally. He was a big part of the reason I ran. Why I left my pack. Why I started over. I didn't tell you because I thought you'd hate me for it—and maybe I was right."

Dan turned toward her, his eyes glowing faintly in the light, his wolf close. "I don't hate you. That's the problem." His voice broke. "I want to. God, I want to. But my wolf still wants to claim you, even knowing who you are. Even after all of it." He stepped closer, cupping her jaw. "I wanted you—us—to be different than everything else in my life. The one thing I didn't have to second guess."

"I am." She placed her hand over his heart. "But if you walk away now, I won't stop you. I've lived my life in fear of men like Dolan. I'll never go back to the McTier pack willingly. But I won't beg you to believe me."

Dan studied her, eyes flicking to her lips, her tears. He just wanted to kiss them away. But he didn't. "I don't know if I can forgive you... but I'm not walking away. Not yet."

CHAPTER 41

The following afternoon Connor Morrigan sat across from Dan at his desk in the offices of Bertrand Enterprises on the top floor of the River Building, a ten-story office building in downtown Rivelou. It was late afternoon, and he'd stopped by to discuss the latest contracts with one of the company's top clients. Connor had his own office near the courthouse, but he was a frequent visitor at Bertrand Enterprises. He had just taken off his jacket, loosened his tie, and pulled out the paperwork for the two of them to look over when the office door banged open and Hank barged in, followed by Remy, who was trying in vain to quiet his father.

"Look at this. Just look at this!" Hank slammed a national news magazine onto the desk.

"What? I didn't know anyone still read paper magazines," Dan said dryly. "You know, if you had something for us to read, you could have just emailed a link."

Connor shook his head. Dan was usually excellent at defusing tense situations, but in the last few weeks, he'd been strung tight, and his patience was non-existent. While understandable, it was certainly not the way for Dan to handle his grandfather right now. Connor shared a glance with Remy, who was standing in the doorway. The other man just shrugged. It was obvious he, too, was having little success at calming his father.

"Well, I'm an old fart and I still read magazines," Hank growled in angry reply. "Connor," he turned away from his grandson and worked hard to modulate his voice. "I need you to sue these people for slander. Right now."

"Well, Hank, let's read it first; then, I'll have a better idea of what this is all about," Connor said reasonably.

Hank took a step back from the desk, his claws flexing in and out of his curled hands as Connor picked up the magazine and began to read aloud.

"Paranormal Creatures in Our Midst: Real or Hoax?

"Rivelou, Kentucky, has long been known as a quiet town where nothing much ever happened. And the residents liked it that way. The annual magnolia festival brings a few thousand tourists to the sleepy city each spring. Rivelou University has a mediocre Division Two basketball team and a girl's Lacrosse Team that has recently been coming up in the ranks of college sports.

"But on any given summer afternoon, taking a walk along the Rivelou River, for which the town is named, is a study in the meaning of the phrase 'sleepy Southern town.'"

"That all changed a few weeks ago when Daniel Henry Bertrand, scion of one of the local 'first families' was arrested for the second time in as few weeks in the disappearance of nationally-known author and professor Alexander Fontaine. (see sidebar)

"At a press conference announcing his arrest (he was subsequently released for lack of evidence) new charges surfaced that Bertrand is, in fact, a werewolf. And while that statement might sound incredible to anyone who has been living under a rock for the last month, there is a growing concern that not only are Bertrand and his family members from a ruling 'pack' of werewolves, but that other 'paranormal' creatures have been living among us for centuries, masquerading as humans, not only in Rivelou, KY, but throughout the world. Witches, shapeshifters, and vampires are just a few of these so-called paranormal creatures who have been 'outed' in the past few weeks."

Connor put the magazine down and looked at each of the three men in the room. "We've got a problem here, but I don't see how suing anyone is going to fix it."

"They are running our good name through the mud," yelled Hank. "They are tearing apart everything I've worked my whole lifetime for. They're branding us monsters! If we don't stop this, they'll come for us with pitchforks and torches! It's slander, I tell you."

"Well, first, Hank, it's in writing, and that makes it libel, not slander," Connor said mildly. He wasn't trying to be irritating; he just couldn't stand it when people misrepresented simple concepts of law and found it impossible not to correct them.

Hank drew a deep breath readying himself to say something, but Remy, who had sat down in the chair next to Connor, now stood up again and put a calming hand on his father's shoulder.

"Dad, sit down. Let the man have his say. You hire him to know about these things."

Connor sent him a grateful look as Hank sat. Dan, he noticed, had his head in his hands behind the desk.

"The problem, Hank, is the best defense against libel is to prove that what has been written isn't true. And so far, everything I've read here is just facts."

"Well, go on. They talk about PackNet and Gabe. Call him a 'mastermind of an insidious plot to either scam the entire world or create a new dark web even blacker than what we already are aware of.'"

Connor raised his eyebrows, and Dan lifted up his head. "Grandpa, have you memorized this thing?" he asked incredulously.

Connor continued perusing the article as Hank and Dan sniped at each other. When there was a pause in their conversation, Connor stepped in.

"It explains that PackNet, like the dark web, consists of sites not catalogued on regular search engines, and—oh wonderful—tells exactly how to access it. It does mention that the access seems to come and go and speculates that the 'person or paranormal being who has designed PackNet is using magical means to keep it hidden.' Again, Hank, it's all true. And we'd only get ourselves in more trouble and draw more attention by trying to dispute it. Our best choice is to lie low and hope that Gabe and his new experts can get these leaks stopped."

"And that's another thing, Daniel; you gave these elves permission to come into our territory without even asking me."

"Hey!" Dan said, putting his hands up in defense. "They didn't ask; they just showed up and told us they were going to fix the problem."

"And then what will we owe them?"

"They didn't say anything about that."

"Huh! Boy, you don't know a thing about elves. There's always a price to pay. And, trust me, it's always a lot higher than you think it will be."

Remy came to stand between his father and son. "Look, we're all on edge. It's been one thing after another for a month now. But arguing with each other is not going to help anything. I'm more worried about what I'm seeing on the PackNet chat rooms than anything in the non-para press. Dad, a lot of people in our pack are saying you're too old. That it's time you were replaced."

"Well, let's just see them challenge me, and I'll prove who the Alpha of this pack still is."

"Dad, you know that's not what you want. You've always said when the pack wanted someone new, you'd step down. We may not be there yet, but if we don't get things under control quickly, you're going to be challenged. And soon."

"Yes, and I've set it up that it's not just a fighting challenge anymore. I know I'm not as young as I used to be. A lot of these young pups could probably take me. But everyone in this room knows it takes a lot more to be a good Alpha than just being the strongest fighter. It takes brains, and cunning, and a hell of a lot of damned diplomacy. That's what I've been preaching for years, and everyone in the pack has always said they agreed with me."

"The older generation, maybe, who remember the way it was before, and some of the younger ones who understand what you've created here in Rivelou," Connor said, slowly and cautiously feeling for the right words so he didn't set his pack leader off on another tirade. "But Dolan McTier's been hanging around with a lot of the younger wolves, stirring things up, talking about 'the old way,' and how the Bertrands don't follow tradition, and that that's why we've had these problems."

So much for Connor's attempt at cautious words, Hank could stand no more. "Dolan Damn McTier. If I have to hear his name one more time… What is Channing thinking about seeing him in the first place? Remy, can't you keep control of any of your children?"

"Grandpa, that's so unfair," Dan said as Remy also spoke up.

"We talked about this, Dad. If we forbid her seeing him, we're doing exactly what the McTiers have done for years. It would just play into his hands. I'm hoping if we let her run with him for a while, she'll figure it out for herself. Ana was telling me the other day she's already saying Dolan is controlling."

"As long as she isn't telling him any pack secrets, I suppose you're right," Hank said grudgingly.

"Grandpa… Alpha…" Dan came around his desk and stood before his grandfather, head bowed in submission. "I have a confession to make."

"Well, I don't think you can tell us anything worse than we already know. Our plate's pretty full as it is. Out with it."

Remy came to stand next to his son. "Whatever it is, if we stick together, I'm sure we can fix it."

Dan took a deep breath and shook his head. Connor sat still and watched each of the three men, three generations, all of whom he'd known and respected his entire life. He knew what Dan was going to say. What would happen when Remy and Hank found out about Kathleen?

"You know I've been seeing someone, right?"

"Yes, yes, we met her for a few minutes the night you were arrested," said Hank. "Seemed nice. Marianne said she knows the pack. O'Connor, I think? When are you going to introduce her to us officially?"

"Well, that's just it. She lied. She's not part of the O'Connor pack—although her mother was. She's… she's a McTier. Michael McTier's daughter."

CHAPTER 42

The room exploded in noise as all three of his listeners spoke at once. But over everyone else's words, Dan distinctly heard his grandfather's furious hiss. "You brought a McTier—another McTier—into my territory. Do you know what you've done?"

He hung his head. He knew he'd betrayed his grandfather—the man he'd always looked up to. The man he wanted to emulate. The one man, even more than his father, that he always wanted to make proud.

"Our whole damned pack is going to be out for my head now," Hank continued. And I don't blame them. If I can't keep control of my own family... Channing's betrayal has been bad enough, but the other wolves all assume if she mates McTier, she'll go to his pack. Problem solved."

Connor started to protest, but Hank put out a hand to stop him. "Oh, I know, it's old-fashioned. Females are equal to males. They can hold any role in the pack they want to. Hell, they can even become the pack Alpha. It's been done. I'm the one who taught you all that. But the younger pups have been sniffing around Dolan, too, just like Remy said. One of them could easily bring a challenge. And we won't be able to stop them. McTier's been trying to undermine me since the day Channing brought him home. Telling everyone who'll listen that his family's way is better than ours. That's it's tradition—as if that word means the same as sacrosanct—and anyone who says otherwise is spouting blasphemy."

Even as he continued speaking, Hank crossed the room with a raw, animal swiftness so fast Connor almost didn't see it. One second, he was sitting, the next he was in his grandson's face as Dan flinched back instinctively. "Dan, you've put us in the soup with this. I won't be able to stop it if enough of them start spouting this tradition nonsense."

"Dad! Dad! Enough," said Remy. He stepped between

his father and his son, slow and deliberate, his hands half-raised in a gesture of peace. He kept his eyes down submissively while still giving his father flickering glances to measure the danger. "Dan's made a mistake. I'm sure he has a plan to fix it. Don't you, son?"

Dan had started to feel a little better when his dad began to speak. Remy usually didn't go against his father in any way, and Dan was surprised. But then he heard the sentence, "Dan's made a mistake." Nothing had changed.

And he hadn't yet said those four fatal words: "She's my fated mate."

But was she? He'd been so sure. And she'd betrayed him. How could someone who was supposed to be the other half of his soul do that?

Connor watched him as if he knew exactly what Dan was thinking. He probably did. Connor and Gabe were the only two he'd spoken those words to—except Kathleen.

Connor tried to play peacemaker now. A difficult role for the young lawyer, the only one in the room who did not share the Betrand last name, no matter how indispensable he was to the pack.

"Look, we need to all sit down and look at this calmly." He went to the bar in the corner of the office and poured bourbons for Hank and Remy. "Let's look at this strategically instead of emotionally."

He went back and brought two more bourbons for Dan and himself, then sat down. "Dan, what do you know about Kathleen?"

Dan took a sip of bourbon and tried to decide how to answer that question. His first thought was how soft her hair was. How good it felt to have her in his arms. His wolf chimed in with a picture of Kathleen spread out naked on his bed as he kissed her. He tamped that thought down fiercely. It wasn't what Connor was asking, and it certainly wasn't something he planned to share with his father and grandfather.

"She's shy. She's scared of her family—of her pack. At least most of them. She hasn't said much about them. Yes, she always avoided talking about them when the subject came up. But I could tell she was afraid. Didn't want them to find her. Hadn't told them where she was."

"Humph, that's the line she's been feeding you, all while she played you—probably laughed with her brother the whole time about how gullible the Bertrands are—you and Channing both."

Dan felt himself growing angry. His fangs grew as a low growl sounded in his throat.

"Don't give me that sass, boy, unless you're willing to back it up."

"Dan, Hank, this isn't helping," said Connor. "Dan, what makes you so sure she's been hiding from her pack? And what made her finally confess who she was to you?"

"She didn't confess. Dolan found her. We ran into him when we were eating at a restaurant. And the look of surprise—of terror—on her face. It wasn't faked."

Remy made a soft sound of concern. Dan was sure he was thinking of his own daughters being in that situation with no one to turn to. He nodded his appreciation toward his father. "She's alone, Dad. When Dolan walked into the restaurant, she was terrified. He was with two other pack members. Dolan threatened her. And I did nothing to stop them." The self-loathing in his voice was evident. "I'm telling you she's not like the rest of the McTiers. I know how it looks, but she's with me, not them."

"I've met her, too." Connor stepped in to play peacemaker again, knowing he could get his head bitten off by any one of the three other shifters in the room. "I'll admit I was suspicious at first, too, but she's done nothing that would lead me to believe..."

"Have you lost your mind, too, Connor? I expected better of you. I taught you to look at things objectively. And here you are siding with Dan just because he's been your best friend since childhood." Hank's hands were clenched on the arms of his chair, his claws flexing in and out.

"It's not like that, sir." Connor bowed his head to his Alpha as he spoke.

"Oh, isn't it? I've been trying since you were children to raise you, and Gabe, and Dan right. To make you ready to take over the leadership of this pack. And look how you all have repaid me. Gabe's PackNet is causing a worldwide crisis. Dan is taking a McTier into his bed. And you. You're just sitting here watching it happen."

Connor took a deep breath, recoiling in his chair at Hank's words. The man had been like a father to him since his own parents had passed away when he was still in high school.

"Dad, that's not fair," Remy stepped in front of Hank, blocking Connor from his view. "Connor's been nothing but loyal to you, and Gabe only started PackNet with your approval. And if Dan says this girl is not a spy for the McTiers, then I trust him.

"But we do have a problem. The Bertrand family— and you, Dad, are fast losing the trust of our pack. I know you don't want to hear it, but we can't go on this way. You're going to have to call a meeting. We need to lay everything on the line for them. Be totally honest. The McTiers are a threat, and the pack needs to know it, especially these young pups he's got trailing after him.

"Dan," he turned to his son to stop him when it was obvious he was about to jump in. "I don't mean Kathleen. But I also don't like this plan of Dolan's to start branching out right across from us on the Indiana side of the river. That's been neutral territory for over a century. We have threats from all sides—the non-paras, the McTiers, even some of our own pack members. If we don't get it under control soon, we're going to lose the pack. And I don't like what I see might come next."

"You're right," Hank said, surprising everyone in the room. "I've been prideful. I've ignored what's been happening right under my nose. It hurts me to say, but maybe it's time for me to think about stepping down."

"Grandpa, that's not we're saying," Dan protested.

"Oh, yes it is. And you're right. Ida's been telling me she wants me to retire. We need to get the family together—

and I mean you, too, Connor. After the family talks, we'll schedule a council meeting."

At that moment, Connor heard a commotion out in the hall. Just as he turned his head, there was the loud crash of shattering glass. Two men in tactical gear came roping in through the window at the same time as the door flew open, and two other cops burst in. "Daniel Bertrand, you are under arrest."

PART THREE
RECLAIMED

CHAPTER 43

"Everyone down! On the ground! Hands where we can see them!"

Connor recognized Sheriff Walker's voice instantly, sharp and commanding, with an edge that said he wouldn't hesitate if crossed.

"Don't make us put you down!" snarled the sheriff behind him, his weapon already half-raised. It was Ricci, Connor realized with a sneer, as usual in a safe place behind his boss. He raised his hands automatically even as he was processing who the men were. His heart hammered against his ribs as he saw he was the only one who had raised them. Dan, Remy, and Hank had already begun to shift, muscle and bone sliding into something half-animal, their deadly teeth and claws in evidence in an instant.

He heard a sharp crack—someone had fired a taser. One of the deputies, a dark silhouette against the window's light, had aimed directly at Dan.

The charge hit, and Dan collapsed on the floor. His shift back to human form happened unnaturally quickly. It would have felt as if every bone in his body had broken, rather than the pleasure-pain of stretching and contracting bones and muscles that was the usual shift. Dan bit back a cry, and the scent of scorched hair hung briefly in the air.

Silver, Connor realized. The taser used silver. That was the only thing that could force a wolf to shift back to human that quickly. How had these cops gotten up to speed so fast on exactly what would be most effective against a werewolf? Two weeks ago, they hadn't even known they existed.

The thought triggered a memory in Connor, but he didn't have time to process it just then as he noticed the fourth officer was already on Dan, yanking his arms behind him with sharp, efficient movements. Once he was handcuffed, the cop snapped a thick collar, glinting with silver studs, around Dan's neck with a metallic click.

Dan growled low in his throat.

"Hank, Remy—shift back. Now," Connor ordered, keeping his voice low and firm. "Don't antagonize them."

The room crackled with tension and noise—boots stomped, radios crackled with static. Still near the door, Connor saw Ricci's finger twitch near the trigger of his rifle. He moved his hand away from it, and Connor let out a quiet sigh of relief.

"Damn, Sheriff, I thought you were crazy loading us up with all this gear, but I guess you were right," the man said, letting out a low whistle.

"I told you, Ricci." Walker's voice was calm, too calm. "They're more dangerous than a Venezuelan gang member. My expert told me just what to bring to subdue them."

Connor made a mental note of Walker's comment. Who was Walker's expert? He'd have to think about it later. Right now, it was more important to defuse this situation before anyone else got hurt. He stepped forward carefully, his hands still raised high, the eyes of every cop in the room following him.

"Sheriff," he said, working hard to keep his voice even. "Why is my client being arrested—again?"

"For the murder of Alexander Fontaine," Walker replied.

Hank laughed roughly as he sank back down in his chair. "Ever hear that old saying about insanity, Sheriff? Doing the same thing over and over and expecting different results? You've arrested my grandson twice already, and it didn't stick. What makes you think this time will be any different?"

Walker's mouth thinned into a hard line. "Because this time we have Fontaine's body. And it's pretty damned clear he was killcd by a large animal."

Across the room, Remy's hands flexed once, then stilled. His face had gone pale, Connor noticed, as he experienced the same emotion he knew Remy was feeling. Ana. Sheriff Walker wanted Dan to be the werewolf who had killed Fontaine, but Remy and Connor knew differently. And if Connor couldn't get Dan released quickly enough, Ana was going to be at the jail turning herself in.

***

Dan lay face down on the carpet, the rough fibers scraping his cheek. A heavy boot ground into his spine, pinning him harder than the silver collar tight around his neck. He tried to move, to shift, but his muscles spasmed uselessly, twitching from the aftershocks of the taser blast.

It hadn't been a normal taser. He knew that much. Copper wire carried electricity. Silver wasn't supposed to. But this shock had been silver-laced; he could still feel it under his skin like burning needles digging into his bones. Only magic could have made silver carry a charge like that. Only magic could have forced his wolf to shift and left him stranded in this broken human form.

Through the haze of pain and anger, he caught part of a conversation nearby, Walker's gruff voice telling Ricci that his "expert" had arranged the special equipment.

Beatrix, Dan thought bitterly. It had to be her. Dolan wouldn't have handed over a weapon that could be turned against his own pack. He was too smart for that. Beatrix, though... she'd love to see him, any Bertrand really, on the ground like this.

Two pairs of shoes came into focus next to his face. Walker and Ricci loomed over him. Out of the corner of his eye, Dan saw Ricci draw back and kick him sharply in the ribs.

Connor surged forward. "Do not attack my client," he snapped, voice cutting across the room. "He's restrained; he's no danger to you."

Walker held up a hand to stop Ricci in a casual gesture of authority before turning a cold look on Connor. "He'll live," he said. "Can't say the same for Fontaine."

"You have a body," Hank growled from his chair. "Doesn't mean it was killed by a wolf." His claws flexed in and out, in and out, in subtle defiance.

"Save it for the judge," Walker snapped.

Hank started to rise, pushing his chair back sharply, but Remy quickly clamped a hand on his shoulder and shoved him back down. Hank muttered something low and furious but stayed seated.

"We don't need you arrested too," Remy said.

Connor stepped between them all, his voice low but firm. "You're not helping," he said, looking pointedly at Hank, before addressing Walker again. "This is unlawful treatment of a suspect. You'll answer for it."

Walker didn't bother replying. He just nodded to Ricci, who hauled Dan roughly to his feet.

Dan staggered, the unexpected weight of the silver collar making it difficult to breathe. He felt half-drowned, his limbs heavy and numb. As they dragged him toward the door, his gaze caught on the office window.

For a second, he saw his reflection—hair mussed, blood trickling from the corner of his mouth, hands cuffed behind his back.

Not a man. Not a wolf. Just another criminal under arrest. The wolf inside him howled in despair, a desperate, furious sound muted by the silver cutting into his skin.

Dan clenched his jaw and forced himself to stay upright. Forced himself not to give them the satisfaction of seeing him fall.

Behind him, Hank continually muttered curses under his breath. Connor and Remy exchanged looks, silent but grim, and then Connor followed close behind as Ricci and another deputy shoved Dan out into the hall.

Dan hung his head. His pack was in disarray; the group needed an alpha, and his grandfather clearly was too emotional to lead right now. Kathleen was in danger. How long could Shannon keep her hidden from Dolan? And unless Connor could get Dan released soon, his sister would turn herself in for Fontaine's murder.

CHAPTER 44

"I've got to go home and get dinner started for Chris and Sophie, but it's so relaxing here, I just don't want to move," said Ana. She was sipping tea in Shannon's kitchen as she chatted with Shannon and Kathleen. A few days ago, she had learned from Dan that her friend had been hiding out with Shannon for several days. She'd been surprised to find out that Kathleen was Dolan McTier's sister, but as she thought it over, it made sense.

"I knew she was afraid of something," she told Dan when they talked. "Hiding from the McTiers explains it perfectly. The more Channing tells me about her relationship with Dolan, the more concerned I am. You know Jonathan didn't win any awards in the husband department when I was married to him, but Dolan is even more controlling. A lot of what he's saying to Channing borders on emotional abuse. And it will only get worse as it goes along.

"He's cutting her off from her family and friends. Dan, we've got to make sure we keep in touch with her all the time. Make sure she knows we support her so when she's ready to leave him—and I'm hoping it will be sooner rather than later—she knows she can come to us."

Dan agreed, and that was one of the reasons for Ana's afternoon visit to see Kathleen. She wanted to learn more about Dolan and also let Kathleen know that Ana was on her side. That the Bertrand pack would support her if she wanted to run from the McTiers.

"I know Dan is still upset now, Kathleen," she said as they continued their conversation. "But he'll get over it. He already has, really. It's just his pride that is in the way."

"I understand, I really do, because I feel the same way. Dan was keeping as many secrets from me as I was from him. I want to forgive him, but I'm just not ready."

The white noise of the small TV Shannon kept in the kitchen was a background to their conversation along with a decoction simmering on Shannon's stove. She was brewing a potion as a part of the cure for Chris. She, Dave, and the three elves hoped that tomorrow they could perform the ceremony that would cure Chris and free him from their mother's control.

"Men!" Shannon laughed now in response to the conversation. "Can't live with them, can't turn them into toads. When Dave and I first started dating we had a lot to work through, too, you know. Mostly it was my…"

Shannon stopped as a local TV announcer's voice broke into the drone of the program they'd had on in the background.

"Breaking news out of Herndon County. Daniel Bertrand, CFO of Bertrand Enterprises and member of the influential Bertrand family, was arrested this afternoon and charged with the murder of well-known author and professor Alexander Fontaine…"

The tea mug slipped out of Ana' hand and fell to the floor, but she didn't even notice. Kathleen turned as white as a ghost, and Shannon jumped to turn up the volume on the TV set.

"It's Dolan. He did this," said Kathleen. "Dan and I heard Ric and Sean—they're other pack members and good friends with Dolan—talking about how they were going to make sure Fontaine's body was found soon. Oh God, this is all about me. Dolan wouldn't be after him if it weren't for me."

"Stop that!" demanded Shannon. "This is not your fault, or yours Ana, or mine. The people responsible are Dolan and my mother."

"Your mother?" questioned Kathleen.

"We've known if she ever got free of the prison I made for her, that she would come after Chris and me. She found an ally in Dolan. They've been working this together. I can't prove it, but it's got to be what's happening. It's the only thing that makes sense. My mother wants revenge on Chris and me, and Dolan wants to take over the Bertrand pack. What better way to accomplish all of it than to frame Dan for Fontaine's murder?"

"But Dan didn't kill Alexander. I did," said Ana. "And I'm the only one who can fix this. I'm going down to the sheriff's office right now and confess."

She got up from the table and began to gather her purse and jacket.

"No, you are not, Ana!" Shannon took the purse from Ana's hands and pushed her back down in her seat. "Think about it. That's just playing into their hands."

Ana hesitated.

"And what about Sophie and Chris? They need you."

With tears in her eyes Ana said, "I haven't told Sophie anything about Alexander. I know she's heard some rumors, but I've tried to keep her away from all of this…"

"And Chris needs you right now, Ana," Shannon continued. "We won't be ready to try to reverse the curse until tomorrow, and we aren't even positive it will work."

"She's right, Ana," Kathleen spoke up. "I don't know everything that's going on with Chris, but know my brother's involved with finding Fontaine's body. I heard Ric and Sean talking about it, but it would be just as useless for me to march down to the sheriff and tell what I heard. It wouldn't prove Dan didn't kill the man; no one would believe either of us and we'd just be putting ourselves in danger without helping Dan."

Ana brushed at the tears which had gathered in her eyes. "I know you're right, but it's so hard to sit here feeling useless."

"I know, honey, but Connor's going to take care of him. He always does," said Shannon.

Ana nodded as her phone rang. "That's Sophie. I wonder if she's heard."

As she answered the phone, the other two could hear Sophie's voice clearly. She sounded panicked.

"Mom, Mom, you've got to get home quick. It's Chris. He just fainted or something. And now he's twitching. Mom, I'm so scared."

Shannon grabbed the phone from Ana's hand. "Sophie, listen to me; it's Shannon. We're on our way; we'll be there in just a few minutes. Keep an eye on him until we get there."

She hung up the phone and turned to Kathleen. "I've got to go with Ana. I'm the only one who can help my brother right now."

She turned to the stove and began ladling the potion she

was making into a large plastic storage container. Kathleen almost laughed at the incongruity of the ancient potion being stored in something so modern and mundane, but she quickly stifled it.

"Go on, Shannon, I'll be fine here."

"I hate leaving you by yourself, but we don't have protections set up at Ana's house to hide you."

"Go. Don't worry about me. Chris needs you now."

"I'll see if Abby can come over. Just don't open the door to anyone while I'm gone," she said as she and Ana hurried out.

CHAPTER 45

The scent of burning rosemary and moonflower root hung heavy in the air as Shannon poured the potion she had brought with her into the iron cauldron resting on a circle of carved runes. They had been afraid to move Chris; he seemed too ill, so Kai, Theo, and Dave had quickly moved all of the furniture from the living room of Ana's home. Shannon looked around and wondered where they had stashed it. It didn't seem to be anywhere in the small house. Had they sent it off to Otherworld to get it out of the way?

They tried to get Sophie to go over the Lessing's house next door, but the 14-year-old insisted she was old enough to stay. "My father doesn't want me anymore," she said. "Chris is my father now, and it's important I be here for him." Ana had agreed, drawing comfort from her daughter's presence as they both knelt beside Chris, lying unconscious in the middle of the circle of salt Dave had spread as soon as he arrived.

The living room pulsed with the low, rhythmic chant from the elves—Kai and Sierra standing just inside the protective circle, Theo standing over Chris while Dave and Shannon knelt opposite him, Dave's expression set with grim determination.

Ana hovered near Chris's head, one hand gently stroking his damp hair. Her other was clenched around the silver locket engraved with a crow that Shannon had found among the items she had kept from her mother. Theo hoped it would help anchor Beatrix's magic here in the room with them and keep her from accessing it. It was their only chance, he said, to sever the tether that linked Chris to his mother.

"I'm afraid he doesn't have much time," Ana whispered, her voice shaking.

"He'll make it," Shannon said, louder than was necessary in the small living room. Maybe she was reassuring Ana. Maybe herself.

Theo's voice rose again, low and melodic. Shannon

didn't understand the Elvish words, but the rhythm was somehow both soothing and powerful. His hands moved gracefully as the Elvish syllables weaved through the room, creating smoky threads that hung in the air and laced back and forth, weaving a net of Elven symbols that surrounded Chris. The fire in the hearth roared higher, blue at its heart. Shadows flickered and danced across the walls.

Dave added his voice next—sharp, clipped English, magic born of blood and will, a counterpoint to Theo's song as he drew a circle of powdered hematite around the pallet.

"By root and stone, by flame and sea,
I call the powers—bring aid to me.
From east winds swift, bring cleansing air,
From south, let fire burn through despair.
West waters flow, release what's chained,
North's steady earth, restore what's strained."

He threw a handful of lavender and crushed quartz into the cauldron, and it flared violet.

"Unbind the mark, reverse the tie,
Let truth break through the binding lie.
With leaf and thorn, with salt and sage,
I banish shadow, still the rage.
Beneath the moon, above the tree—
This curse undone, So mote it be."

He scattered red salt across the circle, each grain flaring as it hit the floor. The overlapping chants began to form a counter-harmony—Elven memory and witch motion, intertwined.

Chris's body arched. The crow-shaped rune on his chest began to glow red-hot.

"Now!" shouted Shannon.

Kai stepped into the circle, hands raised. Light burst from his palms, wrapping Chris in a cocoon of shimmering energy. The rune fought back—dark tendrils lashed out, trying to claw their way into the surrounding magic.

"He's fighting me!" Kai shouted.

"No," Shannon said, stepping closer. "That's not Chris. That's her."

Beatrix's voice echoed from Chris's mouth again, cold and mocking. "He'll never be free of me, Daughter. And neither will you. I've rooted myself deeper than you know."

Theo's voice never faltered.

"Keep going," Dave said as Shannon reached into her pocket and withdrew a single black crow's feather. It had come from an old cloak of Beatrix's that Shannon had found along with the necklace that Ana held. Shannon pressed the feather to the brand on Chris' chest.

Dave struck the floor with his staff. "Spiral unbind. Now!"

The room exploded with light. Sophie gave a small shriek and grabbed her mother's arm. The air grew thick and electric. The symbols Theo had woven around Chris flared into life. The Heart Flame, for purification by fire. The Celtic cross, symbolizing spirit and body, the Thread of Memory, weaving the ancient and new magics together, and a golden spiral within a silver circle. Created by Lireal himself, it would hold back the corruption of Beatrix's blood magic. The rune on Chris's chest cracked, splitting like glass under pressure.

Chris screamed.

Ana reached out for him, but this time it was Sophie who held her back.

"He has to do this himself," Shannon said, nodding in approval at Sophie's actions.

The magic surged as chains of tarnished silver and shadow rose from Chris's body. They twisted around his limbs like living things as he struggled to free himself.

Theo sang louder. Dave threw both hands into the air, their combined incantation sounding like thunder and wind combined. Shannon placed her hand over Chris's heart, her voice steady and calm as she chanted.

"With memory and motion
We unmake the mark.
With blood and bond
We break the curse
With fire and will, we call him back.
As we will,

So mote it be."

The chains shattered.

Chris convulsed once, then collapsed as the fire died down to embers, and the air stilled.

For a long, terrible second, no one moved. Sophie clutched her mother's arm tightly. Ana's eyes never left Chris' face. Finally, he took a breath. Then a second one. His eyes fluttered open, clear and alert, and very, very human.

"Is it… over?" he whispered.

Ana collapsed into his arms, sobbing. "Yes. Yes, it is."

Theo gave a slow nod, finally allowing himself a breath. "He's free."

Dave sagged back, sitting hard on the floor. "Next time," he said between gasps, "We're going to bind the curse to a stuffed animal instead."

Kai gave a shaky laugh. "We did it."

Shannon looked down at her brother, her hand still on his chest where the brand had been. It was just a scar now. Red and ragged, but the mark of the crow could no longer be seen. "No," she said softly. "He did it."

The moment of celebration was short-lived. Dave's phone buzzed. "Hey, Abby, what's up," he said.

Shannon gasped. "Oh no, "I forgot to call Abby. I left Kathleen alone."

CHAPTER 46

Dan couldn't believe they'd arrested him, let alone paraded him out with a collar around his neck and his hands cuffed to a silver-impregnated chain around his waist, like he wasn't just a criminal, but a very dangerous one.

"Walker's finally got what he wants," he said gloomily to himself as he was pushed into a car, a cop's hand rough on the top of his head. It would look to those watching as if the man were protecting Dan from hitting his head, but in reality, he'd pushed him in a way to make him lose his balance and fall forward into the car.

Despite all of the cops surrounding him, he could see and hear the reporters gathered outside the Bertrand Enterprises office. And they could see him. Walker made sure that everyone who wanted to had the opportunity to videotape the perp walk. He could hear questions called out to him by members of the news media who conveniently had been notified of his arrest in time to be here to watch. He pretended not to notice and kept his mouth shut. It was hard, but he knew that's what Connor would want him to do.

As the car pulled out, he could see that Connor had stopped to address the crowd. Walker noticed, too, and laughed. "Looks like your boy is trying to convince the good folk of the media that you're just some poor guy whose rights have been abused, not the murderer I know you are."

Dan bit back more words, wishing Connor could see it. He'd never believe Dan was actually taking his advice and keeping his mouth shut for once.

Hours later he'd been read his rights, booked, photographed, and fingerprinted. One of the cops had expressed awe that his image showed up in the photo; it wasn't just a blank screen. "That's vampires, idiot, whose photos aren't supposed to show, not werewolves. And only in books. Do you think we could have kept ourselves secret for centuries if every time someone took a picture of us there was a big blank?" he snarled. His outburst got him a hard pull on the collar around his neck, just as if he were a dog on a choke chain. It set off a blast of pain as the silver studs pulled at his skin.

He was stripped and given an orange jump suit to wear, then put in a cell by himself where he'd paced restlessly back and forth the entire night. Now, it was finally morning, and he'd been taken out and paraded in the orange suit in front of a judge.

He'd had just a few minutes to talk with Connor before the hearing.

"What's happening, man?" he asked.

"Well, your whole family is here except Ana—and Channing."

"Thank God Ana didn't come," Dan said.

"Yeah, not so much. She would have been here and none of us could have stopped her. But Chris collapsed last night. Shannon, Dave, and the three elves were with them. They called me a few hours ago. They broke the damned curse—finally, but Ana wanted to stay with him today, make sure he's okay. That's the only thing that kept her from coming here and shouting out that she's the one who killed Fontaine."

"You'd better make sure that doesn't happen, Connor. I know how you feel about her. You make sure she doesn't try and take the blame. I'd rather go to jail for life than see her here. And this thing with Chris. You said they broke the curse but if something happens to him…"

"I know, man. I won't let her do anything stupid. Chris needs her right now. Even though they broke the curse and got Beatrix' claws off Chris, he still needs time to recover."

There was no time to say anything else as an officer came to escort him into the courtroom. His family was sitting right behind the defense table. Dan noticed his grandmother had a tight grip around his mom's shoulders. He hoped she could keep her from saying anything she shouldn't. That was a full-time job on a good day, but if anyone were up to the task, it was Ida. Tyler caught his eye, placed his fist on his heart, and mouthed the word, "Alpha."

Dan had to blink quickly several times as he saw his

younger brother's signal.

At that moment, the judge entered the room, and the bailiff called out, "All rise." When the charge of murder was read he heard his mother gasp. He clenched his hands tightly, willing his wolf to stay quiet. No claws. No fangs. Connor had warned him to do nothing that could even remotely be considered violent by a non-para.

"How do you plead?" Judge Lorena Wilson asked.

"My client pleads not guilty," said Connor.

The district attorney, Sheriff Walker sitting next to him, requested no bail on the grounds that Dan was dangerous. Connor immediately jumped up.

"My client is an upstanding citizen, well-known in the community He should be released on his own recognizance."

"Your client is a dangerous werewolf," Walker said. He was immediately reprimanded by Judge Wilson but still turned and looked at Dan with a sly smile. He'd made his point for the media, who sat at the back of the room. And that was all that mattered to him.

"Your Honor, the sheriff is attempting to prejudice the court and the public against both my client and paranormals in general. This is the first time since the Witch Trials of the 1600s that a paranormal has been charged with a crime in open court. Your decision to deny or grant bail today won't just affect Mr. Bertrand; it will send a message to every paranormal citizen in this country."

"Mr. Morrigan, I will remind you that this court is not a platform for political commentary."

"I respectfully disagree, Your Honor. The moment Sheriff Walker used the term 'dangerous werewolf' in open court, this became political. He's not just trying to convict my client. He's trying to paint all paranormals as threats to society, as monsters in human skin. That's not justice. That's a warning shot.

"If Mr. Bertrand were not a shapeshifter, he wouldn't have been detained with silver-laced tasers or a silver-lined collar around his neck. But that is exactly how the sheriff and his men arrested him. And he wouldn't be facing calls for pretrial imprisonment without cause. The state's case is circumstantial at best, inflammatory at worst. If you allow this to happen, you have shown yourself on the side of those who are prejudiced against people strictly for what they are rather than for their actions."

Dan winced. He hoped Connor hadn't gone too far in suggesting the judge herself might be prejudiced.

The prosecutor, who until now had kept quiet, letting the others make his case for him, spoke up. "Your Honor, we're not here to debate the broader implications of this new phenomenon of paranormals—a species that has worked hard to keep itself hidden for centuries. If that doesn't cause enough concern, this one man—pardon me—werewolf—is charged with killing a man and hiding his body for months. We would not yet know what happened to the eminent professor if his remains had not been discovered by hikers. There is clear cause for concern that the defendant is a threat to everyone in the area."

"The state wants to treat this man like he's a weapon. What precedent does that set?" countered Connor. "Do we put all paranormals in collars now? Do we assume guilt based on biology? You do this today, and tomorrow a student gets arrested for 'aggressive energy.' A business owner loses their license because a customer felt 'uncomfortable.' Is that the world you want?"

"Mr. Morrigan, you are admonished again. I will not tolerate your editorializing in this courtroom. That said, Mr. Bertrand is granted bail in the amount of $500,000. He is allowed to go to his home in Kentucky, but he must remain in the Herndon County/Rivelou area. He will surrender his passport. And Sheriff Walker…" the judge turned to the man.

"Yes, your honor?"

"No further magical or physical restraints are to be used in this jurisdiction on *any* suspect without additional order from this court."

CHAPTER 47

As the bailiff called, "All rise," and Judge Wilson swept from the bench with the rustle of black robes, the courtroom erupted into chaos. Reporters surged to their feet, scrambling to be the first out the door, already barking into phones or tugging camera crews behind them. The air crackled with noise and the scent of sweat from too many bodies. For Dan, his wolf still close to the surface and his senses heightened, it was overwhelming.

He sat still for a moment, letting everything wash over him. He was relieved, of course, that he wouldn't be forced to stay in the jail, but he knew, realistically, it was only a postponement. There would be a trial, and he could very well be found guilty. What would happen to his family? To Kathleen? He needed to see her. He wished she could have been here, but he was glad she was safely locked away at Shannon's house.

There was something Connor had said about Shannon... So much had happened he was having trouble keeping it all straight. That's right, he remembered, Shannon was working to help Chris. But she wouldn't have left Kathleen alone. She'd had to go out before and had always made sure that someone had stayed with Kathleen to protect her. He didn't have to worry. He'd just feel better once he saw her, held her, and made sure she knew that everything was right between them. This last twelve hours locked up had proved at least one thing to him: he needed Kathleen. It didn't matter who her family was. She was his. *Yes! Finally! Now let's go get her and make her our mate,* his wolf told him.

He had been vaguely aware of the guards beside him, ready to escort him back for processing; now he wanted to hurry them along. He needed to get out of here. Maybe he wasn't truly free yet, but he was no longer a prisoner.

He stood and let the deputies lead him from the room.

The hallway echoed with their footfalls, and no one spoke as they walked him back to the sheriff's office to change out of the jumpsuit. The scratchy fabric was too familiar now, and he peeled it off with grim satisfaction, armoring himself again in the suit and tie of the respected business executive. Not the prisoner. Not the werewolf. This was the costume the world would respect.

***

He blinked in the late afternoon sunshine as he stepped out of the Sheriff's office door. How had it gotten so late so quickly? Connor had assured him the bail hearing would only take an hour, but the day was almost gone. And he still had to brave the army of media in front of him. He blinked against the barrage of camera flashes. The media hadn't thinned out, and now that the verdict had been rendered, if anything, the gang of reporters had grown. And they were ravenous for sound bites and scandal.

He smiled when he saw his grandfather waiting for him next to Connor, patently ignoring the media's attempts to get them to answer questions. His mother and grandmother were gone, his father, too. He'd probably escorted the women and Tyler home, he thought, relieved that at least some of the family was away from this mess. Then his grandfather moved, and Dan realized Tyler was there behind him. The kid's stance was solid, his arms folded across his chest, eyes steady behind his glasses.

"Tyler," Dan said, striding over. "You shouldn't be here. You've still got classes. I don't want this circus screwing up your future. Your professors…"

"I'm not going anywhere," Tyler interrupted, his voice firm. "Dad took Mom and Grandma home. But I'm staying. You think I can just sit in some lecture hall and pretend this isn't happening?" He glanced toward the crowd of cameras. "We've got to stand up. For you. For all of us. You're just the first, Dan. The rest of us need to make sure you're the last."

Dan blinked. "You sound like…"

"Connor," Tyler said with a grin. "Yeah, I know." He shoved his hands in the pocket of his suit pants. "I've been thinking. Law school. Advocacy. Maybe even a nonprofit for paranormal civil rights." He met Dan's eyes. "I want to fight for our future. I want to make sure we get to have one."

Dan's throat tightened, but before he could respond, the reporters spotted him.

"Mr. Bertrand! Do you still have your job?"

"Does this mean Bertrand Enterprises condones violence?"

"If you didn't kill Fontaine, who did?"

Delaney Dark's voice cut over the crowd like a whip. "Was Fontaine a werewolf, too? Was this a pack challenge gone wrong? Or is this how you Bertrands handle challenges to your authority?"

Another reporter shouted at Connor, "Mr. Morrigan, you say paranormals deserve rights. But why should non-humans have human rights?"

The crowd surged, microphones shoving forward.

Before Connor or Hank could speak, Tyler stepped forward, shoulders square. "You want to know why paranormals should have rights?" His voice carried easily in the sudden hush. "Because we are just like you. We're not non-human. We're not animals. We just have different abilities. Just like you. Yeah, some of us can turn into wolves or cast spells. Some of us have other abilities. But that's no different than being good at football, or tennis, or playing a musical instrument. We've always been here. The only difference between today and last month is that now you know we are here."

A few camera lenses swung toward him, and several people in the crowd shouted out, "What's your name?" "Are you a werewolf, too?"

Tyler started to answer, but Dan put a hand on his shoulder. "Let's get out of here." They walked to Connor's car and got in, ignoring the shouted questions behind them.

As the door slammed shut, Dan exhaled. "I need to see Kathleen," he said. "Now."

CHAPTER 48

"That girl's a McTier. She's bad news. You need to get over her, Dan," Hank said flatly from the front passenger seat.

Dan, sitting in the back with Tyler, flexed his claws with a low growl. After twenty-four hours of constantly restraining his wolf, he finally let it out—just a little. Tyler turned toward him, surprised, as Dan snapped, "She's my mate. My fated mate. I'm not getting over her, and I'm not giving her up."

"I'm still your Alpha," Hank barked, twisting around. "If I say you give her up, you give her up. That's it. You're not thinking straight, or you'd know I'm right."

"And that's worked so well in the past, hasn't it?" Dan replied, his sarcasm sharp.

"We all know Dan's thinking straight," Tyler offered helpfully. "If Kathleen were a threat, she'd have taken him down already."

"Not helping, Kid," Dan muttered, just as Hank let out a warning growl of his own.

Connor took a hand off the wheel and raised it in a calming gesture. "Look, he's not claiming her tonight. We all agree we need to check on her—make sure she's safe from Dolan. But first, we stop at Ana and Chris's. Shannon said the ceremony went well, but we should still check in."

Dan exhaled slowly. "You're right. Family first." He looked out the window, jaw tight. "We check on them. But after that, you can drop me at Shannon's. And Grandpa, I'll find out if Kathleen knows anything about Dolan's plans."

At that moment, Dan's phone rang. He glanced at the screen and brightened. "Hi Grandma, I'm out. We're almost at Ana's…"

His expression shifted. "You're sure? Have you checked with her work? No… no… we'll look into it right now. I'm with Connor, Tyler, and Grandpa. You stay put in case she shows up at the farm. I'll let you know the moment we find anything."

He ended the call and turned to the others. "It's Channing. She's missing. No one's seen her since Sunday."

Hank's face darkened—not just at the news, but at something that troubled him even more deeply. "Your grandmother should've called me, not you," he muttered.

Dan met his eyes in the rearview mirror. "She called the one she thought could fix it."

Tyler reached forward and rested a hand on Hank's shoulder. "You're still our Alpha, Grandpa. But Dan's the one we need right now."

Hank gave a dry laugh. "Just drop me off at home. I'll pack a bag and head to Gulf Shores. I hear there's a nice retirement community there for old shifters."

"Grandpa, no," Tyler started, but Hank waved him off. "We need you," Tyler said softly. "It's just... it's time."

Dan didn't say anything. There wasn't anything to say.

Connor broke the silence. "Let's go to Channing's. Find out what's going on." He turned at the next light, steering the SUV out of town and toward Channing's apartment complex.

The four men gathered at her door a few minutes later. Hank knocked, waited, then pounded harder. "Channing, it's your grandfather. Open the door."

No answer.

He pounded again. "Channing. Open the door right now."

Connor turned to Dan. "We can break it down."

"I thought you were the law-abiding one," Dan said, a half-smile twitching at his mouth.

"Whoa, wait. Don't get excited—I have a key," Tyler interjected. The others turned to him in surprise.

"What? Channing gave it to me when I started at the university. Sometimes I need a quiet place to study."

He pulled a key from his pocket and unlocked the door. "Hey, Channing?" he called as he stepped inside.

The apartment was silent.

The drapes were drawn. No lights on. No dishes, no coffee mugs were set out or in the sink. The air held that faintly stale scent of absence.

"She hasn't been here in days," Connor said quietly.

Tyler walked into the small kitchen. "Here's a note," he said, lifting a folded piece of paper from the counter. "It's addressed to me."

He read aloud:

"Tyler,

You're the one most likely to stop in, so I wanted you to know I've gone to the McTier pack with Dolan. I just don't think I fit in with this family or pack anymore. Tell Mom and Grandma I love them."

The room was silent. Only the creak of the floor under Hank's shoes as he shifted uncomfortably broke the stillness. "So, she left. She left with a McTier. That's it," he said harshly.

Dan looked closely at the older man. His face was turned away, and he was blinking fiercely. He took the note from his brother's hand, reading it over silently.

"No. I can't believe she left with him. Not of her own free will. Ana said she was upset with him. Was starting to realize he was trying to control her."

Then he looked at Connor. "We need to move. Now. We'll check in at Ana's first."

CHAPTER 49

Ana opened the door and hugged Dan fiercely as soon as she saw him. "Come in. Tell me everything that happened," she said, ushering the four of them into the living room. Chris was leaning back against the couch pillows, still pale, but obviously feeling better than they had seen him in weeks.

"Don't stand up, man," Dan said as Chris started to do just that.

He sank back on the couch, but held out his hand, shaking Dan's, then the other three. "Good to see you're not in jail," he said.

Shannon and Dave came in from the kitchen, both also looking exhausted.

"Good to be seen not in jail," Dan replied.

"But you're not free yet," Ana said as they all sat down. "They'll still be coming after you."

Shannon offered to get everyone drinks and headed back into the kitchen.

Dave said, "I hate to say Ana is right, but we just heard a news report. It's streaming on my phone if you want to see it."

He set the phone on the coffee table, and they all leaned in to watch. A tinny voice could be heard: "Wealthy Bertrand Enterprises CFO just received bail after being accused of the murder of noted author Alexander Fontaine." The announcer went on to explain the details of the hearing, then called on a legal expert to discuss the technicalities of this first paranormal murder case since the Witchcraft Trial of 1878.

"We're not witches; we're werewolves, idiot," muttered Tyler at the screen.

"Hey, speak for yourself, Kid," joked Dave.

"Yeah, yeah," replied Tyler.

Chris held up his hand. "Wait, I think they've got you."

The expert spoke about lycanthropy trials in Germany in the 1500s.

"This guy knows his paranormal history," added Chris, obviously impressed. "I wonder if he…"

"What? Another Alexander Fontaine? Studying paranormals while pretending not to be one?" said Dave.

"Yeah, I'm going to have to look into him. He may be an asset or…"

"That's not what's important right now," said Dan, jaw clenched. "It's the Bertrand name. Grandpa, you've worked your entire life to make sure we had a good reputation—with paranormals and non-paras alike. Now it's gone, and it's my fault."

"Then you clear it. You lead us through this."

"It's not Dan's fault; it's mine. I'll turn myself in." Ana stood behind the sofa, her hand on Chris' shoulder as she spoke.

There was silence. Just then Sophie, who had been helping Shannon in the kitchen, entered with a tray of iced tea. "What?"

"Sophie, I didn't want you to hear it this way. Your uncle didn't kill Alexander. I did."

Shannon took the tray from Sophie and set it on the table. "I know your mom didn't want you to find out, but she did it in a good cause. She saved my and Chris' lives that night. Fontaine was about to kill us."

"It's time I stop hiding," added Ana.

Everyone protested at once.

Sophie grabbed her mother's hand. "Not yet. Please. We've just got Chris back. And I know Connor's not going to let Uncle Dan go to jail."

"Let the facts come out. If you walk in now, they'll make you out to be the villain," said Shannon.

Chris agreed.

"Look, I've got some legal tricks up my sleeve. As the defense we can order a second autopsy. Nathan Lazard is a national expert. No one will dispute his findings," added Connor.

"Vampire coroner. Always good to have one on retainer," muttered Chris.

"And that's why I've cultivated this coalition of

paranormals all these years. We may be out now, but most of the alliances I've built up will stand," said Hank.

After they talked for a few more minutes, Dan said, "Chris, I'm glad you're okay, but that's only one of the reasons we're here. Ana, have you heard from Channing recently?"

"Channing? No. Not for a few days. I assumed she was at the courthouse with the rest of you today, so I didn't even try to get in touch with her."

Dan slowly pulled the note from their sister out of his pocket and handed it to Ana. "We found this at her apartment. The place didn't look as if anyone had been there for days.

"I don't understand. This doesn't sound like Channing. She has a job she loves. Friends. She wouldn't just run off without telling one of us."

"That's what I say," put in Tyler.

"Look, I need to go see Kathleen. Maybe she knows what Dolan is up to."

Shannon nodded. "Abby has been with her since early this morning. I forgot to call her when I came first got her last night, but she would have let me know if anything was wrong. She should still be there. She's a skilled witch and she's able to keep Kathleen safe."

Connor offered to drive him, but Dan said it was just a few blocks. He'd walk.

"You're going to need someone to negate the spells before you can get in. Dave and I will go with you," Shannon said. "I think it's time we let Chris, Ana, and Sophie get some rest."

They left Connor to take Hank back home and walked the few short blocks to Shannon's house. The evening air was crisp with the feel of early autumn. Dan would have enjoyed it if he weren't so worried about other things.

"What do you think I should do?" he asked Shannon and Dave as they walked. "If you haven't realized it by now, there is dissension in the pack. People want a new leader. They are tired of Hank. It probably would have happened without Dolan here, but he's been stirring up trouble, causing everything to blow up right now."

"You've got to do what you've got to do," said Dave.

They continued to discuss the situation as they walked to Shannon's home.

When they arrived, Shannon entered the magical passcode and opened the door. Lying on the floor was Abby.

Shannon ran to her. Abby stirred. There was blood on her hair.

"Abby, what happened?"

Dave knelt down to help.

"Kathleen!" Dan called. There was no answer. "Abby, where is she?" he asked when it became obvious that no one else was there.

Abby was dazed. She groaned. "Beatrix… and Dolan. They took Kathleen. I tried…"

"Channing? Was she here, too? Was she a part of this?" Dan's heart was racing. He didn't know whether to hope his sister was fine but a traitor, or if she, too, had been taken by Dolan and Beatrix.

Abby shook her head weakly. "Didn't see her. I don't know if she was part of it or not."

Dan's eyes went gold. His voice grew low and lethal. "Then I'm done waiting."

He pulled out his phone. "Connor, we've got a problem."

CHAPTER 50

The house was wrong, evil. She knew it even as they were driving through the gates. Channing didn't know what she'd expected of Dolan's ancestral home, but this wasn't it. Bertrand lands were open and sun-drenched, a sprawl of barns, cottages, and renovated houses with smoke curling from chimneys and kids' bikes leaning against porches. This house, this place, was cold.

Massive iron gates clanged shut behind them. The car curved along a brick drive flanked by tightly clipped hedges whose leaves were already turning brown, despite its only being mid-September. There were no flowers, no life. She shivered as if the cold she felt was physical rather than merely emotional. At the end of the drive stood a mansion with Gothic bones, its stone exterior darkened by time and smoke, ivy choking the corners like claws curling into flesh. The front entry loomed like a warning.

Channing's breath hitched beside Kathleen. "This is where you grew up?" she whispered.

Kathleen nodded.

"No wonder your brother turned out twisted."

Kathleen snorted. She sometimes wondered how she hadn't turned out that way herself.

Kathleen had only met Dan's sister—her brother's girlfriend—briefly once or twice, but in the three-hour drive from Rivelou to the McTier pack lands, they had a chance to get to know each other a lot better. After they'd both woken up from the spell Beatrix had cast on them, that is. They whispered quietly, hoping not to attract Dolan's attention, but Kathleen had had a chance to tell Channing a little about what to expect once they arrived.

They sat in the back of the Infiniti QX80, the scent of leather almost suffocating Kathleen. While her father called the luxury SUV "his truck," it had nothing in common with pickups and practical work vehicles that most people in the area—paranormal or non-para—drove. The interior was all deep red leather and chrome—the color of blood—with dark wood accents polished to a high shine. The seats were deep and wide, more like thrones than chairs, and the faint scent of cologne and ozone from the air vents mixed with the sharp tang of silver. It was a luxury cage

Both their hands and feet were bound with silver-impregnated ropes. Beatrix had laughed as she waved her staff and tied them tightly, making sure the silver cut into their skin. She'd disappeared then, leaving Dolan to drive them to the family home.

***

They pulled up at the front entrance, and Ric and Sean hurried out to meet them. "Your father is waiting for you," Ric said as he opened the back door of the car and carefully extracted Kathleen, making sure not to touch the silver bonds, while Sean pulled Channing from the other side. Ric gave her an evil smile. "He's very anxious to see you, too, Princess." The sarcasm was heavy in his voice.

The two men pushed Kathleen and Channing ahead of them into the front hall of the mansion.

Inside, Kathleen noted the familiar odors of leather, whiskey, and old blood. She shivered. Channing's nostrils flared at the scent, and Kathleen fought the urge to reach for her hand. The only warmth they could feel in the house came from each other.

She watched as Channing straightened her spine and put on her haughtiest "granddaughter of the Alpha" expression. Kathleen forced herself to do the same even though being back here made her feel like a small child again, not the confident woman she was when she was with Dan.

The thought of Dan almost made her break. Would he realize she'd been kidnapped? Or would he think she'd gone with her brother willingly? And Abby. She hoped Abby would be alright. The last glimpse she'd had of her had been lying unconscious on the floor, struck down by one of Beatrix' spells.

Ric and Sean pushed them forward into the mansion's

great hall, used as a meeting room for the pack. It had the look of a medieval castle, complete with large table and a raised dais where the Alpha and his family sat. It felt more like a museum than a living space: velvet-covered chairs, portraits of severe men, and a fire that seemed to burn too hot, too high, casting everything in gold and shadow. Her father was there now, sitting in his chair. He stood when Dolan came to him, giving him a simple nod as Dolan bowed his head to the side submissively.

"You've done well, my son," Michael McTier said. "You've brought the Bertrand girl as we planned and have even managed to find your recalcitrant sister."

"Thank you, Father. I always try to do your bidding."

"Girl, come here!" Michael said commandingly.

Kathleen found herself taking a step forward out of long habit, then forced herself to stop. She wasn't that person anymore. She wasn't the cowed, submissive daughter. She was Dan Bertrand's fated mate, and she would prove it.

When she didn't move at once, Michael nodded to Ric, who pushed her forward. She stumbled and almost fell to her knees but managed to keep her feet. Sean, she noticed, gave her a sympathetic look but didn't intervene. That look was new. Was he getting tired of the McTier ways? Was it something she could use?

"What do you have to say for yourself, Daughter?"

Kathleen met his gaze. "My mate will come for me. And when he does, you'll regret ever touching me."

"Your mate?" Michael scoffed. "Show me." He commanded Ric, who forced her neck to the side, exposing it to her father. "He hasn't marked you yet. If he were really your mate, he wouldn't have hesitated to already have claimed you. You have no bond with him; you cannot connect with him. And you are still my daughter, and I can choose whoever your mate will be."

"Now you, Girl." He turned to Channing, who in turn was brought to the dais. "She is quite pretty, Dolan. I can see why you want her—not even counting the advantage of her being a Bertrand. Have you marked her yet?"

"Not yet, Father, I was waiting for your permission."

Dolan turned toward her, his smile as sharp as a blade.

Channing's eyes flashed. "I'm not a damned doll. You can't force me to mate him." She put all of the scorn she could muster into the sentence.

"Oh, I think we can. You will be my son's mate. And if you aren't, well, you might resist if I threaten you, but will you resist if I threaten her?" He nodded at Kathleen.

"You wouldn't," Channing gasped. "She's your daughter."

"Oh, he would, Channing. Don't doubt him," said Dolan. He moved fast toward Channing, but Kathleen stepped between them before she even thought. Her heart thundered, but she stood her ground.

"You'll have to go through me," she said. Her voice didn't shake. Not once.

Dolan's eyes narrowed. "Are you threatening me, Little Sister?"

"No," Kathleen said. "I'm telling you I've changed. I'm not the girl who ran away. Not the girl who let you and Father make her choices for her."

Dolan's silence sliced through the room like a knife.

Behind him, Sean cleared his throat. "This isn't what our pack stands for," he muttered.

"Then maybe the pack needs to remember who's in charge. No one disputes my word," said Michael.

Before anyone could react, he'd bared his claws and slit Sean's throat. Sean fell to the floor, blood flowing, dead almost as soon as he hit the ground.

CHAPTER 51

Dan stood in the center of the barn, the same one where he'd danced with Kathleen for the first time at Ana's and Chris' engagement party only months ago. Tonight, the fairy lights were dimmed, and the laughter had vanished. This was no celebration. It was a war council.

The basement of the old family farmhouse was too small to hold this many bodies. More people had shown up than for the meeting about the PackNet breach. Tension crackled like lightning.

Familiar faces ringed the space: Gabe with Ramona, Landon, and Jace from PackNet, his brother Tyler, Channing's friends Nova and Brittany. His grandmother and mother stood shoulder to shoulder. There were others he barely recognized. But he noticed who wasn't there—the three younger shifters who had been sniffing after Dolan. Had they gone with him to the McTier lands? That would be a loss. Especially Jax, the son of Councilman Tim Means. Dan didn't want to see a pup get hurt, but if they stood with Dolan, they would fall with him.

He hoped it wouldn't come to bloodshed. But knowing the McTiers, he wasn't counting on it.

His father, Remy, came up beside him, clapping a hand on his shoulder. "You ready for this?"

Dan nodded, and together they joined Hank and the council on the raised platform—the same one where the band had played not so long ago.

Their allies stood with them: the heads of the eagle, deer, bobcat and bear shifters—Talon Storm, Maris Wood, Kaia Strickland, and Beau Alden. Cassandra and her coven. Nathan Lazard. Chief Anderson and a few other lone paranormals who had no allegiance but had chosen to come. Their followers stood in the crowd, mingling with the wolves. The largest group were the witches. Winnie Thorne next to Tyler. Dave and Shannon standing near Chris with Ana and Sophie. Abby Mohr and Jake

Waseaux. Jessa Vance with the other members of Gabe's crew. And in the shadows at the rear of the barn were the three elves: Serelith, silent as smoke; Theolin, standing sentinel; and Kailin, bristling with energy. They would not step onto the platform, but their presence spoke volumes. Together, this coalition represented a power Rivelou hadn't seen in generations.

Hank raised his hands, and the crowd began to quiet. "Some of you know why we're here. Two of our females have been taken by the McTier pack."

A voice cut through the barn. "How do we know they didn't leave on their own?"

Dan recognized Isaac Means. Ambitious, loud, and itching for a challenge. Dan knew he had ambitions of becoming the next Alpha of the Bertrand pack.

"She's not even one of us," someone else shouted. "Kathleen's a McTier. Isn't it her pack's right to bring her home?"

Other voices followed. "Channing's been hanging around Dolan for weeks. Maybe she chose him. Maybe she wants to be there." "Is this about the pack—or just the Bertrands?"

The barn buzzed with discontent. Hank lifted his hands again, but this time, the pack didn't quiet. The old Alpha's authority was waning, and he knew it. So did Dan.

If he didn't act now, everything would fall apart—his pack, the alliances, his chance to get Kathleen and Channing back unharmed.

He stepped forward, lifting his hands. The room fell silent, recognizing his authority.

"We know Dolan took them," he said, "because we have a witness." He gestured to the side, where Abby Mohr stood. "Abby Mohr was guarding Kathleen. She saw everything."

The young witch stepped onto the platform, lifting her chin. "Kathleen ran away from the McTier pack to escape their oppressive ways—especially their treatment of women." Murmurs broke out among the crowd, especially from the females as Abby pressed on. "They don't allow women to lead or fight. They're treated as breeders. There are no women on their council. They're forced to marry who the Alpha chooses."

The angry murmurs turned into low growls.

"She's still not one of us," someone shouted.

"She's my fated mate," Dan said, his voice steady. "I knew it the moment I saw her. Maybe I should've claimed her. But I didn't. Because I didn't want to be like them. I wanted to give her time—time to choose me." His voice faltered. He looked down, pain tightening his jaw. Remy put a hand on his son's shoulder.

Dan took a breath and turned to Abby. "Tell them the rest."

"Last night, we had protections around the house," Abby said. "Strong ones. They were broken—by a witch. Beatrix Spier."

Gasps rippled through the room. All eyes turned to Shannon and Chris. They stood rigid among the other witches. Shannon lifted her chin defiantly. Dave slid an arm around her waist. Ana and Sophie moved to flank Chris.

Fear crept into the murmurs.

"One more thing," Abby said. "I saw Channing. Bound. Gagged. Thrown into the back seat with Kathleen. She wasn't there by choice."

Cassandra stepped forward. "Dolan didn't act alone. He took Kathleen and Channing with help from Beatrix Callich Spier—the last of the Callich coven. A coven that once tried to destroy this pack and every paranormal who stood for peace. We must stop them now. And we won't let you do it alone."

She turned and pointed toward the elves. "You don't just have the paranormals here. The elves are with us."

A charged silence followed. Then Dan stepped up beside her.

"You know what's at stake. This isn't just about the Bertrands. It's about who we are as a community. As paranormals. If we let the McTiers and Beatrix Callich tear apart what we've built, then everything my grandfather worked for—everything your families bled for a hundred years ago—will be lost."

The energy in the room began to shift from doubt and

fear to support. Power hummed. Heads nodded. A low growl of agreement spread, fierce and rising.

Hank stepped forward again. This time, more slowly. He carried his age like a mantle, no longer trying to hide the wear in his joints or the silver streaking his hair. His voice, however, was unshaken. "Then it's time."

He removed the copper-and-leather cuff from his wrist—the mark of the Alpha—and held it out toward Dan.

"I've led this pack for decades. I've made mistakes. Held too tight. But I see now—what we need right now isn't a protector. It's a leader who fights with us and fights to win. That's you, Dan."

Dan looked out over the crowd—his family, his pack, his allies. Tyler's proud gaze. Remy's quiet nod. Connor's steady approval. Chris's tired, trusting stare.

He took the cuff and slipped it onto his wrist.

"I'm not letting Dolan take them—either of them. I'm not letting the McTiers win."

A moment passed. Then Dan raised his chin, voice fierce and unshakable.

"Tonight, we fight for every woman who deserves to choose. And for every pack that dares to stand free."

CHAPTER 52

"You know this violates your bail."

It was Connor who spoke as they stood in a corner of the barn, away from the crowd, his voice low but firm, eyes locked on Dan. "If you leave the county, you forfeit everything. They'll come after you."

Dan didn't flinch. "Let them. Walker's as much a part of this as Dolan and Beatrix. I can't prove it yet, but I will."

A tense silence followed as Connor just stared at his friend.

Gabe, leaning against a support beam, gave a slow, crooked grin. "Well, if you're gonna do something illegal, at least you're doing it as Alpha now."

Over in the center of the barn, Ramona let out a sharp clap. "We'd better hurry and suit up because no one kidnaps a member of our pack and walks away."

That was when the barn transformed. What had moments ago been a gathering place now morphed almost instantly into a war room. Orders flew back and forth across the space, shouted over shoulders or growled between clenched jaws. The scent of adrenaline and magic laced the air.

The wolves needed little in the way of supplies. They would shift and attack with claws and fangs. In their wolf forms they could communicate telepathically with other wolves, but not other paranormals. The bears, bobcats, and eagles were similarly prepared. But there were others here who weren't as war ready. The deer shifters were a peaceful herd. Yes, the bucks had horns, and their hoofs were dangerous but nowhere near as lethal as the other shifters. The witches and other paranormals had varying abilities and skills.

Jessa pulled into the barn in a truck Gabe had brought from PackNet. She hopped out, and with Jace, Ramona, and Landon began handing out supplies, including radios and earpieces especially adapted for the shifters to use in their animal forms. Gabe had been working on them for a while, but after his difficulty in communicating with Chris when they were working together to locate Fontaine's body, he'd stepped up his work and finished them. There weren't enough for every shifter, but still, a good many of those there would now have better communication with the rest of the small army that was assembling.

There were enchanted flashbangs Jessa was particularly proud of, too, and a few other little surprises she and Gabe had worked out. Landon and Jace double-checked everything they handed out. Ida and Donna worked nearby with Marianne Legato to distribute water and first aid supplies.

In another corner of the barn, Ana stood arguing with both Chris and Sophie. "Chris, you're barely healed. You still look exhausted. You need to stay behind. We need guards here, too, you know, in case the McTiers or some of their allies try to attack us."

"I'm going, Ana. My mother is at the heart of all of this. I'm not sure anyone but Shannon and I can stop her."

As he spoke, Dave stood next to him and drew a complex rune on Chris' forearm with a stylus. "For protection. And speed," he explained.

"Thanks, Man," Chris said, clasping him on the shoulder. "I think I'll need both."

"I'll be right there with both you and Shannon," he assured him. "And I promise, I won't let your sister out of my sight."

Shannon huffed. "As if I need it. I bested our mother once, you know." But she smiled as she said it and leaned in to give Dave a lingering kiss.

Serelith approached Dan, slipping a folded map into his hand. Theolin stood next to her. "We've tracked movement near the western border of the McTier territory. There's a trail hidden under illusion wards. It leads to a cave at the confluence of several ley lines. That would be the perfect place to hide the two girls."

Dan scanned the map, nodding grimly. He understood the significance of the ley lines. The magic there would be perfect for Beatrix to use, and even shifters, whose only magic was their ability to change form, were stronger near the lines.

The sun had come up as they had strategized and planned. It was now midday. "We'll begin moving everyone as close as we can to McTier lands, but I don't want anyone attacking before moonrise."

"That's when they'll be strongest," objected Theolin.

"But that's when we're strongest also. Unfortunately, in this case, their weaknesses are also our weaknesses.

***

But not everyone could go.

"We'll need to leave a guard behind," Remy said, stepping up beside Dan. "For the elders. The children. The ones who can't fight."

"I want to come," Sophie said, appearing like a ghost behind them. Her voice trembled, but her eyes didn't waver. "I'm a Betrand, too, and they took my aunt."

Ana was at her side in an instant. "Sophie—no."

"I'm not a child anymore. I can help."

Chris joined them, his expression serious. "We need people here, too. Strong ones. You'd be protecting more than just this barn. You'd be guarding the Bertrand pack future."

That gave Sophie pause. She looked to Dan, who nodded once. "Guard the home front. Keep the perimeter tight. Use everything you've learned."

"You mean everything Grandma taught us in Were Scouts? Cool!" Sophie straightened, her shoulders set. "I won't let anyone through."

Dan turned to Ramona. "Make a list. We want it balanced. Pick the squads for a combination of magic, muscle, and strategy."

Ramona nodded and pulled a small notepad from the back pocket of her jeans. "Donna, Ida, and Marianne are staying, Abby, too. She'll reinforce the wards around the farmhouse. Sophie, Casey and his mate, Claire: they've got twin cubs, but they can hold a line if it comes to it. And we should leave a few of the eagles behind. They can scout from the skies. They're like live drones; we don't even have to worry about their batteries running down."

Dan smiled at her enthusiasm. "Check with Talon on who he can spare. They'll act as an early warning system in case anyone from the McTiers tries to take this place thinking we've left it undefended."

From the back of the barn, Talon Storm heard them and gave a sharp nod. "My second, Damaris, will stay behind. She's lethal from the air."

Outside, the autumn sky was beginning to darken. They were two hours from McTier pack lands. Even traveling at magical speed, it would take time to get there.

Dan tightened the cuff on his wrist; the mark of leadership was now burned into his skin in more ways than one. This time, they weren't walking into a trap. This time, they knew what they were up against. Beatrix. Dolan. The twisted remnants of the Callich coven. The archaic brutality of the McTier way.

And this time, they were ready.

CHAPTER 53

The air in the cave hung thick and damp with the scent of moss, limestone, and decay. Kathleen sat with her back pressed against the cold rock wall, her arm around Channing's shoulders. The other woman had finally stopped shaking, but her face was pale and drawn, her eyes rimmed red from silent tears. Kathleen understood how devastated Channing was. She'd believed in Dolan, maybe even loved him, and he had betrayed her. Maybe if Kathleen had ever had so much as a kind word from her brother or father, she might have felt that same betrayal now, but she'd long since realized she was nothing but a pawn to either of them.

She and Channing hadn't spoken much since Dolan moved them from the mansion. Kathleen might have thought of her old home as a prison, but at least it had windows, light, a bed—even one of which she would gladly take now. Down here, buried in damp rock and silence, it felt like a tomb.

She knew where they were. The Hidden River cave system on the far western boundary of McTier territory. But would Dan know about it? The McTiers had been quietly expanding west, pressing closer to Bertrand land. Why hadn't she told Dan who she was earlier? She could have warned him of her father's expansion plans. She exhaled slowly, letting the silence stretch. Magic pulsed faintly through the air—subtle, steady, wrong. That had to be Beatrix. While there were no visible bonds keeping the two of them chained, they couldn't move. They were forced to sit here on the rocky ground and wait for whatever Dolan had planned for them.

"They don't mean to let us out," Channing said at last, her voice hoarse. "You know that, right?"

"I know that's what they think," Kathleen replied. "But they're wrong."

"You really believe Dan's coming for us?"

Kathleen looked down at her own hands—scraped,

trembling slightly, but steady. "Yes," she said, and the word came out stronger than she expected. "And even if he weren't, I wouldn't give Dolan the satisfaction of seeing me afraid."

Channing huffed a bitter laugh. "I thought you were kind of mousy when I met you. I didn't understand what my brother saw in you."

"I was shy and mousy when I first got here. But I've changed."

"I thought you might be pregnant, too?" She made it a question.

"What! No! Why would you think that?" Kathleen didn't know whether to laugh or be offended.

"Well, you did almost faint."

"I was faking. I realized my brother was suddenly living a few doors away from me. I knew I had to get away as quickly as I could before he came out and saw me."

"Well, that explains it. I guess you have some of that McTier ability to lie, after all."

Kathleen bit her lip to keep from saying anything. "I guess I deserve that," she said softly. "I did lie to Dan. He has a right to be angry at me. But I know he'll come for us even if he no longer loves me. That's what your brother is, you know. Honorable."

Channing nodded. "I think being raised around men like my brother, and father, and grandfather made me assume everyone was honorable."

"And I lied to Dan because I assumed he would be like my brother and father." She gave a bitter laugh. "I think the one thing we've both learned is we have to look out for ourselves. We're strong females. We can't wait around for the males to come and save us—whether they love us or not."

"Great, but how are we going to save ourselves when we can't even move?"

"We just have to be prepared to take care of any opportunity that comes along," Kathleen responded.

They sat for a few moments in silence.

"They'll kill him. Dan, I mean," Channing said. "Dolan will kill him if he has the chance. I don't think our pack is ready.

And my grandfather… he'll never allow an attack. He's always stood for peace. Said we should negotiate, not fight. But Dolan—he doesn't negotiate."

They fell silent again. Kathleen shivered as she stared into darkness so complete even her enhanced werewolf vision couldn't pierce the thick black of the cave.

Suddenly she looked up. She heard footsteps echoing, the slow, deliberate tread of several people. Both the women sat up straighter.

A mage light flickered into view as Dolan entered with Ric and several McTier shifters close behind. The glow of the light made their shadows monstrous on the cave walls.

Dolan had heard what Channing said. "Then you'd better hope your pack comes armed," he told her coldly. "You're right. The Bertrands use words. We use claw and fang."

Channing bowed her head in despair. Kathleen sat up straighter, struggling against the invisible bonds that kept her seated. Her eyes locked on Dolan. But her defiance was laced with dread for Dan. Before she could say anything, the air shifted.

Beatrix entered like a shadow stitched into human skin. Her eyes glowed faintly with power, her presence both wrong and dense. Even Ric and the other shifters recoiled as she passed.

Kathleen's stomach churned as the witch drew close. Her skin crawled when Beatrix brushed a finger across her arm.

"Leave her alone," Channing said, voice wavering but brave.

Beatrix ignored them, turning on Dolan. "I warned you," she said in an icy tone. "But like a fool, you continued your little games of dominance. This is not why I helped you."

Dolan's jaw clenched. "I brought you bargaining chips. You know your children won't stand by and let these innocents be harmed."

"Too late," she snapped. "Shannon and her pet elves undid the curse. My son no longer hears me in his sleep. I cannot control him. You've ruined everything I worked for."

She raised her hand in a sharp gesture. Energy crackled

between her fingers, and Kathleen and Channing both flinched. Even Dolan backed up a step.

Beatrix sneered. "You are a child running around with a match in a forest. You'll burn everything down before you understand how dangerous that little light can be."

Her gaze flicked to the two women. Contempt curled her lip. "I should just kill them now."

Kathleen sat up straighter. "Then do it."

Beatrix smiled slowly, cruelly.

"I'm not afraid of you," Kathleen said.

A long, terrible pause followed.

"Brave little bitch," Beatrix murmured. "Let's see if your mate gets here in time to bury you properly."

She turned in a swish of black and vanished into the shadows.

Dolan lingered a moment longer, his gaze resting on Channing.

"You chose the wrong side," he said quietly. "But it's not too late. Come with me now, and you won't just be my Luna. You'll be my queen. The McTiers won't be a pack. We'll be a kingdom. And my father?" His smile was sharp as a knife. "He won't be the king. I will."

Channing lifted her chin. "You're insane. Why did it take me so long to see it?"

His face hardened. "Then you'll die here."

CHAPTER 54

As darkness fell, the Bertrand pack and their allies approached the Hidden River cave system cautiously. Moonrise was still an hour away—a blessing and a curse. The wolves and their shifter kin could transform more freely once the moon rose, but until then, they remained in their human skins, nerves taut and senses half-muted. The same held true for their enemy.

They'd arrived early, but that didn't mean it had been easy. Coordinating a paranormal strike team of ten units with five or six paranormals each came with its own challenges. Once shifted, the wolves, bears, bobcat, and deer could outpace any vehicle. The eagle shifters had taken flight first, soaring overhead to scout before them, reporting back almost immediately. Witches, vampires, and others had their own limitations. Some teleported. A few astral projected to avoid delays. But others, including Nathan Lazard, their designated medic, had to travel the old-fashioned way—by truck or car. And Gabe had insisted on bringing his PackNet communications vehicle to ensure they could coordinate across magical and non-magical lines.

The plan had nearly derailed in a heated argument—until Kailin stepped forward with a solution. "We'll create a portal—yes, large enough for your truck," he added, turning to Gabe before the wolf could even raise the question. "The three of us can hold it until everyone's through." He nodded to his sister and cousin.

Dan hadn't spent as much time with the elves as Gabe. Their presence still unsettled him. He approached Theo awkwardly. "Thanks," he said, then added, a bit stiffly, "We owe you."

Theo gave a subtle nod, accepting the words without ceremony.

Hank, on the other hand, clasped the elf's shoulder like an old comrade. "Knew we could count on you," he said with a grin. The gesture was easy and familiar—too familiar for Dan's comfort. A flash of realization hit him. These two had seen battle together in the past. Real battle. And it showed.

With calm precision, Serelith, Theolin, and Kailin opened a shimmering silver portal, wide and stable enough to move the entire force. It took only minutes to send the small army through, saving hours of travel time. The portal delivered them into a forest clearing a few miles from the cave's true entrance—far enough to avoid detection, close enough to strike.

The first wave through the portal were the scouts: witches Jake Waseaux and Chief Anderson, along with two stealth-trained deer shifters. Above, two eagle shifters flew silent and sharp-eyed. Jake and Anderson had already neutralized a pair of McTier sentries—clean, quiet kills. Their bodies lay hidden under an overhang near the main path. Now, as the teams gathered in the trees, final preparations began.

Ramona stepped into the center of the clearing and raised her voice. "You all know your assignments. Five or six to a unit. Use your strengths together—don't compete. And no heroics. No solo runs. If you get separated, fall back to your rendezvous point. If you encounter Beatrix or Dolan, notify Gabe immediately. Do not engage either alone. We're here as a pack—not lone wolves. This is a rescue mission, not a takeover... at least not yet."

She aimed a meaningful glance at Dan. He didn't flinch. She knew if he found Dolan first, there would be no waiting. Dan planned to finish what Dolan had started.

"Well said," Gabe called. "You'd make a hell of a master sergeant."

Ramona smirked. "Guess all those hours of Counter-Strike 2 finally paid off." She turned to check gear placements. Jace joined her, sliding a headset over his ears. It looked like standard military tech, but Jessa had spelled it to transform with their shifts. Once the mission started, Jace and Ramona would embed with one of the forward teams to coordinate field comms.

At the truck, parked near the portal drop-point, Gabe and Landon were still buzzing from the ride.

"That was insane," Landon said. "Driving through magical space? I think my eyebrows are still tingling. Just like the Delorean time machine."

"You're just glad you didn't crash it," Gabe muttered, adjusting the satellite transmitter.

"Hey, what's up with you?" Landon frowned. "You've been quiet since this whole thing started."

Before Gabe could answer, Ramona approached to grab more headsets. As she turned to go, Gabe reached out and caught her wrist. "Be careful," he said, his voice low. "I don't like you out there by yourself."

"I won't be alone. Jace and the whole team…"

"You know what I mean—without me." He pulled her in and kissed her—hard, fast, and full of feeling.

She blinked, stunned. Then kissed him back with equal heat. "Now I have to come back," she whispered, her voice hoarse. She turned quickly, not wanting him to see the emotion she hadn't meant to show.

A few feet away, Connor spoke quietly to Chris.

"I'm going in with Dan. You stay with Ana. Protect her—and protect Sophie. No matter what."

"Sophie's back at the farm," Chris reminded him.

"I don't just mean tonight."

Chris studied him. "You sound like you don't expect to come back."

Connor shrugged. "No one ever expects not to. I just want to know Ana and Sophie are in good hands."

Chris clasped his shoulder. "They will be. You have my word."

Connor nodded and moved to join Dan, Hank, and the elves.

Shannon stood beside Chris now. She took his hand and gave it a brief squeeze. Behind her, Dave was uncharacteristically solemn, checking the straps on his small satchel of magical supplies. Their team—Shannon, Ana, Chris, and Dave—would enter through the eastern tunnels, where they'd sensed dark energy along an underground stream.

Theo approached them, his tone grave. "I've found

Beatrix's power signature. She's holed up in an old tunnel of the cave. It's wrapped in veils—almost invisible. I doubt anyone but an elf could even detect it."

Shannon's chin lifted. "She's my mother. If anyone can find her, it's me."

Theo's eyes met hers. "You are young in magic. We've had centuries to learn what you're just beginning to grasp."

She bristled but bit back her retort. From Theo, that was as close to an apology—or a compliment—as she was likely to get.

Dave stepped forward, sensing her frustration. "I think we can unravel the veil," he said. "But I'll have to move slow. Once I start, she'll know. We only get one shot."

Chris nodded. "Then we make it count."

"It's time." Dan's voice echoed across magical channels and through the comms. Some saw him. Others were far enough away that they only heard him.

He looked at his grandfather, who nodded once.

Dan shifted.

It was the signal.

Fur burst across bodies. Antlers sprouted. Claws glinted. Growls and low snorts filled the forest. The air shimmered with magic as wolves, bears, and deer emerged in force—coats red, grey, black, and tawny gold beneath the rising moon.

Above the cacophony, the witches lifted their hands. A flicker of silver and green light shimmered around their fingertips—protective spells, curses, wards, all woven and ready. Where shifters brought teeth and strength, the witches brought will and power.

Behind them, the last of the shifters transformed.

And together, they turned toward the cave—and the final confrontation waiting inside.

CHAPTER 55

With a howl that split the night, the attack began. Serelith raised her arms, silvery blue light flashing from her hands as the magical veil that hid the cave entrance dropped.

Behind Dan his wolves surged, some even before they completed shifting. Claws lengthened; fangs dripped. They leaped forward on two legs and came down on four. Red, black, grey, and white fur glowed in the moonlight. The bobcats came next as the bears followed, a rear guard of brute strength.

Several McTier shifters were lounging near the entrance, still in human form, their surprise at the sudden attack showing just how lax these sentries were. Dan's wolf howled in triumph as he slashed the first unsuspecting guard's throat. The others were taken out quickly, but Dan saw one running toward the back of the cave. He howled in protest and watched Connor quickly take off after him, his grey fur making it clear to Dan who had given chase.

Magic sizzled in the air as the witches struck next. "Save one for questioning!" Dan demanded; his telepathic voice came through Gabe's magically enhanced comm units so all could understand him, no matter their powers or their pack. "We need to know where they're keeping the girls."

Hank pulled back from striking at a wolf's throat, catching him in the side instead and shaking him like a dog with a toy. The other wolf howled in pain and surrendered. Two deer shifters immediately herded the wolf toward Gabe's command vehicle.

From the depths of the cave more McTier wolves burst forth—snarling, snapping, savage. The Bertrand allies fought back with everything they had. Theolin's sword flashed with power and enchantments as he pushed his way through the enemy line. Jessa, next to him, let out a witch's howl of her own that stopped both friend and foe alike. She mowed down the McTier wolves, enchantments flashing from her hands. Jace turned to give her a wolfish grin, then focused back on the battle and took out two more wolves.

Some of the McTier pack faltered, unprepared for the scale of the assault. They'd heard for years that the Betrand pack was weak, unwilling to fight; now, they learned how wrong that belief had been. Others fought back with ferocity in savage clashes with the Bertrand allies. The air filled with growls, yelps, the crack of bone, the wet sound of claws raking into flesh. Glittering runes hung in the air like fireflies— binding spells cast by Serelith and Kai.

Gabe's voice cut through the comms, calm but firm. "Push east. Team Five, collapse the northern tunnel. Ramona— status?"

"South ridge secure. We're moving forward."

"Good. Keep the perimeter tight. We don't know what's waiting deeper in."

They didn't. Because inside the caves, something darker stirred.

***

As the assault on the main entrance to the cave system got underway, Chris, Ana, Shannon, and Dave moved quietly through the eastern tunnel. Dave's mage fire glowed in his hand, giving them just enough light to navigate the tunnel without showing too far ahead.

The passage twisted before them, the stone slick and pulsing with unnatural warmth they could feel even without touching it. The ley lines were wrong here. Something or someone had tampered with the magic.

In the past months Chris and Shannon had both studied and practiced their magic with David, their expertise growing as they embraced the power they had shunned for years, afraid it would corrupt them like it had their mother. With Dave and Ana's support, they had embraced their true selves. Chris knew when he found his mother she would be in for a surprise. He was no longer the young boy, weak in magic, that she remembered. The crow sigil she had branded him with might have allowed her to connect with him, to drain him, but it had also allowed him to take from her. He could sense Beatrix through that bond, her magic calling to the scar on his chest where she had marked him. She was waiting for him. She wanted to capture him, her son, even more than she wanted Shannon. But she was going to be surprised when she found him.

They continued to creep slowly along the tunnels, Dave first, mage light in hand, Ana guarding their backs in wolf form. The tunnel expanded suddenly into a large cave with a small pool of water near the center. Beatrix stood there, waiting for them.

"Christopher and Shannon. My beautiful children. You have come back to me. It is so good to finally see you again." She raised her arms, and dark smoke flowed out from her hands, putting out Dave's light and leaving them only with the greenish evil glow that emanated from her own magic.

Runes spiraled and twisted around her body. A stalactite above the lake drip dripped water in a constant, irritating sound. Shannon had to shake her head to clear it, knowing her mother had enhanced the sound just to distract them. A dark ley node pulsed at the lake's center. Beatrix fed off it, hands raised, eyes burning.

"I knew you would come back to me." None of them spoke.

"Do you still think you're more than what I made you? You wouldn't be here if not for me. Neither of you. And you, Christopher, that brand on your chest—that's your truth. It's who you are. You're mine."

Chris breathed shallowly. "Never," he panted. The scar flared red-hot, the pain lancing through his body almost as great as when she had first attacked him. She twisted her hand, and the pain doubled. His knees started to buckle. Through it he heard Ana whine. She moved quickly to support him, nosing his side. He twisted his hand in her fur and leaned on her for support.

Beatrix laughed. "You think your little puppy is going to protect you?"

Ana leaped at the witch as Dave used his magic to throw up a protective shield around the wolf. Ana fell back, panting.

Chris started forward, his own pain forgotten as he knelt by his love. "You will not win, Mother!" he shouted.

"You can't stop me, Christopher. You're my weapon. I'll use you against your lover, your sister, your friends. You're mine. All those years as a child, you thought I didn't love you. Thought I was ignoring you, that I loved Shannon more. But I was forging you for something greater—to be my weapon. Greater even than your sister, standing helpless over there. No matter how far you run, you'll always be mine."

"I'm not," he growled through clenched teeth. "I never was. You could never control me, and it killed you to know that."

She stepped forward, her smile vicious as energy coiled around her. She raised one hand—and Shannon burst forward.

"Don't touch him." She slammed a binding sigil into the ground, then another and another, just as she had ten years before. "I bested you once, and I can do it again."

Chris surged up from his knees and came to her side. Pain lanced through him from the attacks Beatrix continually threw at him, but he didn't stop. He stood with his sister, hands raised to send his own magical attack back at her.

Beatrix broke through the binding spell. "I had years to master your weak attack," she snarled evilly. "Do you think you can stop me by using the same trick again?"

"We have to end it," Shannon whispered to Chris. "She'll never stop otherwise." The siblings raised their hands just as Beatrix pulled Ana in front of her, stopping them from using more magic against her. Ana lay quiet, whimpering. Injured. As Shannon, Dave, and Chris looked on helplessly, Beatrix was gone in a flash of green light, leaving Ana lying on the floor.

CHAPTER 56

Kathleen pressed her back against the damp stone, scooting closer to Channing. Every rumble overhead made her flinch. The sounds of claws, howls, and snarled curses blended into a violent symphony, echoing faintly through the tunnels to where they waited. If they could see, it would have been better, but in human form they could make out nothing. Here in this cave, no light leaked from cracks or fissures leading to the surface. Kathleen wondered just how far underground they were. How long it would take Dan to find them. They could do nothing to help him right now, nothing to help themselves. They couldn't even see the ropes that bound them. The magical chains Beatrix had placed on them kept them from shifting into wolf form. They might as well have been trussed like Christmas turkeys; they could barely lift a finger.

She shared a frightened glance with Channing as a particularly loud boom cracked through the stone, shaking the walls and raining down dust and pebbles from the cave ceiling.

Who was winning? There was no way to tell. When the first cries of battle had reached them, they'd clung to hope. Dan and the Bertrand pack had come. But time seemed to stretch and bend strangely in the dark. It could have been one hour since they'd first heard the sounds of battle, or it could have been many. And no one had come to find them.

"At least Dolan hasn't come back for us," Kathleen muttered, twisting against the invisible chains that bound her wrists. Beatrix had used their blood when she'd cast the spell, cutting them both with a ritual blade and whispering words that tasted like rust and ash in the air.

"What if no one finds us?" Channing asked, voice cracking. "What if they just leave us here forever? Or worse, what if Beatrix comes back instead?"

Every second that passed tightened the knots in their stomachs. After a while, Channing's fingers twitched against

Kathleen's leg. "That didn't sound like a McTier howl," she whispered. "Did you hear it? That one—it was Dan. I'd know my brother's howl anywhere."

"You're sure?" Kathleen breathed. "I... I don't know what he sounds like as a wolf. We only had a few runs together. I didn't give him a chance. I lied to him. Pushed him away." A tear slipped down her cheek. She rubbed her face against her shoulder to brush it away. "And now I might never..."

Channing's hand closed gently around hers. "He's your mate, and he's my brother. I know he won't give up on either of us. Besides, I'm seeing what a good match you two are. You're just as stubborn—and brave—as he is."

Kathleen gave her a watery smile. "But Dolan..."

Channing's face darkened. "I was so stupid. I thought he cared. I thought..." She shook her head, disgusted with herself. "I thought he loved me when really he was only using me. And I was such a silly little fool that I let him."

"You're not the only one he fooled. Most of the pack thinks everything he says is right. They're ready to follow him to hell and back. Ready to follow him against your pack."

"Still, I wish I'd seen through him sooner."

"I'm just glad you see it now," Kathleen whispered.

Suddenly Channing stiffened. "Shh."

They heard footsteps, quick and uneven as claws skittered on stone. Someone was coming. They weren't alone anymore.

Dolan burst into the chamber; his grey and white fur was streaked and matted with blood. His flanks heaved. His eyes gleamed with wild fury. Without pause, he shifted, fur shrinking back into flesh, bones cracking with the change. In an instant, he was human again: bare chest slick with blood. And he was livid.

He swept a hand through the air, muttering something sharp and guttural. The spell on their bindings snapped, and they were free. Kathleen looked at him in surprise. "Since when..."

"Do I know magic? Beatrix taught me a few tricks." He smirked, and Kathleen wanted to wipe the smile from his face.

"On your feet," he barked. "Both of you. Now."

"What's happening?" Channing asked as she stumbled upright, wobbling, her legs cramped and numb from hours sitting in one position.

"Is your side losing?" Kathleen rose more slowly, spine straight. "Planning to run, Dolan? Leave your pack behind? That's always been your way."

He bared his teeth. "They brought witches and elves. You think Father and I planned for that? It's an ambush. It's not fair."

"And your answer is to drag us deeper underground?" she shot back. "For what? To use us as leverage? As shields?"

"If I must; I'm not leaving you here for Dan Bertrand and his pack to find," he growled, grabbing Channing's arm. "You're mine. Both of you."

Channing jerked free. "I was never yours."

His eyes flashed gold, the wolf surging just beneath his skin. For a heartbeat, Kathleen thought he might strike Channing.

Just then the cave groaned. A low, seismic rumble passed through the stone beneath their feet. The ground buckled. Dolan stumbled.

The walls seemed to stumble with him. Rocks tumbled down. Kathleen threw an arm around Channing, covering both their heads as they were knocked sideways. Pebbles rained from above, followed by a sharp crack like the stones themselves were tearing. A low, throbbing hum rose from deep within the tunnels, vibrating through the stone and settling deep in their bones.

"What is that?" Channing gasped, backing against the wall. "It feels like... like something's waking up."

"Beatrix must've tampered with the ley lines," Kathleen said, struggling to stay upright. She noticed Dolan shifting back into his wolf and taking off down the tunnel. She didn't have time to worry about it now, she realized. "She's broken something. Or wakened it. It's..."

She didn't get to finish. A massive slab of stone dropped from the ceiling.

"Move!" she shouted, shoving Channing out of the way as it slammed into the ground behind them, shattering.

Dust filled the air. Kathleen's skin buzzed with static. The ancient magic that slept here, once buried, was unraveling. The ley lines Beatrix had fed on were fraying like a torn net. Kathleen could feel it: the pulse of something vast and wounded writhing underground. This wasn't just energy. It was awareness. The cave was alive; it felt pain and rage. A surge of greenish light streaked through the tunnel behind them, quick as lightning. Somewhere in the distance, Dolan howled and screamed.

Then silence.

"Channing?" Kathleen coughed, struggling to breathe. "Are you okay?"

"I... I think so." Channing crawled toward her, face scraped; she trembled. "What the hell was that?"

Kathleen turned to look. The tunnel Dolan had fled down was collapsed, its entrance now only a small hole in the stone. But behind them, where there had only been wall before, there was now a faintly glowing path—stalactites formed arches along the roof lit by a strange silver-green pulse.

A new tunnel. Opened by the rupture.

Or conjured by something else.

"We can't stay here," Kathleen said, helping Channing to her feet. "Whatever Beatrix broke—it's still breaking."

CHAPTER 57

Dan rounded the corner of a tunnel, dodging falling rocks and sliding as the floor beneath him shifted. Thank God he was on four feet, not two. His werewolf senses sharpened in his wolf form; he could smell blood, both old and fresh. And magic. Beneath it was the unmistakable scent of Kathleen. Just ahead.

Then he saw him.

The grey wolf stood near a jagged arch of broken rock and splintered wood framing the entrance to what must have once been a prisoner's dungeon. He recognized Dolan instantly although dust clouded the air like smoke. Large boulders had fallen behind the wolf, but there were still gaps in the opening to the cave beyond. Dan could glimpse Kathleen and Channing huddled near the far wall of the cavern, battered but alive. His heart surged.

Dolan snarled, blood streaking the fur on his side. *I should've known you'd come crawling.* Dan heard the other wolf's voice in his head. *You always had a hero complex.*

You always had a victim complex, Dan growled.

Dolan lunged, meeting Dan in a thunderous clash, their claws ripping, teeth snapping, neither one holding back. It was an Alpha challenge. A fight to the death. There would be no prisoner taken here. Kathleen screamed as the sound of their bodies slamming into each other, into the stones, echoed in the tunnel. Dan let out a growl of pure fury as he drove his shoulder into Dolan's gut, lifting the wolf off his feet and slamming him into the wall. Dolan twisted free, raking his claws down Dan's back.

Dolan circled; his lips curled back in a snarl. *You don't have the stomach for this. You were always too soft.* He lunged again, striking Dan in the side with both claws and fangs. It was a glancing blow but still did damage. Dan's side burned from Dolan's strike, blood flowing down his side. His front legs collapsed under him, but then he heard Kathleen.

"Dan!"

He looked up.

She was watching him, eyes wide and scared but still shining with belief. In him. Not because he was her Alpha. Not because he commanded her. But because she loved him.

Dan roared back to his feet. Rushing Dolan, he caught him and slammed him into the floor. Dust exploded around them. Dolan bucked and bit, clawing at Dan's throat, unable to break the other wolf's hold on him.

I should kill you now, but I won't, Dan told him. *I want your pack to see you broken and defeated.*

At that moment, the cavern trembled again, groaning with the weight of the fractured ley lines.

Dan shifted back to his human form, body shaking, blood dripping from a dozen wounds. Kathleen and Channing ran to him, helping him up, throwing arms around his neck and shoulders.

You came," Kathleen whispered.

"Always," he said.

Behind them, they heard the scuffle of footsteps and saw Shannon and Dave, followed by Chris, staggering as he carried Ana in his arms. Her wolf form was limp, her flank torn open; blood trailed behind them.

"Dan!" Shannon shouted, her eyes widening as she saw Dolan unconscious and broken at Dan's feet. "We found Beatrix. She escaped. She hurt Ana badly. We couldn't stop her…"

Channing ran to her older sister, placing a hand on her head as she lay in Chris' arms.

"Where is Beatrix now?" Dan asked, his voice a snarl as he stepped toward them. His chest constricted as he saw his two sisters together. Had he just rescued one only to lose the other? He gathered Channing and Kathleen to him, hugging them both.

"I don't know," Chris answered, setting Ana down gently on the floor of the cave. "She disappeared through the ley lines, but she's close. I can feel her."

Ana stirred weakly at Channing's touch but didn't

move.

Then the air shifted, cold and wrong once more. Green light pulsed from the walls. Runes shimmered in the stone. The earth groaned again.

Beatrix emerged from a crevice in the rocks, tall, terrible, and triumphant. Her eyes were flames. Her voice was a blade. "You ruined everything." Her gaze took in all of them, falling last on Chris as he knelt at Ana's side.

Dan pushed Kathleen and Channing behind him. Shannon and Dave raised their hands instinctively, magic crackling at their fingertips. Chris stepped protectively in front of Ana, but Beatrix's gaze had locked on the injured wolf—and she smiled.

"Move," she commanded. "She's mine."

"No." Chris didn't hesitate. He, too, raised his arms, powerful magic surging from his fingertips in a way Dan had never seen him perform before.

Beatrix raised a hand and hurled a blast of force toward him.

And then, Connor was there, emerging from a small side tunnel. His fur was streaked with blood and gore. The same McTier wolf he'd chased earlier now lay dead in the tunnel behind him. He'd followed the sound of Ana's cry. He saw Beatrix raise her hand and didn't think. Just moved.

He dove in front of Ana and Chris, shielding them with his body. The blast hit him squarely in the chest. Connor hit the ground, blood spilling from his mouth, eyes wide in shock.

"No!" Ana shifted back with a scream, her human form raw and bruised as she crawled to him, Chris right behind her. "Connor—Connor, stay with me."

He coughed; the pain of his injuries had forced his shift, and he lay in his human form as he tried to speak.

Dan ran to them, knees hitting the stone beside his friend. "Hold on, Friend. We'll get you help. Nathan can…"

Connor's eyes locked on his, then Chris'. "You take care of her, Chris; I know you love her like I did."

His breath caught. And stopped.

Ana let out a sob that echoed through the cave.

Shannon turned, fury radiating off her in waves. "Enough. I'll end you this time, Mother."

Chris came to join her, and with him and Dave beside her, they raised their hands. Beatrix saw the magic gathering and hissed.

"I will return," she snarled, and vanished into a flash of green light just as the tunnel trembled above them.

She was gone, but the damage was done. Dan bowed his head over Connor's body. "We have to get out. Now."

He tapped the comm unit, still in his ear. "Gabe, what's the status?"

"The north and south exits are secured, but there are still McTier wolves unaccounted for. Especially Dolan."

"We can account for him. We're coming out. And Gabe..." But he couldn't speak the words. He couldn't tell Gabe, the third part of their trio, friends since childhood, that Connor was gone. "This ends now," was all he said as they began the long way back to the surface, with Connor in Dan's arms.

CHAPTER 58

The night sky had never looked so vast.

Dan stepped out of the cave mouth, Connor's body in his arms. Behind him, the others followed—bloodied, bruised, but alive. Kathleen and Channing emerged together. Ana, supported by Chris, came next, and Shannon and Dave brought up the rear, with Dolan on a magical, silver-impregnated leash that Dave had conjured to keep him from shifting.

The silence was heavy around them as the Betrand pack and their allies gathered. Wolves, bears, deer, bobcats, and eagles stood in skin or fur or feathers. They scanned the trees intently as they waited, a few of the eagles still circling on guard duty overhead.

The wolves bowed their heads as Dan passed, acknowledging not only their new Alpha, but the death of Connor, their friend.

Gabe was the first to approach. His face crumbled as he saw Connor in Dan's arms. "No. No. Not Connor. He was the best of us. Damn it, what are we gonna do without him?" He turned away as Ramona came up to him and put her arms around him.

"He saved Ana and Chris," Dan said quietly. "Beatrix tried to kill them. He stepped in front of the blast."

As several shifters took Connor's body from Dan, Ana and Chris approached. Chris grasped both men's shoulders while Ana hugged them. "I'm so sorry. He believed in the law, not violence. It shouldn't have happened this way."

Dan hugged his sister back. "He loved you, Ana. He only wanted what was best for you and Sophie. And he knew you'd found that with Chris."

Ana nodded, and Chris took her in his arms. "We need to get you over to Dr. Lazard and let him have a look at you before we go home. You, too, Dan."

"In a few minutes. I need to check on everyone else first.

See how many wounded we have and if anyone else…" He closed his eyes and took a breath, trying to say the words but unable to.

Kathleen approached him then, and he hugged her to him. "I'm so sorry, Dan. So sorry that I'm the cause of you losing your friend."

He turned on her fiercely, holding her shoulders so she had to look him in the eyes. "You are not the cause. Neither you nor Channing. No one caused this but Dolan and Michal McTier. I'm sorry, Kathleen. I know they're your family, but they will have to pay."

Kathleen nodded. She didn't want to feel good about that, but she did. Her father and brother had abused her and many other pack members for years. It was time they got what was coming to them.

As Nathan Lazard triaged the injured, the elves set up the portal again, shuttling everyone back to the Betrand farm as quickly as possible. No one celebrated. This was not a victory. With Connor's death it was just survival.

They reached the main house just as dawn touched the horizon. Ida, Donna, and Sophie stood on the porch, watching for them.

Sophie ran to Ana, hugging her tightly. "Mom, I was so scared."

Ana gasped as Sophie's arms pressed on her injured side. "Mom, are you hurt?" She tried to pull up Ana's sweater to see her side.

"Don't worry, Honey. It's already starting to heal. That's one of our perks, remember? We heal quickly."

Chris pulled the girl into a hug. "Your mom will be fine by this afternoon; Dr. Lazard promised."

Dan brought Connor inside. They laid him in one of the guest rooms. Someone lit a candle. No one spoke for a long time.

Outside, the rest of the pack dispersed slowly, several of the bears and witches remaining to guard the ten McTier prisoners, including Dolan, in a magical cage the elves created in the barn. Dan knew that others had fled back to the McTier mansion. Michael would be on the lookout for them, but they'd have to deal with that later. For now, he allowed space for mourning.

On the edge of the woods, Shannon stood beneath an elm tree, Dave beside her, Chris leaning against the trunk. Ana sat at his feet. Other than to reassure Sophie, she hadn't said anything since Connor's death.

"He was good," Chris said softly. "Better than we deserved."

"We'll honor him," Shannon replied. "But we have to prepare. Beatrix isn't gone."

"No," Dave agreed. "Just hiding. And she'll come back stronger."

Shannon looked back toward the house, the people inside it, and the light beginning to break over the trees. Once she'd been alone in her fight against her mother. Now she had allies, friends, and loved ones. "So will we."

In the kitchen several of the shifters who'd stayed behind made breakfast for those who had fought. Marianne came up to Kathleen. "I'm so sorry I didn't help you more when I first met you. I wish you had felt you could come to me."

Kathleen gave her a hug. "I'm sorry I didn't tell you, too. Maybe if I'd been honest with you and with Dan, we could have prevented this."

Marianne hugged her tightly. "Oh Honey, no. Do not blame yourself. I know Dan's already told you that. You need to listen to him. Now tell me, how is your mother?"

Kathleen bit her lip. "She loves my father," was all she finally said.

Marianne nodded. "And that means she believes as he does."

Kathleen nodded.

Marianne hugged her again. "I can only imagine what it was like for you growing up. But you're a part of our pack now, and you'll see. It's going to be different."

As Dan came up to them, a coffee cup in his hand, Marianne turned to add him to her hug. "Dan, I'm so sorry about Connor. I know you and Gabe are going to miss him terribly."

Dan gave her a one-armed hug back. "You're right, Miz Marianne. I don't know what we're going to do without him."

She patted his back for a minute. "Right now, you need to take this girl home and both of you get some rest. There will be a lot to do in the next few days, and you need to be ready for it."

"That's exactly what my grandmother just told me. Kathleen," he said, turning to her, "let's go home."

He put his arm around her shoulder and guided her out of the house.

CHAPTER 59

Dan hadn't been home in days, maybe longer. The air inside the condo was stale with disuse, tinged with the faintest scent of sweat, but underneath it all lingered him—cedarwood soap, worn leather, the ghost of beer and laughter shared over late-night video games with Gabe and… Kathleen stuttered over even thinking Connor's name. She stepped through the door and paused, hugging her arms around herself as the morning light poured through the windows, striking the hardwood floor like gold. Dan set his keys on the counter and went to open the door to the balcony. The cool air of early autumn rushed in along with the song of birds and the sound of people, and the faint lapping of the river waves along the shore. The world had moved on, oblivious to their war.

Dan turned to her. "You okay?" he asked softly.

Kathleen nodded. "Are you?"

He gave her a weary smile. "Not yet. But I will be. If you're here." She crossed the room to him and rested her head against his chest. She could hear the echo of his heartbeat, feel his chest move as he breathed. "I'm not going anywhere."

He kissed her hair, breathing in the familiar scent of her, fresh lavender and mint. Then he stepped back and cupped her face in his hands. "Come with me," he said, and led her into the bedroom.

The curtains were still drawn. In the soft dimness, the world felt far away. No battles. No pain. No heartbreak. Just the warmth of two people who had survived. Here it was only the two of them. Dan kissed her slowly, reverently, as if reacquainting himself with something sacred. His hands skimmed her sides, patient and gentle. There was no rush, just the need to feel. To connect.

Dan kissed her like he had all the time in the world. Like she was something fragile and sacred, not a woman who'd fought and bled and survived. His hands ghosted along her sides, tracing her ribs, her hips, memorizing her.

Kathleen lifted his shirt slowly, baring inch after inch of the body she'd feared she'd never see again. She let her hands explore him—familiar, but new all over again. Her fingers trembled as she unbuckled his belt and slid his jeans and boxers down. He stood before her, all muscle and raw desire, eyes dark with emotion. His need for her obvious.

"You're beautiful," he whispered, slipping her blouse from her shoulders. His hands paused at the bruises along her side. "These don't scare me. They remind me how strong you are."

She touched the angry red scar on his ribs. She knew it would fade to nothing in a few days, but for now, it was a reminder of all he'd risked for her. She knew it would fade soon, but right now it was a reminder of how close they had come to losing each other. "I was so scared I wouldn't see you again. That you wouldn't come. Or you wouldn't find us."

He kissed her, a slow claiming that stole her breath. When their mouths opened and tongues met, the kiss turned hungrier, needier. "I did find you. I'll always find you."

She answered with a soft moan, rising on her toes to pull him closer. Their mouths opened to each other, lips brushing, tasting. When his tongue slid against hers, she let herself drown in the kiss, her fingers scraping along the skin of his back.

She gasped when his thumb found her nipple, teasing it until her body arched for him. His mouth replaced his hand, warm and wet, sucking until she whimpered. She dragged him closer, anchoring herself to him with her nails, needing his weight, his warmth.

"I need you," she whispered into his ear, voice ragged.

"You have me," he growled, kissing a path down her neck. "You always have."

His fingers slid between her legs, slicking through her wet heat, circling her clit with devastating precision until her thighs trembled and her hips rocked into his hand. When he finally moved over her, thick and hard, she welcomed him with a cry of relief. He pushed in slowly, deeply, stretching her, filling her. The pleasure bloomed through her in waves, her fingers digging into his back as he began to move.

Make me yours, Dan," she breathed. "Claim me."

He stilled above her, his breath caught. "Are you sure, Little Wolf?" he asked, fearful she didn't really mean it, that it was the only the emotion of the moment.

"Yes, yes, I'm sure. I should have listened to you before," she said, rising up and kissing him over and over. "If I'd let you claim me…"

"Shh, don't. Don't think about what we could have done or should have done. All that matters now is that we're here, together."

She framed his face with her hands. "I was always yours. I just didn't know how to admit it."

Emotion surged in his eyes, and then his mouth was on her neck, hot and wet, kissing, nipping, tasting. His fangs extended, brushing her skin, waiting. "I love you," he said aloud this time, his voice breaking. "I'll never leave you."

"Do it," she whispered. "I want it. I want you."

He kissed and licked her neck once more, his teeth scraping the skin. She felt his fangs grow longer as she moved against him. The pain was sharp, but only for an instant. Her wolf howled, meeting and joining with Dan's in a dance of ecstasy as they came together at last, truly mated, bonded. A rush of emotion—love, fear, devotion, desire—flooded her senses. She felt him everywhere.

Their rhythm turned urgent, bodies slamming together with frantic need. When she came, it was as though her soul shattered open—white heat pulsing through her, her cry raw and real. He followed her with a low, guttural moan, burying himself inside her, spilling deep, collapsing against her with a shudder.

Dan kissed her throat, her collarbone, her lips. *I love you.* She realized she heard him in her mind; he'd said nothing out loud.

I love you, too.

They were together now, forever. Their minds, thoughts, feelings linked.

They lay tangled, limbs entwined, breath mingling. Dan stroked her arm with trembling fingers. He brushed his fingers down her arm. *You're mine, Kathleen. In every way that counts.*

She smiled sleepily and traced the edge of his jaw. "And you're mine, forever."

Outside, the river whispered past, the world still turning. But in this room, time had stopped. And started again, two wolves tangled in the wreckage of love and war—and peace.

CHAPTER 60

A few days later, when everyone had had a chance to rest and heal, Dan, Gabe, and a group of pack members and their allies returned to the McTier pack lands. When they reached the heavy gates of the mansion, they found their way barred by half a dozen shifters, some in human form, others already shifted into wolves. Ric, their spokesman, stepped forward, a pistol at his belt, a rifle over his shoulder. He was flanked by two snarling wolves, their fangs bared toward the Bertrand entourage.

"You're not welcome here," Ric said.

"What, you don't want your heir back?" Dan replied coolly from the driver's seat of the first of three vehicles. In the van behind them, the McTier prisoners, including Dolan, were shackled together. The other vehicles carried Bertrand allies: Cassandra, Shannon, and Dave for the witches; Dan, Kathleen, and Gabe for the wolf shifters; and Talon Storm, Maris Wood, Kaia Strickland, and Beau Alden for the eagle, bear, bobcat and deer shifter communities.

Dan nodded to Gabe, who stepped from the second car, hauling Dolan out and to his feet and forcing him to stand beside him. "I think your Alpha's going to want us to deliver this particular package," Gabe smirked.

Ric turned to confer with another guard behind him, then gave a curt nod. "Okay. But no funny business. We're right behind you."

They drove slowly up the long, tree-lined driveway. The towering evergreens blocked out much of the sun, casting the road into shadow despite the bright morning light. The air grew thick with tension. The gloom felt tainted.

When the mansion finally came into view, more shifters waited. One stood in front of the rest—Michael McTier. Dan would have known him anywhere, even without the sharp breath Kathleen took beside him.

Michael had once been a striking man, but the years, and his own cruelty and anger, had etched hard lines into his face. He stood at the top of the stone steps, arms folded, defiance still clinging to him like an old coat. The six members of his council flanked him, each one older than the next.

"I see you brought an audience," Michael sneered as the Bertrand group exited their vehicles. Gabe again pulled Dolan with him, the prisoner silent and furious. Michael's gaze scanned the newcomers before settling on Kathleen. "And my daughter, parading herself like some pack trophy."

Kathleen stepped forward, her chin held high. "No," she said. "I'm your consequence."

Michael's lip curled.

"You tried to teach me obedience," she said, her voice rising so the crowd could hear. "Tried to teach me to stay quiet, stay pretty, be useful."

Faces appeared in the mansion windows—pack women, including her mother, watching. Kathleen raised her voice even more so that they would be sure to hear her. "You called it tradition. But what you really wanted was a puppet. Someone you could control."

Murmurs stirred in the crowd of shifters behind her, and she could see the women inside turning to each other in surprise and wonder at her temerity.

"But you couldn't control me. And I'm not under your control anymore."

A man broke away from the group on the stairs and approached her. Dan stepped forward instinctively, but Kathleen stopped him with a hand. "It's okay," she said softly, and moved to meet the other man.

He hugged her tightly. "I'm glad to see you safe."

"Uncle Brendan," she said. "Thank you—for everything you've done to help me. You taught me so much over the years." She turned back to the people with her. "This is Dan Bertrand, my mate and the new Alpha of the Bertrand pack."

"The Alpha, huh?" Michael cut in with a sneer. "Did you finally kill the old coot?"

"No," Dan replied. "He stepped down. He knew it was

time for a new kind of leader. You might consider the same."

"You were never meant to lead," Brendan said, turning to Michael while keeping one arm protectively around Kathleen. "You might be my brother, but I never understood you. You ruled by fear for twenty years. I didn't challenge you because I feared what would happen to my family—what would happen to Kathleen—if I lost." Brendan's voice strengthened. "But I'm not afraid anymore. Your daughter's fight against you has given me the courage to stand up to you. You turned this pack into a weapon, Michael. And now it's turned on you."

Michael laughed. "You think they'll follow you? You've always been the weak one. Hiding behind decency like it's something to be proud of."

"I don't need to be feared to lead," Brendan said. "I just need the truth. And your pack has realized that." He looked directly at Michael. "Michael McTier, I challenge you for leadership of this pack."

From the rear of the crowd, someone stepped forward. Then another. Voices rose in unison.

"I stand with Brendan."

"He protected us when you didn't."

"You left us to bleed."

Michael's jaw clenched, but he said nothing. His power was crumbling before his eyes.

Dan stepped toward the mansion stairs, voice calm but sharp as a blade. "By the laws of our kind, your power is broken. The pack has chosen Brendan. You can accept it or fight your brother for it. Which will it be?"

As even Michael's councilmen stepped away from him, the weight of reality seemed to settle on his shoulders. Even if he defeated Brendan, others would rise against him. Their fear of him was gone. "What about my son?" he asked tightly. "What do you plan to do with him?"

Dan turned to Brendan. "That's up to the new Alpha."

Gabe dragged Dolan forward. The younger McTier scowled, teeth bared.

"I'm sorry for you, Boy," Brendan said evenly. "You listened to every lie your father told. And you became worse than he is. If I let either of you stay, you'll poison everything we're trying to rebuild."

He looked from Michael to Dolan, then addressed the pack. "As Alpha of the McTier pack, I declare that Dolan and Michael McTier are no longer welcome in any sanctioned territory. From this moment on they are lone wolves. They have no pack."

Dolan lunged against his bindings. "This isn't over. You think banishment means I'll stop?"

Brendan's expression was stone. "No, Dolan. We think it means you'll die alone."

At his nod, the McTier wolves who had once obeyed Michael now stepped forward to enforce Brendan's order.

"You have one hour to leave this land," Brendan said. "After that, you'll be hunted as rogues."

Michael looked once more at Kathleen. For a heartbeat, his eyes seemed hollow and bitter. Almost human.

She didn't flinch. "You taught me to fear you," she said, "but I'm not afraid anymore."

Michael said nothing. He turned and walked away, Dolan beside him, the gates closing behind them with a sound like the end of an era.

Silence held for a breath; then, Brendan stepped forward and raised his hand.

"I never wanted this," he said. "But I will serve you, not with power but with respect."

The pack responded. Howls. Nods. Something heavy lifted, leaving the air a little cleaner than before.

Kathleen turned to Dan. "I need to see my mother before I go."

He nodded.

As she climbed the steps to the mansion, the front doors opened, and several women emerged. Her mother stood among them.

"I'm so proud of you, Daughter," she said, moving forward to hug Kathleen. "You fought when I was afraid. You are so much more than I ever was."

They embraced, and Kathleen whispered, "Come with

me. You could join my new pack."

Her mother smiled sadly. "No. There is much for me to do here. I think I should stay and help rebuild what your father destroyed. But I will visit you. Often."

They hugged once more, long and hard.

When Kathleen returned to Dan, he opened the car door for her. She paused, looking back at the mansion, then forward at the road ahead. "Let's go home," she said. "There's a future waiting to be built."

CHAPTER 61

The basement at the Bertrand farm was heavy with tension. The sofas and chairs may have been made for comfort, but everyone's posture was tense, their expressions strained. Hank Bertrand sat facing the group, surrounded by his council. His son, Remy, and Marianne Legato, the sharp-eyed elder shifter and grandmother to Gabe. Tim Means had a bitter frown creasing his lined face. He wanted his oldest son, Isaac, to be considered as the new pack Alpha but already knew that wasn't going to happen. Maddie LeBlanc, the youngest but perhaps the most politically astute among them, sat next to Dan. This meeting had been called to discuss the intricacies of declaring the new official Alpha.

"I know that Dan has been voted the new Alpha by the acclimation of the pack, and he led us to a victory over the McTiers just two days ago. But there are some problems with making his status official and public," Hank began.

"I didn't expect this from you, Hank. I thought you'd be all for pushing it through before the first growl."

"I'm aware of how it will look, Tim," Hank said testily.

"Then I think before we just push this through, we should open it up for a pack challenge."

"You just want Isaac to be leader. But do you really think he can take Dan in a challenge?" growled Remy.

"Gentlemen, let's keep the fighting for the challenge ring—not here," said Maddie reasonably. "And since the pack has already spoken, I think it is obvious they want Dan." She nodded to him graciously, and he smiled back. It was good to know there were some shifters besides his family on his side.

Hank cleared his throat to bring everyone's attention back to him. "We can put it to a vote of confirmation, but we must clear the accusation hanging over his head before we make it public. The Fontaine murder is like an open wound on the pack's reputation."

"So what? You are going to play pack Alpha in public, grab all the attention, while your boy here does the work?" Means continued his belligerence.

Marianne spoke up reluctantly. "I'm afraid I have to agree with Hank. It's not like the old days. The whole world is watching us; it's not just the packs anymore. We need to be seen as respecting the non-para laws."

"So we're gonna send out press releases now announcing our officers, just like we're some bigshot corporation? If Marianne's grandson hadn't mucked up his job, we wouldn't have to worry about this," Means grumbled as Marianne shot him a nasty look. She kept her mouth shut though, and for that, Dan was grateful. They needed the council united, and his grandfather spoke wisely. If he were confirmed as Alpha before clearing his name, it would just cause another media storm. And that they did not need.

"Connor should be here for this," Tim muttered. "We need him more than ever."

The mention of Connor's name brought a hush over the room. A wave of pain washed over Dan. He felt responsible for Connor's death. If he hadn't called for the raid on the McTiers, his friend would still be alive. He hung his head, unable to look at the others in the room.

"We don't have Connor," Remy said quietly. "But we do have resources. I've reached out to an old... associate of mine. I was going to wait to mention this until later, but now is as good a time as any. I've asked Cochran Bailey to represent Dan."

Even Marianne, usually unflappable, blinked. "Bailey? The Bailey?"

"Yes," Remy confirmed. "He's... unconventional. And expensive. But he wins. And he knows how to work both sides of the veil."

Tim scowled. "You're bringing in a bloodsucker to fix this?"

"Better a vampire lawyer than a dead pack," Maddie snapped.

Dan said nothing. He agreed with them all. Bailey's

name was whispered in both para and non-para circles. Rumors said he hadn't aged a day in fifty years. No one had confirmed his status as a vampire since the breach, though, at least not officially. While the paras knew him as one of their own, in the non-para world he was infamous for taking down entire state governments, clearing some famous movie stars of every kind of wrongdoing and scandal, including murder. If Bailey were taking the case, there was still a chance that he wouldn't spend the rest of his life in jail for murder.

"And what about the autopsy?" Marianne asked carefully.

"I spoke to Bailey. He suggests we have the answer right here in our own backyard. Nathan Lazard has a national reputation. Bailey says we can get a private autopsy, a second opinion. Nathan will attest that Fontaine wasn't killed by a shifter."

"And what about the fact that he *was* killed by a shifter? "You're asking Nathan to lie for us?" Dan asked, his voice low and tight.

"I know it's not ideal, but I don't plan on either of my children going to jail for something that's only a crime in the non-para world. Any shifter—any witch, vampire, elf, or banshee would agree Fontaine's killing was justified. It's just the damned non-paras we have to worry about.

Hank sighed. "When can Bailey get here? I'll talk to Nathan about the autopsy later today." He looked around the room at the other council members; there were no objections. He could tell neither Maddie nor Tim were thrilled with the idea although he suspected each had different reasons.

"And what about Ana?" Dan asked, his voice tight.

"She will not be touched," Hank said firmly. "We all agree?"

The council nodded again, and the rest of the pack added their agreement.

"We protect our own," Hank finished.

CHAPTER 62

The courtroom was crowded. Reporters, both national and local, non-paras, and delegates from other packs or covens watched the pre-trial hearing as Dan sat at the defense table, Kathleen and his family behind him, even Ana. Bailey had insisted she be there when he heard the whole story.

"If she's not there, people will wonder why. Wonder if she knows something. It will look a lot more suspicious for her to be absent," he'd explained. Chris sat beside her, his arm around her. He'd promised Dan that he would keep her from panicking and confessing to the killing of Fontaine.

Across the aisle, Sheriff Walker sat with the Herndon County district attorney, Randall Coleman. A young non-para, practically fresh out of law school, he was over-matched by the showy, nationally-famous lawyer. He knew it. He'd been elected by the small, rural county to handle the minor burglaries, car thefts, and domestic crimes typical of the area, not a national show-trial of the first paranormal accused of murder in four hundred years. But what could he do? The mayor had insisted that they not bring a big name in to replace or even help him. "It's not in the budget, Kid; besides, how would it look if we got some bigwig lawyer in here to face Cochran Bailey? It would look like we had no faith in you. And it's good PR, too. The smalltown lawyer up against the crafty paranormal guy. It's gonna look great."

Coleman was more worried about what the mayor would say when he lost the case. But here he was on the first day of the pre-trial hearing.

Cochran Bailey stood at the defense table, a tall, pale man in a perfectly tailored dark suit, dark black hair slicked back, gold cufflinks gleaming under the courtroom lights. He had a theatrical air; his eyes were cold and unreadable.

"Your Honor," Bailey was saying, his voice like a razor on silk, "We have new evidence. Dr. Nathan Lazard has performed a secondary examination of Mr. Fontaine's remains."

The judge nodded. Lazard entered the room, his pale face unreadable, his suit immaculate. The spectators buzzed with speculation. Lazard made a stir wherever he went. In his late thirties, several inches over six feet tall, he wore his usual all black: black suit, shirt, and tie. The stark contrast with his blond hair and pale skin only heightened his unnerving presence. He presented his findings with clinical detachment. He removed his ever-present dark sunglasses as he reached the witness stand and raised his hand to be sworn in.

Bailey began by questioning Nathan about his credentials and the national cases on which he had consulted. The audience seemed unimpressed at first. They obviously knew this information already. Then came the surprise.

"And when did you get your medical degree?"

"In 1770 at what is now Columbia University although I'd been practicing medicine for about fifty years before I was granted a degree."

The courtroom erupted into chaos. Gasps, whispers, shouts of disbelief filled the air. The judge hammered his gavel repeatedly, his voice rising over the commotion. "Order! I will have order in this court!"

The district attorney called, "Objection," repeatedly.

"Gentlemen, please approach the bench," the judge said as the two attorneys came forward.

"Are you attempting to pull a fast one?" the judge asked Bailey.

"No Sir, I am not. I'm attempting to verify my witness's credentials."

"And we are to believe he has been a doctor for over two hundred years?" questioned Coleman.

"Now that paranormals have been forced out of the closet, I think it is relevant."

"He has a point," the judge said to Coleman. "What type, er, species, er what term do you use?" he asked Bailey.

"He is a vampire, as am I. I know it has been rumored for years; I just thought I'd make it clear now so that there can be no question later," Bailey said arrogantly.

"I know we are in new legal territory here," said the judge. "I appreciate your candor."

"If we don't acknowledge Dr. Lazard as a paranormal now, and it comes out later, his findings in this case could be called into question. Instead, we would like his status as an expert—possibly the only medical expert—on paranormal crime we have right now."

"Your Honor, I must object to a paranormal coroner giving evidence in this case. He may obviously be prejudiced in favor of the defendant," Coleman said, helplessly throwing up his arms.

"And that is why we have called him. As I said, what better doctor to identify the difference between a paranormal killing and an animal attack than another paranormal? Particularly one with as much experience as Dr. Lazard?" Bailey questioned smoothly.

"Gentlemen, please return to your seats. Mr. Bailey, I'm going to allow the testimony of Dr. Lazard."

"The wounds, as previously reported, were characterized incorrectly," Lazard said when they returned to the questioning. "They are consistent with a large predatory animal. But I must emphasize the word animal here. Dr. Fontaine was not killed by a shifter. The marks are much smaller than those that Mr. Bertrand would inflict. The assumption that Mr. Bertrand was involved is scientifically invalid."

"In other words, Sheriff Walker's case was made based on assumptions, prejudice, and a personal grudge. Am I right?"

Before Nathan could answer, Coleman jumped up to object again. "While the Rivelou, Kentucky coroner may be an expert in paranormal animal bites, he cannot know what the sheriff was thinking when arresting Mr. Bertrand."

"Objection sustained," said the judge. "Mr. Bailey, I caution you against such grandstanding techniques. They won't work in my courtroom."

"Yes Sir, please forgive me," Bailey said penitently. But there was a gleam in his eye that said he had made his point with the audience. This was not a jury trial, but Bailey knew the people of real importance here were the media.

The judge made it official moments later. Dan Bertrand was cleared of all charges.

The room erupted, some in applause, others in hushed murmurs of anger and disbelief.

Dan shook Bailey's hand. "Thank you. I owe you everything."

Bailey smiled, but it didn't reach his eyes. "Justice, Mr. Bertrand, is often an illusion. But sometimes illusions are what keep the world spinning. It's not always about truth, but about what people believe." He left the room so swiftly, Dan didn't even see him go.

***

Tyler caught up with Bailey as he headed down the courthouse steps. "What will happen to Walker?" he asked. "He started this without any evidence."

"Son, sometimes you have to leave well enough alone. The sheriff didn't follow his own laws; he let his pride and his grudge against your brother cloud his judgement. But that's not illegal. As paranormals, sometimes we put our own laws ahead of those of the non-para world. Is that fair?"

"Well, when you put it that way…"

"Exactly. For centuries we've skirted the non-para laws whenever we could. Now that they know we are out here, they're going to be watching our every move. Sometimes that will mean injustice—for them or for us. We're going to need good young men like you to help keep both sides on the straight and narrow."

As Bailey headed down the steps, Tyler stood quietly, watching the crowd disperse.

Ana came up beside him. "You okay?"

"I'm going to law school," he said, voice steady.

Ana blinked. "That's sudden."

Tyler shook his head. "No, it's not. Connor always said the law was more than words. It's power. And someone needs to make sure no one like Walker ever gets to do what he did again."

Dan heard his brother and clapped him on the shoulder.

"Bailey's right. The world needs more fighters like you, Tyler. On both sides of the courtroom."

Tyler smiled faintly, his gaze lingering on the spot where Bailey had stood.

"I'm going to learn from the best," he said. "Then I'll do better."

As the sun dipped behind the courthouse, Dan knew the battle was over— for now.

But as long as people like Beatrix still played in the shadows, they'd need more than alphas.

They'd need champions who could fight with truth, lies, and law. Maybe his little brother would lead that fight.

CHAPTER 63

The Samhain moon hung heavy and golden over the Bertrand farm. It was Halloween and shifters, witches, elves, and even a few cautious but friendly non-paras gathered on the lawn, the crisp night air was softened by bonfires and the warmth of the pack's unity. Some shifters wore their fur, enjoying the cool evening; others mingled in human form, their breath fogging under the glow of lanterns holding candles lining the clearing. Tonight, the old ways mattered more than ever. No strings of fairy lights or electric heaters. Only candles, firelight, and the glow of the moon.

Dan stood before the gathered pack, Kathleen at his side, her hand steady in his. The copper and leather wrist cuff that had passed from father to son, Alpha to Alpha, for nearly four centuries, now gleamed on his wrist. Hank had placed it there as the pack howled their approval.

"Tonight," Hank's voice rang over the assembled crowd, "we name Daniel Henry Bertrand our Alpha. By blood, by bond, by choice."

The howls rose like thunder, wild and raw, vibrating in Dan's bones. It was official. Finally.

He turned to Kathleen, their hands still joined, the bond between them now seen and accepted by all. She was a Bertrand now, no longer a McTier. They'd hold a wedding ceremony later, Dan had told her, if she wished. But she was a traditionalist. This traditional shifter ceremony, naming Dan the Alpha and Kathleen as his Luna, meant more to her than a wedding.

"Ready for the next chapter?" she whispered to him now.

Dan smiled. "With you? Always."

They kissed softly, briefly, the crowd erupting again as the new Alpha and his mate took their place at the heart of the pack.

***

After the ceremony, the tone shifted. The pack prepared for the next event of the night—not the traditional Halloween run though many of the wolves would surely indulge later.

It was Ana and Chris's wedding, long delayed, long needed.

Ana, radiant in a simple ivory dress, took a quiet moment alone in the woods before the ceremony. Moonlight bathed the clearing in shadows as she closed her eyes.

And there he was.

Connor stood as she remembered him—strong, laughing, his dark eyes warm.

"You look beautiful, Ana."

She blinked back tears. "I miss you."

"I know. I miss you, too. And Sophie. And Dan and Gabe. I'll miss them every day until I see them again."

He stepped closer, but not close enough for her to touch. "But I found her, Ana. My mate. She was waiting for me. It was worth it—saving you, finding her. I'm not alone anymore."

A woman stepped into the vision beside him, young, with dark hair and almond eyes. She smiled gently at Ana before taking Connor's hand.

Ana gasped softly. "I'm glad, Connor. So glad. I needed to know."

"I wanted you to be happy, Ana. You can be. Know that I'm happy too, and I'll see you later, Little Wolf."

The pair faded into the starlight, hand in hand, leaving only warmth behind, wrapping around her like a blanket.

The pack gathered once more in the clearing that had been transformed into a makeshift woodland chapel. The flicker of torches lined the aisle where Sophie proudly led the procession, wrapped in a copper velvet gown with a silver faux fur to ward off the chill of the evening. Monica and Shannon followed behind as Ana's bridesmaids. Monica looked around, wide-eyed, finally convinced that paranormal creatures were real as she watched wolves, deer, bear, and other creatures mingle with paranormals in human form.

The wedding was tender, intimate, and filled with

laughter and tears. Chris's vows were soft, Ana's voice shook, but when they kissed, the pack cheered, and for the first time in months, Ana smiled without shadows behind her eyes.

The pack danced, ran, howled, the night alive with celebration. For a while, the world's troubles, the looming threat of Beatrix, the politics, all faded into the music of wolves under the Halloween moon.

But as the fires burned low, and the pack drifted away, Dan and Kathleen remained in the clearing. It was their moment now.

Dan let the quiet settle around them. It was their pack now, no longer his grandfather's, and it was strong. Their future might be uncertain, but it was theirs to claim.

"She looked happy," Kathleen said softly, watching the last of the dancers head back toward the farmhouse.

"She deserves it." Dan wrapped his arms around her. "They all do."

They stood in silence for a moment, the cold night wind brushing over them.

"The world's still watching us," Dan murmured. "Beatrix is still out there."

Kathleen smiled, leaning into him. "We've faced worse. We'll face whatever comes next. Together."

They swayed to the faint echoes of the music, just the two of them under the watching moon, their shadows stretching long into the night.

For the first time in a long time, Dan let himself breathe.

The wolves would face this new world. They were done hiding. He and Kathleen would face it together.

EPILOGUE

The Samhain moon rode low in the sky as the night faded toward dawn. It smeared its shadow across the surface of the Rivelou River like an old bloodstain.

Beatrix stood alone on the Indiana side, where the mud still bore the scars of her earlier work. The car was long gone, the battlefield quiet, but still she lingered. She liked this place. The water remembered things even if fools like the Bertrands had already forgotten.

She knelt, trailing pale fingers through the sluggish current. The river was colder now, but she didn't mind. She had always preferred the cold.

"Let them think they've won," she whispered to no one, to the water, to the crows watching from the skeletal branches overhead. The birds shifted restlessly. They, too, knew the truth. This was just one move in a much longer game.

Beatrix smiled faintly, her reflection twisting in the ripples like an echo of something ancient and hungry. "They celebrate their little victories. They dance under the moon. Good. Let them. It makes breaking them all the sweeter."

Far downstream, a single crow screamed in the night, a harsh note against the hush of the river.

Beatrix rose, smoothing her cloak, her expression as calm as the still, black water as she walked away.

The river never stopped flowing. And neither did she.

A Note to My Readers

Dear Reader,

I hope you have enjoyed my Unleashed series—complete with sexy werewolves, witches and vampires, oh my! I hope you had as much fun reading it as I have had writing it.

I hope you enjoyed Kathleen and Dan' story. It took me awhile to find the right girl for Dan, but once he met Kathleen, I knew she was the right wolf for him.

While this book concludes the "Unleashed" portion of the stories of Rivelou, don't think that I'm leaving this world. I've become too fond of the inhabitants of Rivelou. And you may have noticed that several couples have been hinted at, or have yet to find their Happily Ever After. I'm still trying to find just the right mate for Monica. What do you think? Should she find a sexy shifter? A romantic vampire? Maybe be introduced to Otherworld and the elves?

And that brings me to my next series. The Elves of Rivelou. The first book is titled *The Elf Knight,* and right now I can only say it will be out in early 2026.

Keep watching my Facebook page to find out more about publications dates and other information. You can find me at: https://www.facebook.com/profile.php?id=61574782089215

I'm also on Instagram, or you can check out my website at: www.LeeKRogersauthor.com

An author's best friend are reviews. If you enjoyed this book, please leave a review on Amazon or Goodreads. And thanks once again for reading.

Acknowledgements

Every author I know wishes they could spend all their time writing, and never have to think about marketing their books. Unfortunately, that is just as much a fantasy as my world of Rivelou. So my first thank you goes out to Noelle Stary and her assistant Allison Lange of www.20Lemons.com marketers extraordinaire. They help keep me on track and take care of all the little details I miss.

Also, thank my excellent editor, Cheryl Garayta for not only reading and critiquing my work, but for being willing to listen to my new ideas and tell me when they are either great or terrible.

Thanks to my Zoom writers group, Sherri A. Lynn, Janice Detrie, and Wendy Wyatt. Even though they are not normally readers of fantasy or romance, they have read every word and pay attention to all the tiny details I miss.

And of course, thanks to Eric Labacz, for his beautiful covers.

I couldn't do it without all of you.

ABOUT THE AUTHOR

Lee K. Rogers has been reading fantasy since she discovered the Brothers Grimm, and her love of the genre has only grown from there. From classics such as the Narnia series and *The Lord of the Rings* (before the movies came out of course!) to Charlaine Harris' series, Pamela Clare, and of course Rebecca Yarros—she reads it all. When she discovered urban fantasy romance she found her passion. She particularly loves adding a little spicy sex to her fantasy adventures.

In her other life, Lee's name is Karen Hodges Miller and she writes books designed to help other self-published authors achieve success. She recently won a FAPA award for her memoir *Hibiscus Strong*.

Lee has lived in many places, and while she currently resides in North Carolina, She once called the Kentucky/Indiana border city of Evansville, In, home. If you've ever been to the Evansville/Henderson area, you may recognize a few of the locations in the book. While she never met a werewolf there, she was convinced there was an entrance to the land of Fae just down the street from her house.

The Wolf Revealed is the third in the three-part Unleashed Series. Readers will be able to return to Rivelou and its many paranormal inhabitants in her next book, *The Elf Knight,* due out in early 2026.